And Then There Was You

by

Barb Warner Deane

A Harper's Glen Novel, Book 2

This is a work of fiction. Names, characters, places, and incidents are either the product of the author's imagination or are used fictitiously, and any resemblance to actual persons living or dead, business establishments, events, or locales, is entirely coincidental.

And Then There Was You

Cover Art by *Kim Mendoza*

The Wild Rose Press, Inc.
PO Box 708
Adams Basin, NY 14410-0708
Visit us at www.thewildrosepress.com

Publishing History
First Crimson Rose Edition, 2019
Print ISBN 978-1-5092-2591-0
Digital ISBN 978-1-5092-2592-7

A Harper's Glen Novel, Book 2
Published in the United States of America

Dedication

To my family, friends, and neighbors
in Watkins Glen and Schuyler County—
thanks for your love and support
and the fun memories you shared about the craziness
that was the Summer Jam in July 1973.

~

To Wendy Byrne, talented author,
fantastic critique partner and brainstormer,
and my personal cheering section.

~

To Nan, Stacy, Lori, Lisa,
and everyone at The Wild Rose Press
for their help in the publishing process.

~

To my sisters, Kate, Cim, & Patty,
as well as my best friend Jane,
for their support, suggestions, and celebrations.

~

And, as always,
to Chris, Elizabeth, Samantha, and Miranda,
with all my love

Author's Note

Welcome to the second book in my Harper's Glen series. This story, the town, and the characters are fiction, but some of the events are factual.

The Summer Jam rock concert was truly one of the largest rock concerts ever presented. Summer Jam took place at the Raceway in Watkins Glen, New York, on 28 July 1973, four years after and more than 200,000 people larger than Woodstock.

Watkins Glen, a village of approximately 2,000 people, is the home of American auto racing. As such, residents were used to crowds of 100,000 for the Formula One races.

When the promoters of the concert approached the town, they estimated 100,000 young people would attend the one-day Summer Jam. Instead, over 600,000 people came for more than a weekend, blocking roads, over-running the racetrack and adjoining campgrounds, depleting the water, food, and restroom facilities, and occupying the entire area for more than a week.

People began arriving a full week before the festival. Many hitchhiked or drove microbuses, campers, or vans there early to select the best camping locations. Cars were stuck in traffic up to fifty miles from Watkins Glen, with the impact of the traffic felt for nearly a one-hundred-mile radius.

Nobody realized how huge Summer Jam was going

to be. It was a chance at being part of an event for the younger generation, especially for those who missed the legendary three-day Woodstock festival in 1969. The Vietnam War was still going on in 1973, the '60s counterculture was still hanging on, and this nomadic group of young people was up for anything.

Over the weekend, there were more than fifty arrests, mostly for fights, property damage, and drug charges, but also including charges against five people for the theft and slaughter of a local farmer's pig. They intended to barbecue it. One man died attempting to skydive into the crowd with flares strapped to his legs that exploded before he touched ground. And one baby was born during the weekend. On the whole, the concertgoers were an easygoing crowd, although many needed treatment for drug-related illness and other health issues at local hospitals.

Of the one million dollars spent by the promoters, Shelly Finkel, 29, and Jim Koplik, 23, little was spent on advertising because they didn't need it. Because all the tickets were sold out, the gates at the concert site were left open, and eventually fell down, and the overflow of nearly 500,000 people got in without any attempts to check for tickets.

For three to four days, the Village of Watkins Glen and some surrounding areas were without mail, fire, and police services. Local hospitals were overrun and few public services were available. There were abandoned vehicles left for miles in all directions, and tons of garbage.

The three bands stayed eighteen miles away in a small motel in Horseheads and had to fly by helicopter to the concert ground for their sound check on Friday.

Over 200,000 people had already swarmed the track area, so these sound checks turned into concerts, with The Band playing for about forty-five minutes, The Allman Brothers pushing close to two hours, and the Dead doing an almost complete show.

While it was larger than Woodstock, Summer Jam never received the same notoriety, except among the residents of the Finger Lakes area of New York, who had lived through the chaos.

Barb Warner Deane

Chapter One

State Trooper Scott Randall yanked open the door of the Stevens County Youth Center. His rain-soaked uniform pants chafed against his thighs, while droplets hung on the shoulders of his leather jacket.

He stopped at the director's office but found it empty. Following the sound of chatter, he walked to the main room, which was both a gym and a study area. Small groups of kids sat at the eight long tables around the room, while others played catch along the far wall. The kids ranged in age from about six up to teenagers, although there were more little ones. How hard could it be to find a blonde sixteen-year-old girl?

Nick would not be happy he was chasing the girl down, but if she wouldn't come to him, he'd have to find her. Though he didn't want to scare her, he had no choice but to investigate his brother-in-law's off-handed comments.

He started walking toward an older blonde woman in the front of a glass-walled office but stopped in his tracks when his gaze swept over a petite brunette surrounded by seven kids all talking at once. She laughed, smiled...hell, she practically sparkled as she responded to questions and listened through the chaos. Even the gray sky seeping through the old cracked windows didn't dull the glow she radiated. He couldn't move one step farther.

"Can I help you?"

Snapping himself back to the present, he turned to find the blonde woman standing at his elbow.

"I'm Linda Porter, Director of the Youth Center."

"Uh...I'm Scott Randall." He held up his badge. "I'm an investigator out of the Horseheads State Police office. I'm looking for a teenage girl and have reason to believe she's a regular of the Center."

"Which teenage girl?"

He shook his head. "I don't have a name, just a general description."

"Can I ask what this is in reference to? If one of the students has been involved with a crime, I need to be notified."

His attention was pulled back to the feisty brunette as her laughter erupted amidst the circle of smiling teens. He hadn't been so distracted by the mere sight of a woman in a long time. This engaging woman couldn't compare to the mousy librarian-wannabes he usually dated. She was tiny, no more than five one and one hundred and ten pounds, but full of animation and spark. He'd guess her to be early forties, probably a few years older than he was. In mere moments, she'd bewitched and beguiled him.

"Uh, no." He had to pull himself together. Turning back to the director, he met her gaze. "I don't believe she's committed a crime, but I need to talk to the girl in connection with an ongoing investigation."

"Let's ask Marnie Edwards. She's been tutoring math here for years, started when she was a teenager herself, and knows the kids better than anyone. She's nearly done for the day, but perhaps she can help you before she leaves."

He could have kissed the woman when she not only named the brunette fireball but also took him over to where the small woman stood with a large group of kids. Maybe he'd be able to get some information, help out Nick, and do himself a favor at the same time.

****

A shot of current charged the air as Marnie turned to greet Linda and the visitor. She stopped mid-sentence, losing her train of thought.

The leather jacket curved from the man's broad shoulders to his narrow hips, where wet, navy pants took over, plastered to his long, muscular legs. She couldn't stop herself from wondering where those cowboy boots came from, as Harper's Glen, New York, was a long way from the Wild, Wild West. When a picture of those boots under the edge of her bed filled her mind, she shook her head.

A lock of dark hair fell across his face. His midnight eyes seemed oblivious to it, but her hand itched to brush it back. When his gaze turned her way, the power of the contact hit her as if it were a physical force.

In a town of less than one thousand people, how was it she'd never run into this guy before?

The instantaneous connection rocked her. Even with everything she knew about chemistry and electricity, she could have sworn there was a current running from his eyes to hers.

"Take a break, kids. I need Marnie for a minute." Linda motioned for her to follow them to the office.

The director pulled her glass door shut. "This is Scott Randall. He's a state trooper."

Marnie turned to face him and took his offered hand. His smile was stiff but softened as they shook. She should be saying something but couldn't quite figure out what, so she smiled back.

"Scott, this is Marnie Edwards."

"Nice to meet you, Ms. Edwards."

He glanced down at their joined hands, and then back up at her. That's when she realized they'd stopped shaking but her tiny fingers were warm and content, still nestled inside his rough grasp.

She grabbed her hand back, turning and taking a seat quickly in the hopes he wouldn't notice the embarrassment heating her cheeks. "Please, call me Marnie."

"Thanks, and I'm Scott."

If he noticed her blush, he didn't comment. Just to be safe, she addressed her question to the director. "What's the problem?"

"Scott is looking for a teenage girl and has reason to believe she regularly hangs out here, but he doesn't know the girl's name." Linda shrugged her shoulders and slanted her head toward the trooper.

Marnie also turned to face him, embarrassment replaced by protective reserve. "What do you want with one of our girls?"

"I simply want to ask some questions. As it is an ongoing investigation, I can't divulge the details." He pulled a notebook out of his pocket and flipped it open. "She's about sixteen, long blonde hair, thin, and apparently comes here for math and science tutoring. Does this mean anything to you?"

A number of faces flashed through her brain, including Carly's, because the girl hadn't been herself lately. "That could be any number of girls. Mostly all are too thin, their hair color changes weekly, and they all come here for some kind of help. Can't you tell me anything more specific? Do you have a name, a photo, anything?"

He glanced out the wall of glass, looking at the kids bunched in small groups around the center. "No. If I had a name, I'd have been able to find her myself." He turned back to face her. "Sorry, but in fairness to everyone involved, I can't tell you anything more. All I can say is that I need to talk to her as soon as possible."

She started to shake her head but stopped when he spoke again.

"Don't worry. I don't think she's participated in any illegal activity, but I have reason to believe she has information I need."

The concern in his voice was enough to convince her to try to help him, at least without endangering the kids.

"How about if Linda and I make up a list of those that might meet your description. Would that help? Of course, if we find the girl you're looking for, one of us will need to be with her when you talk to her, unless she has a parent here."

Linda stood behind her desk. "Please remember, the kids that come here usually have nowhere else to go. They have to feel safe. We won't impede your investigation, but we also won't allow anything to hurt these kids while they're here. Otherwise, they won't come back, and who knows what kind of trouble they'll get into out on the streets."

He sat down next to Marnie. His long, muscular

body had trouble adjusting to the flimsy, wooden folding chair. He leaned forward, resting his elbows on his knees. "I understand, but I have to do my job, too. She may have information vital to my investigation, so I have to find her. And it would be better if I could do it today, if she's here."

She darted her gaze toward the corner where Carly sat, working on her homework. What was the girl hiding? When her boss nodded in recognition, she turned back to face him. "Why don't you hang out here for a while, help some kids with their homework, and Linda and I will see what we can come up with, okay?"

"You want me to help these kids with their homework?"

His surprised expression almost made her laugh. "That's a big part of what we do. If we are working on your list, I won't be tutoring my kids. You can fill in for me."

He stood and turned to the door, although he hesitated and his hands floated at his sides. At least he was a good sport about it. He drifted hesitantly to her math table and sat among the kids. She shared an amused smile with her friend before turning to the task.

Linda pulled out a pad of paper and handed it to her. "This is going to be a short list."

"I know. We don't have many teenage girls, but at least we can talk about this before giving him any names."

"I noticed Carly's back today but wasn't sitting at your table. Did she talk to you at all? Has she been ill?"

Shaking her head in response, Marnie tried not to get caught looking at the girl. "I planned to go sit with her when I was finished helping the others with their math. I called her last night, but her phone must have been off. She doesn't look good to me, but she might not have any homework today."

"I had a suspicion something was wrong, but I don't know if it has anything to do with whatever the state trooper is investigating. Still, she's the first girl that came to mind when he described who he's looking for."

"I agree, although there are a couple of others who could fit that description. So what do you think we should do?"

"I think you should talk to her before we give him any names, to see if she tells you anything first. You said she's been acting strangely, so maybe you can figure out what's going on and if it's something that would concern a state trooper. Why don't I go help him with fractions, and you can talk to her?"

Marnie approached the girl, smiling, and tried to keep her voice light. "Hey there, girlfriend. What, no math homework today?"

The girl smiled woodenly, dropping her gaze to her notebook and snapping it shut. "Nope, not today."

Marnie slid into the seat across from the teen, leaning back in as casual a way as possible. "So, what's new? We've been missing each other the last couple of days. What have you been up to?"

The pale girl glanced nervously around the room before meeting her gaze. "Nothing."

"Everything going okay at school?"

Her shrug told Marnie little. The girl was bright

enough, but school and academics weren't valued at home.

"Is something wrong, honey? You're a little anxious today. Do you want to talk about anything? We could take a walk, just you and me."

"In this rain? No, thanks!"

She smiled. "Well, a drive then? I'm leaving soon anyway, so I could drive you home, or to work."

Linda came racing over to the table with Marnie's cell phone, and whatever the girl was going to say was lost.

"I'm sorry to interrupt, but I recognized the hospital number on your caller ID, and so I answered your cell. It's your father."

Marnie scooped up the phone, her hands already shaking and her breath stuck in her throat. "Dad? Is everything okay?" While she wanted to scream, her voice barely rose above a whisper.

"Well, honey…I'm at Schuyler Hospital with your mother."

Her palms sweated and fear clenched her stomach. "What's wrong? What's going on? Are you and Mom okay?"

"I'm fine. We drove over from Ithaca this afternoon and were going to meet up with you at your house. Your mom blacked out in the car, so instead, I just drove up here to check her into the ER."

Her mind raced. "Did she have another stroke?"

"I don't know. The doctors haven't said anything yet."

She grabbed Linda's arm. "Okay, Dad. I'm on my way. I'll be there in about fifteen minutes." She snapped her phone shut and turned back to Carly. "I'm sorry, but I've got to go to the hospital. Can we talk tomorrow?"

Carly's big eyes showed worry. "Is everything all right?"

"My mom's not feeling well, but I'm sure she'll be fine. I need to go be with my dad right now."

"Okay."

The high, shaky tone of the girl's voice nearly broke Marnie's heart. "You'll be all right until tomorrow, won't you?"

Her eyes wide, Carly nodded, saying nothing.

"Why don't we plan to take our walk then? Maybe the weather will be better. I'm sorry to have to run." She squeezed the girl's hand, hoping to reassure her, then rushed to the office to grab her coat and purse on her way out.

Scott came and helped her on with her coat. No one had done that for her in so long that she almost pulled it from his grasp.

"I'm sorry, but I have to leave. My mother's been taken to the hospital."

"I'm sorry. I hope she'll be okay."

"Thanks. Me, too. But Linda and I didn't get a chance to finish your list."

"No problem. I'll come back tomorrow. Right now, why don't I drive you to the hospital? I'm sure you're upset. Maybe you shouldn't drive in this rain."

Again, he took her by surprise, but his offer sounded sincere. "Thanks, but I'll be fine. I'm a careful driver."

He walked her to the door, his hand resting protectively on her elbow. She didn't have time right now to think about why it felt so natural.

13

"I'm sure you are, but it's a rainy mess out there, you're understandably anxious, and I can use my lights and sirens to get us there quicker."

She pulled the heavy door open, and stinging shards of icy rain bombarded her face. She put her full weight into the door, closing it again. "You win. I'm in enough of a hurry that 'lights and sirens' sounds good right now. Thank you. I accept."

He unzipped his leather jacket, crouched down close to her, pulled the fabric over their heads, and whipped open the door. They ran together to his Jeep, and he got her settled in the passenger seat before racing to his side and jumping in. By the time he got the door shut, he was dripping wet. He pushed some empty M&M wrappers off the seat before starting the car, flipping on his emergency lights, and pulling out of the parking lot.

****

As he turned onto the rain-soaked street, he chanced a glance at his passenger, who hadn't made a sound since leaving the center. She was so small and delicate, but he sensed a strength within her. Worry etched her face, replacing the joy and animation he'd seen there when she joked with the kids.

"Linda said you've been working at the center since you were a teenager. You must enjoy it."

She glanced up at him, a vague smile breaking through. "I do. I always feel like I make a difference there. Even on the hardest days, those kids give back much more than I give them."

"But you're not there full-time, right?"

"No, I'm only a volunteer. I'm the general manager at Davis Winery. I've been there a little over fifteen years." She wrung her hands in her lap.

"That must be fun. There are so many wineries around here. It's a great boon to the economy, brings a lot of welcome tourist traffic into the area."

"Hmmm."

Distracted and tapping her right index finger on the face of her watch, she might have forgotten he was even in the car. Not great on his ego, but certainly understandable. She had to be worrying about her mother.

"We're almost there."

She nodded but said nothing. She stared out the windshield, but appeared to be holding it together. In fact, even at the two different ends of the emotional spectrum he'd seen tonight, she'd maintained control. What a welcome change. Darlene would have been ballistic by now.

His ex-wife had been a drama queen, milking every situation for all it was worth, making everything that happened all about her. Even worse, every emotion she displayed, every crisis she encountered was all a fake.

Darlene cared about nothing but having a good time. It had never mattered what he wanted or needed. She expected life to be one big party, and if something came along that threatened to change her plans, she ignored it or eliminated it. With him, she'd done both.

Silencing his memories and the siren, he pulled into the hospital parking lot and drove to the covered entrance of the emergency room.

She hopped out almost before he came to a stop. As she turned to close the car door, her gaze met his. "Thanks for the ride. It was kind of you. There's no need for you to stay."

Suddenly, he hated the thought of her going in there alone. Who knew what news awaited her? He threw the Jeep into Park and left the lights flashing. Sometimes being a cop had its perks.

He raced around the front of the vehicle and ushered her into the ER. "I want to make sure you find your father. Let's check in at the desk."

She nodded, saying nothing, though she leaned on his arm. He led her to a small glass window in the center of two short hallways. Leaning into the open side of the glass, she gave her mother's name.

While they waited for the room number, she scanned each hallway. Just as the nurse started to speak, Marnie ran down the hall on the left. He followed at a distance, watching as a distinguished older man pulled her into a tight embrace.

She immediately took over the situation from the man who was obviously her father. She began speaking in a low voice, walking him back down the hall with her arm around the man's waist, since she wasn't tall enough to get them around his shoulders. While her jaw was clenched and her face pale, she became the caregiver, nonetheless.

She didn't appear to notice Scott was still there, so he decided it was time to leave and give her time alone with her family.

He left the ER and jumped into his Jeep. Pulling out of the parking lot, he decided to head back down into town to meet Nick at Minnie's Diner for a late supper, as previously arranged. He'd have to convince his ex-brother-in-law to give up as much information about the mystery girl as possible.

And hopefully, everything would be all right with Marnie Edwards' mother.

She'd made an impression on him in record time, and the thought of getting to know her better was enticing. In fact, everything about her was enticing.

****

"Dad?"

Her father pulled her into his warm embrace as they took seats outside the I.C.U. No matter what happened in the outside world, she felt safe and secure in her father's arms.

"I'm so glad to see you. I was worried you'd have trouble finding me once they moved her from the emergency room."

"I'm glad, too. I got a ride from the Youth Center, but..." She glanced around the hall. Scott must have left. "Anyway, I'm glad I could get here so quickly."

The cold, orange plastic seat creaked under her slight weight as he pulled her hand into his; she was grateful for the continued contact.

"No problem. Any news on Mom's condition yet?" She shifted in the chair, and the static electricity raised the hair on her arms.

"Not much. They ran a bunch of tests and decided to move her in here but haven't come to any definite decision about what's going on—at least, nothing that they've told me about."

She squeezed his warm, wrinkled hand. Her heart lodged in her throat as she fixated on the sterile, white room on the other side of the window. Tubes, monitors, and other machines gurgled, blinked, and beeped but didn't tell her a thing about the woman in the bed. It all reminded her too much of the spring day when her mother had suffered a stroke.

She prayed that this, whatever it was, wouldn't be as bad. Her mother wasn't that strong, but they weren't ready to lose her.

Holding tightly to her father, she tried to impart as much strength as she received. She huddled with him, watching the nurses shuffle in and out of I.C.U., hearing doctors paged, mesmerized by the ebb and flow of illness and recovery, life and death. She lost track of the time and was surprised that almost an hour had passed by the time her mother's doctor approached them and took a seat in the gold plastic chair facing them.

"I apologize for the delay. We got the results of some of her blood work that we wanted to double check and a bone marrow test that took a while to analyze. I know this is a long process and the waiting is difficult."

"What's wrong with my mother?" She winced at the sound of her own voice, sharp and demanding, but wouldn't—couldn't—apologize for her impatience.

The doctor didn't act offended. In fact, he smiled. "Let's not waste any time, then. First, Susan has not had another stroke. I know that's what you were worried about, Roger, but that is not the case here."

Her father sighed, shaking his head. "Thank God for that."

The relief in her father's voice was at odds with the tight grimace on the doctor's face.

"So what is it, then?"

His gaze shifted to her. "I'm sorry to say that Susan has acute myeloid leukemia."

The mere sound of the word, combined with her

father's pained gasp, echoed in her ears. "Leukemia? How is that possible?"

"There's no way to say what caused it, although I'm afraid it's not that uncommon, especially in elderly patients. Your mother is well over eighty now, Marnie, and that makes everything more challenging."

"But she's been in good health since she finished rehab after her stroke."

"I understand that, but it doesn't change the fact she has leukemia. Again, I'm sorry."

Her breath came in rapid gasps. Fearing she was in danger of losing control, she closed her eyes for a moment and took three deep, cleansing breaths before returning her gaze to the doctor. "Okay, so what do we do now? Does she need chemo? Radiation? A bone-marrow transplant? I mean, I don't know much about leukemia, but there has to be a standard plan of action for this type of thing. What do we do first?"

"Your mother is not a candidate for a bone-marrow transplant because of her age. There are treatments we can try, and I'll discuss them with you, all in more detail, when she is conscious and stable. At this point, until she regains consciousness, the best thing we can do for her is to provide IV meds and saline and give her several units of blood to build up her red blood cells and improve her body's natural immune system."

His complexion a shade grayer than usual, her father raised a concerned gaze to the doctor. "Is she in any pain?"

"No, not at this point. That will change, but we can address any pain that develops with a host of different medications. We will do everything we can to make her comfortable."

Comfortable wasn't enough, not nearly enough. Marnie didn't want to discuss maintaining; she wanted to know what to do, how to fix it, how to get her mother *better*.

There had to be something she could do, right now, instead of sitting there worrying. "She needs blood now, right?"

The doctor turned back to her, his smile kind but faintly patronizing. "Yes, that's the best thing for her right now. She will need transfusions on a regular basis to keep her strength up."

"Should I go to the lab and give blood? I mean, this is a small hospital, and I'm sure you'll need more blood to help keep up with demand, right?"

"That's true, and close relatives are the best chance of a match. It would be helpful if you encouraged your friends and family members to donate blood, too. If we find a match locally, it will help ease the strain on our blood donation system."

Standing, she clasped her hands at her waist. "Okay. I'll donate some now, and then I'll make some calls. With all the blood she might need, it'd be good to have other people come in and donate, too."

Her father stood and drifted toward the window, leaning against the wall.

Hating the strain obvious in his every muscle, she went to join him, looping her arm around his waist. "It'll be okay, Dad. Don't worry. I'll call everyone after I finish giving blood. We'll beat this thing, you wait and see."

The doctor joined them. "Do you know if you are the same blood type as your mother?"

She turned back to face the doctor. "Not really. I'm O negative. That's the universal donor, right? That's what they said at the blood bank last time I gave. What are you, Dad?"

He didn't answer.

"Dad? Did you hear me? What's your blood type?"

Again, he paused. "I'm A positive, sweetheart."

She turned back to the doctor. "Mom must be O negative, then, right? So I'm a match."

"Marnie…"

Checking the chart, the doctor glanced up. "Your mother's blood type is AB positive. If your blood is O negative, you can donate to your mother, but you're not a match."

She shook her head. "That can't be right. Are you sure about your blood type, Dad? Maybe you were thinking of Mom's. One of you has to be O negative for me to be O negative." Turning back to the doctor, she asked, "Are you sure about my mother's blood type? Maybe they made a mistake in the lab."

"No, I'm sure. We double-checked before we started giving her blood. She's AB positive."

When she turned to her father, he would not meet her gaze. "Dad?"

"This isn't the time, sweetie. Let's not get into this right now, okay?"

He barely spoke above a whisper, but his words caused a chill to race down her spine nonetheless.

"What are you talking about? This isn't the time for what? Mom needs blood. This is definitely the time to make sure she has access to all the blood she needs."

Her dad dragged himself back to the orange plastic chair and crumpled into it. If he hadn't leaned forward and met her gaze, she would have feared for his health, too.

"Dad? What's the matter? What's going on?"

She turned back to ask the doctor, only to find he'd disappeared. She was alone with her father, whose whole body had deflated, like the world was about to end. The tingle of fear that had merely warned her of trouble before now became a cold grip on her very core.

She knelt on the cold, hard linoleum at his feet and rested her arms on his knees. "I don't understand, Dad. Tell me what's going on."

He cupped her cheek in his cold, weathered hand, as he used to do when she was a little girl. The unshed tears in his eyes made her heart pound in her chest.

"Mom and I should have told you years ago. It was selfish of us not to, but you have been everything to us from the day we first laid eyes on you. You are a wonderful daughter. You've given us every happiness and made us proud. Nothing could ever change the love we have for you. You know that, don't you?"

She swiped at the tears leaking from her own eyes for some as-yet-unknown reason. "Of course I know that. I love you, too, both of you. But tell me what's wrong, please? You're scaring me, Daddy."

Her father pulled her up into the seat next to him, holding both of her hands between his own. "You are the daughter we always wanted but never thought we would have. You know your mother and I were around forty when you came into our lives. We had given up hope of having children and figured it wasn't in the

Lord's plan for us."

She smiled, having heard this story a hundred times. "I know, I know. And then I came along when you least expected it. It's okay, Dad. I know all about this."

"No, honey, you don't." He stopped and pulled out his white cotton handkerchief to blow his nose. "You see, we figured there was no way Susan could get pregnant, so we signed up with an adoption agency."

The word hit her stomach like a stone. "Adoption?"

"Yeah. We knew we wanted to be parents and decided to find a child in need of a family. When Mom got the call you were ready and waiting for us, we knew it had to be the Lord's will. I came home from work one day, and there you were, all pink and pretty, and it was love at first sight, for both of us. There wasn't a moment from then on we didn't think of you as our little girl. And that's what you'll always be, even though some other woman gave birth to you."

She stood, stunned. Somehow, she found herself at the hospital room's window, even though her legs and feet were suddenly numb. Staring at the woman she'd always thought was her birth mother, she shook her head. This was unreal.

She was forty-five years old. No one found out at forty-five years old they'd been adopted.

It has to be a mistake.

The machines beeped, the pumps pumped, and her mother slept on, as if nothing had changed. Meanwhile, she felt as if time had stopped.

"I'm adopted?"

Her father jumped up and stood mere inches behind her. "I'm sorry, honey. I know this is a hell of a way to find out. There's no excuse for not telling you long, long ago. But we didn't think of you as anything but ours."

She couldn't face him, and she darted her gaze to the doorway, the hall, the nurse's station, anywhere she might find normalcy. But it didn't exist—everything was slightly askew, as if nothing would ever be normal again.

"But...but I had a right to know. How could you keep this from me? My God, Dad. I'm a grown woman. More than half my life is over, and *now* I find out I'm adopted? This is unbelievable."

"At first, we thought it would confuse you. Then, when you were a teenager, Mom was afraid of losing you if you found out. You know how uncertain and rebellious those years can be. And, well, then it got harder as the years passed. I know we should have told you a long time ago, but it didn't seem to matter as much to me, because I couldn't be prouder of you if you were born of my flesh. You are *my* daughter and always will be."

She watched the lights on the monitor board, the movement of nurses from station to station. The sounds of the I.C.U. faded and swirled into the void in her brain. She couldn't remember ever feeling as cold or weak as she was in that instant. Her father's eyes stared back at her from his reflection in the window, but she couldn't bear to meet his gaze.

She ran her fingers through the crown of disheveled curls on her head. She'd always believed her mother when she said the curls were inherited from her dad's side of the family. But her mother had been lying. What else had she lied about?

"Honey, are you okay?"

"Uh...I...I don't know. It's such a shock. I don't know what to think."

He offered her his arm in comfort this time.

"I know, and I'm as sorry as can be that you had to find out like this. I know it will take some time for you to think it through. I want you to know your mother and I love you more than life itself. You have always been the light of our lives, and that hasn't changed one bit. Please remember that."

She leaned her head on his shoulder and welcomed the familiar scent of Old Spice and peppermint. *How is this possible?* This man, the daddy she worshipped, treasured, and loved more than any other human being on the earth, had been lying to her for as long as she'd been alive.

And somewhere out there were two other people, people whose lives were foreign and unknown to her. Nonetheless, those two people had given her life. She was a part of them, intimately connected to them...and didn't even know their names.

It didn't make any sense.

****

"Things won't go well for you or the baby if anyone else hears about our little talk," the woman said. She was sure the girl would take the bait. With her pale skin, listless eyes, and furtive behavior, she definitely had all the earmarks of a scared, lonely teenager facing an unwanted pregnancy.

Chapter Two

When Scott pulled up in front of Minnie's Diner, his ex-brother-in-law Nick stood in the doorway. Even though the aluminum overhang gave a sliver of protection against the weather, he couldn't believe the boy didn't have sense enough to go inside, out of the rain. He jogged to the front door and pulled Nick inside with him.

"'Bout time you got here."

Nick's wire-thin teenaged body was soaked to the skin, and he shook his head side to side, sending water flying everywhere and rattling the three silver hoops hanging from his left ear. Three truck drivers at the counter glanced up when they got hit with raindrops.

"What? You didn't see the rain out there? You couldn't wait for me inside?"

Nick glanced around the diner before turning back, and his bravado slipped a bit, revealing the insecurity hiding behind it.

"You said to meet out front. Figured you'd blow me off if you drove up and I wasn't out there."

He gave Nick's shoulder a gentle shove as the hostess directed them to a booth in the back corner. He took off his jacket and hung it on the hook at the end of the booth before taking his seat.

"Coffee, fellas?" Alma, according to the waitress's name tag, gestured toward the mugs on the table, a filmy coffeepot in her hand.

"Please." He flipped his mug over and she filled it for him.

Nick did the same and grunted in the woman's general direction. It only took a quick kick under the table and his ex brother-in-law looked up at Alma and smiled, sort of.

After she took their orders and left, he slid the laminated menu back into the metal holder attached to the end of the table. He added sugar to his coffee and took a sip, giving himself a moment to calm his nerves before starting in on Nick. "Mind telling me what your problem is tonight?"

Again the boy grunted, or maybe it was a snort. Whatever it was, it wasn't an answer, that was for damn sure.

He reached across the striped Formica table and placed his hand on the teen's wrist. When his grip didn't budge despite a sharp tug, Nick's eyes filled with mild panic.

Scott asked, "What's the deal, dude? You're as cross as a bear. Why don't you tell me what's got you so ticked off?"

Sighing, the kid shook his head. "Just my stinking boss. He's such a prick."

Scott gave the boy the eye and almost enjoyed the way he sheepishly looked around to see if his language offended anyone sitting near them.

"What happened?"

"He enjoys making my life miserable. It's a stupid job, but if I'm going to need to go full-time, I have to figure out a way to please the little p...pinhead."

Knowing this was about more than just work,

Scott shook his head and smiled. "Don't worry about it right now. You need to concentrate on finishing up and graduating before you worry about the working world."

Alma interrupted them to deliver their meals. Nick dug into his turkey and mashed potatoes and gravy as if he hadn't had a decent meal in days. Of course, it could be true. Darlene's father was rarely around, other than to take a swing at his wife and kids, and her mother had given up long ago. Life in that house was anything but predictable or ordinary.

Taking a bite of club sandwich, Scott watched Nick unnoticed. Now a high school senior, the boy wasn't a child anymore, as hard as that was to believe. He hoped to grow a little taller, but had to be about five feet ten inches by now. He needed to fill out his gangly form, so it was satisfying to watch him eat.

After wolfing down his dinner and most of Scott's fries, he finally started to slow down. It should be safe to bring up the girl now.

"Any news from your girlfriend?"

Nick's head snapped up mid-bite. "No. Why?"

"I wondered if you'd seen her lately or had a chance to talk over what you're going to do about the baby. You said she'd been sick. Is she back in school?"

His fork poised in midair, the teen focused his gaze. "Yeah. She was back in school today. Seems fine."

"Did you have a chance to talk her into meeting with me?"

Dropping his fork back onto the plate, the kid's temper rose. His eyebrows narrowed and his face colored, working up to outrage.

Scott held up a hand. "Listen, I'm not trying to get into your business. Yes, I want you to have all the facts before you change your life for this girl and the baby. You can't put off talking it out, making a decision. The baby will come no matter what you two decide. But this is bigger than even that."

Nick squirmed in his seat, as if he planned to bolt any second.

"You told me someone tried to buy her baby, and then you clammed up. I need to know everything so I can start investigating, figure out who is behind it, and lock them up. Tell me who your girlfriend is, and I'll see what I can find out. That's all I ask."

Nick's face reddened. "That's it, huh? Just let me sic a state trooper on her. You won't scare the piss out of her, now, will you?" He snorted. "Come on, man. I told you, she's scared. I told you I'll talk to her, try to get her to agree to meet with you, but she's not ready. Okay?"

He reached across the table, his fingers barely brushing the kid's arm. Nick had never been demonstrative, but in the three years Scott was married to Darlene, and even in the five years since, he had worked hard to get this neglected boy comfortable with affection.

"My main concern is you. If you love this girl enough to make a baby with her and to consider marrying her, I want to make sure she's okay. I don't want anyone coming after her or your baby. Let me keep you all safe."

Remaining silent for a few moments, a scared little boy showed briefly before the angry man took over in Nick's expression.

"You don't think I can keep her safe, her and the baby? You think I'm not man enough?"

He shook his head. "I'm not questioning your manhood, dude. Although how you ended up getting her pregnant after all the safe sex talks we had, I don't know."

"Accidents happen, man. You told me so yourself."

He took a drink of his coffee, hoping to swallow a lump in his throat. Yeah, accidents did happen. He'd told Nick that Darlene had gotten pregnant when the condom broke. At least, he liked to think that's how it happened.

Of course, since it wasn't his baby, or his condom, he could never be sure.

"If you are so into this girl, whatever her name is, why didn't you tell me about her? Why haven't I met her? What's the deal?"

Maybe Nick was finally going to come clean, but then he glanced out the window and quickly got up from the table. He started for the door, hoping to catch the object of his attention, but already whoever was out there was gone. When he turned back, he was digging into his pocket, pulling out some loose change.

"No, dinner's on me."

The boy seemed to relax a bit but still acted guilty. "I gotta run, man."

"Where to?"

Nick inched away from the booth. "Uh…I've got some homework. Ya know, midterms. I worked all day, so I'd better get to it."

Scott stood and grabbed the boy's right arm with his left hand. The deer-in-the-headlights expression in the boy's eyes made him appear younger than his eighteen years.

"Be careful, dude. And call me."

He reached his right hand out to shake Nick's, stuffing some bills in the kid's hand.

"No, really. I don't need any…"

His expression was cool, but once again, the boy and man seemed to be at war in his gaze.

"Just take it. Buy two lunches tomorrow. Put some meat on those bones."

The boy smiled and shoved the money in his pocket. "Thanks, man." He turned and was gone.

Scott returned to his seat at the booth as his friend Jack approached the table.

"I thought I saw you over here, Randall. Can't stay away from Minnie's, can you?"

"Hey, Finelli. Guess you can't either, huh?" He reached out to shake Jack's hand. "Have a seat. I'm almost finished." He tilted his head toward Nick's empty half of the booth.

Jack slid into the seat, a to-go cup of coffee in his hand. "I only have a minute. The wife called asking me to meet her at the hospital."

He put his sandwich down. "Is Kate okay? Is it Deke?" Deke, the former sheriff, was like a second father to Jack but had been losing his battle with cancer for months.

Jack smiled. "No, not yet." He took a breath and continued. "Deke's at home. He doesn't have much time left, but he's hanging on. Kate's fine, too. She went to be with a friend of hers whose mother's there.

She drove the friend's car up, so I need to go pick her up."

"Her friend isn't Marnie Edwards, is it?"

Jack startled, nearly spilling his coffee. "Yeah, how'd you know?"

He took a sip of his now-cold coffee. "I was at the Youth Center when she got the call. I drove her to the hospital."

Jack gave him a knowing look. "I didn't realize you even knew her, never mind well enough to be driving her places. What's the deal?"

"There's no deal, Sheriff Finelli." Suppressing his mirth, he tried for fake outrage. "I was there on business, and she was too upset to drive in the storm. It was just a little community service, that's all."

Jack chuckled. "Yeah, right. I've seen Marnie Edwards. I can imagine the service you had in mind, and it had nothing to do with the community of Harper's Glen."

Scott couldn't help himself. His mind pictured her—petite, vivacious, totally together. Yeah, he had some ideas about that woman. He'd have to be dead not to.

"How do Kate and Marnie know each other?" he asked Jack. "She's got to be more than ten years older than your wife."

Jack nodded. "Yeah, but when Kate started teaching self-defense classes at the Youth Center, Marnie took her under her wing, and they became the best of friends."

Scott shook his head. "She sure seems dedicated to the Youth Center." He had to wonder if she'd give him a list of names if it would risk alienating any of the kids.

"Here comes my food." The server dropped off a paper bag in front of his friend, grease stains already soaking through.

Scott threw a tip on the table, following Jack to the cash register.

"Wait 'til I tell my wife you have the hots for her friend. She's been looking for the right man to fix her up with. She'll be in matchmaker heaven."

"Can't you keep your wife busy enough she doesn't have time to meddle in other people's lives?"

Jack slapped him on the back. "No woman is that busy, dude."

He laughed. "I'm going to tell her you said so, Jack. You'll be sorry."

As they exited the diner, he stopped on the sidewalk and turned to Jack. "Have you ever heard anything about someone buying and selling babies in town?"

Jack stepped out of the diner doorway and joined him under the awning. "Why do you ask?"

He stuck his hands in his back pockets, walking to stand next to Jack. "I've heard some rumblings in the past, but was never able to substantiate anything. I've got a lead on something current and wanted to see if you've been hearing anything."

Jack nodded. "Deke told me he'd heard rumors to that effect over the years but could never get anyone to give him specifics. But this goes back a long ways. I haven't heard of anything recently." He shifted his takeout to his other arm. "Are you interested in sharing what you've got?"

Scott fished his keys out of his pocket and an

M&M wrapper fell to the ground. He picked it up and then twirled the key ring around his finger. "I don't have anything concrete yet, but once I do, I'll give you a call and we can go from there."

"Fair enough." Jack waved and headed through the rain down Main Street, probably heading for the county parking lot.

Climbing into the Jeep, Scott started the twenty-minute drive back to Horseheads. He could only hope he'd get enough information to share with Jack.

That she was friends with Kate was another point in her favor. Jack and Kate had struggled to make a life together, and he'd seen it nearly wrenched from them. The odds hadn't been in their favor as Kate struggled to escape her abusive marriage to Jack's brother, but she was a special woman, and they found their way back to each other. They were finally happy.

Which was exactly the kind of peace he wanted in his life. A wife, a family, the normal things a man wanted in life. Maybe he'd stumbled onto a good thing when he went looking for Nick's girlfriend.

It'd be fun to figure it out.

****

Marnie dragged herself out of her car and up the back steps into her house. She and her father had passed a few tense hours together at her mother's bedside but effectively avoided discussion of anything other than leukemia. Once the doctor convinced them her mother would sleep through the night, they decided to head back to her house. She was able to send him on ahead; she wanted time to talk to Kate about her mother's illness and the adoption madness. Their talk helped her work through the initial shock, but she had little energy left to talk to her dad afterward.

When her parents moved to a retirement facility in Ithaca, she had bought their house from them. While it was less than an hour's drive to Ithaca, her father had agreed to sleep at her house while her mother was in the hospital, rather than make the drive alone after dark.

As she pulled the screen door open, however, the day's earlier tension returned full force. Her father sat at the kitchen table, waiting for her.

She tried to paste a smile on her face but knew she couldn't fool either of them. Hopefully, he'd let it pass.

After she hung her coat on a hook in the mudroom, she squared her shoulders and walked into the kitchen. "Dad, you must be exhausted. Why don't you go to bed?"

He smiled up at her as he had a million times before. Tonight's smile was slightly more bittersweet, his gaze somehow more frail and tired.

"I've been waiting for you, sweetheart. I think we need to talk." He pulled out the chair next to him, her usual seat at the table.

There was nothing she could do but sit.

"It's late, Dad. We're both tired and have another long day ahead of us tomorrow. I don't want you to wear yourself out. You should get some sleep."

He wasn't buying it—he held her in her chair with his gaze, those eyes that always were her port in a storm. She could hardly resist the urge to run to him with her troubles, like always. Except this time was different.

"We need to talk about the adoption. I know we managed to ignore the issue all evening, but it's there nonetheless."

"There's nothing to talk about right now, Dad. Mom's health, her recovery—that's the most important thing. Everything else can wait."

He shook his head slowly, sadly.

Suddenly the napkin she was shredding absorbed all of her attention.

"No. This cannot wait. I know how upset, angry, and confused you must be. I know Mom would handle this better, if she could. But right now, she can't, and I can't let either of you down by brushing it under the rug."

He reached his hand out and placed it on hers, calming the nervous energy. She fought the tears threatening to spill out.

After a moment, she found her voice again. "What do you want me to say, Dad? I'm still in shock. Everything I knew about myself, my family, my life…well, it's not what I thought it was. Not what you and Mom have been telling me for forty plus years." She swiped at her tears. "Am I angry? I don't even know yet. Mostly, I'm confused. I have to digest this and get used to it. It'll take some time."

He squeezed her hand gently until she raised her gaze to meet his.

"Of course it will take time for you to deal with this news. But please remember, nothing about your place in our hearts, *nothing* about our love for you has changed in any way."

"I know you love me, Dad." She tried to temper her tone. "That's not the issue." She took a breath and got her nerve back. "It's just I thought I knew who I was, based on who the two of you are. Now I know there are two people out there, somewhere, who are complete strangers to me but are the reason I look like I do, act like I do. I mean, they are the reason I even exist, and I don't know anything about them. Not even their names."

She stood and walked to the sink, pouring herself a drink of water. She needed the moment to rein in her temper. She'd never yelled at her father—or, at this man who had always been her father—and she didn't want to start now.

"Do you want to find out their names? Find them? Meet them? Is this what you're thinking?"

His voice remained calm, but he hesitated. She recognized the worry coming through.

She turned to face him, leaning against the counter. "I don't know. I haven't had time to think about it."

He almost smiled. "I know you, sweetheart. I know how your mind works, and I know a part of your brain has been working on this all evening, thinking of all the angles, all the possibilities, all the variables to this situation. You must have given some thought to finding your birth parents, right?"

She walked back to the table and sat. He knew her well.

"Of course I thought about it, briefly. But it isn't a priority right now, not with Mom unconscious and struggling to fight leukemia. Maybe later, after we know what her status is, after she gets started on her treatment, maybe then I'll have time to think about whether or not I want to find them. But I can't think about it right now."

Her dad nodded. "I don't want you to feel like it's disloyal to your mother and me to want to find these people, to find out about them or even to meet them. It's perfectly natural for you to want to know about your roots. We knew this could happen at any time, even if we tried to pretend it wouldn't. Your mother's illness is no reason for you to feel guilty because you have questions."

He draped his arm across her shoulders, and she leaned in and let her forehead rest on his. Her body, her mind, and even the deepest recess of her heart were too tired to move.

Her father reached down and tipped her face up. "You need to get some sleep, sweetheart. Let your thoughts go. Don't hammer this out tonight. When your mother wakes up, we can discuss this situation with her. I know she'll want you to do what feels right." Placing a kiss on her forehead, he gave her a squeeze and pulled her to her feet. "And, in the meantime, all I ask is you try to find room in your heart to forgive us for being too weak, too scared, and too selfish to tell you about this years ago. We never wanted to hurt you. That's the last thing either of us would ever want to do. We love you so much. We didn't want to risk losing you."

His gaze held all the fear, the love, the worry he clearly felt. Even though she wished she could say she wasn't angry and she understood, it wasn't true. She wasn't there yet, and they both knew it.

"Okay, Dad. Let's go to sleep. Tomorrow will be another long day."

He didn't say a word but nodded, turned, and

walked into his room.

After switching off the remaining lights, she went upstairs to find her bed and try for mindless sleep. She needed escape more than anything.

****

The next morning, Kate appeared at the doorway of the I.C.U. waiting room, and Marnie pulled her into a hug. Her friend convinced her to sneak away for a coffee break in the cafeteria.

"Has the doctor given you any more information on your mother's prognosis since last night?"

She carried her cup of bad coffee, following her friend to a small round table in the back of the room. "No, nothing new. I researched her leukemia online last night, when I couldn't sleep, but didn't find anything I wanted to know."

Kate smiled and placed a hand on her arm. "Give it some time, kiddo. You're probably on sensory overload about now. Why don't you take a break and get out of here for a while?"

Marnie sipped her coffee and shook her head. She relished the care and support in her friend's gaze. "I know it would be smart, but I can't seem to do it today. The doctor said she should wake up soon, so I guess I'm afraid if I leave the hospital, something will happen to her. I need to be here when she wakes up." She shrugged. "I left a message at work that I'd be out for at least a couple of days. At some point, I'll have to deal with...you know, the adoption issue, too. Although I'm not ready to face that."

After taking a sip of her coffee, Kate said, "So don't. Concentrate on keeping yourself healthy and sane while you deal with your mother's illness. Unless

39

you've changed your mind since last night, you're not really ready to do anything about the adoption stuff right now anyway."

She sighed. "At this point, I don't see there's much for me to do about it, other than get used to the idea. Finding my birth mother, discovering a new family, learning I have siblings—well, that all sounded possible when we talked last night. But in the cold hard light of day, the reality is the mother I know and love is critically ill."

"You mean, you've already decided not to search for your birth parents?"

The disbelief in her friend's voice surprised her.

"That's not much of a decision, is it? I mean, my mother, or at least, the woman I've always known to be my mother, is lying upstairs, possibly dying, based on the research I did and what the doctor had to say. It may not happen this week or this month or maybe not even this year, but the reality of the situation is that she's terminally ill. How can I add more stress to my parents' life by rejecting all they've done for me to search out my biological parents, especially at a time like this?"

Kate placed her hand on Marnie's arm. Her tender touch was like a warm hug.

"Don't make any rash decisions. You aren't being disloyal to your parents by needing to know where you came from and who gave birth to you. You can be their loving daughter and still search for your birth parents. It doesn't have to be either/or. The only thing that matters is what feels right to you."

She twisted her hands together on the table, hoping to keep them from shaking with stress or fear.

"Nothing feels right. It's as if everything in my life has been built on the wrong foundation. I don't even know who I am, so how can I know anything else? Everything I've done, everything I ever knew, is all a lie."

Kate put her arm around her shoulders. "Oh, Marnie…I know it must feel that way right now, but it's just the shock. Give yourself time to digest all of this, and then you'll know what to do."

She nodded, unable to speak without her voice shaking. Between waiting to see if her mother would wake up, finding out who her birth parents were, helping Carly with whatever was going wrong in her world, and staying on top of her job, Marnie thought her head might well explode. Still, she had to keep it together, as she wasn't the kind of person to lose it in public or create a scene. Well, at least she didn't think she was, but now, who knew?

****

A note fell to the floor when Carly opened her locker. She bent to pick it up, looking around for but not seeing anyone walking nearby who might have slipped it there. Cold chills ran down her spine as she read the words, *You haven't been talking, have you? Don't do anything you'll regret.*

She glanced up and down the hallway again, but nobody was there. They were watching her, and she didn't know what to do to protect herself and her baby.

Chapter Three

Her father was plastered in the orange plastic chair outside her mother's room in the I.C.U. He placed a kiss on her cheek when she hugged him.

"Any change, Dad?"

"Nothing. The doctor was in about an hour ago, but he didn't have an update. We're supposed to wait and see if the drugs take effect. There's nothing more we can do, besides hope she wakes up soon."

She laid her hand on her father's shoulder. They sat in front of the window of her mother's room. "I'm sure Mom will wake up today. Everything I've read says the lethargy she's been experiencing recently is related to the leukemia. With a couple of days of rest and treatments, she should be strong enough to wake up soon."

Her dad rose, standing at the window, his hands on the glass at shoulder level, as though he planned to push his way through. She went to him and placed her hand on his back. "I think she might be giving up. She's been so tired, so out of sorts, maybe she knew something was wrong. I'm afraid we're losing her already, that she's not going to wake up, ever again."

She wrapped her arms around him. "Don't say that, Dad. She doesn't want to leave us. Give her a little more time, let her get a little stronger, and she'll open those eyes. You have to believe it."

They settled in for the afternoon watch, taking turns using the ten-minute visits allowed each hour. By six o'clock, her father was a little gray around the edges.

When she finished her allotted visiting time, she took his hand. "I'm hungry, Dad. Let's go down to the cafeteria and get some dinner. Then I think you should go home. You've been here all day. I'll cover the evening. Okay?"

His gaze shifted from her to her mother, still and quiet, only the hum and beeps of the machines breaking the oppressive silence of the room. He appeared torn but tired.

"Okay. I'll go home after dinner, but promise me you'll call if she wakes up."

"Of course. She'll want to see you when she does."

They walked down the hall to the cafeteria. "And you won't stay too late yourself, right? I know you're going in to work early so you can have time here with your mother, so you'll need to get some sleep."

She smiled. "I'll be home before eleven. I promise."

After making sure her father ate at least some of his turkey sandwich, and picking at her own dinner salad, she sent her father home and returned to the I.C.U. The hour was nearly up, so she only had time to glance through a magazine briefly before she went back in to visit her mother.

"Hi, Mom." She took her mother's hand and stood next to the bed, keeping up a stream of conversation, even if it was only one-sided.

"Dad was tired, so I sent him to my house. The

worry is getting to him, and I don't want him to get sick now, too. You need to wake up, you know. He's not going to be able to get a good night's sleep until he believes you haven't given up. He needs you. We both do."

She talked about her job, the vineyards, the new spa, and the local gossip. After running out of small talk, she picked up the couple of get-well cards her mother had received and began reading them aloud. It was kind of Jack and Kate, and Linda from the Youth Center, to think of sending some.

"We're waiting for you to wake up and come back to us, Mom. We need you. I need you. I need to talk to you, to understand why you kept the truth from me all these years. I want to know what you know about the woman who gave birth to me. I want to be able to wonder about this without feeling such immense guilt over it. Please, wake up and set things straight. Okay?"

When she leaned down to kiss her mother's cheek before leaving, her mom's eyelids fluttered.

"Mom? Are you there, Mom? Wake up. Come on, open your eyes."

Without taking her gaze off her mother's face, she pressed the call button.

The young nurse was there immediately. "Is there a problem?"

"I think she might be waking up. Her eyelids were fluttering, and she seems to be breathing differently, better somehow."

She stood back as the nurse moved in to tend to her mother. During the exam, her mother opened her eyes fully.

"Hello, Mrs. Edwards. Welcome back."

Marnie quickly moved to the other side of the bed, grateful to stare into those light blue eyes again. "Mom?"

"What…what happened?" Her voice was hoarse but strong.

While Sandy, the evening nurse, continued to check her vitals, she turned her head slightly. Her gaze met Marnie's. "Why am I in the hospital?"

She reached in and took her mother's hand again. "You passed out. That was two days ago. You've had us pretty worried waiting for you to wake up."

Sandy closed her file. "Everything seems fine. I'm going to call the doctor, and I'll be back in a few minutes to check on her. Don't stay long."

Her mother watched the woman leave and turned back to Marnie. "What's going on? Why did I pass out?"

Being a straightforward kind of woman, her mom always preferred the facts. Her mother wouldn't appreciate it if she gave vague or incomplete answers to her questions.

This was something they shared, something she'd always thought she inherited from her mother.

"I'm sorry, but the doctor says you have acute myeloid leukemia."

"Leukemia?"

She took a deep breath before continuing. "Unfortunately, it's not uncommon at your age. That's why you have been feeling so run down and exhausted lately."

Her mother didn't respond for several tense moments. Marnie started to fear the worst, but relaxed a bit when her mother started nodding.

"Hmmm...that makes sense." She pulled herself up a little in the bed. "I haven't felt like myself in weeks, but it wasn't anything specific. Nothing I could point to and say, gee, I need to see a doctor about this. Just general malaise. I guess this explains why." She met Marnie's gaze. "So now what?"

She pulled a chair close to her mother's bedside and sat. "I've been researching the treatment options, and there are lots of things we should talk about over the next few days, when you're a little stronger. We need to figure out how to attack this thing, make our plan, and then you'll feel better in no time. But right now, you need to rest and get stronger, and I need to call...I need to call Dad and tell him you're awake."

She leaned in and kissed her mother's cheek, preparing to leave. Her mother grabbed her hand with surprising strength and wouldn't let her go.

"There's more, isn't there?"

She froze, afraid to let the jumble of thoughts racing around in her brain spill out onto her weakened mother.

"We'll talk tomorrow, when you're stronger. Now, get some rest."

"No." Her mother tugged on Marnie's hand again. "Now."

She sighed. "What? You want to go over the treatment options? The prognosis? What? I don't think there's anything that can't wait until tomorrow."

"I know enough about cancer to guess what my treatment options are and to understand the prognosis for someone my age, especially someone who had a stroke several years ago, isn't very good."

Marnie tried to swallow the lump in her throat, but

her mouth was suddenly dry as dirt. "Then what?"

"I want to know what's wrong with you. I can see it in your face, in your eyes. Something's changed, and I want you to tell me what it is."

She ducked her head, trying to hide her eyes from her mother's probing gaze. "I've been worried about you. Dad and I both. I'm tired, I'm worried, and I haven't been sleeping well. So why don't I go home and get some sleep and see you tomorrow?"

She tried to pull her hand free, but the old woman held on tight.

"Nice try." Her mother's voice was quiet but not soft. "But I can see there's something more. You look at me in a way you never did before. I want to know why."

She sighed again and shook her head. "I don't want to go into this now."

"Tell me."

"Fine. Because you will require a lot of blood transfusions as part of your treatment, I offered to donate blood for you." She paused, but her mother gave a tug on her hand, forcing her to continue. "I can't do it. We're not the same type."

Her mother's face went whiter even than it already was. "And?"

"Dad told me the reason is because…I'm adopted. After forty-some years, I find out I was adopted, and I never knew."

Her gaze darted to the older face, wiping at the tear running down her cheek.

Her mother smiled sadly but there was no change in her monitors.

Again her mother tugged on her hand. "I'm so

sorry, sweetheart. I never wanted you to find out like this."

This was not the time or place to lose her temper, so she took a deep breath and strove to keep her voice level. "You never wanted me to find out at all."

Her mother paused, swallowed, and Marnie began to fear the conversation was too much for her. "Let's finish this tomorrow."

"We can talk about it tomorrow, but give me a few more minutes right now." Her mother took a breath and continued. "I have to make you understand how much I wanted you, how much your father and I love you. I never wanted you to find out you were adopted, because I didn't want to believe it myself. The day you arrived in our house was the happiest day of my life. And every day after has been even better."

"It's okay. I know you and Dad love me. I think this is too upsetting to talk about tonight, especially for you. Dad and I had to put it away for now. When you're feeling better, the three of us can sit down and talk more. I'd like to hear about how you found me, what you two know about my birth parents, everything there is to know. But not now. You need to rest."

Her mother finally released her grip on Marnie's hand, and she pulled back, preparing to go.

"Okay. We'll talk more tomorrow, but don't press your father for details, okay?"

"He's in better shape right now than you are, so I think if there's something I can't wait to talk about, I'd rather ask him. Okay?"

"No, you don't understand."

The urgent tone in her mother's fading voice made the little hairs on the back of her neck stand on alert. "What don't I understand?"

"Your father. He doesn't know...he doesn't know the truth."

She felt the walls closing in on her again.

"What? What doesn't he know?"

"He thinks we got you from an adoption agency. He doesn't know my mother brought you to us. I never told him."

Her mother's voice was faint and thin, but the path it cut along her skin left fear in its wake. "What are you talking about?"

"Grandma Gill, she brought you for me. She knew how much we wanted you. But no one was ever to know."

"How did Grandma Gill get a baby? Where did she find me?"

Her mother rolled her head to the side and sighed. "They found you at the Summer Jam. She told my father she'd take you to a foster home, but she brought you to me."

The rock concert in Watkins Glen back in the early seventies? "What was a baby doing at the rock concert?"

"You were born there, sweetie. Your birth mother gave birth to you that weekend, in the back of somebody's VW microbus. The police found you there and, after you were checked out at the hospital, they gave you to my parents."

Her mother started to fade again, her voice growing more wispy, but Marnie couldn't stop herself. "I was born to some hippie during a rock concert? Why give me to Grandpa and Grandma?"

"Because he was the mayor, sweetie. And then

Grandma brought you to me."

Her mother's breathing changed. She pushed the call button and waited anxiously as Sandy checked the vitals again.

"She's sleeping," said the young nurse. "She needs her rest, and if you don't mind me saying, so do you. Go home. You can talk more tomorrow."

She followed the nurse from the room and then walked out of the hospital to her car. Her fingers were too cold to get the keys into the ignition. They fell to the floor, and she hit her head on the steering wheel when she tried to find them.

She laid her head on the steering wheel and burst into tears. Tears of relief, frustration, worry, and betrayal—they wouldn't stop. She cried herself dry but didn't feel any better.

Unsure of how long she'd been sitting in the parking lot, she retrieved her keys, started the car, and drove home. Thankfully, her father was asleep when she arrived. She dropped her coat and purse in the kitchen, climbed the stairs to her room, and crawled under the covers fully dressed.

Her brain had finally hit overload and couldn't process another thing. For once, she slept the sleep of the dead.

****

"Hmmm...it smells wonderful in here, Kate." Marnie followed her friend through the house to the kitchen, setting a bottle of red wine and her big brown leather purse on the counter before taking a seat at the ceramic-topped breakfast bar. The warmth of the kitchen and the smells of her friend's homemade dinner did more to revive her flagging spirits than even sleep could do at this point.

"Thanks so much for convincing me to come to dinner. I couldn't look at hospital food again, and when I get home, I have no energy to cook."

Kate stopped at the stove to stir a pot of something that smelled delicious and then turned to lean against the counter, smiling at her. "I could tell when we talked on the phone the last couple of days took their toll on you. Especially given your mother's latest revelation, you needed a break. And a good meal with friends always helps."

She blinked back the moisture appearing in her eyes, tears that surely should have been cried out by now. She smiled. "Good friends help a lot."

As her friend poured them each a glass of wine, Jack strolled into the kitchen, placed a kiss on his wife's neck, and then crossed to the breakfast bar, giving Marnie a quick hug. "How's your mom?"

She swallowed the lump in her throat. "She hasn't woken up again today, but the doctors are encouraged she woke up last night. They think she's getting some much needed sleep."

Kate handed a wine glass to Marnie and poured another for her husband. "What about you? How are you holding up?"

When she opened her mouth to answer, a laugh bubbled up from somewhere, sounding a bit hysterical. She took a sip of wine and tried again. "I'm okay. I'll be better when my mother's consistently conscious. But for now, I'm hanging on."

Jack sat next to her while his wife sliced a loaf of Italian bread. "Kate told me about the adoption. I'm sorry you have to go through this, especially with your mom so sick. If there's anything we can do to help, just ask."

"Thanks. I appreciate it. There's nothing to do right now but wait."

After she carried the bread basket to the table, her friend stopped and nudged her elbow. "Jack thought maybe Deke would be some help in tracking down your birth parents. He was sheriff back then and may remember something helpful."

"I don't want to bother him. I know his condition is not good these days. He doesn't need to waste his energy on me."

She turned to Jack, who thought of Deke as a surrogate father. The old man's battle with cancer had prompted Jack to come back to town to serve as Deke's undersheriff. As Deke's health deteriorated, Jack took over as sheriff. While Deke was still hanging on nearly two years later, even Jack admitted it was only a matter of time.

"He's not strong enough to do any digging on his own, but he still likes to talk. He'd love a visit by a pretty lady like you."

"I'd be happy to go see him. But I don't know if I want to start a search for my...for the woman who gave birth to me. With Mom's terminal disease, I think I'll have my hands full. I don't want to put extra pressure on her or my dad right now."

Jack put his hand on hers and gave a gentle squeeze before turning to help his wife with the rest of dinner.

Her friend started setting the table for four, and before she had a chance to ask who the extra plate was for, the doorbell rang.

Jack ducked down the hall, and soon his laughter came rolling back toward the kitchen. When he walked back into the kitchen, his smile was enormous, as was the bouquet of flowers he carried to his wife. Close on his heels was Scott Randall.

"Look what I got you, honey…"

Scott pulled the flowers out of Jack's hands and carefully carried them to Kate. "Don't listen to him. I brought these to thank you for taking pity on me and my horrendous cooking once again."

"But, but…"

"Don't even try it, Finelli." Kate took the flowers, gave Scott a kiss on the cheek, and then kissed Jack on the mouth as she waltzed by. Pulling a glass vase from the top of the pantry, she winked at Marnie. "Aren't these beautiful?"

"They certainly are." She would have said more, but the words flew from her brain when Scott turned and bestowed his devilish grin on her. His expression changed to something softer, warmer.

"Marnie, hi. I didn't realize you'd be here. How's your mother?"

Startled, she smiled and took a deep breath. What was he doing there? "She's holding her own, thanks."

"I'm glad." He shoved his hands into his back pockets and glanced around the suddenly quiet room.

His shoulders appeared even broader in his hunter green polo shirt than they'd been in the leather jacket. That one lock of hair slipped down over his eyes again. Realizing she was staring, and probably drooling, she quickly averted her gaze. Her tight neck muscles relaxed when Jack announced dinner was ready.

As she carried her wine glass to the table, she tried to calm her racing pulse. It had to be lack of sleep and an overabundance of stress making her picture the wild and reckless things she wanted to do whenever she got near him. She had more than enough on her mind right now without a man complicating things by starting something up between them. Even if he was a fine-looking man.

Kate took her seat and started dishing up the linguine in clam sauce. As she passed a plate to Scott, she asked, "Now, how did you two meet again?"

"I stopped by the Youth Center a few days ago. When Marnie got the call about her mother, I drove her to the hospital."

"And I never had the chance to thank you." She set her own plate down, wiping her hands on the napkin in her lap. She brought her gaze up to meet his. "The rain was awful, and I was glad not to have to drive through it. It was sweet of you to take me."

His mouth curved into a pasta-filled smile, and he nodded.

"What were you doing at the Youth Center?" Kate passed the bread around but didn't take her gaze off him.

"On a case. I'm looking for a witness, a teenage girl." He turned to her. "Even though you've been busy with your mother, I hoped you'd have a list of names for me."

Although his warm chocolate gaze was alluring, she wasn't going to give him any names until she'd talked to Carly.

"I haven't had a chance to talk to Linda yet. I've been at the hospital most of the time, with my mom.

I'll try to get to it tomorrow."

"Thanks. I'd appreciate it, or I can go see Linda myself, if that's better for you."

She felt that current of connection between them again. The instant heat warmed her tired, aching body and gave her a renewed sense of energy. "I'll talk to her tomorrow, and one of us will call with that list of names."

"So," said Kate, filling Scott's wine glass, "do you handle a lot of missing person cases?" Her smile was sedate but the twinkle in her eyes showed mischief.

"It's not a missing person's case, really," he started.

"Honey..." Jack gave his wife the eye.

Marnie's face grew warm. Her friend might be meddling in something that ought not to be meddled in, at least not yet.

Kate finally looked at her, nodding. "I'm sure Scott would be happy to help you with your search."

He set down his wine glass, turning back to Marnie. "Are you searching for someone?"

"I-I don't know." She paused. "I just found out I was adopted." Giving her friend a pointed look, she continued, "I haven't decided yet whether I want to find my birth parents." She waited, expecting a laugh, a gasp, something. But he sat still, waiting, his gaze patient and sympathetic.

"My mother told me I was born and abandoned during the Summer Jam rock concert. I don't know much more than that."

Kate reached over and placed her hand on Marnie's arm, glancing at him. "I thought you could help her with this, Scott, as an experienced investigator, if she decides she wants to find her birth mother."

He nodded but didn't speak. Did he think she was crazy to even try? She could almost see his brain working behind his intense gaze, but couldn't tell which direction his thoughts were taking.

Finally, his gaze met hers. "I'd be happy to help you, if you decide you want to look for your birth parents."

She fiddled with her napkin but eventually raised her eyes and smiled at him. "Thank you. I'll let you know if I need any help." Working with him could be fun, if she decided to search for her birth parents, but she seriously doubted she'd want to do that any time soon.

His face relaxed a bit, breaking into his crooked smile. "Just say the word."

"Thanks."

He fished a business card out of his pocket and slid it across the table to her. "I forgot to give you one at the Center, after the call about your mother. Please call or email me when you get the list of girls together, and if you decide you want to start your search."

She grasped the card, curling her fingers around it. "I will."

The rest of the meal was a bit of a blur, as she tried to swallow some of Kate's great cooking along with her fears and conflicting emotions over the search and her developing attraction to Scott.

The guys talked about work, and Kate asked Scott about some case that was still open, but Marnie only listened with half an ear. No matter what her father said, a search would hurt her parents. And when the truth came out, whatever the truth turned out to be, would she be sorry she'd ever started to look? Whatever happened, did she want to risk the shame it might bring to her own mother to find out Grandma Gill was involved in illegal activity?

That thought made Marnie think it probably wouldn't be a good idea to work with a state police officer on finding the truth.

Their hosts carried dishes to the sink and loaded the dishwasher. The love between them showed in everything they did, each touch they shared.

The truth had literally changed their lives. When stuck in an abusive marriage to Jack's brother, Tony, Kate had feared the truth because of the pain and shame that came with it. Neither she nor Tony wanted anyone to know what went on within their marriage. But when Kate took the steps to free herself from her abusive husband, to stand on her own and bring their dirty little secrets to light, she had found not only her self-esteem and freedom but also Jack's love. The truth had brought them together.

She wanted to believe it would turn out as well for her. She wanted to know who she really was, and she couldn't do that without knowing where she came from.

Scott took a sip of the coffee Jack handed him and leaned back in his chair. The breadth of his shoulders and the warmth of his smile struck Marnie again. She enjoyed the good-natured way he teased Jack and buttered up Kate. And he'd brought her friend flowers.

To be honest, she liked everything she'd seen of him so far. She wanted to get to know him better, even though he seemed younger. Of course, maybe it wasn't such a big deal to the new Marnie, the daughter of a hippie.

If she hoped to have a new man in her life someday, she had to know who she was and what she wanted. To do that, she had to know where she came from, who her parents were—and she didn't know if she could trust the facts behind her "adoption" to him.

Dinner and dessert were long over by the time she rose to leave. "This has been wonderful, but I have to get going. Between work, visiting Mom, and making sure my father doesn't overdo, I'm running out of steam."

Kate smiled, wrapping her in a hug. "We completely understand, sweetie. It can't be easy balancing everything right now, but it will get better." Kate pulled back to meet her gaze. "Your mother will recover and have many more years with you, I know it. Give her my love when you see her, please."

Marnie swiped at an escaping tear, then pulled her friend into another hug as the guys stood and bid Marnie goodnight.

****

After she left, Scott knew the best thing would be to say his goodbyes and head home too, but he had some burning questions for Jack and his wife, so he sat back down. He didn't miss the shared glance between husband and wife, so he dove right into his questioning.

"So Marnie seems great." He couldn't keep the smile off his face. He wasn't fooling anyone into thinking this was benign small talk. Kate and Jack were smiling right back at him.

"She's wonderful," said Kate, laughter barely

contained in her voice.

His friend stood, walked to the refrigerator and came back with a couple bottles of beer, offering him one. "Our man is finally intrigued."

Scott shook his head, holding his hand up. "Not for me, thanks. I've got to drive back to Horseheads."

Jack set the beer down and stared at him, and Scott chuckled. "Of course I'm intrigued. She's intriguing. What can you tell me about her?"

His friend laughed. "Well, she's single, so what more do you need to know?" He took his seat next to his wife.

Kate poked her husband in the side with her elbow. "She's a great person. She's upset right now, with her mother's illness and the whole adoption bombshell, but she's really great."

"As long as you don't mind a woman who's a little older than you." Again, she elbowed Jack. He winced. "Well, she is, isn't she? She's got to be close to forty-five."

"She still looks good, dude."

Jack laughed, but protected his ribs. "She does."

Kate smiled. "I won't argue with you. She's beautiful, inside and out, and smart, runs a winery, volunteers as a tutor, and is active in community groups. She even finds time to volunteer at the library and was one of the first ones to introduce me to the range of audio books available."

Jack wrapped his arm around his wife's shoulders.

"So why is she single, then, if she's nice, beautiful, and smart?"

She leaned her head on her husband's shoulder. "She's picky, I guess. Since her divorce, she's had a lot of first dates, even some second and third ones, but she hasn't gotten serious about anyone. She said she knows early on if he's not the right one for her, and she's not interested in stringing a guy along, making him think he has a chance when she knows he doesn't."

Jack chuckled. "Ooh, no pressure there, Randall. If you don't make it to a third date, now you'll know why."

Kate made a half-hearted attempt to elbow him again. "There's nothing wrong with a woman knowing what she wants and doesn't want. She's not under any obligation to date a guy she doesn't want to have a future with."

He sat for minute, imagining her telling him she didn't want to see him anymore. He hoped it never came to that, as he was definitely interested in her. "When you say she's had a lot of dates, do you mean she gets around? I mean, she works at a winery, so is she a big partier?"

Jack shook his head. "She's nothing like Darlene, dude."

His shoulders relaxed. Jack knew what he had been through.

Kate sat up straight. "Marnie is not a party girl. She's a woman in her forties with a good job, a beautiful home, loving parents, and loyal friends. She's been on a lot of first dates because she's been divorced for years. But she's not promiscuous or easy. She's a great person, and I think you two would have a good time together. You'll have plenty to talk about. Give her a call and ask her out." She sat back, curled back into her husband's arm, and that was the end of that.

He thanked his friends, grabbed his coat, and headed home. He couldn't get Marnie's smile or the sparkle in her eyes out of his mind, so he'd have to take Kate's advice and ask her out to dinner. He was glad he needed to talk to her again about work, so he'd have an excuse to follow up with her.

****

When she picked up the check and cash from one of the restaurant tables, Carly noticed writing on the back of the paper: *"You wouldn't want anything to happen to those pretty little sisters of yours, would you? Keep your mouth shut."*

Her hand shook, but she shoved the note into her pocket before anyone could see. She closed her eyes, trying to remember who had been sitting at that table.

What did they want? She hadn't told anyone but Nick about the woman. She never even went to the cops.

How could they be everywhere she went?

How could she protect her sisters?

Chapter Four

"Want a ride, girlfriend?"

Turning toward the voice, Carly closed her hand on the door handle behind her. She squinted to see who waited outside the restaurant, her arms and legs already shaking. When she saw it was Marnie, she breathed a sigh of relief.

"Sorry, I didn't mean to startle you." Marnie gave her a quizzical look. "Are you okay? I was driving by and realized you'd be getting off work soon. Thought you might like a ride home." Leaning against the door of her car, Marnie dug her hands deep in her jeans pockets. She had a smile on her face and a Shania Twain CD pouring out through the open windows, definitely "a sight for sore eyes."

Hoisting her backpack onto her shoulder, Carly ran to the passenger side and jumped in. As Marnie buckled up, she passed over a can of cola.

"Thought you might be thirsty after such a long day. Did you eat?"

Carly closed her hands on the cold can, trying to steady her breathing. She popped the top, took a deep swallow of the sweet pop, and felt the bubbles lift her spirits. "Uh…yeah. I had some meatballs. They weren't selling much tonight."

But those meatballs were good, and she had several more tucked away in her backpack. Her sisters would be hungry when she got home. After another drink of cola, and another deep breath, she remembered about Marnie's mother. "Uh…is your mom any better?"

Marnie smiled at her, although a sad smile. "She's about the same, but thanks for asking. I'm sure she'll be doing better in a couple of days."

Linda at the Youth Center had told Carly Marnie's mom had a stroke a few years ago, and maybe this was another one, she didn't know for sure. Her mom must be old, although Marnie still seemed pretty young.

"Did she have a stroke?"

Marnie turned, surprise showing in her eyes.

"Uh…sorry. Linda said she might have had one."

"It's okay. No, it wasn't a stroke. Unfortunately, she's got leukemia."

Not good. "That's some kind of cancer, right?"

"Yeah. It's basically cancer of the blood. It makes her weak and is affecting every part of her body."

"Oh, man, it sounds bad. I'm sorry."

"It is bad, but we'll figure out a way to fight it."

She didn't want to ask anything else. The hurt on Marnie's face was too clear already.

"I can give you a ride, kiddo. Do you need to go straight home, or can we stop at my house for a few minutes?"

Other than the warm meatballs in her backpack, there was no reason to hurry. She'd already finished all of her schoolwork, best she could, and would check on the girls when she got home.

"No, I've got time. You've saved me the walk, ya know."

She texted Ashley and Deena to let them know

she'd be late. While they were getting older, at 11 and 12, her sisters still got nervous about being home alone for too long. And since their mother left, and their father was barely there himself, she was in charge of making sure the girls had something to eat before bedtime.

Marnie drove back toward the heart of town, "the flats," as people called it because it was on the flat area of land at the end of Seneca Lake, nestled between the two hills and east of Watkins Glen. The houses on the flats were mostly fixed up nice, not like the beat-up shack her family lived in.

They pulled into the driveway, and she dragged her backpack from the car. Her eyes widened as she climbed up the back steps, through the kitchen door, and into the warmth of the old house. What would it be like to live in a house like this?

The place was huge. "Do you live here all by yourself?"

Marnie nodded. "I grew up here, but when my parents moved to a retirement home, I bought it from them. I love this place."

Who wouldn't?

She took a seat at the kitchen table as Marnie suggested. Such a warm and cozy room.

"Want anything? Another cola or something to eat?"

Her stomach wasn't exactly normal these days. "No, thanks. I'm fine."

After grabbing a diet cola from the fridge, Marnie sat near her at the end of the table. "So how was school today? Need any help with homework?"

"Nah, I'm good."

Marnie took a sip and gave her a once-over that had her almost squirming in her seat. "I haven't had a chance to get to the Center in a couple of days. Anything new happening over there?"

She couldn't meet Marnie's gaze, so she stared at her fingernails. She'd almost completely chipped off the blue polish, but kept picking at it. "Don't know. I haven't been there the last couple days either."

Marnie laid a hand on her arm, so she stopped fidgeting, but didn't look up.

"What's going on? I can tell something's wrong. Can you tell me about it?"

Tears burned behind her eyelids, but they were always just below the surface these days. She didn't want to cry, didn't want anyone to think she was helpless—even though she had no idea what to do.

If she told Marnie what was going on, it'd make it more real. Of course, she might be able to help. She usually could.

She took a deep breath. It was time to come clean, even though the concern in Marnie's gaze almost brought on more tears.

"I'm pregnant." Her palms were clammy. As tough as it was saying it out loud, she'd been wanting to tell Marnie for days.

The quick, tight hug nearly knocked her off her chair. "Oh, honey. I'm so sorry. Are you okay?"

Overcome by the exhaustion, the overwhelming fear, the sense of being alone in the world, she sagged against Marnie. It felt so good to be held, to have a motherly figure patting her back, murmuring soft nonsense words, making her feel a little better.

When she'd cried all she could, she pulled back,

wiping her nose on the back of her hand. Marnie thrust some tissues at her, so she blew her nose. She was still tired, but felt a little better. At least no one had yelled at her.

Yet.

"Did you do a home pregnancy test?"

She nodded.

"Just one? Sometimes they aren't accurate, you know."

She sighed. "I did three. They were all positive."

"Okay. Have you been to a doctor?"

Shredding the wad of tissues in her hand, she nodded. "I went to Planned Parenthood, over in Montour Falls, you know, for the blood test."

Marnie stood and walked to the desk in the corner of the pretty blue-and-white kitchen, pulled out some paper and a pen, then returned to the table. "So we have to figure out what to do from here."

Carly stared as her mentor started numbering down the left side of the paper. On the top, she wrote "Carly's Plan" and underlined it. Next to the number one, she wrote "doctor."

If only Marnie knew everything, she'd add a few more items to her list.

"First, you need to see a doctor, to make sure everything's okay. You can go to Planned Parenthood again, they're good, or I can take you to my gynecologist. She's young, hip, and good. Do you want me to make you an appointment?"

She nodded, unable to find her voice.

"Okay, good. Once we know how far along you are, and if you're healthy, you can review the various options available and decide what you want to do."

Number two was pregnancy options, with a question mark next to it. She wasn't sure whether it meant questions she might have, questions about what she was going to do, or who the father was. She hadn't even asked.

"How are you feeling?" Marnie patted her back gently. "Are you nauseated? Vomiting at all?"

"Not really. Mostly, I'm tired all the time."

Nodding, Marnie made more notes. "From what I hear, it's perfectly normal, especially in the first trimester. Try to get as much sleep as you can."

Yeah, right. She couldn't sleep in school, at the Youth Center, or at work. Those were the only times she got out of the house. There was too much to do at home, taking care of the girls, her father, and the housework, never mind her schoolwork.

Her father didn't want to hear about her being too tired. He sure as hell wouldn't want to hear she was pregnant. They definitely didn't need another mouth to feed.

Marnie wrote a few more things on the list, such as vitamins, naps, and school issues. She got up and got another diet cola, tossing her empty can into the recycling bin on the way.

"Have you talked to the baby's father at all? Does he know? Do you want him to?"

She tried to push the knot of panic back down her throat so she could speak. "We talked about it some. He wants to get married, but I don't think it's a good idea."

Marnie smiled, care and concern showing through each little line around her eyes and the soft light of her gaze. "What are your reasons for thinking so?"

She smiled and didn't make it sound like Carly was doing something wrong. Just asking. It was nice.

"We're too young, and I don't even know yet if I want to have this baby."

"You don't have to tell me who the father is, unless you want to. You can take your time to decide what you want to do, and what's best for you." Marnie reached out and took her hand. "Let's think about you for now, okay?"

Nobody had ever said that to her before. "Okay." She checked her watch, and a wave of panic prickled up her spine. "Uh, I'd better be getting home."

Marnie folded up the list and put it in her purse. Of course, that purse was so huge, and so full of stuff, who knew if they'd ever see the list again. How did the woman ever find anything in there?

"Of course. I'm sorry, I didn't mean to make you late. I wouldn't want to worry your father. Do you want to call and tell him we're on our way?"

"Uh…no. That's okay. He's probably not home yet." Or *too wasted to hear the phone.*

When they walked out the back door, out of the warmth and light of the kitchen and the comforting feel of the house, it was like a physical ache. Marnie was so lucky to have grown up here.

At the same time, she knew she couldn't change things. She needed to get home, to give the girls their meatballs, and tuck them into bed. They could fill her in on their days while they ate, and hopefully, they'd drift off to sleep soon after.

Then, maybe she could sneak off to bed herself. She needed sleep. She could do the dishes and pick up the house in the morning, before school. She didn't want her father to figure out anything was wrong.

She needed sleep, instead of staying up late worrying about what might happen. She had to come up with a plan.

Her father would probably be furious about this baby. He'd definitely be disappointed in her. He couldn't even know about it, at least not until she'd decided what to do. She didn't know how she'd keep it a secret, but she needed time to make up her own mind.

She needed to keep her sisters safe, to keep herself and her baby safe. Even her father.

She'd have to find a way.

****

The next morning, Marnie couldn't keep from stopping in front of the hospital nursery. She stood at the window, watching the wiggly little red bundles in pink and blue blankets, marveling at the way the nurses knew how to calm and soothe each one.

The thought of Carly having a baby in her teens frightened her. There was so much the girl hadn't had a chance to experience yet, so much growing she had left to do herself. Of course, if she was worried, Carly must be scared half to death.

Would she decide to abort the baby, assuming she wasn't too far along in the pregnancy to make such a choice? Would she want to keep her baby? What was the right decision for her? What was the right choice for the baby?

A week ago, if anyone had asked for her opinion, she would have said adoption was a wonderful option in such a tough situation. Staring at the sleeping babies in the nursery window, panic started to surge through her. How could she recommend giving up a baby for adoption if it meant the child could one day be faced with the shock she'd had to deal with? If it was a closed adoption, the baby might never learn about Carly or her boyfriend or any real roots.

How could anyone do that to a baby? Although the rational, calm part of her brain knew it might be the best option for the mother, and adoption was often best for the baby, too, wasn't the child entitled to someday learn the truth about his or her parents? Didn't a person deserve to know where they came from? Deserve to feel wanted?

She would never want to condemn another person to the hell she was going through, not knowing who she was, where she came from, what kind of people her parents were. There had to be a better way, but she didn't know what it was.

She left the maternity ward and went to her mother's room. Her mother appeared smaller, older, and much more fragile than usual.

If only she'd wake up.

After kissing her mother's cheek, Marnie pulled up the blankets. Walking around the small room, she watered the flowers, grabbed a stack of cards, and began reading them aloud.

"You have the most soothing voice."

Soft, blue eyes and a sad smile greeted her. Marnie dropped the card in her hand and leaned forward.

"Hello again. How are you feeling?"

Her mom shifted a bit on the bed. "Not great, but better, I think. I'm not nearly as exhausted as I was."

"That's a good sign." She wrapped her hand

around her mother's, stroking the long, thin bones. Why hadn't she ever noticed how different their hands were?

"Shouldn't you be at work?"

"I'm going in a little late today. Dad and I are alternating days. That seems to be the best plan for us right now. He'll be along this afternoon, when his class is over."

"I'm glad he went. He needs to keep teaching, even if it's only one class a week. It's much better for him than sitting around here watching me sleep."

Marnie smiled. Her father had said exactly the opposite last night when they made up this plan.

"Besides, we need some more time for girl talk, right?" Her mother's eyes were bright, but her skin was still gray.

Marnie stood, walking to the window to adjust the mini-blinds. As much as she wanted to know more, she wasn't sure her mother was up to talking, at least not for long.

"We've got lots of time to talk, Mom. You need your rest. Do you want me to turn on the TV? Or, if you'd rather, I brought your CD player and a few CDs. I have some of your favorite jazz and classical stuff. What would you prefer?"

"Marnie."

The firm, almost sharp "Mom" voice always stopped her in her tracks. She turned to her mother.

"Sit. I don't need a distraction. I need to talk to you, help you understand how you came into our lives. I want you to know as much as I do, to help you find your birth parents, if you decide to look." While her mother's words were strong, her voice wavered.

"I don't want you to get too tired. You need your rest."

Her mom smiled. "I'm lying down, dear. I can handle it."

She sat, her hands folded in her lap, and sighed. This was harder than she'd thought it would be. "Okay, but promise me, if you get too tired, we'll save the rest for another time."

Nodding, her mother said, "Okay. Now, first, I want you to know how much your father and I love you."

"I could never question your love. I have the best parents ever. You've always made me feel cherished and special. Nothing could change that."

"But…"

She met her mother's dark brown gaze. "But how could you keep this from me?" She took a breath, holding her anger at bay. "I had a right to know, Mom, a long time ago. I need to know where I came from, who those people were, who I am. You should have told me." She clasped her hands together in her lap, trying to stop the shaking.

"You're right, of course." The soft voice shook. "It was selfish of us not to tell you. We couldn't admit there was even a moment when you weren't ours. In the beginning, at least, and for a long time, I was too scared someone would come and take you away. But once you hit eighteen, my fear faded and was replaced by the utter terror of you hating me, rejecting us, never letting us be a part of your life again. That would have killed me, and your father, too. But you had the right to know."

Marnie nodded and waited until she could speak

without her voice cracking. "So tell me, if you're up to it. Tell me what happened."

"Okay." Her mother shifted, a wince momentarily crossing her face. "What do you know about the Summer Jam?"

Shaking her head, she said, "Not much. I mean, I know it was a big rock concert, sort of like Woodstock, at the race track in Watkins Glen."

"When the concert was planned, it was going to be a crowd of about a hundred thousand people, not much different than the races in Watkins at the time. By the time the weekend was over, though, more than six times that many young people swarmed to the village. They abandoned their cars because the traffic was bad, even fifty to a hundred miles away, and walked there. People camped in the grass in front of the post office, along the beach, and everywhere. It was insane."

"Were you there?"

Her mother laughed and then coughed. "No, thankfully. Dad and I didn't live in the area back then. We were living in Tully. We both taught at Syracuse at the time. I remember my parents were livid about the mess the concert made, even in Harper's Glen. Teenagers and hippies overran every town within a fifty-mile radius of Watkins, so you can imagine Harper's Glen was crazy."

"All to see what? Three bands?"

"But remember, the three bands playing were the Allman Brothers, the Grateful Dead, and The Band. They had a huge number of fans. Every kid in the Northeast wanted in on this concert, in the hopes it would be another Woodstock. It turned out to be even bigger than Woodstock. It rained like mad, though, so everything was muddy."

Although her mother was still pale, finally telling the truth appeared to revive her slightly.

"Okay, so somewhere during this mess, I was born?"

Her mom swallowed, and a glimmer of moisture pooled in the loving blue eyes.

"Yes. Remember, this is what my mother told me, and she wouldn't say much, so I don't know all the facts. She said a teenager who was at the concert gave birth to you in the back of someone's VW microbus. The mother didn't stay around, because the owner returned when the rain stopped, and he found you in his van. A cop was nearby—I think he was a village police officer. Anyway, they gave you to him."

Marnie sat stone still, unable to breathe, or utter even one word. The chill that had started in the fingers she had clenched around the arms of her chair began to inch up her spine.

"The police officer found an ambulance, which wasn't easy, given the horrendous crowding and mile-deep mud. They took you to the hospital and tried to track down your birth mother. Apparently, the hospital was so overcrowded they called my dad, since he was mayor of Harper's Glen then, to see if he could find a temporary home for you. He asked Mom to do it, and she brought you to me in Tully."

"Why not ask the Watkins mayor?"

Her mother shook her head. "I guess he had too much he was already having to deal with at the time. All the village services were more than maxed out."

Trying to process the mental pictures in her mind,

Marnie shook her head. "Just like that? Weren't the police worried about what happened to me? Surely they followed up with your parents and realized the baby was gone. I mean, they lost a baby and didn't care?"

Her mother took several deep breaths, reached a hand out to her, and she grasped it.

"Maybe we should take a break…"

"No," her mother insisted. "I'm fine." After another deep breath, she continued. "Mom told them your birth mother returned. She made up some name and hometown, I don't remember where, and told them she'd given the baby to the rightful mother. In her mind, she had, so I'm sure she was pretty convincing. Plus, the whole area was overrun with concertgoers. The people of Watkins Glen and Harper's Glen were up to their ears in drugged-out, drunken young people—lining the streets, cleaning out the stores, eating and drinking everything in sight. My father spent most of the weekend at the track trying to help keep the peace. Remember, my father was the mayor and my mother was the school nurse, both respected in the community. The police probably never gave Mom's story another thought."

It still didn't make sense. "But I've seen my birth certificate. It lists you and Dad as my birth parents. How did you come up with that?"

"My mother gave it to me when she brought you to us. I don't know how she got it. I asked, but she only told me that a friend knew a guy who helped them out. I decided you were a gift from God, and I wasn't going to argue about it."

Her mother fell silent, leaning back against her

pillows and closing her eyes. "I didn't want to know more. I was a coward."

It was too much to believe, too bizarre not to be true, but nonetheless unreal. Not only was she not the person she thought she was, this whole scheme was a tangle of questionable ethics and downright illegalities. The woman—hell, the girl—who gave birth to her had thrown her away, probably hoping the poor schmuck with the microbus would keep her. Then the woman who would become her grandmother stole her, lied to the cops, and got a forged birth certificate. Finally, her mother hid the truth from her father for over forty years. And neither of them had ever bothered to tell her.

And she'd never even had a parking ticket.

"Honey, are you okay?" Her mother's voice was soft, diaphanous, barely there. This was too much for her.

Marnie opened her eyes. Her mother reached for her again. Stifling the urge to bolt out of the room, she leaned forward, grasping her hand.

"That's enough for today, Mom."

Her mother didn't speak, just seemed to be holding her breath.

"It's going to take me a while to process all this, you know?"

Her mom nodded, and her eyes filled with tears again. "I understand. I know it's a lot. And I know it's awful. I'm so sorry, honey."

She squeezed her mother's hand gently. "I know, Mom. I know."

After another few minutes had passed, she met her mother's gaze again. "Do you know anything about her? Did Grandma Gill ever learn anything about the woman who'd had me? If not her name, any more details about what happened?"

Head shaking, her mother sniffed. "She told me she didn't know anything about the mother, and after that she refused to talk about it anymore."

Marnie sighed.

"Are you going to try to find her?" The whisper was so faint, it was almost as if she never asked.

There was no need to think about it any longer. She already knew the answer. "Yes, I guess I am."

Her mother nodded. "Good."

Without another word, her mom drifted back to sleep. Marnie sat by her side, still holding her hand, for a long time before finally deciding to move. She stood and kissed her mother's cheek.

Suddenly, she looked around and found she was in the lobby, with no real memory of how she got there. She needed to let her dad know her mother had woken up. Wanting to escape the hospital for a moment, she burst through the sliding doors and into the sunshine. She found a bench in the garden and sat, allowing the heat of the sun to wash over her.

The hospital sat on a hill above Watkins Glen and had an incredible view of the valley and Seneca Lake as it snaked deep and silent through the farmland and vineyards. Smoke puffed out from the salt plant, and the fire whistle sounded the noon hour. Even from here, the white caps on the lake pounded the shore, and a few brave sailboats cut ribbons across the steel-blue water.

Closing her eyes, Marnie let her thoughts slide to what it must have been like forty-some years ago—

teenage concertgoers lining the roads, sleeping in fields, looking for food. In high school, she'd done some research about Summer Jam, and it sounded exactly as her mother described it. Chaos. Lots of drunk and high teenagers, half-naked and covered in mud, trying to find water, food, and clean bathrooms. Not necessarily hostile, but not really law-abiding, either.

That had been her beginning.

Not the warm little house she barely remembered in Tully, before Grandma Gill died and they moved to Harper's Glen. Not the cozy, sunny kitchen or her pretty, pink bedroom in the big old Victorian in the heart of town. Not the soft, tight hugs of her father or the gentle touch of her mother.

Booze, rain, mud, drugs, chaos, and rock-and-roll. A teenage hippie so stoned she didn't care what happened to her baby. Some guy with a VW microbus. That's what she came from.

Those were her roots, not the picture-perfect life she thought she'd been leading. Not warmth, responsibility, love, and respect. She wasn't at all the person she'd thought she was.

How could anything ever be the same again?

****

Scott pulled into the restaurant parking lot a good five minutes before he was supposed to meet Marnie for dinner. She was already there, outside the door, even prettier than he remembered.

When she'd emailed him that she had the list of girls at the Youth Center who might be his witness, it had felt natural to thank her with a dinner invitation. Jack had already ribbed him that his intentions were clear for everyone to see, but he kept telling himself it was a simple "thank you" between friends. Not really a date, or at least he tried to play it up that way. She'd been kind enough to agree.

She waved to him as he got out of his Jeep, her smile lighting up her face. Waving back, he couldn't help but notice how the little crinkles gathered around her eyes, making her face softer and kinder. She was so petite a strong wind would probably knock her down. As he was getting to know her, though, he had every suspicion she'd jump right back up.

"Hi. It's good to see you again." Just one look at her and the day's stress melted away.

"You, too."

He held the door open for her as they entered the softly lit entry. She'd suggested this restaurant, which was new to him. If the tantalizing aroma of garlic and basil was any indication, it was going to be a great meal.

They sat in a booth along the back wall, which was quiet and private, perfect for this getting-to-know-you-but-not-really-a-date kind of occasion.

After they ordered dinner and wine, he asked her about her mother.

"She's getting stronger, although we have a long row to hoe. The doctors are not as pessimistic as they were on the first night, so I guess that's a good thing."

"Good, I'm glad to hear it."

"Oh, that reminds me..." She opened her giant purse and rifled through, pulling out a small, wrapped gift.

"Your purse must weigh more than you do," he joked, as she let it drop onto the booth with a thud.

"What all do you have in there?"

She laughed. "I know it's huge, but I like to carry a lot of stuff. I never know when I might need my calendar or tissues or a paperback book. I hate to get caught in a long line or a waiting room with nothing to read. Besides, I make a lot of lists."

She handed him the small wrapped box.

"What's this?"

Her smile was shy, even tentative. "I wanted to thank you for helping me the night my mother went to the hospital. I really appreciate your kindness, especially given we were total strangers at the time."

He smiled and pulled off the wrapping paper. Inside the small box was a cork puller with an engraved wooden handle. It read "Davis Wines."

"Thanks. You didn't need to give me anything, but I like it. I've never been to many of the local wineries."

"I work there. You'll have to come visit sometime, and I can give you the full tour."

At that moment, the server arrived with their wine. "You're the expert," he said, indicating the server should pour the first taste in Marnie's glass.

She took a sip and nodded to the server, who then poured wine into both of their glasses and quietly stepped away.

"How long have you been at the winery?"

A fleeting grin crossed her lips. "A pretty long time now. I used to be married to Matt Davis, who owns the place, so I've been working there since before we got divorced."

He shook his head. "Your ex owns it, but you still work there? Isn't it awkward for both of you?"

"You'd think so, but really it's not. We were lucky enough to be friends first and stayed friends after the divorce. Even though our marriage didn't work, we didn't see any reason to end our friendship, or our professional relationship."

"Good for you," he said, nodding. "I certainly couldn't work with my ex. Never mind the baggage we'd have to get past, you know, after she cheated on me and all. It's just that she's so irresponsible, I wouldn't want to work for any place that would be willing to hire her." Taking a deep breath, he checked himself, not wanting to sound too crazy. "So what do you do at the winery?"

Their food arrived, and they started to dig in before she answered. "I'm the winery manager, Matt's the farm manager and the owner of the whole operation, and the winemaker is in charge of the magic which goes into the bottles."

He swallowed a bite of his delicious chicken parmigiana before continuing. "I know the wine business around here is growing like mad and has been a huge boon to the local economy."

This time, her smile lit up her face. "You really should visit some of the local wineries. We have more than a hundred in the Finger Lakes region. Our wineries are competing with, and often surpassing, wineries from California, Oregon, and even international winemakers. I can give you some suggestions."

He took a sip of his wine, which was local and good. "Okay. You've convinced me. Make me a list of your ten top favorites, and I'll start checking them off."

"Beginning at Davis's, of course." She tapped her glass to his.

"Of course." He set down his glass and glanced back up at her. "Maybe you'll take some time to show me some of your favorites personally?"

She blushed a little, and it was a good look on her.

"Maybe." She laughed. "Who am I kidding? I never have to be convinced to taste at any number of local places. And I can call it market research."

She can call it whatever she likes, as long as she smiles at me the way she is right now.

She cut into her lake trout and took a bite. A drop of butter clung to the corner of her lower lip. Before he could think why, he reached across the table and caught the drop on the tip of his index finger.

She didn't pull back or say a word, but a heat in her gaze matched the flame growing in the center of his chest. His finger burned as he sucked the butter into his own mouth.

They ate in near silence, murmuring about the food and tasting each other's dinner. He couldn't take his gaze off her, mesmerized by the way she held her fork, sipped her wine, wiped her mouth.

"I have the list of names for you, uh, of girls at the shelter." Her smile was gone and she became all business as she held out the list for him.

He almost choked on the water he'd just sipped. Yeah, that was why they were meeting. "Thanks."

She offered him a sheet of paper but didn't let go when he grabbed it. "These are good kids."

He shook his head. "I'm sure they are. I'm not arresting anybody. I just have some questions."

Her shoulders dropped, and the corners of her

mouth tilted up slightly. "Okay."

After they finished a shared tiramisu, he paid the bill, she left the tip, and he guided her outside to take a stroll in the evening air. Spring had finally sprung, so the night was cool but clear and comfortable. They walked north on Franklin Street, toward the lakefront, taking in the cool air.

She pulled her jacket around her and then leaned briefly against his arm. "Have you always lived in this area?"

He stuck his hands in his pockets and nodded. "Yeah. I grew up in Odessa and came back after college. When I decided to enter the State Police Academy, I knew I wanted to be assigned to the Horseheads' barracks."

"Do you still have family in Odessa?"

He shook his head. "My mom moved to Florida a few years ago after one too many snow-covered winters. My father passed away a few years before, so she wanted to be near her sister, who lives in St. Petersburg. I visit a couple times each year, and she comes up to see her local friends in the heat of the summer, when it becomes unbearable in Florida."

She shook her head. "I don't think I could ever retire to Florida, but I know a lot of older people like getting away from the cold winter weather."

They walked out the pier at the southern tip of the lake, a tranquil site that had become a favorite of tourists.

"What do you know about the Summer Jam rock concert here in Watkins in the seventies?"

"I remember my father talking about it, the cars blocking the roads around our house in Odessa.

Sounds like a wild weekend. I'm glad I wasn't a trooper then."

She shivered, so he took her arm and turned back toward the restaurant.

After they'd walked a bit, she spoke again. "I heard the town fathers passed an ordinance shortly after that weekend to basically prohibit something similar from happening again."

He nodded. "Yeah. There was a lot of property damage in all of the surrounding areas, more than had ever happened with a race up at the track—even though they used to burn buses during race weekends, up there in the bog."

She laughed. "I've heard about that."

He put his arm around her shoulders. She fit perfectly against his side, like she was made especially for him. The faintest pink blossomed on her cheeks as she snuggled in closer. He escorted her to her car in the parking lot. "I wasn't born yet when Summer Jam happened, but it still affects policing in this area sometimes. Locals have a long memory."

She was quiet but didn't shrug off his arm. He liked the way it felt to keep her warm. "I really enjoyed dinner tonight. I hope we can do it again." He waited, hoping he wasn't pushing her too far, too fast.

She smiled. "Me too. Thanks for suggesting it."

He took that as a good start. As they reached her car, he slid his hand to the center of her waist. Even as tiny as she was, she would fit perfectly in his embrace.

She turned to unlock her door. He pulled it open and then leaned against it, bringing his face mere inches from hers.

When her wide-eyed gaze met his, he wanted to

dive into the hazel pools. Whatever he'd been about to say was gone. He cupped her cheek in his hand, the smooth and silky skin almost his undoing.

Before he missed this chance, he leaned in and laid his lips on hers. It was a moment, the merest touch, but it rocked him to his soul.

She murmured good-bye, dropped into her car, and closed the door.

Still, he didn't move, couldn't look away. Whatever else happened, they needed time to explore this connection between them. He couldn't remember another woman exciting both his body and his mind the way she did, especially so quickly.

****

When she got home and had tucked her sisters into bed, Carly sat at the table and pulled her books out of her backpack. A picture of her walking out of school was stuck inside her chemistry book. There was a big red X centered on her face. She pulled out the photo, but there was no other writing on either side.

She couldn't seem to focus. Her pulse echoed *rat-a-tat-tat* inside her head and her throat went dry.

That picture hadn't been in her chemistry book in tenth period.

Whoever was following her, stalking her, had gotten into her backpack when it was inside her locker. Her palms went clammy and her throat dry.

She'd have to work harder to keep the girls safe and her baby safe. They could find her anywhere.

Chapter Five

By the time Marnie got to the Youth Center the following day, homework time was over, so she popped into Linda's office. "Sorry I'm late."

The director glanced up from her computer, her brows raised. "I'm surprised to see you at all. How's your mom?"

"About the same. I stopped at the hospital after work, but she was asleep, so I decided to drive back down here. Anything I can do?"

Linda motioned her to a chair while she got up and closed the door. "I'm worried about Carly. She asked for you when she first got here. I tried to talk to her but got nowhere. She's been off in the corner working on her own, but I think she's upset."

"I'll talk to her." Although she ought to tell Linda about the girl's pregnancy, she wanted to give the girl more time.

She stood and followed Linda into the main room.

"We've got things handled in here. You see what you can do for her." Linda gestured in the girl's direction.

Marnie headed off to the far table where Carly sat. The girl's already too-thin frame was even frailer. Her hair was greasy and her skin pale. She might not have any morning sickness yet, but she was definitely exhausted.

The frightened expression on the girl's face eased a bit as Marnie approached. She wanted to pull her into a big hug but knew it might spark more tears, causing the other kids to notice. Best not to do anything that would lead to uncomfortable questions.

"Hey, girlfriend. How ya doing?"

Carly gave her a wan smile as she took a seat across from her. "Okay. What about you?"

"Good, thanks." The pregnant teen needed more food, more sleep, and fewer worries, but there was only so much Marnie could do to help. "Listen, I wondered if you'd take a walk with me today? I'd like to continue our talk of the other night, only with a little more privacy, you know?"

"It's okay if we leave? You don't have to stay and help anybody else right now?"

She smiled, the little-girl insecurity on the thin but beautiful face almost doing her in. "Nope. It's just you and me, okay?"

After stepping out onto the sidewalk, she directed the girl north toward the lake. The Youth Center was located in an old church fellowship hall, right over the town line from Watkins Glen. It was off the main drag and a little quieter, but still convenient for the kids to walk to after school.

When she asked about homework and school, Carly's answers were emotionless and mundane. She'd finished her homework, nothing was new at school, and her job was fine. From the park at the end of the lake, they could see the sun slip down to a sliver of pink shining over the west hill.

After walking through the parking area and crossing behind a pavilion and basketball court, they wandered down toward the water's edge.

Marnie motioned to a bench, taking a seat after Carly plopped down. "I love sunsets on the lake, don't you?"

The girl first turned to Marnie, her gaze confused and questioning. Then she glanced at the lake, as if seeing it for the first time. After a moment, she turned back. "Yeah, I guess. It's pretty."

Marnie had missed this view when she moved to New York City after college, so she appreciated the way the lake nestled between the hills, reflecting the glorious pinks, corals, and reds of the sunset on the waves.

"How are you feeling? Have you had any morning sickness? Are you getting enough sleep? Any cramping or pain?"

The girl's slender shoulders dropped, as if her chest suddenly deflated.

"I'm fine…tired, but it's no big deal."

"Have you given any more thought to your options and what you might want to do about the baby?"

Carly slowly shook her head. "No, not yet."

"No problem." Marnie put a hand on her back. "It's your decision, sweetie. I want to help in whatever way I can."

After a few moments, Carly spoke up again. "I saw your doctor. She said I'm about nine weeks now, so I don't have long to make up my mind."

"But you still have some time, so take all you need."

They stood up and strolled along the water's edge in silence, stopping to skip a few stones along the way.

Marnie took a deep breath, knowing her next question might set the girl off again. They stopped at a picnic table and sat.

"Is there any reason you can think of why the police might want to question you?"

Carly shot up straight, dropping her backpack off her lap. "The police? They want to talk to me?"

Smiling her most reassuring smile, she put her hand on the girl's shoulder. "A state trooper stopped by the center looking for a blonde teenage girl, and his description made me think of you. I wondered if there's anything we should be concerned about."

Carly turned slightly, her shoulders hunched and face drawn. "Do you think he'll come back?"

"Yes, He's looking for a witness, and we gave him a list of names of all the girls who come to the center. He'll have to sort them out."

"What's his name?"

"Scott Randall. He works out of the State Police office in Horseheads. Do you know him?"

Carly sat so still Marnie began to wonder if she was going to answer. Just when she was about to shake her, the girl's eyes filled with tears, some of which escaped to slide down her hollow cheeks. Nodding, she leaned her head down and began sobbing in earnest when Marnie pulled her into a hug.

Rocking and soothing her as best as possible, she let the girl have her cry. She tried not to panic at Carly's reaction to Scott's name. She pulled a tissue out of her purse and handed it to the sobbing teen.

When the sobs melted into hiccups, Carly pulled back and wiped her eyes and face. Marnie left her arm around the girl's shoulders, waiting for her to speak.

"Sorry. I got you all wet."

She chuckled. "No problem. A little water never hurt anybody."

After blowing her nose, Carly walked to the nearby trash can, tossed her tissue, and came back, sitting on the bench facing Marnie.

"So?" She waited.

"So, Nick is..." the girl hesitated. "He's the baby's father."

"Okay."

"Well, this Scott Randall is Nick's brother, or brother-in-law, or something. Nick talks about him, thinks the dude walks on water. He's probably looking for me because..."

"Because..." She fought to keep the desperation from her voice. She waited for a reply, her hands folded tightly in her lap so as not to shake the answer loose. What did he have to do with Carly?

"Because Nick told him someone tried to buy my baby."

Marnie shook her head. "What?"

Carly sank onto the bench, her answer muffled as she talked into the neckline of her sweater.

Rubbing her palm between the girl's shoulder blades, Marnie asked, "What's going on?"

Carly's eyes were wet again, but she held in the threatening tears. "Somehow this lady found out I was pregnant and said how she could find a good home for my baby and maybe I could make a little money for my trouble."

"When did this happen?"

She shrugged her shoulders. "A couple weeks ago."

Marnie placed her hand on the girl's arm. "Do you have any idea who the woman was or how she found out you were pregnant?"

Shaking her head, she said, "No, I never saw her before."

"Hmmm." She dug a pad of paper and a pen from her bag again. "Tell me what you remember. What she looked like, where you were, what she said, like that."

"I don't want to get you in trouble, to bring you into this."

She rubbed the girl's back. "Don't worry about me, sweetie. Let me help you."

Despite her scared expression, Carly took a deep breath and started talking. "She was old, you know, way old. Over fifty, maybe even over sixty. She had brownish hair that was pretty gray. She wasn't as tall as me, and she was really skinny. She kinda reminded me of a mouse. Not the kind of person you'd really notice unless you were looking right at her."

She wrote as quickly as she could. "Good, that's excellent. Do you think you'd recognize her if you saw her again?" If she identified the woman, the police could arrest her.

The teen laughed, making a tight little sound. "I'm not likely to forget someone who tried to buy the baby I haven't even decided whether I'm having or not. And before I'd told almost anyone, too."

Nodding, Marnie stopped writing and gazed into the girl's eyes. "Who had you told before this woman approached you?"

Still for a moment, the teen finally said, "Just Nick. Nobody else."

She wrote it down. While a teenage boy might

have told a buddy, she couldn't believe he would be behind someone's attempt to buy the baby.

"Oh, and the people at Planned Parenthood."

"Okay." That could be the connection. "How soon after you went to Planned Parenthood did this woman talk to you? And where? We need to figure out how she found you."

Carly shrugged. "She waited for me at the curb when I walked out of school, probably about three days after I'd been to Planned Parenthood. I have no idea how she found me. But after I said no, her face changed."

"What do you mean? How did it change?"

Carly stared down at her hands, waited a moment, and then met Marnie's gaze. "She stopped smiling and got a real cold look in her eyes, like I was trying to steal something of hers or hit her car or something. And she sorta threatened me."

Marnie sat up straight, dropped the pen on the table, and placed a hand on the girl's arm. "What did she say?"

The girl mumbled, her voice low. "Something like I was to keep this all to myself and not tell the cops or anything, if I knew what was good for me."

Wrapping her arm around Carly's shoulders, Marnie bowed her head down to rest her forehead against her hair. "I'm so glad you didn't let her frighten you into keeping quiet about it. That's so smart, and brave, of you. She's probably done this to other girls before." She pulled back, meeting the girl's gaze.

"But..." Carly's lips thinned to a line, her eyes filled with tears.

"But what?" She could feel the shiver that ran through the teen and wanted nothing more than to protect her from whoever wanted to hurt her.

"I'm not supposed to tell anyone, go to the police, whatever, or something bad might happen, ya know, to me or the girls."

"Is that what the woman told you?"

The girl nodded, her head almost resting on Marnie's shoulder before she pulled herself away.

Marnie slipped her arm around the girl's shoulders. "Don't worry. You'll be safe, the girls, too. It'll help to tell the police. They can keep you safe."

Carly shook her head and pulled away. "Yeah, well, I didn't want to go to the cops. I'm still not sure I do. If this trooper wasn't Nick's brother or cousin or whatever, I doubt I'd be even thinking about talking to him."

Steepling her fingers in front of her lips, Marnie paused. "Let's concentrate on this woman. Are you sure you didn't see her at Planned Parenthood?"

"No. I told the receptionist I was there for a pregnancy test. Then I saw a nurse, who made me pee in a cup. She did the test and told me I was pregnant. After she gave me a bunch of pamphlets, I left. I didn't see anyone else."

"Okay." She set her paper and pen down and took one of Carly's hands in her own. "Honey, I know you're scared, but you really need to tell all of this to Scott so he can find this woman. Buying and selling babies is illegal, and there's a good chance you weren't the first and you won't be the last young mom she approached."

The girl's eyes filled with tears. "Do I have to?"

She nodded slowly. "Yeah, you do, if only to protect you, your sisters, and your baby. I can go with you, if you want. And if he's related to Nick, you can decide if you want Nick there too."

Carly pulled her hand away to blow her nose, shaking her head. "No way. Nick gets so wound up about all of this. I haven't even decided if I'm having or keeping this baby, and he's already starting to plan a wedding and completely change our lives."

Marnie rubbed the knot at the base of the girl's neck, her heart aching for the pain Carly was suffering. No wonder she hadn't been herself lately.

"How long have you and Nick been together?"

"I don't know if we're really together. Nick and me, we've been hooking up since maybe early fall, when I'm not working, he's not working, and I don't have to be home taking care of the girls. He's an okay guy, not like most of the jerks at school."

"You've been dating Nick for what, five or six months?"

Carly laughed. "I wouldn't call it dating. We meet up after school sometimes. We talk, get something to eat, hang out, you know. It's not like we go out to the movies or he's taking me to the prom or something." A blush crept up her face. "We hooked up and...you know, he's nice. It's nice."

"How do you feel about him? Regardless of what you decide about the baby, would you want to go on dating him, for lack of a better word?" She could practically feel the heat from the girl's blush now.

"I guess so. I mean, he understands about how I have to take care of my sisters and don't have a lot of spare time. He treats me nice, and we work on homework together sometimes. He never comes to the house, like I asked."

Cocking her head to the side, Marnie quizzed, "You asked him to come to your house and he won't?"

"No!" The teen nearly yelled. "I definitely don't want him to come to my house, and I told him so. I meant he listened to me and never has." Carly looked at her out of the corner of her eye, her face turned slightly away. "We don't have much, ya know, and you can barely call it a house. I don't want anybody from school to go there."

Her heart broke for the girl. Frank Johnson, Carly's father, was in and out of work, and her mother had died several years ago. Like so many families in the hills surrounding town, the family had barely enough to get by. Without the free breakfast and lunch at school, Carly and her sisters would probably go hungry. She knew where they lived but had never been in the house. The house was little more than a shack and she'd never wanted to embarrass the girl.

"Okay." She stood, eager to ease Carly's discomfort. "Why don't I call Scott and arrange for the three of us to meet? I'll ask him to come to my house tomorrow after school. Does that sound okay to you?"

The teen nodded again but seemed more wary this time. "But don't tell him about any of this until tomorrow, okay?"

"Okay, I promise. It's your story to tell. How about I pick you up after school tomorrow?"

The girl shook her head. "No. I'll be fine. I'll grab a ride with Nick but tell him you're tutoring me."

Marnie smiled and sent up a silent prayer to keep the kids safe.

Carly stood. "Uh, listen, I need to get to work. There's Nick now." She gestured toward a car just parking on the street beyond them.

Looking at her watch, Marnie nodded. "No problem."

Instead of heading back to the Youth Center, Carly walked toward downtown and turned to wave as she climbed into the car she had indicated.

Marnie used the solitary trip back to the Center for thoughts of how best to approach the problem, where to begin, and how to give Carly the support she'd need. Good thing, too, since Scott was waiting in Linda's office when she returned.

As she entered the room, his smile radiated warmth and welcome. Her heart fluttered as her lips remembered his touch. Silly how a simple kiss could resound in her dreams all night, but she'd vividly remembered his face, his voice, his touch when she woke up in the morning.

She needed to tell him about the threat to Carly, but she'd promised she wouldn't. It was only a day, so she had to pray all three girls would be okay until tomorrow.

She stared at his lips but quickly moved her gaze up to his eyes, and a smile she couldn't contain poured out. She moved to the chair next to him, taking a seat without ever breaking his gaze. His pull was almost magnetic.

"Marnie?"

Linda's soft voice pulled her back to reality.

He wasn't about to kiss her again.

This wasn't a date.

She had responsibilities to the center, to Linda, to

Carly and the other kids. She couldn't go all moon-eyed over the first good-looking state trooper to enter the office, even if he did kiss like a breath of spring with the heat of summer. Maybe she was just too tired from her late nights at the hospital.

She fumed with herself, forcing her mind back to her duties and, ashamed of herself, turned to face Linda. "Sorry. I know who he is looking for and what it's about. If you don't mind, I think we should discuss it privately. Would it be all right with you?"

The pleading in her eyes must have been enough to convince Linda to agree. She left the office.

After she was alone with him, she took a deep breath and stood. Distance was good. If she kept the kids in sight, she'd keep them in mind, too. She faced the windows, her back to him.

"If my information is correct, I think you're looking for the girl your brother has been dating. His name is Nick, right?"

She turned when he chuckled.

"Nick's actually my ex-brother-in-law. I was married to his sister, Darlene."

"But you're looking for his girlfriend?"

He leaned back in the chair, crossing his right ankle over his left knee. "Yes. If you know that much, you probably know why, too."

"Yes."

"Okay. So you know why I need to talk to this girl. What's her name?"

She took a deep breath. "Carly Johnson. Why didn't Nick give you her name?"

He shook his head. "He's so secretive these days, especially about anything important. I can't get him to open up to me the way he used to. He told me she didn't want to talk to me, so he wouldn't give me her name."

"She's scared, but she did agreed to meet with you. She'd like me to be present, if that's possible."

He nodded. "That shouldn't be a problem. She told you about the woman who approached her?"

She inhaled. What to tell him? The police needed to be able to protect the girls, but she had to respect her promise. "Yes, she told me about it. She says she doesn't know who the woman is, and I believe her. She wouldn't lie about something so upsetting to her."

He paused, his lips pursed. "I can accept that. I'd like to meet with her soon. Is today or tomorrow, okay?"

She dropped back into the chair. "Yes. I told her we could all meet at my house after she gets out of school tomorrow, if it works for you."

He dropped his foot to the floor and leaned forward, his muscular forearms resting on his knees. "Sure." He handed her his notepad. "Give me your address."

She did. Her hand brushed his as she gave the paper back to him, sending shivers down her spine.

"Good." He smiled. "Makes it easier to pick you up the next time we go out, too."

She smiled back, heat rising in her fact. "The next time?"

He winked.

She stood, looking up into his face. "One more thing. Carly doesn't want Nick to be there tomorrow, so it might be best if he doesn't know we're meeting."

"Okay. Mind if I ask why?"

"Apparently, Nick is acting a little possessive and already making long-term plans. I think she's feeling a little overwhelmed by it all."

"Thanks for your help with this. I appreciate it." As they stood at the office door, he reached out to shake her hand.

She tried to contain her disappointment. Maybe she'd imagined the kiss last night. Or maybe he just didn't feel the same connection she did every time they so much as shared air.

When he turned away without another word, she couldn't even fake a smile anymore—until he just as quickly turned around, pulled her in for a quick kiss and a wink, and bolted out the door.

Her smile came back in spades and didn't fade for hours.

****

"Where the hell do you think you're going?" Scott put his hand on the boy's arm.

"I'm thinking it's none of your business." Nick shook off his hand, pulling away.

Nick grabbed his backpack and made to jump out of the Jeep, so Scott flipped the locks.

"Not so fast. I want to know if you asked the girl, Carly, isn't it? Did you ask her to marry you?" He looked into Nick's eyes. "Did you?"

While the boy seemed surprised he knew her name, he quickly changed his expression to a perfect teenager sneer. "What's it to you? This is none of your business."

The parking lot of the high school was quiet at this time of night. He planned to work out in the weight room with the boy tonight. But first they needed to talk.

"You're my business."

Nick turned to his window, not meeting his gaze. "So?"

Although the boy said nothing, he pulled the door handle a few times and then punched the dashboard.

"Talk to me, man. What's going on?"

When Nick still didn't answer, he began to worry. What had happened to the little boy who used to tell him everything? The close relationship with Darlene's little brother had been the only good thing to come out of his failed marriage. Pain radiated from the boy, but he didn't know how to make him talk.

Finally, as he pulled his keys from the ignition and flipped the locks, Nick spoke.

"I asked her, but she said no. She said it's too soon, we're too young, we don't know each other very well, yadda, yadda, yadda. She doesn't want to marry me."

He put his hand on Nick's arm. "Has she decided she wants to have the baby? Whether she wants to keep it?"

Nick shook his head. "No."

"Then give her time, dude. This is a hell of a lot for her to deal with right now. You see it from your side, but remember, the baby's growing inside of her, and the hormones are already playing havoc with her body."

They grabbed their bags and started walking to the gym. Maybe the workout would help.

Sure, Nick was in pain right now, wanting to do the right thing but not knowing what it was or if he could do it. It was difficult to accept you couldn't control everything in a relationship. It'd been hard for Scott to accept how many other men Darlene had slept with, even when she admitted it to his face. Once you gave a woman your heart, you didn't expect her to stomp all over it.

He put his arm on the kid's shoulders. Although Nick might think he was ready for a man's responsibility, he wanted to protect the boy as long as possible.

"You're going to have to give her space and time. I know it's hard—I've been there. But the fact is, she's dealing with a heavy load right now, and the best thing you can do for her is be there when she wants to talk and help her decide what to do about the baby, if she'll let you."

Nick stopped in his tracks, tears running down his cheeks. "I want the baby, man. I really want it. I know it's crazy, and we're too young, and I don't have any money. But I want her to have our baby."

Scott stepped closer again, keeping his voice soft. "You need to tell her that, but she's got to decide, dude. Let her know you'd be there for her if she has the baby, even if she won't marry you, if you can make her a promise. It's about all you can do, right now."

Nick wiped his face on his T-shirt and pushed his way through the double doors of the gym.

"I don't think she wants to have our baby, or keep it. Or maybe it's only me she doesn't want." Pain filled his eyes. Wrapping his arm around the boy's shoulders, Scott led him into the school.

****

Scott tossed his doughnut-shop coffee cup into the

public trash can on his way into the Stevens County sheriff's office the next morning. He showed his badge to get through security and stopped at Thelma's desk to deliver a large tea he'd picked up for her.

"Good morning, ma'am." He flashed her a hundred-watt grin and handed her the tea.

"Good morning to you, Investigator Randall." She smiled back, something Thelma didn't do often enough. "You know you don't have to bring me something every time you stop in our offices, don't you?" There was the slightest blush creeping over the lady's face.

As Jack stepped through his office door, out into Thelma's domain, he leaned against the doorframe and crossed his arms over his chest. "Are you attempting to steal away my administrative assistant, Randall?" Jack smiled at Thelma. "You know our county government would grind to a halt, right?"

Scott smiled and knelt next to the woman's chair, holding his arms out to her. "If only I thought I had a prayer of convincing her to leave your office for mine. Please, Thelma, reconsider." He laced his fingers and held his hands over his heart, pumping as if his heart beat only for this efficient septuagenarian. How could she resist him?

She smiled at him, fully blushing now, pushing him away. "You boys are crazy. Go on with you now."

Jack straightened up. "You heard the woman, Randall. Leave her be."

He stood and bowed to Thelma. "If ever you change your mind, all you have to do is call." He tipped an imaginary hat to her, turned, and followed Jack into his office.

Jack walked to his desk chair. "Every time, dude? Do you have to bring her something every time? You're really showing me up here."

Laughing, he settled into one of the guest chairs. "You don't deserve her, Finelli. She makes you look good."

Jack shook his head. "Too true. I hope she never retires."

"Yeah, you would be so screwed."

Nodding, Jack said, "Don't I know it?" He leaned back in his chair. "So what's on your mind today? I mean, besides a certain little winery manager we both know." Jack chuckled.

Scott smiled but tried to keep his expression mild, even when her sexy little laugh rumbled through his mind. "Never mind about that, Finelli." He took out his notebook. "I wanted to pick your brain about this possible baby-selling ring. I read over the files you sent me—and thank you, by the way—but I'm having trouble believing the rumors and allegations in your files from the seventies and eighties are connected to whatever is going on today."

Jack sat forward, leaning on his desk. "Well, I'm not saying they are. That would be a hell of a long time for the same crime ring to be operating."

He choked out a laugh. "Yeah, forty-some years. How many sixty or seventy-year-old felons do you think we have in these parts?"

His friend laced his fingers together, resting his joined hands on his desk. "There hasn't been much talk since I took over as sheriff, but rumors came and went during Deke's time in office. He never found much to substantiate the claims, though. Back in the seventies and eighties, teenage pregnancies were a real problem in the area. Access to birth control was limited, and the nearest Planned Parenthood office was either Ithaca or Elmira. Apparently, Schuyler and Stevens Counties had the highest teenaged pregnancy rates in the State of New York for several years running."

"I remember even when I was in school a lot of girls dropped out of school, as early as seventh or eighth grade, because they got pregnant." Back then, there weren't enough activities for teens in the county, other than underage drinking and unprotected sex.

Shaking his head, Jack sighed. "And you would think, given all those babies over the years, our population would have been growing instead of declining."

He leaned forward, his forearms braced on his thighs. Too true. Where did all the babies go? "It looks like Deke got a fairly credible complaint about eight years ago but couldn't nail anything down. Do you remember discussing the Simmons case with him?"

Jack pulled open the bottom drawer of his desk and pulled out a box full of small notebooks. He dug through and pulled one out, flipping through the pages. "I don't...okay, here it is. Regina Simmons got pregnant at fourteen, but it was ten years ago. She delivered the baby at Schuyler Hospital and took the baby home with her the next day, but when Social Services went out to check on them three days later, Regina claimed the baby died."

He started taking some notes of his own. "Did they suspect abuse? What did the medical examiner have to say?"

Jack glanced up, meeting his gaze. "There was no body. Regina claimed her daddy buried the baby, but she didn't know where, and he was out hunting. They don't have a land-line out there, and he didn't have a cell phone. Every time they went out there to talk to him, he was never home. After six months, they gave up."

He shook his head. Sounded like the Simmons family had played the system. "Did Deke call in the state troopers?"

Jack looked back at his notes. "No, he said there was no evidence of foul play, so there was nothing to go on."

He crossed his arms over his chest, leaning back in his chair. Had someone taken that baby away, or was the poor thing really buried somewhere out back, like an old coon dog? He flipped farther down in the file. "It looks like there was an anonymous complaint about two years later alleging Regina's baby didn't die but that instead she sold the child. Deke's notes indicate they followed up with Regina, the hospital, the Social Services workers, even the school, although Regina was out of school by then, as she was pregnant again. Anyway, looks like they came up with nothing."

Jack flipped through his notes again. "Regina was pregnant again at what, sixteen?"

He nodded. "And guess what—she didn't raise that one either."

"What did she say happened to the second baby?"

"According to Regina, she gave the baby to her cousin." He turned the page in his notebook, reading it off. "Misty Tremble, over in Bath. The file indicates

Tremble verified this when contacted by the Steuben County sheriff's office. There aren't any copies of adoption records in the file, however, so I have an investigator following up on that."

Jack leaned back, hands on the armrests of his chair. "What made this stick out for you?"

Scott ran his left hand over his chin as he thought. "I guess the fact the death was never verified of the first baby, no death certificate, or funeral home, and the fact her second baby left the county. I want to take a run up there and talk to Regina and her father, if we can find them, and the cousin in Bath. Make sure everything is kosher, after all."

His friend rifled through his file. "Regina still live up on Sugar Hill, as far as you know?"

"I haven't found a more current address, so I think that's the place to start."

Jack smiled. "I think I'll go with you, if it's all the same to you. Some of those families up there can be mighty tight-lipped when it comes to a state trooper, but they might be more inclined to talk to the sheriff."

Scott stood, tucking his notepad away. "You free now?"

Jack stood, picking up his jacket. "Sure. Let's do it. I'll let Thelma know where we're headed."

Scott chuckled as he edged toward the door. "I'd be happy to stop at her desk and tell her."

Jack yelled as he headed out, "Stop coveting your neighbor's secretary, dude. She's an institution in this office."

Scott stuffed his arms into his leather jacket, laughing as he pulled Jack's door closed behind him. "Then what are you worried about?"

As hard as it might be to think the disappearance of babies over the past thirty years had anything to do with Nick and Carly, he had to follow any possible lead. The most important thing was protecting those two and the baby they might be having together.

****

Uneasiness creeping up her spine, Carly felt the hair on the back of her neck tingle and itch. She turned around, glancing in all directions. She didn't know where or even who they were, although one was probably that old woman, but they were out there, watching. She'd told the girls to lock the doors when they got home from school, even though they were so far out of town, and to keep them locked until she got home after work. She couldn't even think about how she'd survive if something happened to them.

She had to protect them.

She packed a bag with a box of granola bars, three bottles of water, clothes for the girls, and a couple of outfits for herself. Then she stowed the bag under the edge of her bed.

If they came after her at home, she and her sisters would take to the woods. She knew the woods around their house like nobody else.

It would be easy to hide there.

They could grab the bag and make a run for it, and they'd stay hidden for as long as they had to.

Chapter Six

The doorbell set off a flutter in Marnie's stomach, as if she were sixteen again. She refused to check the hall mirror as she walked by, but gave in to the urge to smooth her hair before opening the front door. Carly had texted she was running late; it had to be Scott.

When she pulled open the door, there he stood. His black leather jacket hung unzipped, dark sunglasses hiding his eyes. A hint of the bad boy hidden under the good cop image. He pulled off his shades and flashed her a sultry grin.

She stood back to let him enter, and he passed so close it was nearly an embrace. Oh, yeah. Her pulse skipped a few beats. This was no mistake.

"Hi." Was that breathy voice coming from her? If so, where had it been hiding all her life?

"Hi yourself."

His smile turned up at one end, holding promise of secrets she hadn't even dared to consider.

She hung his jacket on the coat tree in the front hall and led him to the back of the house.

Why should she feel so unsettled? Carly was the focus of the investigation tonight, and the teen hadn't even arrived. While the possibility of some sort of baby-selling ring in Harper's Glen scared her, safety for Carly and her sisters was the main concern. Her nervousness now had to be about him, and the one little kiss they had shared.

He surveyed the living room. "Is your father at the hospital tonight?"

Marnie nodded. "Mom's been feeling better, so it's good for them to have some time alone together." She sighed. "My parents moved to Kendal, a retirement community in Ithaca, several years ago, and I bought the house from them. Dad's been staying here while Mom's in the hospital. I don't want him driving back to Ithaca when he's tired, especially after dark."

"Good idea. There's always the chance of deer darting out in front of your car as you go over the hill to Ithaca, and it's hard to see them after sunset, even with young eyes."

"I know it," she agreed. "I've had to make a sharp stop more than once myself."

She led him into the kitchen and motioned him toward a chair at the table, which was already set with silverware and bowls. Since Carly would be stopping in after school and on her way to work, she wanted to take the chance to fatten the girl up a bit. Of course, Scott might enjoy a homemade meal as well.

"I hope you don't mind, but I made an early dinner. Carly is running a little late, and will have to hurry off to work when we're finished, so I wanted to give her a chance to eat while she's here."

Shaking his head, he sat. "I don't mind at all. Whatever makes her feel more comfortable will help with the interview. Plus it smells fantastic."

She smiled. "Thanks. It's just chili, but I thought it was a cool enough evening to get away with it." As she threw together the tossed salad, she motioned toward the refrigerator. "Help yourself to a drink.

There's beer, pop, wine, water. Grab a glass from the table, if you don't mind."

He poured himself a cola and leaned back against the counter, watching her work. She couldn't ignore the warm, comfortable, "honey-I'm-home" feeling which filled her. What would it be like to have this man to come home to every night?

Luckily, Carly's knock on the kitchen door interrupted her daydreaming. She signaled to the girl, who let herself in.

Scott set down his cola and held out his hand to Carly. "Hi, I'm Scott Randall."

Her gaze darted to Marnie first and then, looking down at the floor, she took his hand for the briefest of shakes. "I'm Carly." The girl slid into a chair at the table and immediately took out her phone.

His gaze met Marnie's over the teen's head. She shrugged and brought the salad to the table.

"You made dinner?" Carly set her phone next to her plate, as if just noticing the place setting. "You didn't have to…I'll eat at work."

Marnie wasn't so sure that would happen, and the girl needed to eat. "Well, I made a lot of chili, so I'd really appreciate it if you guys help me eat it. What do you want to drink, honey?"

Carly took a can of seltzer water and popped it open while Marnie spooned up bowls of chili. After adding a basket of corn chips to the table, she carried her glass to her place and took her seat, next to the teen. Carly's eyes lit up as she shoveled a spoonful of chili into her mouth. Nice to have an appreciative audience for her cooking, Marnie thought.

"Thanks for dinner. It looks great; much better

than I'd have at home." Smiling, Scott grabbed his spoon and started to dig in. After they passed the salad and started in on their dinners, Marnie caught his gaze and smiled.

"Carly." He set his spoon down, wiped his hands, and pulled out his trusty notepad. "I know you're uncomfortable talking about the woman who wanted to buy your baby, but I need to know all the details you can tell me. I'm going to take notes, okay? I don't want to confuse anything you tell me."

The girl nodded but took another sip of her seltzer water.

Marnie put her hand on the thin shoulder. "Simply tell Scott what you told me, and anything else you can remember."

Carly told him about the small, older woman who had approached her outside the local high school.

He glanced up from his notes. "Did she tell you her name?"

"No, but she knew mine." Carly shook her head. "She was all shifty-like, talking low, acting like she knew me, but I'd never seen her before. I don't know how she knew I was pregnant."

"So at the time she approached you," he continued, "who knew about your pregnancy?"

Carly focused on her hands, twisting her fingers and picking at the bitten nails. "Just me, the receptionist and nurse at Planned Parenthood, and Nick."

He stopped writing. "But it wasn't either of the Planned Parenthood workers who approached you?"

Carly's spine straightened, and she turned to Marnie. "I told you, I'd never seen her before."

Reaching out a hand to rest on the teen's shoulder, she turned on Scott. "This is tough enough for her; you don't need to make her repeat herself."

He held up his hands. "No problem. I wanted to be sure." Bowing his head, he nodded and took a sip of his pop. "Somebody else knew about Carly's pregnancy, so we have to figure out who. Can you describe what she looked like?" He took notes as she rattled off the description she'd given Marnie. "Would you recognize her if you saw her again?"

Carly nodded, taking another bite of her chili. Dinner had been a good idea, even if only to give the girl a chance to breathe and calm down.

Scott's smile turned tentative. "Would you be willing to work with one of our department artists to create a sketch of her?"

The teen looked at Marnie and then back at him. "Yeah, I guess so."

She hoped he knew what he was doing, because the girl looked frightened. But maybe putting a face on her fears would help Carly get through this. Nodding, she passed the corn chips again. "Do you want me to come with you?"

Shaking her head, the girl smiled. "That's okay. I'll be all right."

Scott and Carly agreed he'd pick the girl up after work the next evening and take her to the station to get a sketch of the woman.

He gently prodded her. "And have you seen the woman again, since that day?"

She bit a loose bit of cuticle, bringing up a dab of blood. "I haven't seen her."

The girl was so frightened, Marnie couldn't help

being thankful the woman hadn't been back. Of course, that didn't mean the danger had passed.

"Carly," she said, putting her hand on the girl's arm to get her attention. "Tell him what's been happening since you saw her."

The young mother looked back up at him, tears in her eyes. "I've gotten some notes, at school and at work, telling me to keep quiet, don't go to the cops, ya know, if I know what's good for me…and my sisters."

Scott leaned forward so his eyes were on a level with Carly's. "Did you keep the notes?"

Carly nodded. "Sure, I watch some of those cop shows. I know about evidence and stuff."

Smiling, Marnie had to admire the girl's smarts, even when faced with something so frightening. And Scott's manner with the scared teen, how sweet and gentle he was being, said a lot about him as a man, in addition to his work as a cop. While part of her brain worried for Carly, she couldn't help but appreciate the light in his eyes and the curve of his smile.

"Do you have the notes with you?"

The girl shook her head. "I don't carry them around with me. They're hidden in my bedroom at home."

"Okay, will you bring them with you tomorrow, when we go to the station?"

Her eyes grew wide and vulnerable as her lip trembled. "But, but…what will they do to me and the girls?"

He held a hand out, stopping just short of touching her arm. "I'll send a police car out to your neighborhood tonight, to keep an eye on your house." He handed her his business card. "Call me if you get scared. We'll make sure you and your sisters are safe."

Scott put his notepad and pen in his pocket. "I really appreciate your help, both of you. There have been rumors of a baby-selling ring in this area for a long time—we're talking decades—but we've never had a witness before. I'm hopeful this will lead us to more evidence and we can finally put these people away."

The slightest edge of unease creeped up Marnie's spine, and she felt goose pimples appear on her arms. "For decades?"

"Nothing specific, mind you." He shook his head. "But both Stevens and Schulyer Counties have had high teenage pregnancy rates for years, so it's suspicious the population has decreased so much instead of increasing. There've been rumors in nearby communities this is the place to come for a baby, as far back as the seventies, but we haven't been able to track down any proof."

Marnie's ears were buzzing, and she felt a headache coming on. She'd never liked coincidences, and this one hit too close to home.

****

Marnie woke on Tuesday morning to a text from Kate.

—Deke passed away yesterday. Calling hours are tonight at Chedzoy's Funeral Home, with the funeral service tomorrow morning.—

Sadness came in a wave. Although she hadn't known Deke well, they'd had some business when he was still the sheriff. More, he was like a father to Kate's husband, Jack, the current sheriff, and the death, while no surprise, would hit her friends hard.

114

After work that night, she found a place to park on Fourth Street in Watkins Glen and made her way into the funeral home, along with what seemed to be most of the neighboring communities.

Soft voices filled the corners of the room, where small groups of mourners gathered. Locals had loved and respected their sheriff and would miss him, but more than one person praised the end of Deke's pain and suffering.

Her friends stood at the head of the line, the closest thing to family Deke had. While Jack's father, Mr. Finelli, had little time for his son's intellectual pursuits, the former sheriff had stepped into the role as if he'd raised Jack himself. It was at Deke's request that Jack had come back to Harper's Glen, helped Kate escape her abusive marriage, and rekindled their friendship, which led to love and marriage. Despite how crushed they both must be at losing such a wonderful mentor, the strength of their love and commitment to each other was obvious.

After making her way through the line and hugging her friends, she touched base with a number of others in the community who'd come out to honor the former sheriff. Many people asked after her mother, and she was relieved to say she was out of danger, working hard on rehab, and moving back to Kendal soon.

She wasn't surprised when Scott joined the receiving line or when he walked toward her after making his way through the line and giving his condolences.

He dropped his leather jacket on the back of the spindly chair next to hers and then spread his long frame over the seat. "I thought I'd see you here. I meant to call, but the day got away from me."

He draped his left arm over the back of her chair, his bicep brushing against her shoulder, causing a shiver to run down her spine. She had to be careful here.

She looked into his dark eyes. "Even though everyone knew it was only a matter of time for Deke, I feel bad for Jack and Kate."

"Me, too."

His right thumb traced patterns on her left arm, igniting small sparks in her that were wholly inappropriate for the setting.

His gaze met hers. "I wanted to thank you again for dinner and helping me with Carly. Let me make it up to you by taking you out on a proper date, please?"

A hint of mischief played in the twist of his smile and the light in his eyes. Maybe he wasn't always the serious, solid, and dependable state trooper. Maybe there was a little of the rebel in him to match his leather jacket and hooded eyes.

She swallowed the tickle of excitement. "Maybe." No need to rush anything. She needed to put some distance between his investigation and her research into the summer of 1973.

"Excuse me." Scott sat up abruptly and reached into his pocket for his cell phone, swiping to answer a call as he stood and started to walk to the back of the room. "Randall…"

He stood against the back wall, speaking so softly she couldn't hear a thing, which made it all the more fascinating to watch his lips moving. His crisp white shirt pulled tight on his shoulders and that lock of hair fell across his forehead. She felt an incredible pull toward this man, even though the possibility of overlap between his baby-selling investigation and her grandmother's role in her illegal adoption made her uneasy. If she could keep him away from that topic of conversation, she would love to spend more time getting to know him. And, frankly, talking wasn't the most interesting thing on her mind anyway.

He hurried back to her, grabbing his leather jacket off the seat next to her as he swung himself back into the chair. "I'm sorry, but I have to go. Carly is done with work, so I'm going to go pick her up." He pushed his arms into the jacket.

"No problem. I hope it goes well." She pulled her bottom lip between her teeth. Hopefully, the teen wouldn't be too anxious about making the identification.

"How about dinner on Saturday? I could pick you up and we could maybe drive up to Geneva. It's supposed to be a lovely weekend, now the rain has finally stopped."

She couldn't think of a way to say no. "Sure. That sounds great."

He leaned in and brushed the faintest of kisses onto her cheek as he stood to leave. "Great. I'll stop by at six, if it's all right."

She smiled up at him. "Okay, see you then."

And, with that, he was gone.

Deciding it was time to head home, Marnie stood up herself, but then a hand tapped on her shoulder.

Kate pulled her into a hug. "We're wrapping things up, now that there's no more line, and Jack wants to talk to you, if you have a minute."

She nodded. Maybe he needed something for the next day's funeral. "Sure, whatever I can do."

Kate led her to some leather sofas and armchairs in one of the side rooms. Jack, looking tired and pale, started to rise.

She placed a hand on his arm. "Please don't get up. You must be wiped out."

He chuckled, obviously grateful. "I feel like a bus ran over me, about an hour ago."

"What can I do for you?" She took a seat as her friend slid onto the sofa next to her husband.

"Nothing, actually. I wanted to tell you I talked to Deke a couple days ago about you. He was frail and tired, but his mind was still sharp." His eyes teared up. "He was a great help."

"We don't have to talk about this now. It's been a rough day for you."

"Actually, it'd be good to talk about something else, right about now." He reached over and took Kate's hand in his.

It was good her friends had each other. "Okay."

"He remembered the baby found during Summer Jam. As sheriff of Stevens County, he wasn't directly in charge, of course, since Watkins Glen is in Schuyler County. But it was such a madhouse, he said, every law enforcement official who could lend a hand helped out. He apparently spent a lot of time at the track."

"Did he see the...well, me? Did he know what village cops were working that weekend?"

He sighed, pulling a notepad from his pants pocket and flipping it open. "Everyone was there—no one got out of it. He didn't remember who found the baby, but he said a couple of the guys were talking about it after the weekend was over, how incredible it was that the birth mother came back and claimed the baby."

She tried to hide her disappointment. "Did he give you any specifics we can use to track down the particular village cop who found the baby?"

"No, but the hospital had a record of it."

She gasped, feeling a surge of excitement skitter up her spine. Kate put a hand on her arm. "Can we get a copy of it?"

Jack nodded. "Since it doesn't name the baby or mother, and we're only looking for the police information, it wasn't a problem."

She swallowed, almost afraid to ask. Did Jack already know? Could it be this easy? "Who was it?"

"Jeff DeMarco. Ring any bells?"

"No." She shook her head, unable to place the name, but hoping the officer was still alive.

"I checked the records. DeMarco was on the force in Watkins for more than thirty years. He's retired but still lives in the area. I called, and he agreed to see you Thursday night, if you want to meet with him."

As she started to shake, she covered her mouth with her hands, trying to take a deep breath. *Am I ready to find the answers?*

Jack ripped a sheet out of his notebook. "Here's his address and phone number. If you don't want to go alone, I'm sure Scott would go with you, if he's free." Jack sank back into the sofa cushions, the stress of the day showing on his face.

She straightened and took the paper he held out to her. Her hands shook slightly as she folded it and stuffed it into her purse. "Thanks, but I can handle it on my own."

She tucked the information into her pocket, knowing she couldn't ask Scott to go with her, not if her grandmother had somehow started a baby-selling ring back in the day. Maybe this retired police officer would bring it up; maybe he knew something that would implicate her grandmother or even her mother. No, she couldn't risk giving him more reason to direct his investigation toward her family.

****

Driving to work the next morning, Marnie realized her mother would have told her she was as cross as a bear, but she couldn't shake her bad mood. Between the research she had found on her mother's condition, the lack of specific information available about people attending Summer Jam, and worrying about Carly and the woman who wanted to buy her baby, she was frustrated. It was too much of a dark cloud for her normally sunny disposition to break through. Then again, maybe she wasn't naturally as optimistic as she'd been led to believe.

Her ex-husband, Matt, pulled out of the winery's driveway as she pulled in. While it was true that he owned the place, he usually kept to the fields and farm buildings. Hopefully, his presence didn't mean there was some kind of problem waiting for her inside. Just what she didn't need to further piss her off.

He stopped his truck next to her car, driver's side to driver's side, and rolled down his window, obviously expecting her to do the same. *Couldn't he come to my office like everybody else if he wants to talk to me?*

When the window lowered below her chin, she squinted at him. "Yes?"

He smiled that good-ol'-boy smile of his, the one he'd had since puberty. Sometimes the mocking implied in that grin really infuriated her. "And good morning to you, too, sweetheart."

She grunted, not wanting to play into his games.

"Okay then." He laughed. "I wanted to see if you'd have time to go over some numbers with me this afternoon. Are you planning to be here all day?"

Her face became warm and was probably red as a beet. Did he think she'd been slacking off, because she took some time out of the office? "Yes, I'll be here all day. I have been putting in my time every day, even if I've been working at home, you know. I haven't been neglecting winery business."

"Whoa." His hands came up in front of the steering wheel. "I didn't say you were, okay? Get off your high horse there, woman."

She hated when he called her "woman."

"I'm under a lot of stress right now."

He shook his head, put his truck in gear again, and started to raise his window. "I hope your mother is doing okay, and I'll talk to you later."

With that, he drove away, leaving her fuming, as much at herself as at her ex.

Marnie parked and stomped into her office. Even the soothing sounds of the soft country music filling the tasting room couldn't smooth out her mood. She dropped her purse and her tote bag on the guest chair in the corner, plopped her unopened can of diet cola on her desk, and closed the door behind her, hard.

There was a stack of invoices in her inbox, a slew of email calling for her attention, and a staff meeting in fifteen minutes. She needed to update their social media page, review the numbers on their latest marketing campaign, and check on the schedule and menu for the next club member event. She couldn't think of one good reason to have a staff meeting today even though she'd been the one who scheduled it.

Most days, she loved her job, liked the mix of front of the house and customer contact with the back-of-the-house strategy, marketing, project management, and finance all rolled into one. She'd never really dreamed of owning her own business, but managing the winery, along with Matt, owner, grape farmer, and ex-husband, gave her the thrill of responsibility and pride in a job well done, but with ability to go home and forget about it if she wanted to.

As odd as most people found the situation, she usually enjoyed working with Matt. He understood the farm, the grapes, and the region, and had a talent for mixing the relaxed gentleman farmer exterior with the shrewd businessman inside. Even after their divorce, she never regretted staying on to work at the winery.

She rarely forgot about work, but with her mother's illness, the revelation of her adoption, her growing attraction to Scott, and Carly's pregnancy, she already had a lot on her plate. All she could think of was the upcoming meeting on Thursday with the retired village cop, Jeff DeMarco.

Steepling her fingers together, she rested her lower lip on her fingertips. Even though her father had called to say her mother was being transferred from the local hospital back to the skilled nursing unit at Kendal today, she needed to figure out when she'd go visit them. She hadn't touched base with Carly since dinner at her house on Monday. She had a date with a hot young state trooper who made her imagination run wild, even though she needed to steer conversation away from babies and adoption.

And she was both in a hurry to meet with DeMarco and wishing she'd never agreed to it. Maybe she wasn't really the cautious, overly organized woman she'd always believed herself to be. How could she know what kind of woman she was? She didn't even know *who* she was.

The knock at her door startled her, mostly because she rarely closed it. Tina stuck her head through the opening, a hesitant smile on her face. "Everything okay, honey?"

Marnie thanked the fates she hadn't lost friendship with her ex-mother-in-law in the divorce. "Oh, sure, come on in." She stood, put some files in her credenza, and walked to her office window, looking out over the vineyard and the blue expanse of the lake. "It's looking good out there."

"Yup, spring is sprung."

Tina reached Marnie and put a hand on her back to rub, such a maternal act it made her throat tighten. She was always grateful for this woman's caring nature, but she couldn't get her mind around how she felt about her birth mother, her adopted mother and grandmother, or, more importantly, about herself.

"How's your mom?"

"I talked to her last night, and she's doing pretty well. They're sending her back to Kendal today. They have a great facility and will take good care of her, but I need to get over there and see her."

Tina rested her hand on her back. "Don't worry. I'm sure your father is on top of everything."

She paused a moment, trying to decide how much to share.

"What's wrong?" Her friend sat on the edge of her desk. "Something's going on in that brain of yours."

She turned and met her ex-mother-in-law's gaze. Her eyes burned with tears, but she didn't want to break down at work. All she seemed to do these days was cry.

"Honey, what is it?" Tina leaned forward, reaching out and touching Marnie's arm.

"I found out I'm adopted."

"What?" Tina's white curls bounced as she shook her head, disbelief in her eyes.

"I know, I'm nearly forty-five years old and I've just learned my parents adopted me when I was a baby. I tried to donate blood for my mother, and the truth came out."

Her friend's normally feisty aura became more subdued. "Are you okay?"

She shook her head, her voice breaking. "I don't know."

"Tell me."

Tina had a mother-earth/goddess thing going on, often dressed in tie-dye and denim, and always seemed to know what was in Marnie's heart of hearts, which had made it awkward and uncomfortable when she divorced Matt. She'd always admired the woman's ability to be both teenager and grandmother with Matt's nieces and nephews.

"Just between us?"

Her ex-mother-in-law nodded. "You know it."

"Remember Summer Jam, the rock concert in Watkins in 1973?"

Tina shook her head, her cheeks going slightly

pink. "My memory of the weekend is hazy, but I definitely remember being there."

"Well, there was a baby born up at the track during the weekend."

Her friend started nodding, a vague smile on her face. "I do remember hearing about that." Her gaze met Tina's. She waited a beat then her head jerked back. "That was you? You're the baby born at the track?"

Marnie nodded, wiping an errant tear. "There's some fishy stuff which went on behind the scenes I'd rather not talk about, especially since I haven't figured it all out yet, but yeah, I'm the baby born to some drugged-out hippie in the back of a VW microbus, in the middle of a stampede of drugged-out teenagers, during a wild weekend rock concert."

Tina wrapped her arm around Marnie's shoulders. "And your parents never told you?"

"Again, because of said fishy stuff...stuff my dad didn't even know about. Also, they 'never found the right time,' they said." She choked out a laugh. "They only had forty-some years to choose from."

Tina leaned her head on Marnie's shoulder. "You're angry." It wasn't a question, and there was no judgment in her tone, just a statement of fact.

"Yeah, I guess I am." She sighed. "And confused. If I'm not the uptight, mildly OCD daughter of two academics, but instead the unwanted offspring of a teenaged hippie, who the hell am I?"

She looked sheepishly at Tina, hoping the teenaged hippie comment didn't offend her.

"Oh, honey. You're *you*, the same as always. You're still the same girl your parents raised. Besides, they aren't in charge of what's in your heart, you are."

She shook her head, pulling away. "Who I am is based on who they are, on what I've always believed to be true. I feel like the rug has been pulled from beneath my feet. In fact, the whole damn floor is gone, and I'm falling. Who knows where I'll end up or who I'll be."

Her ex-mother-in-law turned to her, wrapped her in an all-encompassing hug, and held on. "I'm sorry you're going through this. You know I'm here for you, anytime you need to talk."

Marnie let her hold on a little longer than was strictly necessary, reveling in the feeling of total acceptance, no matter what. But, as big as Tina's heart was, reality was another thing altogether.

****

The old brown car had been parked outside the school every day this week.

Carly watched it carefully, keeping notes in case she had to tell the cop.

There aren't any kids walking over to it, so what's it doing there? There's a guy sitting in the driver seat, but he's alone. If he's not there to pick somebody up, who is he? How does this all connect to the notes, the threats, or the woman who wanted to buy my baby? What does it all mean?

Chapter Seven

Walking up the steps to Jeff DeMarco's house the following evening, unable to decide if she was terrified or excited, Marnie took several deep breaths, just like in yoga class. She rang the bell, staring straight ahead, as though trying to bore a hole through the heavy maple door.

DeMarco answered and showed her into a small, dark living room. Photos, knickknacks, and the memorabilia of a lifetime covered every surface.

"Thanks for agreeing to meet with me, Mr. DeMarco." Her lips were so tight the smile she forced almost shattered.

He offered a hand, and she tried to keep her handshake firm and professional.

"Please, call me Jeff." He motioned for her to take a seat on the couch. "Can I get you a drink?"

She sat shaking her head. "No, thank you." He already had some brown liquor over ice in a glass next to his chair.

"As I said on the phone, Jeff, I'd like to ask you some questions about Summer Jam and the baby who was abandoned at the track during the weekend."

DeMarco nodded but didn't meet her gaze. The big man leaned back in his Barcalounger, a faint smile on his lips.

"I'm not sure what I can remember about that

weekend, seeing as it was forty years ago, but I'd be happy to help."

"But you found the baby, didn't you?" Her voice was unusually high, and her whole body tightened as if poised to jump off the old floral sofa.

His dark brown eyes narrowed a bit, but then he smiled. "Sure did. What a cute little bug she was, too."

She pulled a notebook from her purse and started writing. It helped her focus and soothed the tremors in her hands. "When and where did you find the baby, exactly?"

DeMarco laced his fingers behind his head and settled in, as if for story hour. "Let's see, it was Saturday afternoon, during the pouring rain, I can tell you that much. Really, it rained most of the weekend, or so it seemed. Mud was everywhere, and we could hardly drive or even walk around up at the track. It was a bi—well, a pain in the neck, that's for sure."

He looked over, like he wanted her to hang on his every word. Couldn't he tell she already was?

"So I'm walking down the road that crosses the campground, and this guy starts waving like crazy and yelling for help. He ran up to me, raving that I needed to come with him. I almost slapped the cuffs on him when he started pulling on my arm. Figured he must have been high or something."

He turned, chuckling, but she just stared without speaking, hoping he'd continue.

"I couldn't really figure out what he was talking about, but he was really worked up, so I followed him over to one of those VW buses, parked in the middle of the field. It was sort of sinking into the mud, but nobody could have gone anywhere by that point anyway. There were thousands of drunk and stoned kids, their tents, cars, coolers, and backpacks all over the place."

She could hardly catch her breath. "And the baby? Was she inside the VW?"

He really seemed to be enjoying himself, reliving the glory days, but as long as he gave her the information she needed, he could do that.

"Sure was." He slapped his knee. "It was the darnedest thing. The guy was flapping around me like some crazy bird, but I pulled open the side door and leaned in to look into the back of the bus. All I could think was, 'What the hell?' There lay this brand-new baby, bloody and bawling, wrapped up in a dirty old T-shirt."

"Was the baby's mother there, too?" She held her breath, silently praying for good news.

He shook his head, his right hand absently scratching at his chin. "Well, no, there was no sign of the mother at all. She musta birthed her babe, wrapped her up, and disappeared into the crowd. She was probably high as a kite, just like everybody else."

"Did you question the guy who took you to the VW in the first place? Did he know anything about the baby's mother?"

The large, former cop dropped his hands back to the armrests and sat forward in his chair. "That poor guy owned the VW, but he swore six ways to Sunday he didn't know anything about the baby. His panic was so real, and his confusion as to how a baby got in his van so sincere, I totally believed him."

She wrote a few notes, but then stopped, trying to process and pick the most important of the million questions running through her mind. "Do you remember his name?" She hadn't found it in her research, but it might be worth tracking him down.

Jeff scoffed. "I have no idea. I probably wrote it down at the time, but I couldn't tell you what it is. He didn't know anything about the baby's mother. You have to remember, we made more than fifty arrests that weekend, had hundreds of reports and witnesses to process, never mind trying to keep them kids from killing the neighboring livestock."

That stopped her in her tracks. "What?"

"When they couldn't find any other food, some of those kids got the idea to have a pig roast. We got several calls from the Haverbacks that kids were chasing pigs around their farm. We caught a group of them roasting one of the pigs over at the track."

Shaking her head, she wrote a few notes and then looked back up. "Did you see anyone else around the VW who might have seen the mother? Surely someone noticed an extremely pregnant girl walking around in the rain, didn't they?"

DeMarco snorted, almost sneering. "You don't understand how it was that day at all. It was madness. Everybody was stoned, covered in mud, and dancing, sleeping, screwing, whatever. Their biggest concern was when the bands were going to start playing again and whether there'd be enough food and water for all of 'em. Nobody paid any attention to that girl. She slipped in, had her baby, and slipped out."

Marnie took notes as fast and furiously as she could. "Did you take the baby to the hospital then?"

He turned his smile back on, meeting her gaze. "Sure did. It was pretty tricky getting her out of the bog, I tell ya. There were lots of abandoned cars and half-naked people lining the roads, but we got her out. A group of them kids had to pick up a punch bug that blocked the road and move it out of the way in order for me to drive through. 'Course, the hospital is up there on the hill not far from the track. Eventually, I was able to get her over to the ER. And she was fine, other than some dirt. Mostly the little thing was hungry."

Listening to DeMarco rattle off the details of the checkup, she started to wonder what the man wasn't telling her. Every time she pushed him for specifics, his memory mysteriously faded. But when he got to the parts of the story which told little, he remembered every tiny detail.

"You're so young. You probably weren't even born yet, but let me tell you, the concert was a giant headache for this town. Everything was a muddy mess, lots of kids overdosed, there wasn't enough of anything, including us police to handle all those problems. The whole thing was a nightmare. I took that baby to the hospital, made sure she was okay, and then had to get back to the track."

This much she'd learned from her research. "But you never found out who the baby's mother was?"

"No, and frankly, I didn't look for her. There was too much else for us to do, so I hardly gave the little doll a thought after leaving her at the hospital." He scrubbed his chin with his left hand. "I heard later that week the mother showed up to claim the girl. I always figured she sobered up and realized what she'd done."

Her shoulders slumped. She was writing down everything he told her, but it wasn't adding up to the answers she needed.

He shoved his hands into his pockets. "So what exactly is it that you want to know?" He shook his head. "I mean, after all these years, why are you so interested in all of this? Mostly, that concert was a nightmare for the town that we, thankfully, chose never to repeat."

She took a deep breath, searching for a plausible answer, a way for her not to give away too much, but also not to lie.

"My grandfather was the mayor of Harper's Glen back then."

He nodded, but said nothing. So far, so good.

She tried not to make eye contact, but looked off toward the window. "My mother has just been diagnosed with cancer and, well…" The catch in her voice was a good diversion and would have been a smart choice to sell the diversion, except it wasn't a choice. She couldn't talk about her mom without tears welling in her eyes or emotion seizing her throat.

He reached out and touched her arm. "I'm sorry to hear that."

Nodding, she took another deep breath. "Thanks. Well, anyway, I wanted to put together as much of the family history as possible, kind of a tribute to her parents and mine." She paused, not wanting her voice to shake. "I guess I realized I don't know much about my grandparents and, well, my parents won't live forever."

This was harder than it should have been, given that it wasn't entirely true.

"When I stumbled over some references to Summer Jam, it sounded so crazy; I wondered what it was like. When I heard there was a baby born, I became fascinated." She stood. "I really appreciate your time, Officer DeMarco. You've been very helpful."

Or not.

"I'm happy to help, although I don't really know what became of the baby."

She followed as he walked her to the door, and she said her good-byes, thanking him again.

After she drove about a mile from his house, Marnie pulled off to the side of the road, rested her shaking hands on the steering wheel, and leaned her head back against the headrest. She didn't realize she was crying again until the warm trails of dampness slid down the back of her neck. Once the tears started, she was lost in an ugly crying jag, barely able to catch her breath.

He saw me, he held me—he was really there.

She hadn't known how she'd feel after meeting with him, but somehow the whole thing was even more real. It wasn't some story her parents had concocted to hide something worse—although she couldn't think of anything worse than being born and abandoned in a minibus during a rock concert.

Thrown out like yesterday's trash. Who did that?

As DeMarco said, probably some drugged-up teenager, too stoned to remember who knocked her up or to care about the child she'd brought into the world. She was lucky the girl hadn't given birth in the mud where the baby—*where I*—would never have been found in all the chaos. Not a good start to her life.

Her sinuses were pounding, and her breathing was shallow. She dug some tissues out of her purse and blew her nose. Wiping away her tears, she put the car in gear and drove home.

Twenty minutes later, she pulled into her driveway. As she stepped out of her car, her purse buzzed and vibrated. She'd forgotten to turn her cell phone ringer back on after leaving DeMarco's house.

Pulling it out, she glanced at the screen. Scott. She almost didn't answer, as she felt raw and cranky and didn't want to explain what had her so down tonight, but then realized it could be about Carly.

"Hi."

"Hey. How are you?"

"I'm good." She unlocked her back door and let herself in to her kitchen, dropping her purse on the counter. "What's up?"

"I know it's a little late, but I wondered if you have a few minutes to talk."

She shook her head, trying to dislodge the dark cloud hanging over her. "Sure."

"That's great. Do you want to have a cup of coffee at Minnie's? Maybe some pie?"

His voice was as smooth and warm as liquid chocolate, and she couldn't help but picture how nicely his leather jacket was probably hugging his shoulders.

"I don't think so. I don't really feel up to going back out tonight. Do you want to come here?"

"Sounds great. I should be there in about thirty minutes."

After they hung up, she took out a bottle of wine and a couple of glasses. That sounded much better than pie to her.

But she couldn't get her meeting with DeMarco

out of her mind. While she was glad he'd been able to tell her some of the story, she had to admit she was disappointed. She'd hoped to walk out of there with the name of her birth mother or at least the names of several witnesses who'd been questioned at the time, hoping to spark some memories in them with her own questions. But he didn't have names, or at least he couldn't remember any, if he'd ever written any down. He'd wiped her from his mind once he handed her over to the nurses.

What was DeMarco thinking? How could he be so callous with a baby's life?

Still, she couldn't shake the mental image of a baby lying in DeMarco's big, callused hands. He'd probably saved her life.

Marnie shook her head as she climbed to her bedroom and changed into her softest leggings and a long blue tunic. She stopped in the bathroom, fluffing her curls as she passed the mirror.

When the doorbell rang, she pasted a smile on her face. She didn't want to discuss any of this with Scott, at least not until she had a better idea of what her grandmother had done and how illegal the whole thing was. So when she pulled open the front door, she turned off her thoughts of her birth mother and grandmother and gave him her complete attention.

"Hi," he said, standing at the door with a small bunch of daffodils in his hands.

"Come on in."

As he handed her the flowers, she buried her face in the yellow petals, inhaling the sweet aroma. When she raised her head, she could feel her cheeks warm. "Thank you, but what are these for? Do you always drive around with flowers in the back seat?"

He laughed and followed her back to the kitchen, where she got down a cobalt blue glass vase for the yellow beauties.

"No, but my mother raised me better than to show up at a lady's house without flowers, so I stopped to pick them up on the way." He shrugged off his leather jacket and placed it on the back of one of her bar stools.

After arranging the daffodils in the vase, she set it on the butcher-block breakfast bar and turned to smile at him. "Well, they're beautiful, and I thank you, again."

It was his turn to blush. "They make me think spring is really here, you know?"

She handed him a glass of wine. "I do. They're one of my favorites." Grabbing the bottle, she motioned for him to follow her back into the living room. When he sat next to her on the couch, his gravity drew her a few inches closer.

"So what's up?" In just taking a sip of her wine, she felt the knots in her shoulders begin to release. She drank some more.

"I'm worried about Carly, and by extension, about Nick."

"Did something happen to them?" Pausing, she put her wine glass down on the coffee table. "Is there something wrong with the pregnancy?"

"No." He held up a hand. "Sorry, I didn't mean to make you worry. They're fine and their baby is fine, as far as I know."

Exhaling, the temporary tension leaving with her breath, she picked up her wine glass and took another sip. "Good."

He put his own glass down on the table. "Nothing has happened, but I'm worried about them anyway. First, there's the woman who approached Carly about buying the baby, and the notes she's being left, which concerns me on several levels, but the investigation is moving along. I think we'll find out who's behind it eventually."

Her late grandmother couldn't have been part of this. She just couldn't.

"But regardless of that, they are still teenagers, pregnant, and talking about getting married, having the baby, and who knows what." He grabbed his wine and took another sip.

Marnie exhaled, feeling some of the tension leave her. "I haven't talked to Carly in a couple of days. I should follow up with her and make sure everything is okay."

Realization dawned. She'd been neglecting a lot of important people and things lately, including her mother, Carly, and her job, even though she'd never been irresponsible before. This search for her birth mother was already taking a lot of her time and attention, and maybe giving her a glimpse into the woman she would have been without her parents in her life. The woman she might really be, underneath it all.

Scott stared at her, obviously waiting for her to finish her thought.

"Sorry, I drifted there for a moment. I need to touch base with Carly, see how she's feeling, both physically and emotionally, and if she's made any decisions about whether she's having this baby."

He stilled. "So she's thinking of terminating, then?"

Pausing, she tried to remember the girl's exact words. After refilling their wine glasses, she shook her head. "I don't know. She wouldn't say what she was thinking, the last time we talked. But it may have crossed her mind, given the circumstances. I need to be there for her, but I haven't been doing a good job of it."

"Don't beat yourself up," he said, sipping his own wine. "According to Nick, they haven't reached a decision yet, although he wants to get married. I don't know how Carly feels about it, but it's crazy." He set his glass down on the table and stood, stretched, and then stepped over to lean against the fireplace mantel. His concern for Nick, and by extension Carly, made him even sexier than his deep brown eyes and his leather jacket. When he finally turned back to face her, his eyes were filled with pain. "I don't want Nick to rush into marriage—or Carly, either," he quickly added. "Marriage is hard work, and they're so young." After a moment, his shoulders slumped, and he lumbered back to take a seat on the couch.

Her heart melted a little bit more. Hoping to ease some of his pain, she reached out to touch him. "It's hard work, even when you're not young. I got married for the wrong reasons, to the wrong guy, and I wasn't a teenager. I don't want the kids to go through that."

"It sounds like your marriage ended on a friendly note. That's rare and so completely opposite of mine."

"We shouldn't have gotten married, but we're great as friends." Swirling her wineglass and gazing down into the crimson ripples, she couldn't disagree.

"I started dating Matt in high school, although we broke up when I went to Cornell for college. When I came back to town years later, we started dating again. I went to work for him, and, well, one thing led to another, so we got married." Holding up her glass to him, she said "Davis Winery makes good wine, don't you think?"

He nodded but waited silently for her to finish her story.

"We couldn't hack the marriage thing, but we work together well." Shaking her head, she took another sip of wine, starting to feel it. "Matt had some drinking issues, so we hired a wine maker. I manage the winery, and he runs the farm. It works, as long as we're not married to each other anymore."

He smiled. "I couldn't work for, with, or anywhere near my ex. Darlene was a train wreck who was never on time, under budget, or thinking of anybody but herself. I can tell already that you are about as opposite from Darlene as is possible." He shook his head, as if trying to dislodge some of the bad memories. "The only good thing I got out of that fiasco is Nick."

"And that's why you worry about him." His love for the teen couldn't have been clearer. "I get it. I care about Carly, too."

He smiled. "Let's try to steer them in the right direction."

She put her empty wine glass on the table, leaned back against the couch, and smiled up at him. A man that looked so good in denim and leather, *and* had a soft heart for kids in trouble, was right up her alley. "You're pretty cute, you know."

****

Scott couldn't take his gaze off Marnie. Her eyes were filled with hope and warmth and everything pure and good. She was so unlike any other woman he'd known that he couldn't stop himself from reaching out to cradle her cheek in the palm of his hand.

"You've started to mean a lot to me, Marnie."

If her smile was any indication, he hadn't made a fool of himself. Taking it as a good sign, he leaned in and brushed his lips gently over hers.

She didn't pull back, didn't push him away. Those things he might have expected. He was rushing things, after all.

Instead, she kissed him back.

Her hands slid up to his neck, her fingers tangling in his hair. When she leaned in to his chest, he moved his arm to circle her waist, pulling her closer, moving in deeper.

He stilled for a moment when she gasped, thinking she'd finally found some sanity. It didn't last long, though, since she used her other hand to pull his shoulders toward her until they were lying on the couch.

Her mouth was warm, soft, and welcoming. Her tight little body moved beneath him. Deep in her throat, she made soft little noises, which were driving him crazy. If she was trying to put the brakes on, he was missing those clues completely.

Before he knew what was happening, his hand had found its way under her shirt. He cradled her small, firm breast in his right hand while he used his lips to trace a path from her lips, down her neck, along the ridge of her collarbone, to meet his fingers on the edge of heaven.

Her hands fisted in his hair, but she never tried to push him away or make him stop. Her hips were bucking, pressing against him as her legs wound around him.

Once he'd snapped open her bra and freed her breasts to his touch, he pulled a nipple into his mouth, suckling her softly. She groaned, writhing beneath his taste, pushing him harder against her skin. He stopped long enough to pull off her shirt and bra and get rid of his own shirt.

She reached for his fly, her nimble fingers making quick work of the button and zipper. The touch of her skin against his abdomen nearly sent him over the edge. While he struggled with her jeans, her hand slid into his boxers, sending shock waves through his system and instantly shutting off all rational thought with a touch.

However it happened, they were both naked in record time. Since the couch wasn't nearly big enough for what he had in mind, they clearly needed a bed. Grabbing the condom he'd stuffed into his pocket earlier, he slid his arms under her and picked her up, pulling loose long enough to motion with his head. "Which way to the bedroom?"

He followed her hurried instructions, carrying her there, but grabbing a kiss after every few steps, feeding his need and prolonging their journey.

When he lowered her onto her bed, before joining her on the sheets, he ripped open the condom packet. He hadn't thought he'd need it, when he left the house tonight, but figured he'd bring it along with him, as well as the flowers. He'd learned to be prepared in

Boy Scouts, although his troop leader had never talked specifically about condoms.

He turned back to face her and stopped.

They hadn't uttered a word, either of them, beyond a groan or a sigh. He'd never asked, she'd never agreed, he'd never muttered a single endearment. But every look, every sigh, each time he felt her heart beat, he was pulled deeper and deeper into her spell.

She wasn't the kind of woman made for one-night stands, and he didn't want this to be one anyway. He liked to see her like this, nestled in her bed, all flushed and rosy and ready. He wanted her like this every day for the rest of his life, and he'd never tire of her.

The rest of his life? Where had that thought come from? As surprising as it was, it felt right to him.

How could he jump into bed with a woman he had serious feelings for, someone he might want to marry, without having the decency to talk about what they were doing? Unfortunately, his tongue wasn't working at the moment—at least not for conversation.

She might have sensed his moral dilemma. Or maybe she mistook his intention, thinking he'd paused for effect. Whatever was on her mind, he couldn't say. Thank God, she didn't appear to want to talk about it. She simply raised up on her knees, slid the condom over him, and led him home.

When they were finished, he pulled her into his arms. It felt so right to have her there, he promptly fell asleep.

****

Exhausted, Carly clocked out of work and took off her apron. She should never have stayed late, even though her boss basically had begged her to.

When she walked out of the restaurant, Nick waited for her. Even though she didn't know what to tell him, it was still better to see him than the nagging feeling she'd been having the last couple of days that someone was watching her.

"Carly, we have to talk. You up for a pizza?"

Shaking her head, she couldn't keep the chuckle out of her voice. "I've been working in a restaurant for the past five hours and you want to take me out for pizza?"

He was cute when he blushed.

"We could take a ride down to the lake."

As if. Every time she'd gone to the lakefront with him after dark, they'd always hooked up.

"I don't think so."

He must have realized what he'd said, because he stuttered, "No, I mean…just to talk, ya know."

"Yeah, right."

He grasped her elbow, stopping her in her tracks. Even as she wrenched her arm free, he apologized.

"Sorry, I didn't hurt you, did I? I mean, shit, Carly. I'm sorry for everything. Just talk to me, okay? Don't shut me out of this. I want to help."

She was too tired to talk. "I don't have time to talk to you right now. I'm late, and my father is going be furious. And stop stalking me, dude."

"Okay…wait." Nick held his hands up in front of him. "What are you talking about? I'm not stalking you. I wanted to give you a ride and maybe get a chance to talk. Geesh!" Now his face was red, but he wasn't blushing.

"I don't mean tonight. You've been waiting in the

shadows the last few nights when I leave work, just watching me. Going to deny it?"

Shaking his head, he dropped his hands. "No, I… What do you mean?" He raised his voice. "Has somebody been following you?"

Chills spread down her spine. "It wasn't you?"

He took her hand in his, gazing deep into her eyes. "No. Did you see a car? Was it just a single guy? Have you told anybody about this?" His voice got louder and louder.

"I thought it was you." Now she was yelling. Fighting against tears and swallowing back a lump in her throat, she took a steadying breath. "If it was you…" Her stomach churned.

He touched her arm, but more gently this time. "It wasn't, Carly. I wouldn't do that to you."

Biting her lip, she nodded. "Okay, so I don't know who it was."

His shoulders seem to grow broader as he straightened up. "If somebody is stalking you, I will be here every night when you get out of work. And I'll drive you to school in the morning."

She shook her head. "This isn't your problem, Nick. I can take care of myself."

He cocked his head to one side, looking her up and down. "No offense, babe, but you look so tired tonight I'm not sure you could." He pulled her hand into his, lacing his fingers through hers.

She took a deep breath, preparing to argue, but realized she *was* too tired to fight about whether she was too tired. "I don't want whoever's following me to start threatening you."

Nick didn't let go of her hand as they walked

toward his truck. "As you said, I can take care of myself."

She shook her head. "I think these are bad dudes, Nick. I'm scared."

He squeezed her hand in his. "We can talk about it, but right now, let's get in the truck. I don't want to stand out here in the parking lot."

She hesitated, but it was stupid to fight about it.

When he opened the door of the truck, she climbed in. She wasn't even showing yet, but she was starting to move like an old lady. This pregnancy thing zapped all her strength.

Nick climbed in the driver's side, started the engine, and pulled out of the parking lot. "So when did you first notice somebody following you?"

"Over the last few days, and it was more like a feeling, you know, like somebody watching me. Sort of a shiver sending goosebumps down my spine, like a spidey-sense or something. I didn't really see anybody."

Nick nodded. "Only here at work?"

Even though she'd spoken to Scott about it, she hadn't really told Nick any of the details. "There's been a little weird stuff going on at work and school, but only notes, mostly." While she'd started looking behind her whenever she walked anywhere, she hoped he wouldn't freak out. "I haven't seen anybody following me. I could be imagining it, and I'm feeling all mixed up." His eyes were sorta popping out of his face, so she shrugged and tried to make it seem like no big deal. "Probably hormones, ya know?"

"What do you mean 'weird stuff' and notes? What are you talking about?"

She turned toward the passenger window but closed her eyes. She didn't want to cry. "Just some threats, like 'don't tell the police or else,' that kind of shit." She kept her voice steady, but still got goose bumps at the memory.

"What?" Nick exploded. "Why didn't you tell me about this?"

She turned to meet his gaze. She'd sort of wanted to tell him, but was afraid he'd get all protective about it. "I didn't want to tell you because they said not to tell anybody, Nick."

"I'm not just anybody, babe."

He sounded hurt, but she had to keep her sisters and, well, their baby, safe. "I'm scared, Nick. But I told Scott about it at Marnie's house Monday."

He sighed. "Okay. You talked to Scott about it; that's good. But…" He turned away, his gaze on the road in front of them. "You told him before you told me."

She lowered her gaze, unable to face him. "I'm sorry. I didn't want to put you at risk."

He sat silently for a while, just driving, before he finally glanced at her, his expression turning serious. "Did this start before you found out you're pregnant? Like, before you went to Planned Parenthood?"

Running her fingers over her forehead didn't bring calm or sharpen her memory, but it seemed to ease the headache building there. "I don't really remember."

"Think, babe."

She pulled out her agenda, thumbing through the pages. "No, it didn't start until after that woman approached me about the baby. But I haven't seen her again since that day."

He cocked his head to the side. "She could have people working with her."

"That's what Scott said." The buzzing in her brain seemed to grow louder.

"What's he doing about it? Are you and the girls moving to some sort of safe house or something?"

She shook her head and tried to swallow the lump in her throat. "He has a cop car driving by my house, keeping an eye on the place."

He lowered his voice, now almost a whisper. "Okay. But I'm driving you to school, to work, and back home. No argument, Carly."

She released a breath, which seemed to deflate her entire body, as exhaustion took hold. "Okay." They sat quietly for a while. "What's up with Scott and Marnie, anyway?"

He stole a quick glance at her. "What are you talking about?"

Shrugging, she chuckled. "When I was at her house, there were definitely some vibes running between them. I think they're hooking up."

He coughed out a laugh. "Did you have to put that picture in my mind? Ugh. I don't want to think about who Scott is sleeping with. And I have no idea whether it's Marnie or not."

Even if Nick didn't want to believe it, the glances she'd seen passing between Scott and Marnie were more than just two adults worried over the threats she'd been receiving. There were some serious sparks flying between them.

Nick drove along the lake road, heading up the hill toward her house. He lightly brushed his hand along her arm, in that way he had which calmed and soothed.

She leaned her head back against the seat and took another deep breath, but the headache only grew worse.

When he linked his fingers with hers, turning his irresistible smile on for her, she squeezed his hand. "I…I'm sorry, Nick."

He shook his head, "Don't…"

"No." She sat up straighter. "Listen. I know you're a good guy. You're trying to help and do the right thing, whatever that means. It's a lot right now." Her eyes filled with tears, but she refused to let them out. "I don't know what to do about the baby."

"I know, babe. I understand. I want to help. I'll do whatever I can, as long as I'm part of the conversation." His gaze was concerned and protective, making him look older.

"You are helping, but please don't push too much." She squeezed his fingers again. "I don't want an abortion. I don't know where to go from there."

He smiled again and turned his face away from her. "Good." His voice was deeper than usual.

"I know you want to get married, and I'm sorry." Again she squeezed his fingers gently. "I'm not ready to talk about that yet. Can we give it a rest for now, as we've got more than six months until this baby is born?" He turned back to her, and she added, "I don't want to rush into anything."

His smile somewhat dimmed. "Right."

She'd never been with anyone as nice as Nick, and she didn't want to hurt him. But he didn't understand what her life was really like and what he had gotten himself into, thinking of marrying her.

He deserved better.

They were getting close enough to her house she should have told him to pull over up ahead and let her out. Even in the dark, she wouldn't want anyone to see their house. Not only was she so far out of town it took nearly an hour on the school bus in the morning, but this part of the county was filled with two-bit shacks, rusty old trailers, and more than a few meth labs. She didn't need to tell him her father was a drunk who couldn't keep a job. He could figure it out on his own simply by driving past their house in the daylight.

"You can let me out here." She looked up at him out of the corner of her eye.

Nick smiled, although it didn't reach his eyes. "Don't try that sly look on me now, Carly. I'm driving you home and waiting for you to go into the house, lock the door, and then waiting to be sure you're safe. No argument."

As much as she wanted to argue, she didn't have the strength. Nick wasn't going to make fun of where she lived. He was too good a guy for that. She nodded and pointed to the house on the right. "Okay."

He stopped the truck in the driveway, turning to her again. "I'll be here in the morning to drive you and the girls to school. Don't leave the house until I get here."

She coughed, trying swallow the lump in her throat. He really was a good guy. "Okay. Thanks for the ride, and thanks for watching out for me and my sisters." She opened the truck door but stopped when he reached out and put his hand on her arm.

"Text me when you get inside and have checked on the girls. I want to know everything's good. I'll wait here until I hear from you."

Overwhelmed, she climbed out of the truck and turned to face him. "You don't need to do that, Nick."

He shook his head. "Maybe not for you, but for me I do. I won't be okay until I know you're all safe."

"Okay." She shrugged. "See you tomorrow."

She started to close her door, but he held up his hand, his palm facing her. His expression was so serious, she stopped instantly.

"Good." The smile was back in his eyes as he kissed her cheek. "Remember, I'm here if you need me."

****

She wasn't going to like his excuse, but his hands were tied.

"The girl has a protector now…Yeah, he's with her at school and work."

He spoke softly, but couldn't hide his frustration. It wasn't his fault, so why was she yelling at him? He'd been trying to catch the teenager alone, but she was always with somebody.

"He drives her everywhere. What do you want me to do?"

Chapter Eight

"I'm glad your mom's doing so much better, Marn." Kate smiled at her across the front seat as she drove them to a little dive bar.

"Thanks. Me, too. When Dad called to say Mom is regaining strength and Kendal moved her back into the assisted care area, I felt a huge weight lift off my shoulders."

"You've had a rough time of things, but you'll all make it through. Just wait and see."

She leaned her head back against the headrest and closed her eyes. "From your lips to God's ear, girlfriend."

Kate chuckled. "Any news on the search for your birth parents? Last I heard, you had talked to the retired cop Deke recommended and got some more information. Anything new?"

She nodded, her throat suddenly dry. "Yeah, I met with him yesterday evening. He didn't have a lot of information to add, but I'm following some leads, so we'll see what happens." She rested one elbow on the door handle and cupped her chin in her palm. "I put my information into one of those adoption reunion websites." It was hard to contain the skittering of her nerves.

"What does that mean?"

"It's a website that tries to help birth parents

reconnect with the children they gave up for adoption." Her voice rose with excitement. "I list when and where I was born and birth parents list when and where they gave birth and gave up the baby, and the website tries to match you up."

Her friend straightened. "That's amazing. I had no idea anything like that existed."

Marnie chuckled. "It's sort of like online dating, but with your birth parents. It's a long shot, but at least the information is out there now. We'll see if anything comes from it." If she could be that lucky.

Kate gently touched her arm. "Good luck, girl. I'll be keeping my fingers crossed for you."

As they drove up the hill leaving town, Kate turned down the radio. "So what's new with that handsome trooper?"

Marnie smiled just at the thought of him. "Who knows? It's early days, but it's looking good so far."

Her friend nudged her across the front seat. "Think it could be something serious? When I've seen the two of you together, he looks pretty smitten."

Pausing, Marnie brought to mind his warm smile, soft eyes, and gentle touch. "It could be serious, maybe, depending on how things go. I'm not sure I'm the right person for him, though."

Kate laughed. "Why in God's name would you say that? He'd be lucky to be with you."

While she was not at all impartial, it was nice of her friend to say so. "I'm several years older than he is, really past the age to have babies, if he has a mind to start a family. I'm not sure he has considered that, or even if he's thinking that far down the road."

"Again, he'd be lucky to be with you, and he's a

fool if he doesn't realize it."

She couldn't help but laugh at the woman's loyalty. Good friends were truly a blessing.

Kate pulled into the little lot and parked, then got out, closed the car door, and waited for Marnie to climb out the other side.

Marnie stuffed her license and some cash into her pocket, for once leaving her giant purse in the car. The pounding of the music thumped through her as her foot touched the front stairs. When she joined her friend at the front door, she wrapped an arm around the thin waist. "I think you're a genius for suggesting a night out. I needed it."

As Kate led the way into the Owl's Nest, Marnie tried to think of the last time she'd been out with friends for a girls' night out.

Way too long. She plastered a smile on her face and felt a bounce creep into her step.

Even though she worked in a winery and drank wine with dinner on occasion, she wasn't much of a drinker. She'd never been much of a party girl. In the past, she always figured that was just who she was. Neither of her parents ever drank much, and they certainly didn't frequent the bars in town. She wasn't so much of a prude as it simply had never interested her.

But now, she wasn't her parents' daughter. For all she knew, her genes came from a couple of wild-partying, no-good drunks. Maybe she would enjoy the bar scene more now that she had learned the truth about herself.

Who knew? Maybe it had taken forty years for her real personality to emerge.

The Owl's Nest was literally pounding with noise, smoke, and a crush of people. Normally, she would have turned around and left as soon as she stepped inside. Not tonight. The stress she'd been holding inside—from her mother's illness, the news of her adoption, her birth-parents search, Carly's problems, and the developing relationship with Scott—was enough to drive her into the bar in search of relief. All the people around her appeared to be having a good time. Maybe if she relaxed, had a drink, and danced the night away, she'd be able to think clearly again in the morning.

They found a table in the back corner and hadn't been there long when a couple of other friends whom Kate had invited came and sat down. The music was loud enough that the conversations she didn't really want to have were too hard to hear anyway.

Kate ordered the first round, and Marnie had to laugh when the waiter delivered four drinks with little umbrellas in them. This wasn't the kind of place she thought would even stock frilly paper umbrellas. If she had to bet, she'd say few of the regulars had ever ordered a frozen daiquiri at the Owl's Nest.

The next round was Cindy's. She worked at Kate's salon doing nails and manicures. The waiter kept staring down the young woman's top while she talked to him. Of course, since she was young, single, and unbelievably built, she was probably used to it.

The crowd was crazy. Music blared from the old jukebox in the corner, and people had shoved tables to the sides to make a dance floor. Here were lonely people finding good times in a drink, a song, and a friend. She wanted some of that for herself.

"Who has a quarter for the jukebox?"

By the time Dana ordered them gin and tonics, their attempts at conversation had turned to the lack of decent, marriageable men in Stevens County and their volume had ratcheted up a notch. Dana worked at the county offices and had recently ended a long-term relationship with a man who couldn't, or wouldn't, leave his wife. Everybody sitting near them could hear her talking about it. But, given it was a small town, they probably already knew.

The only problem was that Marnie couldn't shake the picture in her mind of Scott, warm and naked, when he'd gotten up to leave her bed the night before. Actually, it was early that morning, since they'd made love again before dawn. Her skin still tingled with the remembered whisper of his touch.

It had been the most incredible night of her life.

She was no virgin, although she had certainly never slept around. Besides her marriage, she'd had a few longer relationships which included sex, but nothing could compare to last night.

Not only was he a fun and playful lover, she wasn't the same woman she used to be. Maybe it was the wild woman in her whom she'd never known existed, but she'd been more creative, aggressive, and demanding than she'd ever been in her life. And it was wonderful.

Even better, when the amazing sex was over, Scott had folded her in his arms. He fell asleep holding her, protecting her from the evils of life. She'd honestly believed nothing bad in the world could touch her as long as she was in his arms.

And that scared the crap out of her.

She wasn't ready to fall in love, get married, and make a life with a rock-solid, good-guy, steady man. Would the "new" Marnie ever be ready? She'd had a wild woman inside her all these years and didn't even know it. She couldn't lock that party girl away without trying her on for size.

So tonight she wouldn't think about him. He was probably over at Kate's house with Jack, watching a ball game and drinking beer. He might be ready for the solid and steady life, but she felt like she had just woken from a lifelong dream—not the same person she used to be. She didn't even know who she was, but she could have a lot of fun finding out.

Meanwhile, there were exotic drinks to try, gossip to share, and tables to dance on. A little bit of crazy was just what she needed tonight.

When her turn to order the drinks came around, she decided to try Jell-O shooters. She'd heard of them before, learned they were a specialty of the house, and thought they sounded like the kind of drink a wild woman would order.

After downing her shot, she stood, flipped her hair behind her ear, and grabbed the chair. The room tilted a bit as she tried to steady herself. Maybe it wasn't such a good idea. But once she had a plan, she wouldn't be stopped.

So she placed her right foot on the chair and, with it wobbling beneath her, swung her left foot up, knocking over a couple of empty glasses in her attempt to dance on the tabletop.

Whenever she tried to sway to the beat, it felt like the little table was going to topple over. The guys at the bar were laughing and hollering, though. Several had made their way closer to their group, hooting and yelling things at her she couldn't quite make out.

The room was swaying, but so was the table. She shimmied her hips, but her shoe slipped off the edge of the table. Since she was barely able to stop herself from falling off the table, it was possible she wasn't in the best condition for dancing.

This table-dancing thing might be fun for some, but she was a little too tipsy to enjoy it to the fullest. Especially when Scott and Nick came bursting in the door.

"What the hell is going on in here?"

What got his panties in a bunch?

****

Who the hell was this woman sitting next to him?

Scott took a few deep breaths to steady himself so he could give Marnie the details of Nick's call. The trip to the hospital wasn't long enough to waste time talking about her table-dancing escapade. They had more important things to discuss.

"Nick said Carly called him in tears, and he went to pick her up. She was bleeding and afraid she was losing the baby, but she wouldn't let him call an ambulance. She wanted him to take her to your house, but once she got in the truck, she fainted, so he drove her to the hospital."

He turned his head. Was she even listening to him? God only knew how much she'd had to drink tonight. She reeked of cigarettes, booze, and the rank dive bar he'd dragged her out of.

Just like old times.

"She's lucky he was smart enough to do that." Marnie ran the fingers of her left hand through her hair while her right elbow rested on the windowsill. She didn't look up, but took several deep breaths. She was trying to either calm her nerves about Carly or keep herself from throwing up.

"Yeah. And she's lucky he was there when she called him. Who knows what would have happened if she'd waited until she could get a hold of you."

That brought her head flying up. Her mouth opened a couple of times before she actually said anything. "My cell phone was in my purse, in Kate's car. I would have seen her messages when we came out, and I would have called her back."

"Right." *How many times did Darlene give me the same excuse?*

"Listen, I'm allowed to have a night of fun with my friends now and then." She turned away, looking out the side window. "I mean…" Her voice got much quieter. "I'm sorry Carly couldn't reach me when she needed to, but at least she found Nick."

Scott pulled into the hospital parking lot and found a spot more easily than expected. She stalked silently through the front door, and he followed her inside. At least she was sober enough to find her way to the nurse's desk. Darlene would have been puking in the bushes by now.

"Is Carly Johnson here?"

"Are you family?"

Marnie looked chastised by the drill sergeant of a nurse.

She remained quiet, almost frozen. Maybe lies didn't come quite as easily to her as they did to Darlene.

He put his hand on her shoulder. "This is her aunt.

Can we see Carly now, or at least talk to her doctor?"

The woman's glare softened a bit as she met his gaze. "The doctor is still with her, but he'll come out as soon as he has any information. Why don't the two of you have a seat in the waiting area?"

Marnie was about to say something, but he kept his hand firmly on her shoulder and steered her to the line of plastic chairs against the far wall. A magazine on the table and a tiny TV in the corner indicated this was the waiting area.

He glanced up and down the narrow hall, but Nick was nowhere in sight.

She collapsed onto a chair, the urge to argue apparently leaving her in a rush. "You lied to her." Her tone was more tired than accusing.

He took a seat next to her. "Carly's a minor. There's no way they'd let you within ten feet of her if they didn't think you were related. You know that."

She shook her head, as if trying to dislodge the hold alcohol had on her brain cells. "You're right, of course. "But..." She sat up suddenly. "It means they called her father, right? When he gets here, my cover will be blown."

Crossing his arms, he leaned back in the small chair to rest his shoulders against the wall. "Since she was in and out of consciousness when Nick brought her in, they didn't need her father's permission to start care. Unless Nick gave them her father's number, they probably haven't reached him yet. We'd know what's going on if we could find Nick."

She stood again, a little less unsteady, and paced the short length of the chairs. "Maybe he's in there with Carly. God, I hope so. She must be so scared."

At that moment, Nick came out of the men's room up the hall. Although more mature than Scott had ever seen him, the young man started to melt when his tears began to fall. The scared-little-boy expression which covered his face brought Scott immediately to his feet.

"Are you okay?" He resisted the urge to pull Nick into a hug, instead patting the kid on his back and letting his hand linger there a moment longer than necessary.

"I'm fine, but Carly, man..." He sighed, shaking and pale. "I'm scared. She's bleeding and everything. They won't let me see her."

"They said the doctor's still with her. He'll come out when he has anything to tell us."

Marnie grabbed Nick's hand and didn't appear to notice when he tried to pull away. "What happened? Had she been feeling sick? What did she say?"

"Nick, this is Marnie."

The teen succeeded in pulling his hand out of her grasp this time. In fact, he even took a few steps back. "She tried to call you." His voice got slightly louder as he stepped back another foot, glaring at her. "You weren't answering your phone. I thought you cared about her."

As if struck, she staggered back. Her eyes filled with tears and pain at Nick's words. Maybe she was more different from Darlene than he had begun to think. She seemed to truly care about the girl.

"I'm sorry. I'm...I'm glad you were there for her."

She slumped back into her chair looking so beaten down Scott felt sorry for her. But the anger and hurt in Nick's eyes stopped him from comforting her.

Before the teen could lash out at her again, a doctor walked into the hall and called for Marnie.

She stood, her hands clutched in worry. "I'm Marnie Edwards. How's Carly?"

The tall, dark-haired doctor briefly looked at him and Nick, but then turned his full attention on her. Maybe a little too much attention.

"I'm Dr. Connolly." He didn't take his eyes off Marnie. "I'm happy to say Carly's stable. The bleeding has stopped. She's sleeping now."

She hesitated a moment. "And the baby?"

Dr. Connolly leaned in, closer to her than was strictly necessary. "As far as we can tell, everything is fine with the baby. It's still early in the pregnancy. If she makes it through the next twenty-four hours without miscarrying, everything should be fine."

Nick shuddered, and Scott reached out and grabbed his shoulder.

"Is Carly being released, or does she have to stay?" Marnie's voice was nearly a whisper now.

The doctor glanced again at him and Nick, sizing them up. He almost wished he'd worn his trooper's uniform. He was there as Nick's family, but if they didn't start getting some respect, he'd pull out his I.D. and go all official on this guy.

"She can't be alone and must stay in bed. If that's not possible at home, she'll have to stay here tonight. We can't risk her starting to bleed again."

"She can stay with me. I'll take care of her." Dr. Connolly smiled at her as if she were an angel. If only he knew about the tabletop dancing. When she looked into the doctor's eyes, the guy nearly purred. "What about her father? Is he coming to pick her up?"

Dr. Connolly shook his head. "No. Once she was conscious, Carly insisted we not call him. Since she's sixteen and pregnant, we're not required to. The decision is up to her."

"Okay. How long does she need to stay in bed?"

"At least a week." He glanced from her to Nick. "She can get up to use the bathroom, but I don't want her climbing stairs or walking around. And definitely no physical activity, including sex."

Nick blushed and stared at the floor, and Scott wanted to wrap his arm around the kid's shoulders. He stopped himself, knowing Nick would only be more embarrassed.

Even Marnie seemed sympathetic to the boy's embarrassment, as she cleared her throat and pulled Dr. Connolly's attention back to her. "Can I see her now?"

The doctor took her arm and led her back to a curtained area.

Scott watched them walk off. Sure, Connolly could see how upset she was, and maybe he believed she was Carly's aunt, but still, he didn't need to touch her.

He turned and focused on trying to calm Nick, who refused to sit and talk. Instead, he worried a path in the worn linoleum with his pacing.

Finally, his ex-brother-in-law stopped and turned to him. "I picked her up after work and drove her home. She seemed fine then."

Scott rubbed the boy's back again, and they sat in silence until Marnie returned to the waiting area. She was even paler and obviously on the verge of tears. He stood and put his arm around her back. He may have jumped to conclusions about her girls' night out.

"Carly agreed to come home with me." She hiccupped a little and then took a deep breath. "She's getting dressed now. She refuses to call her father, so I guess it's up to the hospital to tell him where she is, if he calls here looking for her."

He patted her back. While she did screw up, she was definitely worried about the girl. "What did she have to say?"

"She's worn out and feels like crap, but she said she started bleeding after she got home tonight." Marnie swallowed. "She was scared, and when she couldn't get hold of me, she called Nick."

She turned to face the kid. "Thanks, again, for getting to her so quickly."

Nick nodded, shoving his hands into his pockets.

Scott took one of her hands in his. "When you're ready, I'll drive you both home."

She walked back to the nurse's station and started signing some paperwork.

Would she be up to taking care of a pregnant, shaky, teenaged girl? The smart, stable Marnie would, but he wasn't so sure about the drunk, table-dancing Marnie. Which one was really her?

A nurse pushed Carly to the door in a wheelchair. The girl might be pretty, but mostly she was too thin and pale. Nick took over the wheelchair and followed him out to his car. As Marnie took Carly's left arm, helping her to her feet, Nick held her other side, and Carly leaned into Nick.

Once they'd helped her into the back seat, Marnie climbed in next to her, and Nick shut the door. He turned to leave, but Scott reached out for him, stopping him in his tracks.

"You did good, dude."

Nick stared at the ground a minute, shuffling his feet on the asphalt.

"Do you want to stay at my place tonight?"

When the teen glanced up at him, there was a little boy fighting the man in his gaze. Wanting to be responsible. Wanting to be held.

The man won.

"I'm fine. Just get them home. Don't worry about me."

"I'll talk to you tomorrow. Let me know if you need anything before then."

Nick started to turn. He held the boy's arm a moment longer. "You probably saved her life, Nick, and the baby's life, too."

The kid stared resolutely at the floor, nudging a gum wrapper with the toe of his sneaker.

Scott pulled him in for a quick hug before letting him go. "I'm proud of you."

****

"I'm fine, okay? Stop fussing."

After tucking Carly up in the first-floor guest room with a water bottle, her phone, and the charger on the bedside table with the TV remote, Marnie double-checked that she was warm enough. She couldn't leave the girl alone. She'd been wrapped up in her own trouble when Carly needed her earlier, but she wasn't going to be among the missing again.

She sat in the upholstered armchair next to the bed, not wanting to be too far away from the girl. "I'll call the school tomorrow, let them know you'll be out this week, and ask them to collect your homework assignments. Do you have all your textbooks at home?"

Carly's expression darkened. "Umm, why don't I have Nick get my books and homework? He's there anyway."

Marnie nodded, not wanting to agitate her. "Sounds good. I'll run out to the grocery store in the morning to stock up on your favorites. What do you want?"

The teen shrugged. "I'm not picky. Don't go to any trouble."

She decided to ask Nick about it when she called him about the schoolwork. She didn't want to leave Carly's side, but she also didn't want to keep the girl awake if she was ready to go to sleep. She leaned forward in her chair. "How are you feeling? Do you need anything?"

Carly met her gaze, a faint smile on her face. "I already told you, I'm fine, but how are you feeling? You look kinda pale."

She leaned back against the chair, her body not up to the effort of acting as perky as usual. "I'm tired and a little worn out. You scared me, sweetie. We were all scared for you."

Carly dropped her gaze, suddenly drawn to examine her cuticles again. "Thanks, but you didn't need to be."

Marnie reached out and placed her hand on top of the thin ones on the bed, pressing down until she looked up again. "I'm so sorry I didn't answer your call. I promised to be here for you and then wasn't there when you needed me. I'm sorry."

Carly didn't move or speak for a long time, longer

than Marnie was comfortable with, the teen's eyes going red, her chin quivering.

"Oh, sweetie…"

"It's not your fault." A tear slid down Carly's gaunt cheek, and she brushed it away. "It's okay, you know. I got a hold of Nick, and he was there in a minute. He took care of me."

Tears were pooling in her own eyes, but Marnie inhaled deeply to try to keep them at bay. She took a second deep breath, looking Carly in the eye. "I know, and I'm so glad he got to you so quickly. He was great. I'm sorry I let you down."

The teen shook her head. "Don't say that." She pulled her hands away, raising her voice. "You don't owe me anything. You're not my mother or even my teacher. It's not your job to keep an eye on me." Peering up out of the corner of her eye, Carly continued, "Besides, you've been a little busy lately, you know, with Scott."

Marnie grimaced. *How does Carly know I have anything going on with Scott?* "Look, we're friends, and I said you could call me any time, and when you did, I was out at a bar, drinking and dancing."

The sound of the girl's laughter caught her unaware.

"You're an adult, you know. You're allowed to drink and dance with your friends. In fact, given what's been going on with your mom, and your job, and whatever it is between you and our state trooper, you probably needed a night out. And I'm fine, so there's nothing to be sorry for."

"What do you mean between me and Scott?"

Again, Carly laughed. "I'd have to be blind not to

see how you two react when you see each other. Even tonight, with all my drama at the hospital, he couldn't take his eyes off you, and it looks to be entirely mutual, from where I'm sitting."

So much for her poker face. How could the teen see right through her? "You're too observant for my own good, I think." She chuckled. "I mean, I'm attracted to him, but he was pretty pissed at me tonight. But maybe that was because Nick was livid."

The teen sat forward. "Did he yell at you or something?"

She smiled, resting her hand on the covers next to Carly's feet. "Nick was scared and upset, and he lashed out, that's all. He cares about you, and I totally understand why he was angry with me. He's protective of you."

"I need to text him. Where's my phone?"

She pointed to the bedside table, and the teen grabbed her phone and texted furiously. Panic passed over the girl's face.

"Why? Can't it wait until tomorrow?"

Carly turned away, fiddling with her ring, a thin silver band studded with three small bits of colored glass.

"Carly? What's going on?"

After another minute or two, the girl finally met Marnie's gaze, her eyes red again. "Nick started driving me to school and work. He plans to do it every day—and the girls, too."

She sat up quickly. "What? Why?"

"When I told him about the threatening notes and the feeling I've been getting of being watched, he said he'll be there every day to drive us all, so the girls and

I aren't alone." Carly's voice was small and sounded young.

Her heart melted a little. "That's nice of him. But why did you need to text him now? I mean, he's had a heck of a night, he's probably tired, and you're not going anywhere, anytime soon."

"I want to make sure he checks on the girls, makes sure they're safe. You don't think your trooper will pull the cop cars he has driving by the house now, do you?"

She shook her head. "I'm sure he'll keep up the patrols. He's looking out for your sisters too." Fear shone from the girl's eyes, despite Marnie's attempt to sound reassuring.

Carly broke down. "Now I'm afraid for Nick, too. What if they go after him?"

She reached out, squeezing the teen's hand. "Why do you think they will? If you're that worried, you need to tell Scott about this." Surely Scott wouldn't let anything happen to Nick.

The girl's shoulders sank. "That's what Nick says."

Marnie climbed onto the bed to sit next to Carly and put her arm around the girl's shoulders.

When Carly nestled her head against her shoulder, a fuzzy peace filled Marnie. Despite the fear and worry of the past few weeks, it was nice to snuggle the girl in tight and lightly kiss her head.

"So has the woman approached you again?"

Carly shook her head. "No, not really."

A faint tingle of fear raced up her spine. "What does 'not really' mean?"

"Well…" the girl paused. "I haven't seen anyone,

but a note waited for me when I got home last night."

"Last night? Is that when the bleeding started?'

Shaking her head, Carly looked at her phone. "I guess I found the note really two nights ago now."

"What did it say?" Marnie tried to stay calm but wanted to call Scott to come over immediately.

"See, Nick picked me up at work, and I asked him if he'd been stalking me. I mean, I thought he was following me around, trying to make sure I'm okay, you know."

Marnie murmured in understanding.

"But when we figured out someone else was following me, he said he'd pick me up after school, take me to work, and bring me home."

"That sounds like a good idea," she said.

The teen nodded. "Yeah, so I agreed and promised to text him when I got into the house. When I opened my door, though, a piece of paper was stuck into it. Someone had been to my house," Carly's voice started to shake. "They came to my house. When the girls were home. If they do something to hurt my sisters, I don't know what I'll do."

"Okay, it's okay. We'll figure this out together." She gave Carly a couple of moments to calm down. "What did the note say?"

Her face paled. "Stop talking to the cops."

Taking a beat, Marnie inhaled. Why hadn't Carly told her about this when it happened? "So it's not only a threat not to tell anyone. They've been watching you, whoever 'they' are."

Carly nodded and started to cry in earnest. "I ran into my room to check on my sisters. Once I knew they were okay, I realized I forgot to text Nick, so I ran to the kitchen to get my phone, and I tripped over a chair. I came down hard on my hip."

The poor kid. "Is that when the bleeding started?"

Shaking her head, the teen wrapped her arms around herself. "No, I was fine then, although there was a little spotting during the day yesterday. It wasn't until last night, when I got home from work, that I noticed it was more than just spotting."

"I'm so sorry, sweetie." She wrapped the teen in a hug and rocked back and forth, trying to calm her tears.

Once Carly had quieted, Marnie sat back against the headboard, tilting the teen's face toward her so she could look her in the eye. "You're fine now, and your baby is too. We'll make sure you take it easy, stay off your feet, and do everything we can to make sure you and the baby are healthy. Okay?"

"Okay." The girl's voice was raspy.

Carly looked down and then quickly raised her head back so her gaze met Marnie's. "What about the girls? I can't just abandon them for a week."

This teenager had more than the average adult's responsibility to worry about. "We'll figure it out, sweetie. Don't worry."

Leaning back into her shoulder, Carly sighed.

"As for the note, where is it?"

"It's in the pocket of my jeans. I stuck it in there as I ran upstairs to check on the girls. I didn't want them, or my father, to see it."

"I'll call Scott tomorrow. I'm sure he'll want to have his people analyze it."

Carly turned back to face her and started to speak, but Marnie laid her index finger against the teen's lips.

"Give me a minute." When the teen nodded, she removed her finger and started again. "These people have probably been buying and selling babies for a long time and getting away with it because they threaten people. If he and his team can track them down and put them away, everyone will be safer, right? In the meantime, you can stay here."

Carly eyes filled with fear, and her brows pinched. "What about my sisters? I don't want them to be alone. Nick will help out, but then the people watching me, they'll know he's helping me, and now you. I'm putting everyone in danger."

"My guess is that the girls are safer if you aren't staying at your house right now, but we'll see what Scott thinks. He could always have an officer drive by there more frequently. Or they could stay here too. Let me talk to Scott."

The teen started to speak, but Marnie continued, "If you're staying here, there's no reason for these people to go to your house. Scott can always have Nick stay with him for a while." She smiled at Carly. "Let's see what he says, okay?"

After not speaking for a moment, the teen finally nodded and said, "We have to keep the girls safe."

"What do you think your father will say about you staying here? Do you think it'd be okay with him for the girls to stay here too? Or do you think he could take care of them?"

Shaking her head, the teen sighed. "If we catch him early in the day, we can ask him, and I doubt he'd care whether I'm staying with you or if the girls do. But by the time he gets home in the evening, if he gets home, he won't be much help in taking care of the girls. If I'm not there, I'm not sure they'll get much dinner."

How could one teenaged girl have to deal with so much? "Let's give him a call tomorrow, after we get some sleep, and we'll see what he has to say." As she paused, the girl's eyes filled with tears again. "I'll talk to Scott about it, too."

Carly sighed. "I can't believe this is happening. Isn't it enough I'm pregnant at seventeen? How much more complicated does it have to be?"

"The good news is you have Nick, and me, and Scott, all pulling for you."

Slipping a little farther under the covers, the girl yawned. "I guess so, but I'm no further along in deciding whether or not to keep this baby."

Her breath caught in her throat. She wanted the girl to open up to her, so she had to temper her reaction. "Are you still thinking of having an abortion?"

"No." Carly shook her head. "I'm definitely having the baby. I don't know if I should keep it or give it up for adoption, though. I don't feel ready to raise a baby, with or without Nick's help. We're still kids ourselves, and I have the girls to think about."

A yawn took over the worried face again. She needed to get this girl to sleep.

"Why don't we save that conversation for tomorrow? You look beat and, as you so kindly pointed out, so am I."

As Carly chuckled and cuddled into the covers, contentment covered her face. "Yeah, I guess we both could use some sleep."

Marnie stood and adjusted the blankets again.

"Get some sleep. If you need me in the night, call me. Don't come upstairs. I'll have my phone by my side and can be down here in a flash."

"Okay." The little-girl voice had taken over again.

"You have the bathroom right here and water if you get thirsty, okay?"

"Good night." The soft murmur trailed away.

Marnie walked to the door, glanced back at the teen, and whispered, "Good night, sweetie."

She texted Scott a short message, telling him about Nick and how Carly wanted a closer watch on her sisters.

His one-word response came through:—*Fine*—

She'd need to talk to him herself, but it could wait until tomorrow. At this point, it really was tomorrow already, but sleep called to her, so Scott could wait.

After double-checking the locks on all the doors and windows, she took her phone and headed upstairs to her own bed.

****

"So now the girl isn't staying at her own house." The house's old windows rattled with the force of the wind, sending shivers up his back.

He didn't want to hear her reply. She was angry again. She was always angry these days. How great would it be to toss the cell phone out the window? He didn't want to listen to her anymore.

He wandered through the darkened living room, stubbing his toe as he moved on to the torn linoleum in the kitchen. Still she griped in his ear.

He'd better get this girl pretty soon so they could go back to business as usual. He couldn't take much more yelling.

"She's moved in with that woman from the Youth Center…I don't know what's going on, only what I see…Yeah, chances are she spilled her guts to the bitch, as well as the boy and maybe the trooper. How are we going to stop this?"

He needed to get some help. This wasn't as easy as he'd thought it would be.

Chapter Nine

The next day when Marnie pulled open the front door, Scott had his hands in his pockets, but his gaze didn't meet hers. He certainly didn't smile, and he didn't seem happy to see her. He pushed himself into the doorway and grumbled a greeting that was only marginally cordial.

What was his problem? Maybe he'd just had a bad day, but he didn't need to share it. If this weren't about Carly, she might have turned him away.

"Carly's in the bedroom back here." She motioned him into the house and toward the first-floor bedroom. She certainly hoped he didn't take out his bad mood on the poor girl.

"Thanks." He bit out the word like he had paid for each letter he spoke.

Luckily, the dark cloud that followed him into the house dissipated when he stepped into Carly's room. Of course, that might mean he was pissy with her, but she had no idea what he could be angry about.

"Hey," he said, as he smiled at the teen. "How are you feeling today?"

Carly pulled herself up to a sitting position and finger-combed her hair. She must have drifted off to sleep again after lunch.

Marnie stood in the doorway, catching Carly's gaze. "Do you want me to stay, sweetie, or do you want to talk to Scott on your own?" His angry air confused her, so she kept her gaze firmly locked on the teen's.

The girl smiled shyly. "Please stay."

She walked to the far side of the bed, opposite of where he stood by the armchair, and took a seat on the foot of the bed.

Carly smiled at her and then turned to him.

"Do you mind if I sit?" Again, he directed his question to Carly, not making eye contact with Marnie. He was as cross as a bear, but only with her. They'd definitely be discussing this later.

Carly smiled but turned to give her a questioning look before responding, "Sure."

"Okay, so when Marnie texted last night, she said I should talk to Nick about you being followed. Thanks for letting me know." Again he ignored her, focusing on Carly, even though it was Marnie's text. "I moved him into my place last night. It's a longer drive for him to get to school and work, but he's safe."

The girl sat up straight. "What about my sisters? Nick was going to drive them to and from school." She looked at Marnie. "They can't be left all alone. They'll be in danger."

Nodding, he held up his hands. "After Marnie texted me the situation, I sent an officer out there this morning to pick them up. For the time being, we'll have someone pick them up in the morning and take them home in the evening."

Carly nodded. "What if someone gets in the house when they're at school?"

"Don't worry. The officer will be sure to clear the house when he brings the girls home."

Marnie put her hand on Carly's arm. It wouldn't do any good to have her get so upset she landed back in the hospital. "I called your father about an hour ago, and he's fine with one of us checking on the girls in the evening, so I was going to suggest that Scott, Nick, or I go by to drop off dinner for the girls, just to make sure everything is okay, at least while you're staying here."

She felt the tension drain from the teen's shoulders and eased her back against the pillows.

Scott nodded. "Okay, so can you give me more details about the person or people following you? Like when it started, what you've noticed, even who you think it might be?" He took out his paper and pen.

Carly explained it to him as she had to Marnie, and he wrote furiously in his notepad.

"You didn't actually see anyone waiting outside the school?"

She shook her head. "No…well, I mean, there are always a lot of cars parked around the school and driving by, you know, picking kids up."

He made a few more notes. "Sure, but picture it in your head. Is there a car, or even a person standing outside the school, someone who isn't meeting a student, or someone who feels hinky to you?"

The girl closed her eyes, sitting still for a few moments. "Maybe. There's a car, sort of brownish, parked down the block a ways. I don't know if it's been there every day, but it feels like it. I don't remember any kids getting in the car or anyone getting out."

Scott leaned forward. "Take a good look at that car in your mind—bring it into focus. Can you see anyone in the car?"

Eyes still closed, she nodded. "Only the driver, a guy. He's not too old, maybe in his twenties, with dark hair. Weird."

Marnie perked up. "What's weird?"

His jaw clenched so tightly, she worried his teeth might crack. "Please let me handle the questioning, if you don't mind."

She raised her eyebrows. *What is his problem?* "Of course." She didn't meet his gaze, but when the teen looked over at her, she smiled and winked.

Scott turned back to Carly. "What do you mean by weird?"

"It's just the dude sat in the car, alone, but he wasn't on his phone. He just sat there, staring out the window."

"Good," he said. "That's great. Anything else you can remember about him or the car?"

Shaking her head, the teen said, "Not really. It was old, brownish, a little dinged up. Nothing special."

"Did you see the license plate?"

"No, I didn't look that closely."

He wrote that down. "What made you think you were being watched?"

"Just a feeling, ya know? Tickling the hair on the back of my neck, giving me the creeps."

She shivered, and Marnie reached out, putting her hand over Carly's on the bed, while he wrote a few more details.

"What about at work?"

The teen explained about accusing Nick of stalking her.

"Why would you think it was Nick?" Scott

seemed worried now.

She paused, biting her lip. "Uh…"

Marnie squeezed her hand. "It's okay, sweetie."

The girl sniffed, and her eyes became slightly red. "It's…well…" She wouldn't look at him. "He's good to me and wants to take care of me, so when I got the feeling somebody was watching me, I figured he might be trying to protect me, ya know, without me knowing about it."

A smile threatened to crack his stone-faced grimace. "But he hasn't been stalking you, right?"

The girl winced, her face slightly flushed. "No. It wasn't Nick."

"Okay," he said. "Now tell me about the note you found at your house. Had you ever seen anything suspicious there before? Either the guy with the brown car from school, or the woman who approached you?"

She shook her head. "No. Nothing. It's…it's pretty remote where we live, so I think I would have noticed something. The first thing I saw was that note last night."

Carly's chin quivered and her face paled. Marnie moved onto the bed and put her arm around the thin shoulders. The tired teen's head fell heavily onto Marnie's shoulder.

His soft expression when he looked back into the girl's eyes made Marnie realize his sympathetic gaze hadn't been directed at her in some time.

"Tell me exactly what happened when you got home."

The young mother-to-be explained about the ride from Nick, walking up on the back porch, the note flying into the house when she opened the door, and her fear for her sisters after she'd read it. Tears filled her eyes as she described racing to check on them, falling, the spotting overnight, and waking up in the hospital.

Throughout, Marnie kept her arm protectively around the girl's shoulders.

Scott reached out and briefly touched the back of Carly's hand. "It's okay. I know what happened from there." He wrote a bit more in his notebook. "Do you still have the note?"

She nodded, tears shimmering in her eyes. Pulling the note from where she had put it in her jeans pocket, she offered it to him. He took out a small plastic bag and had Carly unfold the paper and slide it inside.

Finally, he turned to Marnie, his gaze cool. "I'll add this to the others. Did you touch this?"

She glared at him, not appreciating his accusatory tone. "No."

Once he had covered everything with Carly, and the teen started to fade, she suggested any other questions could wait until later and that he should wait for her in the living room. After she tucked Carly in for a nap, she pulled the door closed and went to talk to him.

As she walked into the living room, he turned to face her, scowling, his arms crossed over his chest. He took a deep breath as if ready to speak.

"Stop." She held up her index finger. "My house. I speak first." She took a deep breath herself, trying to keep her voice down. "I don't know what you're problem is at the moment, and I don't care. But we both want to help Carly, her sisters, and Nick. We're on the same side, at least as far as these kids go. So you can check the attitude, dude."

Suddenly exhausted, she leaned against the side of the floral wingback chair her parents had given her.

He didn't respond immediately, as she expected, but dropped his arms to his sides.

"Okay. Fair enough."

She waited for him to finish.

"But you've taken on the responsibility for a young woman, a pregnant teenager. You are more than a role model now. As long as she's staying with you, you need to keep her safe and healthy. To take care of her." Heat flared in his eyes, but not from desire. "You can't go running out every night to dance on bar tops."

Unable to stop the snort that came racing out of her, she crossed her arms. "I *am* taking care of her. Regardless of what you think, I care about her."

He shook his head, mumbled something, and walked toward the door. She couldn't tell if he was just pissed at her or if he was also worried about the kids, focused on the investigation, or upset about something else entirely. If he thought he had the right to be angry because she was out with her friends the night Carly needed her, he had another thing coming.

She turned away, trying to find something to say. They had something between them, and she hated the thought of it slipping away so soon. "What's going on?" she finally asked, turning around.

But Scott was gone.

She collapsed onto the couch. Walking on eggshells had never been her style.

****

Marnie pulled into the parking lot at Davis Winery around two p.m. on Sunday. While the tasting room was open on Sundays, she normally didn't go in to work. Between her mother's illness, her research on Summer Jam, and dealing with Carly and Scott, she hadn't been putting in her normal number of hours at the office. She got a lot of work done at home, but there were some parts of this business that couldn't be done remotely.

At her desk, with multiple programs open on her laptop and a diet cola at her elbow, she was deep in thought about social media ads and wine club outings when her ex-husband pushed open her office door.

"Hey, stranger. What are you doing in here today?" Matt edged into the room and rested against the credenza opposite her desk.

She winced and glanced up. "If the stranger crack is any indication, you know what I'm doing here. I've been out so much lately, I have a lot of catching up to do."

Chuckling, he shook his head. "I should have known you'd be feeling guilty about taking the time to tend to your mother."

She shrugged. "It's not just Mom, though. I have a teenage girl, a pregnant teenage girl, staying at my house. She's on bed rest after nearly suffering a miscarriage, and I only left her today because her boyfriend decided to come spend the afternoon watching over her. It seemed foolish for both of us to do that. Plus, there are a few other crazy things going on in my life right now. I don't even know which way is up most of the time."

Matt took a seat facing her desk. His six-four frame barely fit and made the comfortable side chair seem like a booster seat. "What crazy things?"

She tried to shake him off. "Nothing for you to worry about. I'm catching up, since I can do a lot of the number-crunching at home. I'll have everything we need for our planning meeting on Wednesday."

He leaned back in the chair, crossing his arms over his chest. "I'll decide what I want to worry about, thanks all the same. What crazy things?"

She let out a deep breath, shaking her head. "Well, I guess you'll hear about it eventually." She lowered her gaze to her desk, frustrated her eyes were again filling with tears and not wanting him to see them. "With Mom's illness...I learned I was adopted and, if that isn't ridiculous enough, I was actually born in the back of a VW microbus up at the track during the Summer Jam rock concert."

Not willing to face his expression, she closed her eyes, then jumped when a hand rested on her shoulder. His touch brought down the gates which had been holding back the tears, and she started to sob. The next thing Marnie knew, she was standing, wrapped in his embrace, crying on his shoulder, or rather practically into his stomach, since he was so much taller, while he murmured nonsense words into her hair.

When the tears subsided and she had gotten her breathing under control, she pushed back and pulled herself out of his arms. She slipped some tissues from the box on her desk, walked over to the couch, and collapsed. She could wipe the tears from her face but couldn't escape the hopelessness that enveloped her whenever she tried to unravel her beginnings.

He followed her and sat at the other end, facing her, his large frame filling much of the remaining space.

"Well." He smiled crookedly at her. "I guess you needed that."

She hiccupped and smiled, in spite of herself. "Yeah, it's been building for a while." The headache that came with those tears, and the anticipated sinus infection, were nothing compared to the loss of her identity, the security she'd always had in knowing who she was.

He held out the front of his shirt, wet from her tears. "I'd say so."

"Sorry," she said with a smile.

"Why is this bothering you so much?"

"What?" She sat up so quickly she nearly fell off the couch. "What do you mean? Of course it bothers me to find out my parents are not really my parents."

"You sound like a petulant teenager." He shook his head. "Of course they're your parents. It doesn't matter where the egg and sperm came from, or whether you were born in a VW or the hospital. Those two wonderful people brought you up, cared for you, and made you into the woman you are today. The rest was just sex."

She had to chuckle at that. "I've never heard you talk about sex in such a dismissive tone before."

His smile returned. "True. But, really, Marn." He put his hand on her forearm. "Nothing has changed, not if you don't let it. Your parents are two eggheads, and you're their eggheaded daughter. Even if you don't have a drop of their blood, you couldn't be more like the two of them. You were always way too smart for the likes of me."

While believing that would be great, she had to face facts. "Forget it. Don't try to pull that dumb-old-farm-boy shtick on me. I know how smart you really are, even if you prefer to stand there scratching your head, kicking the dirt, and projecting the Hector partier image you've cultivated since high school."

"On behalf of the party people of Hector, I take offense at your tone. Even if I don't drink any more, there's no reason I shouldn't enjoy kicking dirt, driving my tractor, sailing, and partying with my friends."

She had to give him that. "Okay, but all of that's beside the point. While my parents are always going to be my parents, I'm not who I thought I was. I don't know who I am or who I would have been if I'd grown up with the woman who gave birth to me."

"Pfft."

Again she wanted to jump to her feet. "What do you mean by that? I'm entitled to feel confused by all of this. If I'm not the super-organized, over-achieving daughter of Roger and Susan Edwards, Cornell professors, the girl who has to be early to be on time, loves calendars and note-taking, and takes responsibility to a new level, who am I?"

He gazed deep into her eyes. "Who says you're *not* that girl?"

Tears slipped from the corners of Marnie's eyes, but she wiped them away. "Me and, well, maybe Scott."

"Scott?"

Sighing, she heard the trooper's cranky tone of voice in her head again. "Scott Randall, a state police investigator out of the Horseheads barracks."

He raised his right eyebrow. "And why does this state trooper get a vote? How well does he even know

185

you?"

While she'd remained friends and colleagues with Matt since their divorce, they rarely discussed their romantic partners. Their divorce had been on amicable terms, but it wasn't right to rub his face in the fact she might be dating someone else. And there'd never been anyone who'd mattered enough for her to bother him with any of it.

"We've only been seeing each other for a little while, only a couple of dates, really, but it's gotten kinda serious, kinda fast. I think part of what drew him to me was my responsible, organized, non-party-girl personality."

Matt chuckled.

She looked up and met his smile with a grimace. "On Friday night, Carly—said pregnant teenager— needed to get to the hospital. She called me for help, but I was out blowing off steam with some girlfriends. He came looking for me and found me drunk and dancing on a tabletop at the Owl's Nest. He's acting all pissy, and I think that's why."

His face sobered; his eyebrows drew together. "You were drunk and dancing on top of a table? At the Owl's Nest?"

She bowed her head. Definitely not one of her finer moments, but the rest of the night had been fun.

He whistled. "I wish I'd been there to see that."

She bristled. "I've been going through a lot and wanted to have a girls' night out with some friends, to relax and forget about everything. There's nothing wrong with that." Until the censure showed in Scott's gaze and the fear showed in Nick's.

He held up his hands, palms out. "Whoa. I didn't

say there was anything wrong with you wanting to relax and spend time with your girlfriends..."

"Damn right!"

He dropped his hands. Shaking his head, he continued, "In fact, I think it was long overdue. But...a drunken, tabletop dancing, wild night at the Owl's Nest is not you, regardless of who your parents are or were. Remember, I was married to you, so I know you pretty well, and I don't think that's who you really are."

"Hmmph." She crossed her arms over her chest. *What does he know?* "Maybe I'm not the same woman you married, Matt. Ever think of that?" *Maybe I never really was that woman.*

His deep, low chuckle was infuriating.

"What's so damn funny?" She jumped up off the couch, standing with her hands on her hips.

He sat forward, looking into her eyes. His gentle smile and soft eyes seem to whisper, *Tell me about it, I'll understand.* She wanted someone to fight with, but he just wasn't cooperating.

"Listen, you're upset, although I think you're making a big deal about something which really doesn't change anything in your life. But, even so, *you* like to blow off steam by taking a run, sinking into a bubble bath, going shopping, or eating chocolate cake with a tall diet cola. Your idea of a girls' night out is the Hangar Theater in Ithaca or a sip and paint at somebody's house. If you didn't work in the wine industry, I think you'd barely be a social drinker at all. Drunk and disorderly is not what makes you happy."

She stomped to her desk and dropped into her chair. While she knew it was childish, she didn't appreciate him acting like he had her completely figured out and there could never be anything new to the story.

"Maybe happy wasn't what I was going for."

He stood and walked to her desk, leaning over to meet her gaze. "Happy is what you should always go for, Marn. You deserve to be happy. If this guy is someone worth your time, he needs to be making you happy, not stressing you out."

She ducked her head, heat rising up the back of her neck.

"Marn?"

Slowly, she lifted her head and met his gaze. "What?" She'd never been able to lie, either to Matt or herself, when she was looking straight into his eyes.

"You're into this guy, aren't you?" He tilted his head, giving her a sideways glance. He knew her so well.

"I don't know," she bit out. He was pretty cute and one of the good guys, at least most of the time. "I mean, he's young. Way younger than we are. Although it doesn't seem to bother him."

He laughed. "What's 'way younger'?"

"He's like thirty-seven or thirty-eight."

"Does he know you're forty-five?" Matt's smile was more of a smirk. Like he knew she was reaching and she knew he knew.

She nodded.

"So I guess he's okay with it, right?"

"Okay, yeah." She glanced down at her hands. Her age might not be a problem, but not knowing who she was, what kind of woman she should be—that might be more of a challenge.

"What else?"

"He's divorced..." She couldn't disguise the tremor in her voice.

"So are you." He laughed again.

"I mean," she sputtered, "his ex was apparently sort of wacko, and she cheated on him. He's carrying some baggage about it."

"And you think that's why he freaked about you doing the wild-girl act at the Owl's Nest."

"I'm not his ex-wife. I never cheated on anybody in my life." Her ex-husband smiled at her. At least that had never been an issue between them. "Just because I wanted to dance and get a little drunk one night doesn't mean I'm going to break his heart. Even if I could."

He sat on the corner of her desk and took her right hand in both of his. "You could. If this guy isn't a complete idiot, he's already more than halfway in love with you."

She didn't say anything as she held his gaze. They had been good friends before they fell in love, and she remembered the falling, the love in those creamy brown eyes, the way his embrace made her feel safe and protected. If only they could have stayed in the warm and hazy new-love phase, the one before reality intruded and drove them apart.

Matt leaned forward and ran his thumb down her left cheek. A tear she couldn't hold back slipped from her right eye, and he caught it. "I'm sorry you're so twisted up about this adoption thing, although I think you're making too big a deal of it."

She started to speak, but he put his index finger against her lips. "No, let me finish. You're the same warm, wonderful, efficient, and organized woman you've always been. If your state trooper has a hold on your heart, you need to work through it with him. I haven't seen you really interested in someone since we divorced, and it's time. You deserve some happily ever after."

Swallowing a lump that had formed in her throat, she sighed. "I'm not sure that's in the cards right now. Everything is just too confusing."

"Just because things around you are changing, it doesn't mean that you are. You might have come into the world in a different way than you thought, but you're still a wonderful person and, if he deserves to spend time with you, he should understand that."

He leaned down, replaced his index finger with his lips, and gave her the barest of chaste kisses. With that he stood, walked to the door, and left.

Maybe she needed to give Scott a chance, talk to him about how she was feeling. She had to figure out what she wanted first, but he was worth fighting for.

****

Scott found himself knocking on Marnie's door again and wincing as he anticipated the tension and arguments that awaited him inside. Nick surprised him by answering the door.

"Hey, man, come on in." His ex-brother-in-law turned and walked toward the back, not waiting for him or closing the door.

He looked around for Marnie as he followed, but there was no sign of her. When he got to the door of the bedroom, only Nick and Carly were inside, both sitting on the bed.

"Hi, guys. Where's Marnie?"

Nick linked his fingers with Carly's. "She asked how long I planned to stay, because she had some work to catch up on. I told her I'd be here all day, so she went to her office."

His feelings were so twisted up inside, he didn't know if she was being responsible or not. It must have shown on his face.

"Cut her some slack, dude," said Nick, shaking his head. "There's no reason for her to be here while I am."

Carly motioned for him to come in and sit in the chair. "Yeah, she's got so many things worrying her right now, she needed to catch up on work before she made herself crazy about it."

Scott sat, not willing to let a couple of messed-up teenagers tell him how to feel. "I know she's busy, but…"

Nick sighed, but Carly stopped him from speaking with a hand on his arm. "What do you think she's been doing? Just because she took one night out to relax, it doesn't make her irresponsible."

Nick was nodding. "And it doesn't make her my sister, either."

When had the kid stopped being angry with Marnie for being out at a bar when Carly needed her? "I know she's not Darlene."

The boy glanced at him out of the corner of his eye. "Are you sure?"

Carly turned to face him, her expression much older than her years. "Marnie has worked at the Youth Center for years, even though she has an important job, runs back and forth to Ithaca at least twice a week to take care of her parents, and has friends and other stuff to do around town. She has been good to me and helps out with…" She lowered her head, paused for a moment, and then glanced back up to meet his gaze. "She knows my father is out of work a lot, and we don't have much money. She makes sure we have food to eat, and the girls and I have warm clothes and boots in the winter. Before Nick started driving me home, she would often make sure I had a ride home from work, even if she had to make up some excuse to be around the restaurant when my shift was over."

Nick handed her a tissue, but she pushed it away.

"I know, but…"

She glared at him. "I'm not finished. She found out her mom has cancer, which is bad enough, but she has something else going on, too. I don't know exactly what it is, but she's been spending a lot of time researching online and making phone calls about something that upsets her. She deserved a night off, a chance to hang with her friends, and if I'm not mad at her for being busy when I called her, what gives you the right to be mad?"

At first, he thought it was a rhetorical question, so he didn't answer. But she continued to glare at him, almost as if she was tapping a toe that didn't even reach the ground.

"I'm not mad." He held his hands up in front of him, palms facing Carly. "I agree she does a lot for other people and has been good to you, and helpful to me, even. But, see…"

Nick leaned back against the headboard and crossed his arms over his chest. "You're mad, all right. You're pissed because you're falling for her and expected her to be little miss perfect, but you've found out she's human, like the rest of us. So she went a little crazy one night. So what?"

How did this kid get to be so smart?

Maybe I have been a little quick to judge her. Still... "Whatever my feelings are for her, or whatever our relationship might be, it's none of your business, either of you."

"Cut her some slack," said Carly. "It's not fair for you to be mad at Marnie for taking a night off. If I'm not angry with her, you sure don't have a right to be."

He held up his hands in surrender. "Okay, Okay. I'll give it some thought, and then I'll talk to her about it..."

The teens looked at each other, smiling. The young mother-to-be rested her head on Nick's shoulder. "Okay."

Scott sighed. "Anyway, I stopped in because I wanted to show you the sketches our guy came up with, both of the woman who approached you at school and the guy in the car. Thanks again for coming in to meet with the sketch artist. I think he came up with a pretty good sketch." He pulled out the folded sheets of paper and handed them to Carly.

The teen's expression changed to something more little-girl than lioness. "That's them."

She started to hand the sketches back to him, but Nick grabbed them. "I've seen her before."

"Okay." He got out his notepad and pen. *Hopefully, this wacko hasn't also been following Nick.* "Do you remember where you saw her? Or when?"

He tilted his head back against the wall, closing his eyes for a minute before opening them again and staring at the sketch. "It has something to do with track."

"When you were on the track team?" Could the woman be scouting pregnant teens at high school sporting events?

"Right." Nick closed his eyes again.

"Did she come to the meets? Like somebody's mother would? Or someone from the school?"

"No," Nick hedged. "I don't think so. That doesn't feel right. I don't think I ever saw her at a track meet."

"She couldn't work at the school or I would have recognized her."

Scott leaned back in his chair. "Right." When Nick made to pass the sketches back, he pushed them into the kid's hand. "Keep 'em. Look at hers every day and try to remember where you saw her or anything that will help us figure out who she is. Okay?"

"Okay, I'll keep trying," he said as he stuck them in his jeans pocket.

"Keep trying to do what?"

All three of them jumped when Marnie walked into Carly's room. He'd been so engrossed in discussing the sketches, he hadn't even heard her come home. He jumped up from his chair and stood awkwardly, offering her his chair.

"Uh," he mumbled, "Nick says he's seen the woman who tried to buy the baby, so he's going to keep trying to figure out where or when he saw her. I brought over the sketches for Carly." His heartbeat sped up when he saw her, but was that a good thing or a bad one? Until he figured it out, he needed some time and space. "Uh, I've got to run. Nice to see you all."

He smiled at Marnie, waved to Nick and Carly,

and practically ran from the house. His emotions were no less jumbled at the sight of her. He needed to get out of there before he said or did something to make matters worse between them.

****

"How the hell do I know what she's told the trooper?" He'd taken to pacing during their phone calls, so he wandered the small kitchen and back to the living room, skating his way over the old matted carpet.

He was pissed, and tired of her nagging him for answers he couldn't know.

"We gotta get rid of her."

Again, she was yelling. He held the phone out from his ear. "I know…no girl, no witness…what she told him won't matter if she's dead." He clicked off his phone and threw it on the couch.

Why does she always blame me when things go wrong? This whole damned thing was her fault to begin with.

He pulled out the laptop and started drawing up some plans. Once he had a basic idea of what to do, he picked up his cell phone again.

"Jimmy?"

Chapter Ten

After Scott dashed from the house, Nick decided to head home and finish his homework, so Marnie went into the kitchen. Shaking her head, she fixed dinner. She couldn't worry about Scott. She had too many other things to think about right now.

Sighing, she carried a tray with two servings, plus glasses of water, into Carly's room.

"How are you feeling tonight?" she asked, before blowing on her portion of chicken stir-fry and taking a bite.

"Not bad," the teen replied through a mouthful of food. "A little tired, I guess."

"I know it must seem like you're not doing anything, so you shouldn't need to rest, but your body is busy, both recovering from your fall and growing a human, so take it easy, okay?"

The girl actually chuckled and shoveled another forkful of chicken into her mouth. "This is good."

"Thanks. It's one of my standard dinners around here. A chance to get a bunch of veggies while still tasting great."

The teen paused. "When you were up at the Winery, did you..." Her voice softened as it trailed off.

"I stopped in at your house and dropped off some groceries on my way to work. Your father was out, but your sisters seemed to be doing well. Did you talk to them?"

Carly shook her head and blushed. "Not since last night. Nick said he checked on them this morning. And then Scott came and it got busy."

Marnie picked at her food. "Scott wanted to show you and Nick the sketches, huh?"

"Yup."

When she looked up, she found her guest staring at her and smiling.

"What?"

Carly chuckled. "I sort of yelled at him."

"Nick?"

Shaking her head, the teen started to examine her cuticles. "No, Scott."

"Why?" Her throat suddenly dry, she took a sip of her water. Scott wouldn't endanger the girl, but he must have ticked her off about something.

The girl put her plate on her lap. "Basically, I told him to stop being a dick."

"What?" Marnie almost shouted, but the teen only laughed.

"Well, not in those words, but I told him to cut you some slack. He's acting sort of pissy about you being out Friday night. I told him he had no right to be mad at you about that if I wasn't."

"Even I wish I'd been there for you that night." She couldn't hide the catch in her voice. Even thinking about it made her pulse race again.

"Don't make me mad." Carly's voice had a hard edge. "I'll tell you to stop being a jerk to yourself."

"It's not that simple, sweetie. Whatever is going on with Scott, I don't know. But I feel terrible that I wasn't there for you."

The "mom" look in the girl's eyes could have come from an experienced mother of three rather than a pregnant teen. "Let it go."

Marnie put her plate on the nightstand and sat on the edge of the bed, facing the teen. "I told you when my mom got sick, right?"

The girl jerked her head back. "Yeah. What does that have to do with this?"

She closed her eyes, took a deep breath, and then met Carly's gaze straight on. "I didn't tell you my mother admitted to me I was born in the back of a Volkswagen bus at the Summer Jam rock concert in Watkins Glen, and then my parents adopted me. But I didn't even know I was adopted, not until she told me that day."

Carly was quiet, staring at her for a few moments before placing her hand over Marnie's. "It's got to suck a little for them to have kept it from you for your whole life."

"Yeah, it sucks a little." If by "a little" she meant shaking her entire world from the foundation up.

"But you like your parents, right?"

"Definitely." She sighed. "They're great, and I've had a wonderful life. I'm very lucky. In fact, I can't imagine growing up with any other parents. But I wish they'd told me a long time ago."

"And does that have something to do with all the hushed phone calls and computer searching you were doing yesterday?"

She smiled. "Can't get anything past you, can I?"

"It was weird for you to keep leaving the room whenever your phone rang, and even though you thought I was asleep, I could hear you typing away on your laptop."

"I'm sorry if it kept you awake."

The girl was silent for a while, and Marnie started to get concerned, especially when tears filled Carly's eyes.

"Are you mad I'm thinking of giving this baby up for adoption?"

Marnie pulled her into a hug. "Of course not. I want you to do what's best for you and Nick and your baby." She pulled back to meet a watery gaze. "I told you, I love my parents, and they have given me a good life."

She released the hug but laid a hand on Carly's. "I know nothing about my birth parents. I may be able to track down my birth mother, but I may not. But the point is I can't know what kind of life she would have given me. Certainly the start of it wouldn't have been great, if she was so messed up she gave birth and walked away." Marnie closed her eyes for a moment, swallowing hard. "I know I have two wonderful parents who couldn't have loved me more."

She gazed into the girl's eyes. "Ultimately, you have to do what is best for you, what you think is best for your baby, whether it's raising the baby yourself or giving it up for adoption. Neither option would be perfect, but both would work out. I know you, sweetie. You're strong enough to handle whichever choice you make."

Carly's eyes filled with more tears. "And you don't think my baby will hate me if I give it away?"

She paused for a moment, trying to bring her thoughts into focus. "I'll be honest with you. I don't think your baby will hate you, although there will probably be moments, over time, when that's true. Honestly, I don't hate my birth mother for giving me away. I feel compelled to find her and learn her story, to ask her why, but I'd still know that growing up with Roger and Susan Edwards was the best of all choices for me."

Quiet now, the teen dropped her head, looking sad but resigned.

Marnie's heart broke a little.

Finally, the expectant mother met her gaze, nodding. "Nick always wants to talk about it, but I keep telling him I'm not ready, 'cause I know it's going to be hard to decide what to do."

"It's a difficult decision, and you should take your time making it." This was too much for a couple of kids.

"I'm afraid," the teen said, her voice soft and young.

"Of course you are." Anxiety skittered over Marnie's skin, too. She wanted to help the teen, but it was not her place. "This is a scary decision to make, no matter how old you are."

Carly wiped away a few tears. "I don't want to mess this up. I mean, I have my sisters to worry about, and my dad, never mind Nick and the baby. I don't know what to do."

Again Marnie moved closer, putting an arm over the teen's shoulder. "You have a lot of responsibility for a seventeen-year-old. I can see why you would worry about taking on more. How old are the girls now?"

Carly smiled. "Ashley is almost thirteen, and

Deena is eleven."

"So they're getting old enough to be a lot of help around the house, aren't they?"

Nodding, the young mother-to-be sat forward, pulling her legs under her. "They help out a lot. Ashley is a pretty good cook, and Deena helps with the laundry and cleaning the house. They're good kids." Pride and love toward her sisters shone on her face.

"They sure are." Carly had done a good job raising them. "And I'm glad they're helping with chores around the house."

Carly's expression sobered. "I don't want to make things harder on them. It's not their fault I got pregnant."

"I know. And, you will be graduating next year and have to think about what you want to do after high school. You're a smart young woman. You could go to any number of different colleges. It would be hard with a baby, but people do it all the time."

"Oh, man, I can't even think so far ahead." The girl shook her head. "I can't afford college, even without a baby, and I need to be here—I need to work and help support my family."

"There are lots of great schools close enough for you to commute if you want to, and you would certainly get scholarship money, but you're right, it wouldn't be easy." She'd thought college was hard when she went to Cornell, but she could see how lucky and carefree she'd really been.

"I don't want you to think your choices going forward are limited if you have a baby in your life, though." She met her gaze. "Especially if Nick helps to raise this baby."

Carly moaned, slid down, and pulled the covers over her head. "You sound just like Nick!"

Marnie chuckled but slid down and pulled the covers over her head, too. Then her gaze met Carly's under the sheet. "What does that mean?"

"I don't know if I want to marry Nick." The teen sighed. "Getting pregnant is a lame reason to get married."

This time, she really laughed. "First, I'm not saying you have to marry Nick for him to be in his child's life. And, for the record, I bet the second most common reason people get married is because they got pregnant."

"Okay." Carly smiled. "I'll give you that. But Nick really wants to get married. I don't know what he thinks it's going to look like. Does he think he'll move into my house? The girls and I share a bed, so that's not happening. And I'm not living with his crazy-ass family."

Again Marnie laughed. A good decision, if any of what Scott had said about his ex-wife were true.

"I know. We'll get some cozy house of our own and live happily ever after. Oh, yeah, with what money?"

Marnie sighed through the overt sarcasm, silent as her mind raced through options available to teenaged parents. "We can find a way to make it work, if it's what you decide you want to do. But first, you have to think about you and your baby, and what makes the most sense to you. What feels right?"

The teen pulled the covers back, and they both sat up.

"I figured you'd have a spreadsheet of reasons for me to decide one way or the other. I thought you were the numbers lady and made decisions based on facts." Carly looked her in the eye. "Instead, you're asking me what *feels* right?"

She bit her lip. "You're right. I used to think everything could be solved with a list of pros and cons. This is too big for that." Nothing like some life-changing news to alter her long-held belief in spreadsheets. "My take on parenthood is there's no way to even list all the pros and cons until you've been there. Even if you and Nick were deeply in love, married, and thirty years old, whether or not to have children is the kind of decision you can research, but you have to make it based on what you feel." She put her hand over her heart. "What your heart is telling you to do."

The mother-to-be sat still, her face pale, her mouth set in a hard line. "What my heart says has to include what is best for my sisters, too. I can't go off to college and leave them to fend for themselves. My father is never going to be the kind of father you can depend on." She stared off across the room, focusing on nothing. "I used to think if we were good enough, if the house was clean enough, if we did all our chores, he'd want to stop drinking and be a father to us. That if we tried hard enough, he'd want to try hard too." Her gaze hardened, and she turned back to face her. "But I wasn't even as old as Ashley when I realized it had nothing to do with us. All he thinks about is himself, and he doesn't care if he lives or dies, despite what he says. It's up to me to make sure the girls and I are okay, that we have food and a roof over our heads.

He's along for the ride and only until he checks out for good."

Marnie knew Frank was an alcoholic, but she hadn't fully grasped the reality of what it meant for his daughters on a day-to-day basis. Over the years since their mother died, she had collected food, clothes, and money to slip to the girls, one way or another, but she had never heard Carly talk this honestly about her home life.

She smiled at the teen, swelling with pride. This kid would conquer anything.

"What?" The teen seemed confused.

"You're so much more mature than I was at seventeen. You never cease to amaze me, sweetie."

Carly ducked her head, a flush rising in her cheeks.

Marnie reached out a hand. "I mean it. You don't need me to give you spreadsheets and lists of pros and cons. You have the reality of your situation down as well as anyone could. What you need to think about is the baby and how you feel about it. Will you be able to live with the idea of someone else watching your baby grow up, teaching him or her to walk and talk? How will you feel about making the decision to let some unknown person experience all of that? Someone who would have more financial means, better jobs, a better house, or whatever you envision the adoptive parents will have. You already know it will be hard to raise a baby at eighteen, whether or not you and Nick ever get married. You know how hard life can be. You have to decide if you're willing to give up all the good things that would come with creating a new family."

"And you won't be mad at me if I decide to give

the baby up for adoption?"

She paused; the lump in her throat almost making her unable to speak. "No, sweetie, I won't be mad at you no matter what you decide."

The teen's eyes swam with tears again, and she pulled her into a hug. "You don't have to decide it right now. You need to get some rest, so why don't I tuck you in and get out of your hair so you can fall asleep."

"Okay." The teen sank down in the covers and closed her eyes, looking like the little girl she probably never got a chance to be.

****

Carly stayed at Marnie's through the end of the week. When she'd suffered no more spotting or cramps for several days, the doctor said she didn't need to be on bed rest anymore. She could go back to school, but she still needed to take it easy.

Marnie made a point of driving out to the girl's house every evening after work, dropping off groceries, checking on all three girls, and sneaking some cash into Carly's wallet. She insisted the girl call her every night so she could verify the bleeding hadn't started again and that no one appeared to be following her.

The first night, when they spoke on the phone, Carly happened to mention that her father had just gotten home.

"Did he ask how you're doing or about the hospital trip or anything? I could talk to him, if you want me to."

The teen sighed. "No, that's okay. He asked how I was feeling, but that's about all. He seemed glad I'm back to cook and take care of the girls."

Carly deserved more from her parent but didn't seem as frustrated by his lack of concern as Marnie felt. She must be used to it.

Since the teen was back in school but not allowed back to work yet, Nick was on hand every day to drive her home and keep a watch out for anyone who might be watching or stalking her. He was a good kid and clearly devoted to Carly and their baby.

Marnie knew Scott was working on tracking down the suspects and finding the connections to the baby-selling ring which had existed in the area for years, but only because Nick told her about it. Scott hadn't been by since Carly moved out, and he wasn't calling her anymore, either.

Whatever had cooled his feelings toward her, it would be nice if he acted as if they were still on the same side when it came to the kids. He cared about Nick, and presumably worried about Carly and her sisters, but he didn't even respect her enough to let her know the status of the investigation.

He had been becoming important to her—and then it ended abruptly. There was a hollow space in Marnie's core that had been filled with the promise of possibility. She'd just have to get used to the emptiness again.

On Friday night, after her nightly stop at the Johnsons' house, she went back to the office to face down a pile of work. Her email and paper inboxes were full and, given that she wasn't planning to drive to Ithaca until Saturday afternoon to see her parents, she had the entire night free to get caught up.

Besides, if she kept busy, she might almost forget

that she had no place else to be on a Friday night and no hot trooper waiting for her to finish her work.

She'd been slogging away at her inbox for half an hour when Matt showed up at her door.

"Burning the midnight oil?" He leaned against the door jamb.

"What?" Glancing up at her ex-husband, she stopped typing. "Oh, yeah. I had some free time and thought I'd get ahead before the start of next week."

Sauntering into the room, he smiled and winked. "You have free time on a Friday night? What's the world coming to?"

"Ha, ha. You're very funny." Her fingers starting racing over the keyboard. "Now, leave me alone."

He apparently wasn't at all discouraged but draped himself over one of her guest chairs, resting his feet on the edge of her desk.

Without looking up, she reached out and pushed his feet off. "Scram, Davis. I have work to do." Knowing her frustration wasn't his fault didn't stop her from letting it build.

He chuckled, a low, deep rumble bubbling out of his chest. "Knock it off, Marn. You don't have so much work to do. This is the off-season, remember? You're trying to make yourself look busy to hide the fact you don't have a date on Friday night."

He still knew how to push her buttons. She slammed her laptop closed. "I'll have you know I'm trying to work out the schedules for the case club events this year, pulling together our social media marketing for the next two quarters, and updating our website. The off-season is when I have time to do all of this."

He chuckled again, and it made her blood boil.

"You arrogant a…"

"Whoa!" He held up his left hand. "Don't start calling me names again or I'll think we're still married."

"I only ever called you names at work, and you know it." She crossed her arms over her chest.

He leaned forward, his forearms resting on his thighs, bringing his face closer to the same level as hers. "All I'm saying is, you don't have to work late tonight. Why don't you call your state trooper guy and go make his dreams come true?"

She exhaled and unfolded her arms, the fight draining out of her. "He's not dreaming about me, that's why. We haven't spoken in a week, not since he stormed out of my house. And really, we haven't had much to say to each other since he pulled me out of the Owl's Nest, the night Carly ended up in the hospital." As if that night hadn't been bad enough.

"What did you do?" He usually was on her side, but even her ex-husband sounded like it was her fault.

"I didn't do anything. He seems to be angry with me for enjoying a girls' night with my friends. I just wanted to blow off some steam, but Carly needed me and I didn't have my phone with me."

"This guy sounds like a jerk to me. You need to forget about him."

She sighed. If only it were that easy.

He sat for a moment, silent. Then he pulled himself up and reached across the desk for her hand. "Come on, then. Let's go have some fun."

She smirked, looking up into his face. "What are you talking about?"

"Let's go do something fun. Working into the wee hours is a dull way to take your mind off everything going on with you. You need to have some fun."

She opened her bottom desk drawer and pulled out a bottle of exquisite Cabernet Sauvignon, one of their medal-winning vintages. After she set it on her desk, she pulled out a glass, nodding to Matt. "I won't take out a glass for you, but you don't mind if I drink, do you?"

"Why do you have a bottle in your desk?"

Waving away his concern, she chuckled. "I was taking some pictures to post on social media. But as long as I have it here, why let it go to waste?"

He shook his head. "Let's go do something else. We can take a late-night walk on the beach, head over to Ithaca for dinner and a movie, even go bowling in Watkins Glen, if you want."

She made quick work of the cork, poured herself a glass of wine, and took a long sip. A little alcohol might help ease the ache in her chest. It would surely help fade the mental picture of Scott naked in her bed. "Those are the fantastic options for non-alcoholic distraction on a Friday night? No wonder so many people go out drinking."

His brow furrowed. "I usually make plans in advance, get together with friends, go listen to a band playing, that sort of thing."

Toasting him with her wine glass, she said, "And it used to involve getting drunk." *Quite a tasty vintage.* While she didn't usually drink much at work, or anywhere else for that matter, no one could argue that she'd been through a lot lately. Maybe she'd always been a drinker; maybe it was in her genes and she'd never given it a fair chance.

He swallowed, sitting back in his chair. The smile was gone from his eyes. "Yes, it always involved getting drunk, as you well know. But it doesn't anymore."

She stood, grabbed her wine glass and the bottle, and walked out into the tasting room. The strains of some soft country song was still playing on the sound system. She emptied her glass and poured herself more, dancing around the big empty space, mostly in time with the music.

She worked in a winery. Why hadn't she tried drinking away her problems long before this? It was good at numbing the pain and stopping thoughts from racing around in her head.

He followed her. "What did you eat for dinner?"

"No dinner," she said softly, as she did a lopsided pirouette.

He put his hand out and grasped her arm as she spun around. "Let's go into town then, get some dinner. I haven't eaten all day and could use some food that doesn't come out of a microwave."

Taking a big gulp of wine, she swayed back and forth. "Still a terrible cook, are you?" He'd never cooked a thing while they were married, not that she really minded. He was good at so many other things...

He nodded. "Some things never change." He pried the nearly empty bottle from her hands and put it on the bar.

She spun out of his grasp, dancing her way across the room into the sunroom addition. "And some things change entirely." She took another gulp of wine. "Who knew deep inside I was a wild child, daughter of an original hippie? I should burn my bra, stop shaving my legs, and buy bell-bottom jeans and a tie-dyed shirt. Find my roots."

Her parents never got drunk and caused a scene, but they weren't her parents after all. Or at least, she didn't share any of their DNA. This was her chance to try a little heavy drinking on for size and see if it was something she'd inherited.

Swaying to the music, she could feel the four or five glasses of wine she'd slurped down in rapid succession. Must be why Matt looked a little fuzzy when he appeared at her side again. He must want to dance.

She turned into his arms, pulling herself into his embrace, and started to dance. Even with more than a foot difference in their heights they'd always been good at dancing together. For that matter, they'd always fit together in other ways as well. She looped her arms around his neck, holding her wine glass in her fingers, laying her head against his chest. His heartbeat was strong and fast, his embrace warm and steady. Why did they divorce? What was it that drove them apart? For the life of her, she couldn't quite remember at the moment.

They danced to whatever slow song came on next, and Marnie's bones were nearly melting inside her. She was fluid and relaxed and having such a good time. If only there were no buzzing in her ears.

He didn't say a word but held her a little stiffly, more awkward than usual. She wished he'd relax and enjoy their dance as much as she enjoyed it.

She hummed along with the song, swaying in his arms, her head against his chest. He didn't sing, even though she knew he knew the words and had such a great singing voice. She loved the way he used to sing to her all the time. Now she had no one to sing to her.

"Matt…" She pulled herself up on her tiptoes, leaning fully against him, getting closer to his ear.

His arms grew more rigid and tense as she leaned her head closer to his. "What?" he nearly barked into her ears.

"Mmm…" Why was he so uptight? How could she get him to relax? "Oh, Matt…"

She pulled his head down, as she pushed up, as if to whisper in his ear. He was so handsome. Why did she ever let him go? Now she was alone, always alone.

She laid her lips on his and let herself fall into a deep kiss, one that brought back so many good memories. Memories that tried to crowd out the ones she couldn't forget—the ones of Scott's arms, Scott's lips, the heat of Scott's embrace.

"Shit!" he yelled and pushed her away in one movement.

She landed on her butt, wincing from both the sting of rejection and the slap of the wood floor. "Jesus, Matt, you didn't have to get…"

"Marnie, look at me." He wasn't yelling quite as loudly, but he still sounded pissed off.

A big red stain started at his shoulder and slid down his shirt.

"Oh, yeah. My wine. Sorry." *Whoops.* He wasn't laughing. He wasn't even smiling anymore.

He turned and stomped away, digging around behind the bar for a towel. He began wiping his shirt, then unbuttoned his shirt and reached beneath it with the towel.

Still on the floor, she watched and wished he'd take his shirt off altogether. He always had a great chest, and his life as a full-time farmer surely had only improved on that. When he did remove his shirt, she enjoyed the view. Farming definitely agreed with him, although he was no cop. State Troopers really had to be built.

"Nice."

His head swiveled quickly. His gaze held storm clouds and misplaced anger, and his lips were drawn into a thin, tight line. "What the hell is wrong with you?"

She tilted her head to one side. He wasn't Scott, but she could still enjoy the view.

He pulled his soaked shirt off the bar, grabbed the towel, and stormed past her, headed to his office. "Idiot!"

He sure seemed mad. What did he have to be mad about? Nobody dumped *him* just for wanting to blow off some steam.

While he had an office in the back of the winery, he wasn't in there often. She started to climb to her feet, although she was a little shaky after her fall, but she stopped trying when Matt came marching back toward her, buttoning up the wine-stained shirt.

"Party pooper," she called to him.

Stopping in front of her, he stared down. Her neck hurt from tilting back so far.

"I thought I had a clean shirt in there, but I can't find any. I guess I'll have to drive you home like this." He sounded angrier than she'd heard him in a long time.

She smiled and held up her arms. "Okay by me!"

He pulled her arm to help her up, a little rougher than was strictly necessary. "Watch it," she winced.

Once she stood, he grabbed both her arms and held her in front of him, bending down so he stared her directly in the eyes. "You're lucky I don't put you over my shoulder like a sack of potatoes and dump you in the trunk of the car, you little fool."

She wrenched herself out of his grasp, although it made her wobble a bit, and smoothed out her sleeves. "What are you so mad about? It's just a little wine. If it doesn't wash out, the shirt is no great loss anyway." She leaned against him, trying to calm him down, reaching her arms up around his shoulders again.

He stepped away from her as she started to lean, so she nearly fell to the floor again. "What...?"

Matt stood a good five paces away from her. The pain and disappointment in his gaze nearly sobered her up.

"I'm not interested in being your drunken plaything. You may think there's a wild child inside you because your birth mother was some type of hippy. But, I'm telling you, you need to stop this, right now."

When she took a few steps toward him, he backed away again. "Stop what?" She gazed up at him. *Was he really mad?* She reached out. "Come on. You don't really want me to stop, do you?" Just because Scott didn't want her any more, it didn't mean other men wouldn't. She was still desirable, even if she wasn't the woman she'd always thought she was. She started to unbutton his shirt.

"Dammit," he bit out as he sidestepped her reach. He started muttering as he went to the bar and poured a large glass of water, then walked back over to where she was and handed her the glass.

"What?"

He shook his head. "Drink it, you idiot. You're wasted."

"I don't need water." Setting down the glass of water, she walked back toward him, doing her best imitation of alluring, although realizing even through her drunken haze she'd never been any good at sultry. "I just want to have some fun." She reached for his shirt again.

He erupted like a firecracker, pushing her hands away. "You stupid fool. Stop playing games with me! Just because your state trooper dumped you and you're having a bit of an identity crisis, don't think you can down a bottle of wine and jump my bones for old times' sake."

His face was beet red, but he said nothing more, apparently waiting for her to respond. Almost as if rooted to the spot, she couldn't move, uncertain of how to respond.

He turned back, looking down into her eyes. His color had started to fade, but pain filled his gaze. "I thought we were friends." When she didn't respond, he walked away.

Suddenly, through her haze, she saw herself as he must be seeing her. Even her wine-soaked brain realized she was pathetic. So overwhelmed with sadness at what could have been with Scott, she was hurting Matt by taunting them both with what used to be. "Oh, my God." She collapsed to the floor again, this time in tears. None of this was his fault, but she had risked their friendship and working relationship just because she'd lost track of who she really was and because she'd gotten dumped. "I'm so sorry." She repeated it over, and over, rocking on the floor, her hands over her face.

Unsure of how long she'd sat there, humiliated, crying and rocking, she hid her face in her hands. She couldn't bear facing him, afraid to see disgust or disdain staring back at her. Once she'd cried herself out, she pulled herself to her feet. Too drunk to drive herself home, she decided she might as well sleep on her office couch.

She came up short in the doorway. He stood at the wall of windows behind her desk, facing out over the darkened farm. He clearly heard her enter the office, as his back stiffened.

"Matt…" She didn't know what to say. How could she have humiliated herself and insulted her boss and lifelong friend?

As he slowly turned, his arms crossed over his chest, her heart sank further. His eyes were suspiciously red. Glaring at her, he didn't say a thing.

"I'm so sorry." She couldn't figure out what to do with her hands, so she tried crossing her arms like his but knew that looked too argumentative. Shoving her hands into her pockets seemed too casual for the pain she'd caused. Finally, she let her arms hang at her sides. "I can't believe I was so selfish, and I'm so sorry for treating you that way." She bowed her head, took a deep breath, and then raised her head to meet his gaze. "Please forgive me. I won't say it was the wine, as the stupidity was all my own. I've let this whole adoption thing make me crazy, but I'm done with the self-pity. I'm so, so sorry."

They'd been lucky to come through the divorce without ruining their friendship or business relationship, and she prayed she hadn't destroyed it all tonight. It wouldn't matter who her parents were. She'd be miserable if she drove all her friends away.

He stood staring into her eyes but not saying a thing. She wasn't sure he'd speak to her again. As much as she wanted him to talk, yell, or even cuss her out, she also understood she'd abused their friendship in the worst way. They'd been very careful, ever since the divorce, to behave more like brother and sister, old friends, or even distant cousins, but never bring a male-female attraction into their working relationship. They'd never had any problems in bed; the sex had always been good between them. But when the rest of the marriage fell apart, they put it aside to come up with the friendship and business partnership which benefited them both. She was a heel for flirting with him, throwing those old feelings, and her old moves, at him as if he had no feelings of his own, as if he didn't matter. She couldn't believe she'd been so stupid and heartless.

"Fine." He finally dropped his hands to his sides and started toward the door. "Let's never talk about this again." He stopped and turned to stare her in the face. "But let me be perfectly clear."

His gaze practically burned holes into her eyes.

"If you ever do anything like this again, we're through. Our friendship will be over, all connections will be cut, and you won't work here anymore. Do you understand?" He didn't move.

She swallowed the lump in her throat. All this because she was sad, confused, and alone. "Yes, I understand. It won't happen again." Even if she was alone the rest of her life, she'd never again risk losing Matt's friendship.

He turned and left, calling out over his shoulder, "Well, come on. I need to drive you home."

****

Thelma wasn't at her desk when Scott walked into the Stevens County Sheriff's Office, so he left his wrapped gift tin of exotic teas on her desk.

"Trying to bribe her away again, Randall? I told you it won't work," Jack called out from his desk chair.

He laughed out loud and walked into the sheriff's office. "I'll never give up, but in the meantime, it can't hurt to have her on my side." Smiling, he took a seat across from the sheriff.

"She'll let you think she's on your side, but don't fool yourself." Jack was trying to look stern, but the twinkle in his eyes gave him away.

Scott sat back in his chair and steepled his hands under his chin. "Thanks for making the time to talk to me. I have some questions about this investigation, and I thought you and I might make some headway together."

"A joint investigation makes sense. We can always call in other local law enforcement, as needed. It sounds like this baby-trafficking ring has been operating for a long time in this area, so let's shut it down once and for all."

He pulled out his notepad while Jack typed away on his computer. "When are you going to get into the twenty-first century, dude," joked his friend. "I can't believe you keep your notes with paper and pen anymore. How old *are* you anyway?"

"Old enough to understand that computers get hacked, dude, and files get corrupted." He put the emphasis on the "dude" moniker, even though he was only a few years older than Jack. "I have my files saved online, which you know, since I shared them with you, but you know as well as I do that a notepad is less intimidating when I'm dealing with witnesses, so my most current notes are in here."

The sheriff sat back, his gaze meeting Scott's.

"Okay. I interviewed the neighbors of Regina Simmons. Luckily, they still live out there by the old Simmons place. I showed the sketches around and each one remembered this woman coming around, talking to Regina at the time of her first pregnancy and of the second. One of the neighbors had an aunt visiting, who used to live there but moved to a retirement home in Elmira." He glanced at his notes. "Helen Nilson. I went to Elmira to talk to her, and even though she's ninety-two and frail as a baby bird, she still has all her faculties."

He glanced up at Jack, who leaned back, balancing on the back chair legs, watching him.

Scott continued, "She lived near the Sugar Hill State Forest her whole life, although in a couple of different spots." He looked down at his notes again. "When she was young, she lived off of Sugar Hill Road. After she got married, they moved to another house, uh…" He flipped some pages. "On Webb Road. And, after her husband died, she moved to Templar Road. She recognized the woman, too. She said everyone up on Sugar Hill knew this woman would take an unwanted baby off your hands and slide you a little cash for it, if you found yourself in dire straits. When I asked her about dates, she said the woman 'placed' a baby in the early to mid-seventies and has been going strong ever since."

Jack shot forward in his chair, the legs crashing to the ground. "Forty years? This has been going on for *forty years*?"

He shrugged. "Looks that way." As hard as it was to believe, and as sick as it made him to think about it, it appeared someone had been terrorizing pregnant teens in the area for several decades.

His friend dropped his head into his hands and waited a beat before looking up, his lips tight and forehead furrowed. "People up there tend to keep to themselves. I've worked side by side with Chris Hoy and several Schuyler County sheriff's investigators in the past, and they've always said they have trouble following a case once the trail leads out there, but this is incredible. How can we all have missed this for so long?"

"There seem to be leads to this investigation in several jurisdictions, which always complicates the situation." Never mind how difficult it was getting answers from some of the people he'd questioned. "Regina Simmons and her neighbor may have lived in Schuyler, but these people approached and followed Carly in Stevens County. It could be the ring originates in Chemung, Steuben, or even Tompkins County. If each jurisdiction only had a part of the story, I can see how the perps could avoid notice."

Jack shook his head. "Now we have facts to work with, we need to shut it down. What's your plan?"

Again he consulted his notes. "I sent investigators

up to Sugar Hill to cover as much of the area as possible, passing around the sketches and trying to come up with some names, either for the sketches or of more girls who may have sold their babies. Hopefully, as state troopers, they'll have better luck than the sheriff's office has had in the past, although that's a long shot." *Why did the people up in the hills distrust cops so much?* "I'm heading over to Watkins to talk to Sheriff Hoy, since I have an investigation going on in his county. I'm also running the sketches through the upgraded facial recognition software. It may take a little while, as this investigation isn't Albany's highest priority, but chances are good this woman has a driver's license, state ID, passport, or something similar, so hopefully we'll get a hit. I have less information for the search on the guy in the car, but we'll see what comes up."

Jack's fingers flew over the keyboard again. "What can I do? I'm thinking I could knock on some doors in the neighborhoods where Carly works and lives, show the sketches, try to jog some memories. It's heading into the dinner hour, so more people are likely to be home."

Scott leaned forward in his chair, meeting his friend's gaze. "Could you get your secret weapon on this tomorrow?"

Jack gave him a quizzical expression for a moment, then started laughing. "What do you want Thelma to do?"

The amazing Thelma had her finger on the pulse of the entire Southern Tier. "I thought she'd be able to track down any reports from the schools—sadly, both middle and high school—of pregnant students, including whether the girls came back to school after the birth of their baby. She can verify them with the local hospitals for records of the birth, and then we can compare that with lists from the various county offices of young mothers applying for social services and home visits from the offices of Children and Family Services." There'd been a lot of pregnant teens in the area over the years. "What do you think?"

"She can do that. It should give us a clearer picture of those who had babies but didn't raise them. Let's have her run adoption records in the county, too."

Scott paused. Despite everything they'd been through, or maybe because of it, he wanted to protect Marnie and her privacy. On the other hand, he could trust Jack. And maybe his friend could give him some perspective.

"What?" Jack stared at him, forehead creased and eyebrows drawn together. "Did you do it already?"

He closed his eyes and then shook his head before opening them again. "I can't help thinking about Marnie. She was adopted in 1973. With everything she's been going through in learning about her history, I wonder if we'll blow apart someone else's world with whatever we uncover, especially as we dig through adoption records." He lowered his gaze to his hands, drawing his lips tight together. "Obviously, we have to take that step, but thinking of her makes me wonder what we'll find." He looked back up to see the concern in his friend's gaze.

Jack leaned forward, resting his forearms on his desk. "Have you two worked out whatever is going on between you?"

"We've only talked about Carly and Nick. Nothing personal. I'm sure she's angry with me for how I acted." Despite the wounds Darlene had left behind, he'd been a jerk. Why couldn't he bring himself to just call her and apologize?

"Which time?"

That stopped him in his tracks. "What do you mean, 'which time'? I'm talking about the night I found her dancing on a bar table. What are you talking about?"

Jack tilted his head to the side, giving him an appraising look. "Kate said Marnie was having fun, blowing off a little steam. What's wrong with a girls' night out?"

Scott pictured her in his head, although not on top of the table, but she'd looked so relaxed, before she saw him. She was so antsy and anxious later, in the hospital waiting room. Angry, and worried, and tired, and…beautiful. "Nothing, I guess."

The corners of Jack's mouth turned up. "Maybe you were more jealous than angry?"

He tried to calm the heat rising in his blood. "I'll concede that as a possibility, but all I could think of, when I saw her, was Darlene." He'd been sure she was a mature, responsible, grown-up, professional woman, nothing like his ex. Had he let Darlene's misbehavior become his standard for the anti-Marnie? Had he decided anything that smacked of wild, uncontrolled fun was immoral?

Maybe.

Jack looked directly into his eyes. "She's not your wife, dude. You've had a few dates. You haven't even known each other that long. You need to take a step back and think about what you're saying."

"Fair enough." In his own mind, he'd seen them rushing off to the altar and living happily ever after. He'd put her on a pedestal as the opposite of his ex-wife. But they'd really only had a couple of meals together before he came down on her hard for having a night out. "I guess I need to give it some thought, without visions of Darlene pounding in my head."

****

"I'll grab her after she gets into her house. The father's never there."

She kept harping on him, making him crazy with her constant phone calls. He slumped down in the armchair next to the couch and rested his shoes on the beat-up coffee table.

"…just never you mind. The little sisters won't do any talking, either…we can handle it. Yes, I think Jimmy can handle it. He's not doing it alone."

He hung up and glanced down at the idiot, asleep on the couch. He hoped they could handle it.

Chapter Eleven

What's taking her so long?

Scott peeked into Marnie's garage window. Her car wasn't there. Disappointed that she might not be home, he rang the doorbell one more time. He'd thought he would catch her at this hour of the day.

He was headed back to his Jeep when the front door opened, and he turned back. A rumpled Marnie, who obviously had just rolled out of bed, didn't appear very welcoming.

"Hi," he said. *Lame, dude.*

"Hi," she responded, clearing her throat. Her voice was raspy and her eyes red. Either she'd been crying or was hung over—or both. He stopped himself from saying something snarky, trying not to jump to conclusions. Maybe she was coming down with something.

She made no move to motion him into the house, nor did she say anything, simply stood in the doorway staring at him.

Stepping forward anyway, he left less than a foot between them. She might be angry, but he couldn't make things right if she wouldn't talk to him. "Can I come in? I think we have some things to talk about, and I have some news on the baby-selling ring."

She moved back to let him walk into her house but still didn't say anything. He walked past her, close enough to take in the scent of her hair and pick up the faint aroma of wine. Maybe she *was* hung over.

Scott stopped in the entrance hall to let her lead. She walked to the kitchen and directly to the fridge, pulling out a diet cola, then looking at him. "Want one?"

"No, thanks," he replied.

Her lips formed into a lopsided grin. "Coffee, then? Not everyone can appreciate the breakfast of champions." She held up her diet cola can.

He smiled. "No, really, I'm good. I already had two cups of coffee this morning." He'd needed the jolt to help build up his courage to talk to her. Now he worried that he'd be too jumpy. He needed to come across as calm and mature and reasonable.

She took a seat at the kitchen table, popped the can top, and took a long drink. He sat in the chair opposite hers, resting his hands on the woven blue placemat.

While he couldn't actually hear her toe tapping in impatience, she crossed her arms and tilted her head, her expression passive as she peered at him expectantly. He'd dug this hole and needed to just plunge forward to find his way out of it.

"Okay, so first, I want to apologize." Her eyebrows shot up and mouth opened for a moment, but she shut it quickly, so he continued. "I've been upset with you since the night Carly went to the hospital." He focused on his hands, his fingers laced together, resting in front of him on the table. "I'm sure I didn't hide it well. The thing is…well…I'm attracted to you." That was putting it mildly. He'd known from the first moment he saw her that she could be the one.

Scott glanced up into her gaze. "Very attracted." He cleared his throat. "I felt a connection from the start, and I saw the kind of woman I've been looking for—someone beautiful, smart, responsible, mature, fun, and, well, someone who makes me feel wonderful."

Her expression didn't soften. "Go on."

In a perfect world, she would have fallen into his arms and declared her undying love. He would have been happy with a smile, a nod, or any hint of positive reaction. Instead, he'd just have to keep talking, hoping that humbling himself and apologizing would bring that warmth to her heart.

"I know it's my issue, not yours, so that's why I'm apologizing." He took a deep breath and met her gaze again. "I went a little crazy when I found you dancing on the table, doing shots, and blowing off steam. All I could see was my ex-wife. I forgot that you're not her. I'm sorry."

She started to speak, but he held up his hand. "I never should have married Darlene. She didn't get the concept of marriage or monogamy or even partnership. It was a sham from the start, and like I said, the only good thing that came of it was Nick. At least I picked up a little brother, a great kid, and hopefully someone I can help through these difficult teenaged years."

Her soft smile eased the feeling of tightness in his chest.

"From what I can see, you've been a great influence on him. He's a good kid."

"Thanks. But it doesn't change the fact I've held on to my scars from his sister long past the time to let them go. I may have put you on a pedestal of my own design because I was so convinced you were the anti-Darlene, nothing like her in any way."

"I don't want to be on anybody's pedestal. And, while I'm not Darlene, I'm also not the anti-Darlene. I'm Marnie." She crossed her arms. "As soon as those words left my lips, though, I remembered that I don't really know who Marnie is anymore. It's fair that you've been confused, since I can't get a handle on my own identity these days."

"I appreciate you saying that, but I think you're the same strong woman you've always been. You're more than enough, just the way you are." He shook his head slowly. "It's my own fault, but when I saw you that night, and knew what Nick had gone through when Carly couldn't get in touch with you, I overreacted." He looked deep into her warm brown eyes. "That's on me and no fault of yours. I'm sorry."

A small smile flashed across her face. "Thank you. I know that's not entirely true, and there was some fault on both sides, but I really appreciate it."

He sighed. Her smile reached her eyes now. If she had truly forgiven him, maybe they had a chance to rebuild what might have been before he messed up.

"I've realized you had a lot going on and deserved a night to cut loose. It was just bad luck you happened to be blowing off steam the same night Carly needed you. I'm sorry if I made you feel guilty for her ending up in the hospital."

"And I'll admit I haven't been handling my stress well for the past few weeks." She shrugged, but at least the smile didn't waver.

He cocked his head to the side. "How's the stress level now?" Unless appearances were deceiving, she still seemed wound up about it all.

She sighed. "Still pretty high. I'm letting it all get to me, twist me up inside. I'm not acting like me, mostly because my foundation of who I am is shaky right now. I'm constantly checking on my mother's health situation. And I'm worried about Carly and preferred having her stay at my house so I could see with my own eyes everything was okay. So, all in all, I'm a mess."

He stared deep into her eyes, trying to send her strength through the power of his gaze. "You're not a mess, Marnie. You're a good person to whom a lot of messy things have happened."

She snorted. "Are you trying to warm my heart with your take on a Harry Potter quote?"

It was nice to get a genuine belly laugh out of her. "Busted." He leaned back in his chair. "But it seemed to fit the circumstances. Right?"

Relief flooded his senses as the level of tension in the room dissipated. She took a sip of her cola, her eyes closed and head thrown back. He wanted to pull her into his arms, kiss her senseless, and carry her upstairs to her bed. He wanted to know he hadn't irreparably damaged what they were building between them.

Nevertheless, he hadn't finished telling her everything he'd come here to say. He hoped what he had to say next wouldn't undo the good he'd done in apologizing, or ruin his chances with her once and for all.

Unsure how to approach what he'd uncovered, he didn't realize he was chewing on his bottom lip until she said, "Okay, what else? You look like a nervous wreck and said you had something to tell me about the investigation, so spill it already."

He met her gaze. "I've been pursuing several different leads. In addition to searching for Carly's stalkers, the woman, the guy in the car, and the car itself, I have been pursuing some old leads on girls who were pregnant but then weren't raising any children. These claims, which span many years, often started with nosey neighbors but ended up raising real questions. For one reason or another, the investigations stalled, but pulling them all together is giving me some perspective and leading to new lines of inquiry."

He pulled out his notepad, more to have something to do with his hands, as he knew what he had to ask her.

She cocked her head, a half-smile on her lips. "Okay. Good. That sounds promising. Once you know who the woman is, and the guy in the car, you can bring them in, right? Arrest them for threatening the Johnsons?"

He flipped a few pages, searching through his scribbles, and then turned to her. "Yes, but I haven't got a name yet, for either of them, although the sketches Carly helped us develop are specific. And very helpful." He cleared his throat. "Have you found any more information on your birth parents?"

A line appeared between her eyebrows and her mouth set in a hard line. "Some, but nothing definitive."

She didn't ask why, which made him suspicious she already knew.

"Did you come across anything to indicate your

adoption wasn't legitimate?"

Some emotion flashed across her face, but she quickly hid it well. "Of course not."

He reached out and laid his right hand on her left one on the table. "Even if you did, it wouldn't change your relationship with your parents or put them in any legal jeopardy. You know that, right?"

Her eyes were red, but her lips were pursed. She picked up her cola with her other hand and took another sip. "I can promise you my parents never did anything which would put them in any legal jeopardy." Her tone was cold as ice.

"Okay. I get it." He held up his hands in front of him. "I'm not accusing them of any wrongdoing. I'm tracing some activity back to the school, back in the time your grandmother was the nurse there. It looks like someone who worked in the school back then might have used knowledge of which girls were pregnant to convince the young mothers to sell their babies. It appears to have been running almost continuously since then."

She stared at him, her face blank and not revealing her thoughts. He didn't want to blow his chance to repair their relationship, but he had to follow where the investigation took him.

"I wondered if she knew what happened back then or used contacts there to help arrange your adoption. She's no longer living, right?"

Shaking her head, she replied, "She died a long time ago."

"Did she leave any journals or diaries? Anything to indicate how your adoption came about or who helped her to make it happen?"

Marnie stood abruptly. "So now not only are my parents criminals but so is my grandmother? I think you'd better leave."

He hung his head, trying to find the words he needed to make her understand. He stood and held her gaze. "I'm sorry if my questions sound accusatory. I don't mean them to be. I'm trying to tie all the pieces of this long investigation together and found a number of threads which lead back to the school in the early to mid seventies. I took a chance there was a connection, given the circumstances of your own adoption. I feel like your grandmother might have known what happened, or at least suspected it."

She threw her hands up and turned away from him.

Scott paused for a moment before walking over to stand behind her, and kept his voice quieter. "But if that's not true, it gives me another direction to go in the investigation. In a situation like this, where there's a possibility a criminal enterprise has been operating in the area for years, more information is always better than not enough."

She didn't respond, but kept her back to him. She was too angry or stubborn to answer him, and he'd probably only make things worse if he pushed her now. He'd have to find his answers elsewhere.

He started to walk down the hallway toward the front door, his head hanging low again. He should have pulled her into his arms when he had the chance. Or saved this conversation for another time.

"All I want to know is…can you keep the girls safe?" He heard her footsteps behind him and turned. She'd followed partway down the hall.

"I'm going to do everything I can to keep Carly and her sisters safe. The sooner we get an identity for both the man and the woman, the sooner we can relax the patrols around her house. But in the meantime, we'll keep a watch on her, both to protect her and, hopefully, to catch the people threatening her."

With that, he opened the door and left, not waiting for her to show him out. Maybe, just maybe, if he gave her some time and space, she might be willing to talk to him about this later.

****

Marnie pushed her mother's wheelchair back to her room from the rehab area. She had blocked out the whole afternoon to spend with her parents. While her father took a class in fly-tying, she had taken her mother off to the skilled nursing wing for a checkup and a rehab appointment. A meeting was scheduled with the oncologist on Tuesday to give them an update on the treatment options available.

"Why don't you stop right up here, in the atrium area, and we can watch the birds in the aviary?"

If her mother wanted to spend some time out of her room, observing the birds in the indoor aviaries, Marnie was okay with that and headed that way.

Once she pulled up a chair next to her, Marnie realized her mother's gaze was on her, not the birds.

"What?" She ran her tongue over her teeth, checking for any stray remnants of lunch, then smoothed her hands over her hair and straightened her top. Funny how her mother could so easily make her feel like an insecure teenager again.

Her mother smiled, one of those serene I-know-you're-not-telling-me-something smiles only she could give, with so-spill-your-guts added into it. "What's bothering you, sweetheart?"

She turned to the aviary. No use giving her more ammunition by looking directly into her eyes. "I don't know what you're talking about, Mom. I'm fine. I'm happy to have the afternoon to spend with you and Dad and, well, okay…" She turned back to face her mother. "I guess I'm feeling a little guilty I haven't been around more often since you got out of the hospital. I'm sorry, both to you and Dad, that I left so much of your care on his shoulders." Kneeling down, she hugged her mother, receiving a loving pat on her back in return.

"That's okay, sweetheart. We're fine. We have so many people here at Kendal taking care of us. We're happy you come whenever you're able."

She sat back in her chair, leaning against the back and lacing her fingers in her lap before grinning. "Thanks, Mom."

Her mother's smile straightened out into a tightly held line, her brows furrowing. "Now, tell me what's really bothering you. You know I can see it and will keep pestering you until you tell me, so save us some time, okay?" The full smile came back, although a little more sarcastic. "I'm an old lady and don't have all the time in the world to wait for you."

She lurched, indignant. "Mom!"

"Spill it, girlie." The older woman's expression changed from Madonna to a Vegas poker player.

She'd never been able to fool her mother, and it was clear nothing had changed.

"It's nothing. I'm tired and burning the candle at too many ends. As I mentioned on the phone last week, I've been worrying about Carly and Nick and what they're going to do about their baby, as well as some friction at work. Nothing to worry about, really."

Her mother smiled and reached for one of Marnie's hands to hold between her own. She made noises that sounded like understanding, acquiescence, and empathy. But when Marnie's hand was gently squeezed and she was pulled so close they were nearly nose-to-nose, she knew her mother wasn't buying her story.

"Tell me. We don't know how long I'll be of this world. Make use of my life experiences and love for you while you can. *Talk* to me."

She briefly closed her eyes and sighed. Maybe she could let her mother in. She opened her eyes again and gazed deep into the brilliant blue ones that had been home for her all her life. "You're the worst, you know that?"

At least she could still make her chuckle.

Marnie continued, all the fight having left her. "Using your illness as an advanced interrogation technique? So unfair." But she couldn't help smiling.

"All's fair in love and war, my sweet."

She leaned back in her chair, crossing her arms over her chest. "So I've been researching what I could find about Summer Jam, the baby born there, other babies who disappeared in Stevens and Schuyler Counties at the time, and adoption records. Even though we were living in Tully, I read through the local newspapers for babies born at Schuyler Hospital at that time. While nothing I've found contradicts what you told me, or what Grandma Gill told you, I also found a lot of other babies born at Schuyler Hospital during the months, and even years, surrounding my birth, babies who don't show up in the school yearbooks, local news, death certificates, or any other public records."

"Okay." Her mom smoothed some wrinkles in the blanket covering her lap. "Your search hasn't turned up any holes in the story I got from my mother, right?"

"No. It looks like they brought me to Grandma's house, and she drove me to Tully. That part is all as you said it would be."

Her mother placed a hand on her arm. "So explain to me where the problems lie."

"Well, another way to look at this is to consider the woman who approached Carly to try to buy her baby."

Her mother gasped. "Someone wanted to buy her baby? Whatever for?"

"I don't think she asked for details. She told the woman to take a hike. But as it turns out, Carly has been watched, likely stalked, pretty much ever since. She even found a threatening note taped to her door, telling her to keep her mouth shut and not go to the cops."

"Oh, dear."

When her mother shrank a little in her chair, Marnie decided this might be too stressful for her. "It's okay, though, as the state police are dealing with it. The Johnsons are protected, so don't worry."

Her mother's spine of steel straightened up again. "Don't brush me off. There's more to this story. I can handle it, so keep going."

Marnie took in a deep breath and released it, trying to give herself a moment to think about how best to handle it.

"So what's with all the disappearing babies back at the time you were born?" Trust her mother to cut right to the chase.

She first raised her gaze to the ceiling and, finally, back at her mother. "See, that's it. It looks like maybe this baby-selling ring operating now was also operating back in the seventies. That it's been going ever since then. And I think the state police are starting to wonder if Grandma Gill was involved."

Her mother leaned her right elbow on the armrest of her wheelchair and cocked her head to one side, silent for a few moments. Then, "Hogwash."

Marnie chuckled briefly. "What?"

A kind smile graced the wrinkled face. "My mother was no more the head of a criminal enterprise selling babies on the black market than she was one of these canary birds who might fly south for the winter. Her job was to help students, to make them feel better. She wanted to be able to help kids in trouble, even if it wasn't always a high-paying job. Money didn't matter that much to her, because she loved what she did and was able to help people. She wouldn't have been a part of selling babies. It just wasn't in her."

Smiling at the defense of her grandmother, Marnie said, "Maybe your parents had financial troubles you didn't know about, Mom."

"No, I don't see how it could be true. Dad was the mayor, in addition to running his construction business. My mother's parents left her quite a bit of money, a good chunk of which passed into that trust of yours. They only had two kids and paid cash for the materials when Dad built the house, so they never had a mortgage. I think this is much ado about nothing, at least as far as Grandma Gill is concerned."

Leaning forward, Marnie took one of her mother's hands in hers. "The state trooper told me they traced the mothers of some of the missing babies to the school nurse's office during the time Grandma Gill worked there. Do you know if she had an assistant or anyone she worked with who might have been involved?"

Marnie reached into her back pocket, pulling out the police sketches. "Do you recognize either of these people, Mom?"

Her mother looked at the sketch of the man and the car without a ripple of recognition. When she flipped to the sketch of the woman, she sat as if mesmerized. She squinted at the drawing, first with and then without her glasses, running her hand over her eyes.

"Mom?"

"She looks familiar, I can say that much. I'll have to think about it, but I may be able to come up with a name eventually, or at least how I know her. Can I keep this copy?"

"Sure. Let me know when you remember anything."

"You should send it to Uncle Don. He might remember." Her mother's younger brother was not young, being in his mid-seventies, but given he still lived in town when Marnie was born, he might have more information about what his mother was up to at the time.

"I'll do that tonight. I would never have thought to ask him."

"Good. So does this all mean you're on the outs with your state trooper?"

She laughed. "He's not *my* state trooper, Mom. Besides, how did you even know about him?"

Her smile was a little like a cat slurping milk from a fine china saucer. "A mother knows. When I heard how he drove you to the hospital the night I collapsed, and walked you in to be sure you were okay, I knew he was hooked."

"We only met that night. Nobody was hooked." Maybe he would have been, was getting there, before she started to implode and lose sight of who she really was.

"Right. Anyway, I heard the two of you were strolling down Franklin Street in Watkins, holding hands. You have never indulged in public displays of affection, so it must mean you're hooked, too."

That had been a magical night. She had no idea if they'd be able to get back to that, but a girl could hope.

She huffed out a breath. "Small towns."

"You better believe it, girlie. I have spies everywhere." She laughed, and the sound sent a flood of warmth up Marnie's spine. It was good to hear.

"Well, we haven't spoken much since Carly fell and spent that week with me. I've been trying to catch up at work and find out whatever I could about Grandma Gill and the disappearing babies."

Her mother's smile tightened. "You need to talk this out with him, after you talk to Don. That should give you enough facts to be able to help him in his investigation and smooth out any problems you've been having."

She looked away. She wasn't willing to risk hurting her parents any more than she already had or tarnishing her grandparents' memory. "I'm not sure I want to give him any more reason to look at Grandma Gill's role in facilitating my adoption or even turn his eye on you, Mom. You knew it was an illegal adoption but went ahead with it. I'm not a minor anymore..."

Her mother pushed at her arm. "Not for a long time, missy."

"Thanks for that. True, I'm a long way from eighteen, so we don't have to worry about the legality of my adoption now, but I don't want him suspecting you and Dad."

She grasped Marnie's hand. "Don't worry about us. We'll be fine. You work things out with your guy and figure out who's behind this. The important thing is to keep the kids safe."

The last thing she wanted to do was face him about this, especially after kicking him out of her house for suggesting her grandmother might have known something about this. But her mother was right. It was the only way to keep Carly, her baby, and all the other girls in the same situation safe. And her mother *was* right, as always. That was all that really mattered.

****

Marnie stepped out of her car in the parking lot of the townhouse complex. The buildings had a stained cedar siding, a color probably in the colonial blue family, with white shutters and trim. The landscaping was tasteful and modest, but could be pretty in the summer with colorful annuals. Not a bad place for a bachelor pad, and certainly close to Scott's office at the Horseheads State Police barracks.

Before she was halfway up the walk to his door, he was there, standing on his front porch, a lopsided grin hesitant on his face.

"Have any trouble finding the place?" Scott shuffled his feet, hands in his front jeans pockets.

In this day and age, with GPS and Google Maps, how many people still had trouble finding an address? It's just off the main road. "No problem."

When she got to the top of the stairs and stepped onto the small front porch, he stared at her, saying nothing. She turned away, unwilling to let him see her mixed emotions. While she was relieved to be able to talk to him about the investigation and, hopefully, help keep Carly and her sisters safe, she had visions of their fights and their lovemaking, conflicting thoughts racing through her mind.

After a few awkward moments, he finally pulled his hands from his pockets, turned to the door, and ushered her inside. She followed him down a short hall, with the stairway on her left, which opened into a nicely decorated living room/dining room combination that flowed into the open kitchen at the back of the house. French doors at the far side of the kitchen gave her a peek of a small backyard area and more buildings in the complex.

"This is nice. I had no idea these townhouses were so big inside." He kept it pretty neat for a single man living alone.

Motioning to the couch, he nodded. "Have a seat. I have a fresh pot of coffee in the kitchen. Can I get you a cup?"

"No, thanks. I'm good."

Sinking into the love seat opposite her, he blushed. "Sorry, there's no diet cola in my fridge."

Chuckling, she winked at him. "Nobody's perfect."

His posture became less tense as he laid his right arm along the back edge of the love seat, crossed his right ankle on his left knee, and turned to meet her gaze.

She swallowed, wishing he *did* have some diet cola. "Okay, so as I said on the phone, I spoke with my Uncle Don, my mother's brother, and he had quite a bit of insight into my adoption."

"Is he willing to talk to me directly?"

"Yeah, he said no problem."

"What'd he tell you?" He pursed his lips, and his eyebrows drew together.

Crossing her legs and lacing her fingers together on her lap, she took a deep breath and dove into the story. "After the hospital examined and released me, the day I was born, the mayor in Watkins Glen asked my grandfather, who was the mayor of Harper's Glen, if he could find someone to watch me until they figured out what to do. There was so much craziness that weekend, the Watkins Glen town fathers couldn't deal with anything more. Grandma Gill said she'd take care of the baby and help find a foster home. My parents had been waiting a long time to adopt, but since they were older, in their forties, there was some question as to whether it would ever happen. My grandmother figured this was their chance."

He nodded but, for once, was not taking notes.

Both uncomfortable and grateful that his full attention was focused on her, Marnie drew in a lungful of air to help steady her nerves. While he needed all the facts to find the guilty parties and keep Carly safe, her stomach churned with anxiety over the light it shone on her family.

"Grandma contacted someone she knew, who created adoption papers and a new birth certificate for me, and then drove to Tully, where my parents were living, and brought me to my mom. Dad was away at some conference, I think. Anyway, she only told Mom I was a gift from heaven and she should tell anyone who asked, including my father, the adoption agency had come through for them finally. My mother was so excited to finally have a child, she didn't ask any more questions after that."

Tears began to fill her eyes. Seeing them, he got up, left the room, and returned with a box of tissues, which he placed on the coffee table.

Though she hated crying in front of people, his concern for her eased some of her embarrassment. Better to just get the whole story out and hope he was understanding and concerned when it was done.

"Thanks." Once he sat, she continued. "That's pretty much all my mother could tell me." After wiping her tears on a tissue, she tried to gauge his reaction by the look in his eyes. She saw care and concern mixed with a professional interest. "She was working, had a newborn, and was over an hour away from Harper's Glen, so she didn't really know anything else. Uncle Don, though, was able to fill in a lot of gaps in the story."

"Maybe like how your grandmother knew someone who could have falsified adoption records and a birth certificate?"

"Exactly." She hoped he didn't think Grandma Gill was in a gang or something. "So as you know, my grandmother was the high school nurse. Don has always lived in town, so he and Grandma talked about her work. She didn't do it for the money, which was almost nothing, but because she wanted to help the kids. So when this pregnant teen came to her distraught, Grandma helped the girl find a family to adopt her baby without going through an adoption agency. Apparently, there was some concern about the baby's father, the girl's uncle, forbidding the adoption if he found out. Anyway, Grandma helped place the baby in a home in the area, although Uncle Don didn't know exactly where. He swears no money changed hands, but it was someone his mother worked with at the school who arranged for the birth certificate and adoption papers at that time. He's sure she used the same connection to create my paperwork as well."

"So…" He leaned forward. "Someone who worked at the school was able to produce counterfeit paperwork. Does Don know who it was?"

"Not exactly." She hoped Scott would be able to find the name.

"What's that mean?"

"Uncle Don said Grandma would never give him the name of the 'girl' she worked with, but said it was a younger aide in the building. He always got the impression the woman worked with Grandma directly in the nurse's office, at least part of the time. The woman was quite young back then, but it's been forty-four years, so she has to be at least in her mid to late sixties now, which would match the sketch. If we can get a list of school personnel back then, you should be able to get a name."

He must have been able to read her thoughts as his lips pressed into a thin line. "You know, as I pursue this line of inquiry, your grandmother's reputation will take a hit, and by association, also your grandfather's, and maybe that of your parents, right?"

She swallowed the lump in her throat. "I know, but my grandparents have been gone a long time, and my parents and I agree it doesn't matter as much as protecting the Johnson girls, and other girls who find themselves pregnant as teens."

"I'm glad to hear you say that."

She didn't want to continue but knew she had to rip the bandage completely off. "Uncle Don said Grandma helped other pregnant teens, at least for a year or two, but he remembers her saying how surprised she was so many girls were either keeping their babies or going through formal adoption proceedings, because they weren't coming to her for help any longer. I think this aide, whoever she was, saw a business opportunity and jumped on it. She got to the girls first, convinced them to sell their babies, and then sold them out of the area or even out of state."

"That's likely what happened."

It seemed they were on the same page with this. Relief flooded through her when she realized she wouldn't have to argue her grandmother's innocence with him.

Rising, he went to the kitchen, leaving her wondering until he returned with his laptop.

"Let's see what we can find." Instead of taking his spot on the loveseat, he sat next to her on the couch.

He placed his laptop on the coffee table in front of them and started typing. "I'm connecting with the state employee records. Let's see what I can pull up for the early seventies."

As he began to type furiously, he stopped long enough to hold up his left index finger. "Would you please go grab my notepad and pen off the counter?"

In the kitchen, she found the notepad and pen on the end of the bar top counter, next to a stack of mail, a bowl full of fun-sized bags of M&Ms, and a house phone. Chuckling, she returned to the living room. "You still have a landline?"

He nodded without looking up. "Useful in an emergency if cell towers are down."

She sat back down next to him and studied the screen. When she realized she was holding her breath, she tried to lean back and relax. Either they'd find the aide or they wouldn't.

While he searched, and muttered to himself in a fairly adorable way, she tried to get a handle on what would come next, both in the investigation and between herself and Scott. She stole a peek at his profile while he was absorbed in his work. If he found the woman who had tried to buy Carly's baby, that could lead to finding the man, arresting them both, and hopefully shutting down the baby-selling ring. If he couldn't find her with the information from her uncle, he might have other trails he was following and, even if it took longer, he could still find the man and woman and shut down the ring. Either way, his investigation could expose her grandmother for her part in some illegal adoptions—but she never took any money or sold any babies, so they could ride that out.

Now they were speaking, and not yelling, maybe they would be able to find their way back to how they had been before everything started to fall apart. She didn't want to be on a pedestal, but she was finally coming to the realization that just because she was born during a rock concert in the back of a microbus it didn't mean she had latent wild-woman genes ready to burst forth. As Matt had told her, she was still the same smart, organized, dependable woman she'd always been. She wasn't boring—surely he wasn't looking for boring—but she wasn't a party girl, either.

Maybe if she was more comfortable in her own skin, and he was less quick to judge, they could start fresh and see where this attraction would take them.

Scott was focused on the screen. She couldn't help smiling at the way he was sucking his bottom lip into his mouth ever so slightly. He must have felt her gaze as he turned to her, smiled, and quickly turned back. He bit his bottom lip and leaned forward, glancing from the screen to his notepad and back. It made her want to take a little bite of his bottom lip as well.

"I think we got her."

She met his gaze, and then focused on the screen where he pointed to a list of names.

"Sheri Jonas." He turned to her, his eyes alight with excitement and a smile on his face. "She was hired in the fall, when she was twenty years old, as a teacher's aide in the Special Ed department. She became a specialized aide in the nurse's office that January, so she would have been working with your grandmother then. It looks like she stayed at the school until retirement, when she was sixty, but she never changed jobs again, in all those years."

"Her position in the nurse's office would have given her access to the names of pregnant students."

He hit a few more keys on his computer and a picture popped up. "Right you are. Especially in the past twenty-five years or so, school districts have kept track of pregnant students in order to facilitate not only access to classes and schoolwork, but also to provide for their health needs. She would have been among the first in the school to know a girl was pregnant."

She cocked her head to one side. "She doesn't look familiar to me."

Walking back into the kitchen, he returned with a print-out of the photo. "Hopefully, Carly will be able to recognize her from the DMV photo."

"I hope so. But how would this Jonas woman have found out about Carly? Sheri Jonas retired a long time ago, but she knew about the pregnancy before Carly had told anyone at school, or anywhere else, with the exception of Nick and the workers at Planned Parenthood."

He scratched his chin. "I can't get into Planned Parenthood's employment records without a warrant, but I'm betting she either has someone on the inside or watches the place to see what teenage girls come out of there looking crushed and scared."

Nodding, she agreed. "I'm sure that's what Carly would have been like after they confirmed her pregnancy. She wouldn't have paid attention to someone outside Planned Parenthood who watched her but didn't approach."

He jotted down a few more things in his notepad. "If Carly can positively I.D. this photo, I should be able to get a warrant for the woman's financials. I'm betting somebody at Planned Parenthood is getting a payoff to let Jonas and her minions, whoever they might be, know when they have another pregnant teen. In the meantime, I'll get a couple of female detectives on surveillance outside the facility to see if anything comes up or if they see Jonas or the guy with the car."

She watched him texting, typing, and writing out notes, his mind apparently going into overdrive. He'd made breakthroughs in the investigation, and she started to believe they would quickly catch the people threatening Carly.

As much as she wanted Carly safe, it was tough to share all these secrets with him. Her mother's face came to mind. Even though she'd encouraged her to talk to Uncle Don, explain everything to Scott, and risk Grandma Gill's reputation, Marnie couldn't help but think having her searching for her birth parents on top of all of this might be too much for the fragile woman.

They went over a few more details. She'd brought him copies of her forged adoption records and the birth certificate her mother had given her. If he was able to uncover the forger, it would help bring the investigation full circle.

Finally, his fingers stopped racing over his keyboard, and he put his notepad away and sat back. She saw understanding and gratitude in his gaze, which helped to ease the ache in her heart.

"Thanks for sharing all this with me. It's going to make a huge difference in finally tracking down the people involved in selling these babies and putting an end to this criminal enterprise." He picked up her right hand with his left one, cradling it on his thigh. "I know how hard it is for you to expose your grandmother's role in this, as benevolent as it was, and risk subjecting you all to criticism and censure. I understand how important your family is to you."

She choked up, tears blurring her vision.

Scott leaned in and wiped away one tear that had escaped. "I'm sorry. I didn't want to upset you more. I wanted you to know I understand there is more at stake here than my investigation and Carly's safety, and you have every right to be upset by what we're uncovering. Your grandmother did something illegal, maybe more than once, but she did it to help others, not for personal gain. Unfortunately, she trusted someone who was unworthy of her trust and proceeded to use and abuse the youth of our area for money."

She wiped her eyes with a tissue and blew her nose. She'd always been a big crier, which used to infuriate her, given her mother was always calm and collected. Now she had to wonder if her birth mother came from a long line of crying fools.

Once Marnie had collected herself, she met his gaze. "Thank you for that. I'm sorry for kicking you out the other night, just for suggesting Grandma might have had some connection to this investigation. I knew enough to know something was hinky back then and to suspect it might be connected, but I didn't want to admit it to either of us."

His smile grew lopsided. "No problem. I've been acting like an idiot lately. I knew I was being a jerk, but I couldn't seem to deal with my feelings." He hesitated, his gaze locked on hers. "I fell for you faster than I believed possible or smart. It made me feel scared and...well, vulnerable. I've been hurt before, as you know, and was afraid I was heading down that road again."

Her mouth went dry. She was scared, too. Maybe the new bit of wild woman in her could help her out here.

She stood up, took his hand, and smiled. "Let's head down that road together."

Scott raised his gaze to meet Marnie's, taking in her sweet smile, her eyes filled with promise, and he couldn't do anything but stand and lead her upstairs. When she turned at the doorway of his bedroom, no doubt or question graced her face; she simply squeezed his hand and gave him a little shove into the room. Her push not only amused him, it opened up his heart. He grasped her around the waist and danced her over to his bed, even though her feet didn't reach the floor.

He placed her gently on the bed, soaking in the sight of her. Her eyes were hooded, her lips barely apart, and he couldn't wait to touch her. How could she be so tiny and perfect, lying there smiling up at him? Everything about her oozed warmth and allure and home; all he'd ever wanted in a partner. He was too far ahead in this, but he was past the falling. He was full-on in love with this woman.

Scott climbed next to her. She reached up and pulled his face to hers, devouring his lips with her own. As her hands began to race over his back, his waist, his arms, he couldn't stop himself from moaning. This was the only place he wanted to be, the only woman he wanted to be with. He melted into her and welcomed the fire, the flames. Before long, he lost coherent thought and went with her touch, scent, and the incredible sight of her, opening for him, meeting him on an equal basis, and taking him home.

Nearly an hour later, when they both lay naked and spent, when he was nothing more than a jangle of nerve endings with smiles, he pulled her to his chest and she rested her head in the curve of his shoulder. This was the point when he normally rolled over and slipped into a relaxed, almost drugged sleep. For some reason, though, he was wide awake in her arms.

Marnie curled against his side, one leg resting casually on his thigh. Her fingers played with his chest hair. While he could tell, with sufficient recovery time, this position was bound to bring about another bout of lovemaking, he couldn't help but feel content for now.

Running his fingers lightly over her back, which raised goose bumps and seemed to make her giggle, he pulled the covers over them. He tangled his fingers in her short dark curls and realized he used to think he preferred women with long, straight hair. He couldn't imagine finding that attractive anymore.

She gazed up at him. "What are you thinking in there? Your face is so serious."

Resting his free hand behind his neck, he winked. "I'm enjoying a little rest before round two."

Her giggle reverberated through his chest and felt almost as if it had come from him.

"Pretty sure of yourself, aren't you?" She gave a few chest hairs a playful tug and then leaned up to kiss him on the lips.

He pulled her close and rolled onto his side to look directly into her eyes. "The only things I'm really sure about right now are how much I want a round two…" He chuckled and kissed her before continuing. "And I'm in love with you." He put a finger over her lips before she could respond. "Wait. I know it's early, and we've been apart more than we've been together—and we've fought more than we've dated—but it doesn't matter. I can't help it. I love you. Even though I don't expect you to feel the same, I hope you will eventually."

Her mouth opened as if to speak and then closed again. She closed her eyes, let out a deep breath, then opened her eyes and stared directly into his. "I can say I'm up for round two myself, but I'm not ready to take the next step. I've been hurt before, too, and may still have too many shields up to let go completely right now."

Not exactly what he'd hoped she'd say, but fair enough. He had all the time she needed to get to the next step.

She kissed him slowly and deeply but pulled back when he started to deepen the kiss.

"I admit there is a special spark between us, something that doesn't come along often. I can see it possibly deepening into a lasting love, but I'm not there yet. Can you give me the time to figure out if it's there for me, too?"

Scott pulled back and admired her beautiful face. He'd give her anything right now. He knew his heart was at risk, because he could get in way over his head before she took the time to figure out whether he was for her. But it was too late for him anyway. He was already all the way gone. He'd give her the world, if he could. Time was easy.

Pulling her close and kissing her neck, her chin, and her nose, he then met her gaze. "You can have all the time you need." He gave her lips a quick kiss, pulled back, and looked deep into those soft brown eyes. "Now for round two."

The joy in her throaty chuckle was the last thought he had as he devoted everything to making round two even more spectacular than round one.

Chapter Twelve

"We're almost there." While she harped at him on the phone, he turned off his headlights and pulled up to the house. "Yeah, I know." Brandon shut off his phone and stuck it in the glove compartment before leading Jimmy to the house.

He stepped through the back door, stopping still to check for any movement. The kitchen was dark, but the moonlight coming in through the bare windows threw shadows across the floor. He had just enough light to avoid bumping into the table and chairs.

He'd been in the house before, so he knew the girls' bedroom was off the kitchen, if you could call it that. The house had only four rooms plus a miniscule bath, with the father's room on the far side of the living room.

Walking silently, and turning to remind to Jimmy to be as quiet as he could, he checked to ensure no one was on the couch. He stood in front of the father's door and motioned to Jimmy to help him place the table in front of the father's door. Even though it wouldn't stop him from pulling his door open, if he even heard what went on in his alcoholic stupor, the table would surely slow him down.

After the last time he was out here and left the note, the teen had moved out for a week, but she was back. He'd been watching the house, and her, every day this week. She continued to meet with the trooper, the boyfriend, and the Edwards woman.

Now, Sheri said the cops were getting too close. They had to stop the teenager from being a witness against them, if either of them was arrested. They had to shut her up.

Relief flooded him at the total silence, despite a dim light showing beneath the door to the other bedroom. He grasped the doorknob in his gloved hand, turning it slowly until he felt it give way. Motioning to Jimmy not to move, he didn't hear any sounds beyond his ragged breathing. Nothing.

He gave the door a gentle push. Only one bed for the three girls sharing the room. Even if they didn't need the little sisters as ammunition to get the older girl to talk, they'd have to take all three anyway. They were all piled in the center of the bed and would certainly all wake up together.

Brandon gestured to Jimmy, praying the dunce didn't screw this up. He wished he didn't have to use the numbskull for anything more than picking up the mail, 'cause this boy was as dumb as toast. But there was no way he could bring all three of these girls out of the house on his own, even if he didn't have to worry about waking the father. And it wasn't like Sheri could help carry the girls to the van.

He pulled the baggie out of his pocket and handed one of the three ether-soaked cloths to Jimmy, who walked next to the bed and leaned over the comforter. Brandon silently counted off three-two-one with his fingers, and then yanked the covers off the bed.

Damn! There are only two little girls in the bed. Where is the big sister?

Lunging forward, he forced the ether over the faces of the two, while Jimmy helped hold them down. Once the girls stopped wiggling, he scooped up one and carried her out the bedroom door, through the back door, and into the van. Luckily, his pitiful assistant was right behind him with the other girl. Brandon eased the door closed as quietly as possible and climbed into the driver's seat. They had positioned the van on the hill so they could get rolling before starting the engine.

Once they pulled onto the road, he turned on the parking lights only. It was so damn dark up in the hills, he needed a little light to stay on the old dirt road. The cinders on the road kicked up and practically exploded noise in the quiet darkness. Brandon was relieved there weren't any other houses close by. When they got to the end of the dirt road and turned to join County Road Four, he switched the headlights on to full just in time to slam on the brakes. A six-point buck stood in the middle of the road, staring at him in the dark.

"Get the hell out of the road," he shouted at the deer, who was apparently unimpressed by the van or Brandon and stared back, unmoving. Finally, he gave up and started to drive around the animal.

"Son of a bitch." The deer, seeming unintimidated by Brandon or his language, stayed in the road until after the van had passed him by.

"What are we going to do?" Jimmy asked. "Sheri won't be happy if we show up with only two of the three girls."

"I know that."

Unless the girl was in her father's bedroom, she

wasn't in the shack she called home. Where else could she be?

He took a quick look at the fool to his right. "You sure she didn't go back to the Edwards woman's house? You've been watching it like I told you, right?"

"Yep. I didn't see that girl there at all the last couple of days."

He wished he could read Jimmy's face in the dark. This idiot was a lousy liar.

"You sure you kept your eyes on her house the whole time? You didn't wander off nowhere?"

"Yeah, for almost two whole days." The dunce coughed. "Well, except when I had to pee, ya know."

He rolled his eyes but kept driving, careful to keep within the speed limit. It wasn't like he'd see any other cars at this time of night, but he didn't want to fall into some speed trap going into and out of the little hamlets along this road.

When he came down the hill into the valley, Harper's Glen was mostly dark and sleeping before him. He turned off on Rock Cabin Road, driving south along the base of the cliff. Sheri had an old house up on this side of the hill where they were supposed to take the girls, the *three* girls, and hold them until she got there later that afternoon.

Maybe if I find the teenager before then, Sheri will never have to know I didn't take her from the house.

He turned the lights back down to parking lights as they made their way up the road, so as not to attract the neighbor's notice. Luckily, it wasn't a long drive, so the two girls were still out. He picked one of them up and carried her into the dark house and down the basement stairs, with his stupid assistant following with the other girl.

Once they dropped the girls on a mattress they'd put down on the floor between a couple of playpens, Brandon turned on the basement light. He and Jimmy quickly taped their wrists and ankles with duct tape, with another piece over each girl's mouth.

Looking down at these girls, he started to fear the whole operation was shot to hell. They'd been moving babies in and out of this house for years, but babies didn't talk. Babies couldn't recognize somebody and give the cops a description. Babies couldn't escape. Even Jimmy was smarter than a baby was.

These girls could talk, would run if they had the chance, and would describe them to the cops if they got away. Nobody wanted that to happen.

But once they started killing people, especially children, they'd turn a big corner. And when push came to shove, the only one who would be getting shoved in a hole would be him. Sheri would weasel her way out of any trouble, or disappear, and this fool, well, no one would believe he was a criminal mastermind.

Yep, it'll be my ass on the line.

"What do we do now, bro?" Jimmy stood with his arms hanging at his sides, his too-big hoodie sleeves covering his hands.

"Why don't you go upstairs, fix yourself something to eat, and I'll watch these two for a while." He gestured toward the girls. "After you eat, come back down here, and then I'll get myself something to eat. We'll take it in turns."

If he actually meant he'd get himself something to eat in town, while he looked for the teenaged sister, this bozo didn't need to know that.

Jimmy's gaze lit up. "Okay, thanks, bro. I saw Sheri bought some of them cinnamon rolls and microwave bacon. I'm so hungry, I'll be quick. You'll see."

Brandon made sure the girls were still sleeping despite the noise of the oaf bounding up the stairs for food. He walked to the shelves against the wall, taking down a brown plastic bottle. He pulled out a couple squares of cotton and a baggie, doused the cotton with ether, slid the damp squares into the baggie, and shoved it into his pocket.

Those girls would be scared shitless when they woke up, but the tape over their mouths should keep them quiet. He needed time to find the big sister. Hopefully, he could grab her and bring her back here by himself. Then, once she was here and saw her sisters, they oughta be able to convince her not to talk to the cops no more. Not only the trooper, though, but also that boyfriend of hers, and the Edwards woman. They all knew too much, but if the girl shut her trap, there wasn't anything they could do to prove any of the stuff she'd already told 'em. She would shut her trap to save her sisters, once she saw how scared they were.

At least, that's what he hoped would happen.

If not, Sheri would tell him to kill 'em all.

****

Long after Marnie had driven home and eaten lunch, she still found herself smiling. Scott had been an inventive and passionate lover and clearly cared about her. They'd spent a good bit of the night, and even the wee hours of the morning, either having sex or snuggled in the afterglow, sharing secrets and swapping stories.

When he told her about his mother deserting him and his father, when he was still in elementary school, she began to understand how Darlene's betrayal, compounded with his mother's abandonment, left him searching for a stable, sensible, reliable woman.

Her walk on the wild side, such as it was, understandably set off some major concerns in his mind. While she wasn't willing to change who she was for any man, she would show him he could trust and rely on her, even if she occasionally wanted to go crazy and have some fun.

She'd originally been worried he was too young for her, that he'd want babies of his own, which was not something too likely to happen at her age. Despite Kate's assurances to the contrary, and Scott's quickly growing attachment, she'd also worried he'd lose interest in her when faced with younger, prettier, sexier women. But, after a night in his bed and his arms, she believed him when he said she was the sexiest, most beautiful woman he knew and was already a little in love with her.

She sat down at the kitchen table, pulled her laptop out of its case, and powered it up. She had some work to catch up on, including checking the status of the winery's latest social media promotions. After she crossed off all the items on her to-do list, she let her focus drift a bit and logged onto the adoption finders website, checking for any responses as she had been nearly every day since she'd posted there.

When she got to her page, her heart nearly skipped a beat at the little red message notification on the top of her window.

When she'd set up her search, she put in the standard information plus a personal message. She didn't mention the Summer Jam specifically but stated she wanted to find her birth mother who had left her in a warm, dry place in the midst of a day of craziness. While her birth mother never formally signed any adoption papers, she wanted her mother to know life had always been good, her adoptive parents were kind, generous, and loving, and no one holds any ill will toward her birth mother. She signed it "Flower Child."

Marnie clicked on the little red envelope icon, and her message box opened.

Dear Flower Child, if the day of craziness you're talking about was an enormous rock concert on a 'Jam'-packed, rainy, muddy day, you may be the baby we've been seeking for years. Hopefully, the policeman who carried you away kept you safe and led you to a happy life...

It was as if the bottom fell out of her stomach, and she broke out in a light sweat. She stopped, reading those words over and over. It sounded like the real thing. She took in a ragged breath, trying to decide what to do next. Call Scott? Email her birth parent? Go visit her parents? Call Kate? Go upstairs, climb in bed, and pull the covers over her head?

It was so hard to know, these days, whether something was real or spam, and she tended to err on the side of deleting anything questionable. She didn't know anyone who was a Nigerian prince, she didn't need penile enlargement, nor did she want to talk to Stacy from customer service about a cruise she never took, a disease she didn't have, or an inheritance from someone who hadn't died. She was internet savvy and computer literate, and had never gotten a virus or even malware on her laptop.

But if this message was spam, it wasn't her hard drive at risk. It was her heart. Her faith in humanity. Her very self.

Was she willing to risk it?

Paused at the computer, she thought about the pro-and-con list she should make, the research she should do, the scans she could run. This wasn't an email; it was an online message. The message was in a secure inbox on the adoption search website. The cautious, methodical, sensible Marnie she'd always been would talk to friends and family before pushing forward with this.

Maybe she was a little bit wild woman after all.

She raced through the rest of the message and then clicked on the reply button and typed out her response.

Yes, I was the baby born during the Summer Jam at the concert in the back of a VW microbus. Are you my birth mother? I just found out I was adopted, which is why I've never searched before, as crazy as it sounds, but I'd love to meet you. I live in Harper's Glen and can be reached by either email or my cell phone number, both listed at the end of this message. I really want to meet you, so please call or email. Thanks. Marnie

She felt a little bit queasy, but her mind raced with possibilities. She ought to be more cautious. If this was a scam, she'd be embarrassed she jumped at the bait.

But it didn't feel like a scam.

Her pulse pounded in her ears. Her mouth was

dry.

How long will it take to hear back?

While going to the refrigerator to get a diet cola, she tried to rein in the wild thoughts going through her mind. All the what-ifs led her back to the need to call her parents. She couldn't forgive herself if they didn't even know she'd placed the ad on the adoption finder and then she showed up one day with her birth mother in tow.

Throwing her phone in her purse, she grabbed her jacket and headed out the door. Before she'd gone far, she called her mom to let her know she was on her way.

Once she hung up, she let her mind wander on the drive. The good news in the spotty cell coverage was she wouldn't be able to check for messages on the drive even if she wanted to. The bad news was she might miss an important call. But that's what voicemail was for.

Half an hour later, she pulled into the parking spot, shut off the car, grabbed her purse, and headed into her parents' home. Realizing she'd forgotten to ask her mom if they'd moved back from the rehab center to their own place, she was glad she had a key to their cottage.

She shouldn't have underestimated her mother. By the time she got to the front step, her father stood in the open doorway.

"Hi, sweetie."

She leaned in as he kissed her cheek. "Hi, Dad."

Backing up, he ushered her in the door. "It's so nice to see you." He smelled like wood smoke and cinnamon; the familiar scent warmed her heart.

Soft sunlight spilled through the garden windows and backlit her mother's smiling face. She held up her arms as Marnie entered the room and went to kiss and hug her.

"Have a seat, sweetie." She patted the couch cushion next to her. "Tell us what brings you over here today. What's wrong?"

She took off her coat, laid it on the back of the couch, and sat next to her mother. Her father went to bring some drinks in from the kitchen.

"Roger, hurry up," her mom yelled. "Marnie has something she needs to tell us."

"How did you know?" Mothers always knew.

A greater wisdom coming through her serene smile, her mother laid a hand on top of Marnie's, patting it. "Don't you think I could hear it in your voice? You're my daughter."

She snuggled into her mother's side, laying her hand on the slender shoulder and starting to choke up. She loved these two more than anything in life, but she was bound to hurt them.

Her father came in with a tray, a pot of tea, three cups and saucers, a bowl of lemon wedges, and some packets of sweetener. "You'll have some tea, won't you?"

Sitting up again, she nodded. "Of course."

Her father's faded beige cardigan with leather patches on the elbows, combined with his slightly rumpled button-down dress shirt, gave him the look of the professor he'd been for many years. The clothes were worn and old but still some of her favorites, as the soft blue of his shirt perfectly matched the color of his eyes.

While he poured them all tea and handed out the cups and saucers, her mother's gaze narrowed on her. *There's nothing like trying to hide something from your mother.*

"Okay, we have our tea, everybody's comfy, and all is good. Now, out with it." Her mother laid her hands across her lap, staring at her.

Her dad glanced up like he wanted to catch up with a conversation he'd just joined. "What?"

"Not you, dear." Smiling, she turned to Marnie. "She's come to tell us something."

Putting her cup and saucer on the coffee table and trying not to let it bump or shake as she did, she took a deep breath. No time like the present. She might as well just forge ahead.

"Okay, you're right, Mom. I wanted to tell you where I am in the search for my birth mother. I don't want you to feel like I'm hiding anything from you." She closed her eyes, took a breath, and opened her eyes again before continuing. "I put a message up on a website dedicated to helping birth parents and adults who were adopted find each other."

"Okay." Her father smiled, but she couldn't be sure he'd understood what she said.

Dabbing her mouth with her napkin, her mother gave her a knowing nod. "And you got a response?"

Trying to answer became harder, as her throat closed up. Tears filled her eyes, as always, but she took a deep breath and tried to swallow the emotion. "I didn't think I'd hear anything soon, if ever, so I planned to tell you guys about it the next time I came over. But, as it turned out...I got a message this afternoon."

"Oh, my," said her father.

This time, it was her mother who looked down at her hands. "So was it her?"

She took her mother's hand, giving it a gentle squeeze until her mom raised her gaze again. "I don't know for sure yet, but I think so. I responded this morning and said to contact me via email or phone, but I haven't heard anything more. I'll call you with more details when I have them."

Reaching across the coffee table and resting a hand on her shoulder, her father's blue eyes were filled with love and understanding. "I hope it turns out to be the woman you're looking for, sugar. We want you to be happy and know you well enough to know you want some answers, some details, any information you can get to help you deal with this."

She couldn't hide the catch in her throat. "You both know how much I love you, right? I don't need to do this, not if it upsets you." As much as she wanted to know who gave birth to her, she'd become the woman these people had raised her to be. She knew that much now and that she was blessed to have them.

Her mother shook her head. "It doesn't upset us, sweetie. We want this for you, to meet her, talk to her, and get your questions answered."

"I know I said I wasn't sure who I am because I'm not who I always thought I was. But after giving this all some thought and time, I think I've figured out I am who I have always been, and that's your daughter." She closed her eyes a moment, trying to pull together what she wanted to say. She wouldn't hurt these two souls for anything in the world. "If the fact I'm adopted makes some sense out of questions I've always had, like where did I get the curly hair, who else was so short, why am I such a crier, well, that's nice. But it doesn't change me. I'm who I am because of the genes my birth parents gave me, but mostly from the love, support, and upbringing I got from the two of you. None of that has changed."

Her mother pulled her in for a hug, and her father stood and wrapped them both in his long arms as well. While she used to take this for granted, she knew how lucky she was to have these two. This was the center of her world, what made her "Marnie." Once he released them and went back to his own chair, her mother let go as well, and everyone wiped their eyes.

"Don't worry about us, dear. We know you love us. You're a mature woman, not a teenager, so we're not really worried about you running away and cutting us out of your lives. We want you to be happy."

Love surged through her, stealing her breath again. *Thank you to Grandma Gill for making sure I ended up with these two.*

She chuckled. "I'm far from a teenager. And after dealing with them for so many years at the Youth Center, I can tell you for sure I'd never want to go back there." She picked up her tea again. The warmth of the cup helped soothe her soul. "But thanks for your support in this. It's scary, but easier knowing I have you both in my corner."

Her dad perked up. "Speaking of the Youth Center, how's that girl you were worried about? How's she doing?"

"She's back home again. She has two younger sisters she takes care of, so she couldn't bear to be away from them for long." And Marnie prayed that all three girls, and the unborn baby, would be safer now that Scott had a better lead on the baby-trafficking ring. "But her pregnancy seems to be out of danger at this point."

Her mother took a sip of her tea. "That's good. And your young man?"

She choked on her tea, almost spitting it out. "My young man?" She laughed. "You say it like I'm sixteen again and bringing home my first boyfriend."

"Maybe I'm thinking he'll be your last." Her mother's face broke into that all-knowing don't-you-dare-try-to-fool-me mother's smile.

How did her mother always know what was hidden away secretly in her heart of hearts? Hopefully her memories of last night's loving didn't show as clearly in her eyes.

Marnie cleared her throat and pasted what she hoped passed for a calm, pleasant smile on her face. "He's fine. We got together last night to discuss the investigation. He was grateful for the information Uncle Don gave me, as it helped him narrow down his suspect pool. He may have identified the woman who approached Carly, offering to buy her baby." Her mother's sudden intake of breath caused her to pause. "I don't think he's got a name for the man yet, but it's definitely progress."

"Do you know the name of the woman suspect? I mean, if she knew my mother, maybe I would know her name, at least."

Hesitating, she wondered how much of last night's discoveries she should share. Even before they ended up in bed. "Let me text him, Mom, and ask him if it's okay for me to share that information with you."

She pulled her phone out of her purse and sent him a text.

A response returned right way.—*Why not? See if she recognizes the name.*—

She met her mother's gaze. "The woman's name is Sheri Jonas." She watched closely for a reaction. "Does the name sound familiar, Mom?"

Her mother tilted her head, lacing her fingers together in front of her. "It sounds familiar, yes. I feel like she worked with my mother at the school. I think it's someone she worked with during her last years there."

"Yes, she was an assistant in the nurse's office. This woman started there shortly before I was born."

"Mom retired when you were about five, right around the time we moved back from Tully." The shaky voice seemed to grow stronger as her mom covered the facts. "My dad was gone by then, so we all moved in together in, well, your house, although it was my parents' house first. I can remember her talking about missing some of the people she worked with, which sounded crazy to me, as it's such a small community there was no way she wouldn't run into them at the Quick-Mart or somewhere around town."

Marnie smiled. Sometimes she'd see co-workers or people from church when she stepped outside in her bathrobe to get the paper off her front stoop. It was a small town, after all.

Her mother continued. "But when she talked about one aide she'd worked with, a much younger woman, she didn't want to see her and actually got upset when the woman came to the house. She was sort of funny about it."

She leaned toward her mother. "What do you mean, funny?"

The gray head shook back and forth. "I don't know, really. I mean, Mom liked most of her co-workers, really most people. She was friendly and patient, and didn't judge other people for the choices they made. But this woman—she didn't seem to like her very much. I guess I remember it because it was so unusual for my mother. She never told me what it was about the woman she didn't like, just said she was no good."

"Did you ever meet her?"

Scrunching up her face, her mother replied, "Well, not really."

"What does that mean, dear?" asked her father.

"I came home from campus early one day. I think you had a doctor or dentist appointment, Marnie." Her mother's gaze met hers. "Anyway, when I pulled into the driveway, there was a strange car parked there, and a woman walking to the car. Mom stood at the front door, yelling, and the woman yelled back. I had to back up to let the woman pull out. When I got inside, I asked Mom what happened, and she refused to talk about it. She told me to forget about it, that the woman would not be returning. I don't think I ever saw her again, at least not until you showed me the sketch the other day."

"Wait." Marnie sat up straighter. "You said you didn't recognize her." Hopefully, that meant they really were on the right track.

"I said I didn't think I did. I've been thinking about it since then, and it finally dawned on me when I'd seen her, if only for a moment." Her mom looked at her, but more past her, as if trying to pull up a memory. "When you said her name, the two clicked in my memory. I'm sure it must have been her."

Marnie pulled out her phone, typing rapidly. "I'm texting Scott to give him an update."

Once she and her parents had covered as much as her mom could remember and she could think to ask, she picked up her purse and rose from the couch. "I have to head home. I want to check on Carly and her sisters. Scott was going to see if Carly could identify that Sheri woman from her DMV photo."

Her father stood, but before he could help his wife to her feet, she knelt down in front of her. "Don't get up, Mom." She pulled her mother into a hug and then kissed her cheek. "Thanks for all your help. I'm sure Scott will want to talk to you himself. The information you and Uncle Don have supplied will be helpful to his investigation."

"I'm glad, sweetie." Her mother patted her head of curls and kissed her cheek.

She stood and allowed herself to be enveloped by her dad's hug.

"Thanks for coming over, sugar." He kissed the top of her head. "Come back soon."

She gave him a squeeze, then grabbed her jacket and headed to her car. After she turned onto the highway, she dialed Scott.

"Hey there." His voice sounded sexier and more relaxed today.

"Hi."

"Thanks for talking about Sheri Jonas with your mother. It's good to know she could identify her as the woman in the sketch."

"She finally put it all together when she heard the name." Excitement skittered through her, and she wanted answers now. She could understand why Scott and Jack liked working in law enforcement, although she'd be exhausted if she had to do this every day.

He hesitated for a moment. "Are you on your way back home now?"

She got off the short stretch of highway, driving through downtown Ithaca. "Yeah, I'll be home in about thirty minutes."

"We could meet up, go over what your mother had to say. And I have news of my own. Um, I'd be happy to come to Harper's Glen. Just name the place."

She smiled. "Why don't you come to my house? If you want to stay for dinner, I can even heat up some soup I made a couple of days ago. That's if you don't mind leftovers." And whatever else they happened to get up to while he was there.

He chuckled. "Sounds great. I love leftovers."

"Good. I'll see you in a little while, then." After she hung up, she still found herself smiling.

****

Marnie had been home only about five minutes before Scott arrived. When she opened the door, he slid in smoothly, shut the door behind him, turned, and pulled her into his arms. It was nice to feel that sense of home, that feeling that this was where she belonged.

He nuzzled her neck and ear, and kissed her again, deepening their connection enough she began to think it was why he'd come to the house. Maybe it was.

She wound her arms around his neck and opened herself to him and the thrill shooting through her.

Once he released her, she grasped his hand and

led him to the living room, her legs a little unsteady beneath her. Her brain was a little fuzzy too, but happiness surged through her.

Realizing that if she stopped at the couch they wouldn't be getting any work done, she decided it was prudent to handle business first, before pleasure. She kept right on walking to the kitchen, and gestured for him to take a seat at the table.

"Can I get you a drink? I have wine, beer, pop, water, whatever." She needed something to do with her hands.

He smiled. "I'm off the clock, so I think I'll have a beer. Thanks."

She pulled out a beer for him, some wine for herself, and set the drinks on the table.

He picked up the beer bottle, holding it in front of him but not yet drinking. "How are your parents? How's your mother's recovery coming along?"

He won points with her for asking about her parents and seeming to be sincere in his interest. With everything that was going on, she wouldn't have been surprised if he got straight to business.

She took a sip of wine. "I think they're good. Mom's doing okay for now, weak, but better. They haven't started treatments yet for the cancer. That will wipe her out, when it starts."

"How's your father handling everything?"

She cocked her head, considering. She was definitely more worried about how her mother was handling everything, given her illness, but her mom had always been strong. "I think he's all right. He's worried about her, and I think, honestly, he's worried about me, too. I'm trying to play down the stalker angle, you know, but he worries."

"Of course." He smiled. "But the information we got from your uncle and now your mother will help us put an end to this stalking business when we make some arrests."

"Sure." She gave him the information her mother had given her about Sheri Jonas and her grandmother's relationship with the woman.

"Thanks for being the go-between on all this. I may need to speak to your mother and uncle directly, you know."

"Yeah, I told them both to expect a call from you eventually." She took another sip of wine. As unhappy as the siblings might feel at the idea of their mother being involved in crime in any way, they seemed more concerned with helping.

He laced his fingers together on the tabletop. "I have some news as well."

She put down her wineglass. "What?"

"We sent a young female trooper into Planned Parenthood, undercover, with a team outside watching the place. As soon as she spoke to the receptionist and sat down with her paperwork to fill out, the receptionist got out her phone and sent a text. Next thing we knew, the brown car pulled up, parked down the street, and watched the door.

"Oh, my God!" Marnie was breathless at the realization that it had to be Carly's stalker.

"Right." He nodded. "So when our undercover officer left the place with a positive pregnancy test, Sheri Jonas approached her and asked about helping to place her baby with an adoptive family. When the officer said she was considering different adoption agencies, Jonas said she could make it worth a mother-to-be's time to work with them."

"You got her!" She raised her hands above her head, wiggling in her chair.

"We got Sheri *and* the receptionist who texted her. We checked both cell phones and found the text confirmation, so we were able to arrest them both."

She took a deep breath, her hands covering her mouth. After a moment with her eyes closed, she opened them again. Staring into his warm gaze, she let loose a yelp of victory. "What a relief. It's over, then."

His mouth thinned in a straight line. "Well, she's not giving up the guy—at least not yet. And the receptionist claims not to know anything beyond that she was to text Sheri whenever a pregnant teenager showed up. I don't think she's involved any further."

She looked into his eyes. "When did this all go down?"

He smiled. "Earlier this morning, after I left your place. I'm sorry I didn't tell you, but I really couldn't, not ahead of time, for the safety of our undercover officer."

She shrugged. "No problem." It was nice he didn't rush off because he just wanted to get away from her. "I'm glad you were able to arrest her and close this down without anyone getting hurt, especially the Johnson girls. Does Carly know?"

He shook his head. "I tried calling her on my way over here, but she didn't answer. I spent most of today trying to get Sheri Jonas to talk, but it was clear the receptionist knew little and had nothing we could use against Sheri. And Sheri decided to ask for a lawyer and wouldn't say another word."

"Maybe if she's in jail for a while, she'll give up the man's name in the hopes of making a deal?" It'd be wonderful it everything was wrapped up that smoothly. Then Carly could relax and only have to worry about being a pregnant teen.

"It's possible," he said. "We wouldn't be willing to make a deal, not with someone who's been selling babies for more than three decades, but she wouldn't necessarily know that."

She reached across the table, taking his hand in hers. "Thank you so much for pursuing this, digging to the bottom, despite me and so many other people trying to shut you down."

He lifted her hand to his lips, a twinkle in his eyes. "Just doing my job, ma'am." He gently turned her hand over and placed a kiss in the middle of her palm as well.

She giggled. Maybe, with the business portion of the evening at an end, the pleasure was due to begin.

He raised one eyebrow and used his free hand to twirl an invisible moustache. "Come with me, my little chickadee."

She outright laughed this time. "Come with you where?" As if she didn't know.

"I have something to show you."

He stood and gently pulled her from her chair. He slipped his arms around her, pulling her close to nuzzle her neck, trailing kisses and gentle nibbles down her shoulder.

Just when she thought he might ravish her here on the kitchen floor, he scooped her up and carried her up the stairs to her bedroom.

"You've got to be kidding," she said, laughing.

"What is this, a fairytale?" She'd never been one of those women who dreamed of a prince to carry her off to his castle, but she could get used to this playful side of him.

He wiggled his eyebrows. "This is no fairytale, sister. You're mine." He chuckled, keeping his voice deep and somewhat sinister.

When they got to her bedroom door, he tilted his head toward the doorknob. "Do you mind? I have my hands full." He squeezed the body parts his hands were holding onto, and she giggled but opened the door.

Once in her room, he lowered her gently onto the bed and lay down next to her. Before he snuggled in, she quickly flipped him over, climbed on top, and began to have her way with him. The relief she'd felt at his news was replaced with desire and excitement as she ran her tongue up the side of his neck.

She laughed, adopted her worst French accent, and started unbuttoning his buttons. "Ah, *ma petit chou*, I think, in fact, you are mine."

****

Nearly an hour later, she lay snuggled with him under the silk comforter. When Marnie noticed the time, she said, "Do you mind if we try calling Carly again? I want to tell her about Sheri Jonas, so she can relax."

Scott reached down, snagged his jeans, and slid his phone out of the pocket. "No problem. Why don't you try her number while I try Nick?"

Climbing out of bed, she grabbed her pants, retrieved her phone, and then dove under the covers again. After punching in the number, she tapped her fingers on her leg, growing anxious as it rang and rang. It was unlike the girl not to answer, so she tried texting as well. Carly always answered a text, no matter what she was doing.

Until today.

Scott seemed to be having no more luck getting through to Nick. "Nothing," he said, as he put his phone on the nightstand. "You?"

"No." *Where could those kids be?*

"I don't like this. Nick always answers my calls, unless he's in class. I can't imagine where he'd be that he wouldn't at least send a 'call you later' text."

She ran through Carly's usual schedule in her mind but couldn't think of any reason the girl wouldn't at least text her.

"I agree. Something doesn't feel right about this."

She climbed out of bed and hurried to get dressed. He did the same, picking up his gun, badge, and phone from the nightstand. She'd have to get used to having a gun in her house.

Maybe they were worried for nothing. By the time they were back downstairs, the doorbell was ringing. Relief flooded her system, but before she could make the five steps to the door, someone began pounding on it as well.

"Coming," she yelled.

Scott jogged past her and looked out the windows at the top of the door before yanking it open.

Carly and Nick came racing in. The girl's eyes were red, her expression frantic. Nick's expression seemed like a cross between a worried father and a carsick kid. Whatever they'd come here to tell her wasn't gonna be good news. Luckily, Scott was here.

"Why haven't you been answering your phones?" Scott started in, as soon as the kids got in the door.

She put a hand on his arm. "What's wrong?" She turned from Carly to Nick and then, when they exchanged a scared expression, she pulled everyone into the living room. "Sit down and tell us what's going on." The hair on the back of her neck stood at attention. Something was very wrong.

The teens sat so close together on the couch, Carly was almost on Nick's lap. Her knuckles were white where she grasped his hand. When she started to speak, her chin quivered and her eyes filled with tears.

"I can't find Ashley and Deena. When I got home, they weren't there. My father said he hasn't seen them since they left for school. He thought they were with me. I've called everyone I can think of, but nobody's seen them. I..." She gulped, and the tears started in earnest.

Nick put his arm around Carly's shoulders, pulling her close, as if he could transfer his strength to her. "We think the baby-buying lady took them, or had the guy do it."

"Did they leave a note, send you a text, or call you?" Scott asked Carly.

Carly looked destroyed, and Marnie wanted to go out and find the girls right now. They had to be okay.

Her pulse quickened. "You haven't heard anything at all? Nothing was left at the house?"

The teen took a deep breath, her watery gaze meeting Marnie's. "Nothing," she managed before burying her face in Nick's shoulder.

He pulled out his phone and walked into the hallway, his voice low.

"Okay," Marnie said, just to have something to say while they waited for him to return. "Let's think this through. If Sheri Jonas, or someone working for her, took the girls, what's the next step?"

Nick's mouth straightened into a thin line. "What do you mean?" He raised his voice. "Are you kidding? She's threatening Carly. She doesn't want her talking to the cops, and this is supposed to shut her up."

She held up her hands, palms out. "Okay, Nick," she said, keeping her voice soft. "I understand that, but Sheri Jonas was arrested today."

Nicks eyebrows shot up. "What?"

Carly sat up straight. "She's in jail?"

She nodded.

"Then who has the girls? Oh, my God, they're going to kill my sisters." The teen started crying uncontrollably. Nick wrapped his arms around her and shot imaginary darts at Marnie with his gaze.

Scott came back into the living room, and Carly took a deep breath, stopped crying, and turned to him. Maybe he had good news...

He sat in the armchair opposite the teens.

"When was the last time you saw or talked to your sisters?"

Carly's eyes filled with tears again, and Marnie reached out a hand to her. Her heart was breaking for the teen.

"It's my fault. I...we...we came home from school together." She nodded at Nick, huddling closer to him. "Nick drove me and the girls to the house. We made dinner for Ashley and Deena, and..." The teen's voice broke, and she started crying in earnest.

Nick straightened up, turning to face Scott. "It's

my fault. I convinced Carly we could leave after the girls were asleep. We went for a drive."

Scott seemed to be sizing up the boy's answer. The kids had been reckless to leave the house at night, but it was a good sign that Nick was trying to protect Carly.

"I just called to check with the team who's assigned to watch your house, Carly, as it didn't make sense to me your sisters could be taken when there was a patrol watching, even if you weren't there."

He glanced at Marnie and then turned back to meet Carly's gaze. "They screwed up, obviously. One car followed you when the two of you left the house yesterday, and they called in to say another car needed to take their place at your house. The message was delayed, and when the second team got the message, they were told they weren't needed because you weren't at the house. It's our fault, entirely."

How could they leave the girls unprotected? Marnie's fear for the young sisters lodged in her stomach.

Nick puffed his chest out a bit, his jaw set, and his eyes narrowed. "What are you going to do about it, then?"

The relaxed, after-lovemaking look in Scott's eyes had been replaced by that of the intense, truth-seeking trooper. He leaned forward, looking Carly in the eye. "I understand how worried you both are about Ashley and Deena." He turned to stare down Nick. "But we all need to stay calm. We're going to do everything in our power to find the girls." The boy looked sick, but he pulled himself together, holding tightly onto his girlfriend.

Scott turned back to Carly. "We *will* find them. I promise."

Marnie believed him, and she thought Carly did, too. She couldn't look at him and miss the total determination in his eyes.

"Now, I need a recent picture of your sisters. The good news is, because we have Sheri Jonas in custody, we can lead her to believe she'll get a better deal on sentencing if she gives us the name of her accomplices and the location of the girls. If she's an accessory to kidnapping, she'll get an even longer sentence than she's already looking at."

Once the teen had texted a picture of her sisters to Scott, Marnie placed her hand on Carly's to ease the shaking. She tried to send strength to the girl through her touch. "Did your father have any idea what happened or when? Does he remember anything?"

Carly snorted. "He was plastered, as always, and only said he doesn't remember seeing the girls when he got home, so he thought they were with me." Her shoulders began to shake. "It's my fault. I wasn't there with them. I didn't protect them."

Nick shook his head. "If you'd been there, baby, they'd have taken you too."

"Nick's right." Marnie shuddered at the thought of all three sisters missing. "Those guys went into your house probably thinking they'd get all three of you, so you would definitely have been kidnapped as well." She squeezed the girl's arm.

"Those guys might have killed you all and made it look like a home invasion." While she didn't want to think about that possibility, she knew the kids needed to hear it, and she was thankful for Scott's authority.

"But you confused them by not being there, so they probably don't know what to do with the girls." His voice was low and calm. "Without being able to grab you, those guys are probably still trying to figure out what to do with them. You may have saved their lives."

Carly's big eyes were open wide, and she obviously wanted to believe what he said. Hopefully, it was true and the girls would be all right.

"I know it's late, but I'd like for us all to go to the station. We need to get an official statement in the record, from both of you." He turned from Nick to Carly. "I don't think we'll be too long, but we need to get things moving on the search. Okay?"

He glanced at Marnie, and she snapped into action. "Okay." Trying to distract the kids from their nerves, she clapped her hands. "Let's go, and then you'll come back and stay here." She wrapped her arm around the girl. "I don't want you taking any more chances by going home. They may come back and try to snatch you again." Hopefully, the teen couldn't feel how she was shaking herself.

Reaching out to Nick, she saw the fear in his eyes. "You're welcome to stay here as well, if it makes you more comfortable."

Not wanting to frighten Carly any more than necessary, she tried to convey her worry to Scott. Was it even possible Ashley and Deena were still alive? Her stomach was in knots, but she couldn't imagine how Carly was holding it together.

His gaze met hers. "Good idea. I'll stay here, too, to keep everybody safe." He turned to the teen. "I'll keep a patrol car out at your house, in case they try to come back, so we can protect your father and apprehend them in the act if they come looking for you again."

Carly's face was pale and streaky as she clung to Nick's side. Marnie wanted to both wrap the kids in her safe embrace and lose herself in Scott's.

The kids headed to the door while she grabbed her coat and purse. When she stepped outside with Scott and started toward his Jeep, the kids had stopped by Nick's truck. The trained trooper was the first to react when the shooting started.

"Get down!" Before she could think, Scott pushed her body to the ground. The loose gravel on the driveway caught on her elbow as the musky warmth of Scott's body protected her from harm.

Although she didn't know where it came from, she was relieved to see a gun in his right hand.

"The kids are hiding behind Nick's truck." Scott's whisper in her ear kept her from jumping back up to find the teens. "They're closer to the front door, so they may be able to get back into the house."

If only the door wasn't locked. Would she be able to throw them the keys? Where did she even drop her purse? "I don't know where the keys are."

Shots were still being fired. Trusting he was looking out for the kids, she burrowed her face into his chest and prayed for them all.

As if by magic, he reached out and pulled her purse toward them.

"Thanks." Sliding her hand down inside, she grasped the keys and stuffed them into her jeans pocket.

Somehow, Scott had the presence of mind to pull

out his cell and call the station. "Shots fired." He rattled off her address and identified himself as a plain-clothes officer on the scene before stuffing his phone back in his pocket.

"Keep those keys out." He started to lift off her. "And maybe fish out the garage door opener, too."

He raised up slightly and looked at her briefly. "I want you to run back to the kids. I'll cover you."

Tension seeped through her limbs, and her mouth filled with cotton. "You'll cover me?"

After giving her a quick kiss, he nodded. "You'll be okay. I want you to keep low and run as fast as you can back to Nick's truck. Once you're safely there, I'll join you. And we'll move back into the house."

Words wouldn't come. Her brain didn't work, so she just stared at him.

"You'll be okay. Trust me."

Trust him? She didn't have to think twice—of course she trusted him. She could do this. Grabbing his shirt front, she planted a kiss on his lips, and then released him. "I trust you."

As he eased off her, she rolled over and lifted up to a crouch. "What do I do?"

"Keep your head down and run as fast as you can to the kids. If I don't join you there or you don't hear sirens in five minutes, get into the house and call the station again."

If he didn't join them? Did that mean if he was shot? Icy fear flooded her veins. He needed to keep them safe but keep himself safe, too.

"Okay, go!"

Keeping her head down and staying as low as possible, she ran to the Jeep.

The next shot came zinging while she was out in the open for a brief moment, between the cover of the two vehicles, but she heard Scott returning fire. Not able to breathe until she was safely behind the truck, relief flooded her when she reached Carly's outstretched arms.

When she looked back at Scott, he was back behind his Jeep and gave her the thumbs up.

"Do you want me to open the garage door?" Keeping her voice low, she pulled the remote from her purse, holding it up for him to see.

From his spot behind the Jeep, he checked his watch. "Backup should be here in about two minutes."

The way her heart was racing, two minutes might as well be an eternity.

Inching closer, he nodded and gestured toward the house. "Yeah, open the garage door, and all of you run for the house door inside, keeping your car between you and the shooter. I'll cover you as you run. When you get in the house, stay low and away from the windows."

Nick blanched. "What about you, dude?"

"Yeah." She looked into Scott's eyes. "Shouldn't we stay together?" They all had to come out of this safe. She couldn't lose him now.

"I'm going to stay out here to wait for the uniforms to arrive and to keep the shooter away from the house." He slid the door of the Jeep open and pulled out his bulletproof vest, wiggling into it. "I can hold off the shooter if he tries to make his way to you guys, but I can't be worried about the three of you at the same time." He peered around the end of the Jeep. "Nick, make sure Marnie, Carly, and the baby are safe."

Nick nodded, his scared teenager expression replaced with the determination and authority of a man of responsibility.

"Okay, go ahead, but don't let the door go all the way up." Scott's whisper was calm and authoritative, but it cut a path of fear down her spine.

Holding her breath, she clicked the remote and the garage door started to rise. Once it was high enough for them to slip under, she stopped it. Urging the kids in front of her, she crouched down and ran through the opening, the barrage of gunfire given and returned ringing in her ears.

The shots rang out but didn't hit the house or them. Following the teens, she raced to the door leading from the garage to the house, her heart pounding and her body covered in cold sweat. How could Scott live through this and get up and go back to work the next day to do it all again?

Once they were all inside, she closed the door and pulled the kids into the laundry room, an inside space with the only windows at the top of the wall. "You need to sit down, sweetie. You don't want to start bleeding again."

Carly's face was white as a ghost already, but Nick murmured in her ear and got her to sit down. He wrapped his arms around her and she leaned into him.

Impressed by his maturity in this crazy situation, Marnie patted him on the shoulder and left them in the laundry room while she crawled out to the living room so she could unlock the front door and also listen to the battle outside. Her pulse pounded in her ears, but she took some deep breaths. *Was he okay out there?*

Was there more than one shooter? Where were the police?

Sirens came blasting from both directions. She closed her eyes for a moment, relief flooding her senses. At least Scott had some backup out there now. It was impossible to distinguish anything above the sound of the sirens, but at least she wasn't hearing gunshots now. She hoped that meant the worst was over and Scott would walk through the door any minute.

After five minutes of waiting, she had almost no fingernails left. *Where was he?* Crawling to the windows and keeping her head down, she peeked out under the curtain. No sight of Scott. As she pulled the curtain back down, the door to the garage banged open.

Scott stood in the doorway.

No blood. No blood was always best.

"He's down. It's over."

Running and launching herself into his arms, crying and smiling, she kissed every inch of face she could reach. "I was so scared," she said, shaking in his arms.

He rubbed her back and murmured into her ear. "I was afraid, too. I couldn't bear it if something happened to you or the kids." He looked around. "Where are they?"

Grabbing his hand, she led him down the hall. "I put them in the laundry room because there's no line of sight from outside." As she pushed open the laundry room door, she sent up a silent prayer that they all were safe.

Nick and Carly jumped as she opened the door,

both blanching, but then relaxed when they saw Scott.

"Is it over?" asked Nick.

"Yes and no." He helped Carly to her feet, and she leaned on Nick as they walked back to the living room.

"What do you mean, yes and no?" Marnie asked.

When they sat, he gazed at Carly, meeting her worried stare. "The shooter was stopped and, well, he's dead. He won't be able to hurt you anymore."

She tried to stand up, but Nick kept hold of her. "What?"

Carly stood, panic covering her face. "What if he was the one that took the girls? How can you find them if you killed their kidnapper? What were you thinking?" Tears continued to run down her worried face.

He leaned in. "The man we shot is not the man from the sketch. This is a third person. The man from the sketch is still out there, and I believe he has your sisters."

Scott glanced at Marnie and then back to Carly. Marnie reached out to rub the girl's back, hoping to calm the rising panic.

"We'll use what we know and what we can learn about this guy to gather more information to pressure Sheri Jonas. She's going to give us the name of the man you saw and where he's keeping the girls." Standing, he slid his hands into his jacket pockets. "It's just a matter of time."

Did the girls have time? Carly couldn't handle the guilt if anything happened to her sisters. She'd surely lose the baby as well.

Marnie ached to keep them all safe. Wrapping her

arm tight around the teen's slender shoulders, she prayed that Scott and his team would be able to find the girls and get to them in time.

Chapter Thirteen

After Scott left and the crime scene techs and
uniformed officers had cleared the scene, Marnie and
the kids again sat in the living room.

"How can he be so sure Sheri Jonas is going to
give him the name of the man in the car? And that
once he has the name, he'll be able to find the girls
and bring them home safely?"

Still shaking and pale, Carly was bundled in a
warm blanket, wrapped in Nick's arms on the couch,
and nursing a cup of tea. Every ten minutes or so, she
would start asking the same questions over again.

"Babe…" Nick rubbed his hand on her back and
placed a kiss on her head. "Take it easy."

Staring at Marnie, silently demanding answers,
the girl rested her head on his shoulder. She had dark
circles under tired eyes, and her skin was pale and
waxy.

"Sweetie." Marnie collapsed in the armchair
opposite the couch, leaning forward with her elbows
resting on her thighs. "We talked about this. You've
got to trust Scott and his officers to take care of it.
They know what they're doing."

"But…" The girl started to wind herself up again.
Nick pulled her in tighter, never leaving her side or
dismissing her. Marnie couldn't help but be proud of
the way he was really showing himself to be more

mature than the average seventeen-year-old boy.

She stood and walked closer, perching on the edge of the coffee table and putting her hands around Carly's on the mug of tea. This girl was so strong, so special. There was nothing Marnie wouldn't do for her, but right now there was nothing she could do but pray the girls got home safely.

"I know how scary this has been for all of us, especially you. When Scott finds your sisters, you're going to want to be strong and rested enough to see them." Her gaze met Nick's briefly as he nodded. "The most important thing for you to do right now is to take care of yourself and your baby. You need to drink your tea, try to eat something, and then get some rest."

"I can't..." Carly interrupted.

She reached out and cupped the teen's cheek. "You don't have to fall asleep, but you need to lie down. You're going to end up on bed rest again, or worse. Why don't you and Nick go back to your room, and I'll bring in a couple of sandwiches and some water bottles. You can lie down, watch a show, relax. I'll come get you the moment I hear anything from him."

The pregnant teen didn't easily give up the fight, but her body couldn't continue to hold out. Murmuring her agreement, she wrapped the blanket more tightly around herself. She almost crumpled when she tried to stand, so Nick scooped her up and carried her to the bedroom. While he got her settled, Marnie went to the kitchen to make sandwiches.

When she carried a tray into the bedroom, the mother-to-be was already starting to nod off. Nick's gaze met Marnie's, and he held one finger to his lips, indicating she should be quiet. She placed the tray on the table where Nick could reach it, adjusted the covers, and tiptoed back to the door. From there she spied on the two of them for a moment, Nick taking such good care of Carly, and she smiled, despite everything they'd been through that day.

She stepped into the hall and pulled the door closed, then returned to the kitchen. Deciding to take her own advice, she made one more turkey sandwich, pulled out a diet cola, and sat at the table. If she were a hundred years old, she couldn't be more tired than she was after everything they'd been through that day.

With her phone at her side, in case Scott called or texted her, she opened her laptop. She realized she should email her parents that she was okay, in case they heard about the shooting.

After she sent off a quick message, she scanned her work email, for something she could do to keep busy and occupy her mind. An email popped up from an unfamiliar address in her inbox. A chill rippled down her spine. She had a response from the adoption website.

She clicked on the email.

Dear Flower Child,

Or should I say Marnie. What a pretty name. I have been searching for you so long. It's wonderful to finally have a name, to know where you are, to be able to talk to you.

Her mouth went dry. Could this be real? Grabbing her diet cola, she took a sip. Both anxious to read on and afraid not to stop, she took a deep breath and braced for what lay ahead.

When you were born, the whole thing was so overwhelming. You came early, and there was nowhere to go, no way to get to the hospital. The VW was the best option. Thank God, the police officer found you when he did.

No one ever planned to desert you; it just happened. I'm so glad you have great parents and have had a great life, but I'm hoping I can be a part of your life.

Can we meet? I have so much to tell you, and I'm sure you have questions. Please, I know you don't owe me a thing, but please agree to meet me anyway. Maybe at Minnie's Diner, late in the evening, like nine p.m., after the dinner crowd thins out. I really want to see you, talk to you, try to explain. Call or email to let me know if you agree and, if so, what day.

Ann

She stared at the screen, running over and over the lines of the email. It didn't feel real. Her mouth went dry and there was a sour taste in the corners of her mouth. She took a swallow of diet cola.

Ann.

Was Ann her mother? The email wasn't explicit, though Ann was clearly talking about her. There was no confusion about that.

Even if Ann wasn't the woman Marnie was looking for, she knew something about it all. She had to meet with her.

Should she go alone? She wanted Scott to be with her, but this wasn't the time. With the girls still missing and Carly and Nick sleeping in her spare bedroom, who knew when the time would be right? Her first priority was the safety of the kids.

She couldn't risk losing the chance to meet with Ann, but it had to wait.

She picked up the phone and dialed Kate, but it went straight to voicemail, so she hung up. She wanted to blow off steam, to explore her options, to rant and wail, and who better to listen to her through all of that but her friend?

Looking down at her computer, she realized it was Sunday afternoon. Kate taught a self-defense class at the Youth Center on Sunday afternoons.

She started to type a reply, but really, what could she say to her maybe birth mother? Her brain was starting to shut down, whether from stress, exhaustion, or overwork. Pulling it together as best she could, she searched for the right words.

Ann, thank you for your email and for responding to my post. I didn't know I was adopted until recently, but if you've been searching for me, thank you.

I would like to meet at Minnie's, but…

What to say? How could she explain what was going on right now?

Marnie glanced around the kitchen, her anxiety an itch she couldn't scratch, a hunger she couldn't feed. She stood up and walked to the bedroom, listening at the door. Nothing but the low murmur of the TV. Hopefully, Carly was napping. It'd be good if Nick got some sleep, too.

Avoiding the email but unable to sit, she walked to the living room, stopping at the front windows. She closed her eyes, not willing to relive those moments of terror as of yet. Continuing into the dining room and back around to the kitchen, she found herself staring at the computer.

Her heart was racing again, although not from the stroll around her house. How could she possibly explain the last couple of weeks, or the last forty-five years, in an email or a single meeting?

She picked up her phone, put it down, sat down, and picked up the phone again.

She couldn't call Scott. He was in the midst of a real crisis. They were all waiting to hear what Sheri Jonas had to say, where the girls were being held, whether he found them, and if they were safe. That was what was important right now.

Not that finding out the identity of her birth mother wasn't important.

If she was being honest, it was incredibly important. It wasn't a crisis and couldn't compare to what happened to Ashley and Deena, but it was important, nonetheless. She needed to know, needed to learn as much as she could about the circumstances of her birth and the people who had created her.

She checked her phone, still in her hand, and before she thought it through, called the winery. Maybe talking it out with Tina would bring some clarity.

"Hello. Davis Winery. How may I help you?"

She took a deep breath. "Hi…" she started, but paused. Was it Tina she wanted to talk to? She shook her head.

"Can I please speak to Matt?"

****

After leaving the kids with Marnie at her house, with a patrol car parked out front, Scott soon pulled into the parking lot at the State Police barracks, jumped from the car, and hurried into the bullpen.

Jack must have left Harper's Glen the minute the call came in, as he'd beat him to Horseheads and currently sat in one of the guest chairs in his office. Sheriff Chris Hoy had not yet arrived from Watkins Glen, but he was happy for the chance to talk to his friend privately.

"You okay, dude?" asked Jack.

He took off his leather jacket and hung it on the hook on the back of his office door before rounding his desk to take a seat.

"Yeah, I'm good. The only casualty was the perp."

"And he wasn't the guy in the sketch, right?"

"Right," he replied. "He was younger, blond, and skinny. Definitely not the guy Carly saw in the car."

Jack turned to him. "Did she confirm it?"

His stomach took a little turn. "Nick was pissed, but I needed to make sure he was not the guy she saw in the car." That girl was exhausted, sick with worry, and pregnant, but she pulled off the identification better than most adults. Nick held her hand the whole time.

"Okay. What now?"

He leaned back, lacing his fingers behind his head. "I've been going 'round and 'round in my head, but I want to bounce my ideas off you and Chris Hoy, so we're all on the same page here. We have to find out where the girls are and, to do that, Sheri Jonas has to tell us who is holding them and where he would take them. How do we get her to talk?"

Jack rested his chin in his palm. "Do we have any idea who this guy is, or at least who he is to Jonas?"

"I think I can help."

He swiveled to the door where Schuyler County Sheriff Chris Hoy filled the doorway, in full uniform, jacket, and hat.

"Thanks for coming, Chris." He stood, stepping around his desk to shake the man's hand. "Take a seat." With luck, the sheriff would have insights or updates to move this investigation along.

"Thanks, Scott." As Hoy seated himself in the other visitor chair, Jack rose slightly and shook his hand. "Finelli."

Scott returned to his chair, sat, and leaned forward on his elbows. "So what do you have for us?" *Please don't let it be bad news.*

"You asked me to find whatever I could on Sheri Jonas, so I got a couple of my investigators working on it. I have one gal who is a whiz with computers, and she did some deep digging." He paused, glancing from Jack to Scott.

"And…" He tried not to sound as exasperated as he truly was when the sheriff paused for dramatic effect.

Chris smiled. "Did you know she had a son?"

"Ah," said Jack.

Scott cradled his chin with his left hand and said, "Do you have a name or age or anything?"

"The son is thirty-three, and his name is Brandon. There's some debate about his legal last name, but I found a lapsed DMV registration for a 1997 brown Buick LeSabre in the name of Brandon Lynch."

He furiously took notes. "And you have reason to believe Brandon Lynch is Sheri Jonas's son?"

Chris nodded. "Yup. We found a record of a birth at Arnot Hospital in 1984 in the name of Brandon J.

Lynch, where the father's name is listed as Edward Lynch, although there's no record of Lynch ever claiming Brandon or accepting paternity. The mother is listed as Sheri O'Keefe."

Scott massaged his forehead. A bone-deep weariness was warring with his drive to find Ashley and Deena and bring them home. "Is Sheri O'Keefe the woman we know as Sheri Jonas?"

Chris pulled a few sheets of paper out of his jacket pocket, unfolding them on the table. "Yep. She was born Sheri Lyndon in Sayre, PA. She married and divorced O'Keefe pretty young, before moving to Schuyler County. Lynch wasn't married to her at all, but she listed him as the father on the birth certificate. Sometime later, she must've married Jonas, or at least taken his name. He died, and she hasn't married again, from what we could find."

"Great," said Scott. "Do you have a current address or location for this son?" It made sense to him that the Jonas woman would have someone she trusted as a partner in such a long-running criminal enterprise. He hadn't found any son in his search, but hadn't uncovered her other names to search under, either. That was why inter-county cooperation was so useful.

Chris shook his head. "That's where it gets tricky. We haven't found anything on Brandon Lynch since his car registration and driver's license lapsed almost ten years ago. No address, current driver's license, registration, employment, or military records. But we found a picture of him from his freshman year in high school."

Jack glanced up. "Where did he go to school? Was he in Watkins Glen?"

"Nope. We couldn't find any records after he was pulled out of Thomas A. Edison High School in Elmira Heights at the end of his freshman year."

"Do you have the picture?" asked Scott.

Chris handed over several sheets of the printer paper. "We printed off the picture for you as well as an age-progression of what he should look like now at thirty-three, which seems pretty damn close to your sketch."

Scott spread the papers out in front of him, and Jack came around the desk to peer over his shoulders. The resemblance was close enough. He looked at Chris. "Did you get an arrest warrant, or should I?"

The sheriff shook his head. "It's your investigation, your collar, so I thought you'd want to do it."

"Thanks. I'll have one of my investigators move on it while we go talk to his mama." Scott was already gathering up the papers and walking toward the door. "I'm going back into the interview with Sheri Jonas. If either of you, or both of you, want to join me, come on."

The two sheriffs followed him out of the office as he strode to the interview room, his jaw clenched and his palms damp. He was too close, wanted this too much, and couldn't afford to mess it up.

He stopped to ask one of his investigators to obtain a warrant and distribute copies of the yearbook photo. When he walked into the interview room, where Sheri Jonas had been cooling her heels and building up steam since they'd picked her up the previous night, she crossed her skinny arms over her chest and leaned back in her chair.

He had to control his temper with her, not lose sight of the end game, the goal of getting the girls home alive. He could rely on Jack and Chris to give him time to cool off if this got too close, too personal. After all, someone working with this woman had tried to kill him, as well as Nick, Carly, and Marnie. Hard not to take it personally.

"'Bout time you got your butt in here, Mr. State Trooper. I ain't got all day to sit in here."

She stood and took a step toward the door.

"Sit down," Scott barked. "You're not going anywhere."

Jack and Chris leaned against the wall, each on an opposite side of the door, arms crossed over their chests like a couple of samurai in khaki. He pulled out a seat at the table, spun it around, and took a seat facing the old woman.

Her mousy brown hair, heavily threaded with gray, fell lifeless and lanky around her wrinkled face.

The first picture he pulled out was of the dead perp, taken at Marnie's house. "Sorry to tell you this genius got himself killed."

The baby seller looked down at the picture, relief filling her eyes. She blinked it away and regrouped. "What do I care about him?"

Excellent. This one wasn't her son. That meant he was still alive and he, most likely, had the girls.

"Wow, cold." He turned to glance at Jack and then Chris. "Glad she's not my boss, aren't you, fellas?"

"Sure am," Jack said.

"Me, too," echoed Chris.

"Boss?"

The old hag tried to widen her eyes, making like

she was surprised, but more than likely nothing had really surprised her in years. "I ain't nobody's boss. I don't know that kid."

He stared her down. "Sure, sure. How about this one?"

He slid over the sketch of Brandon.

The seasoned criminal was ready this time, already shaking her head before she looked at the picture. "Nope. No idea."

He whistled. "Wow," he said, as he shook his head. "Not mother of the year, are you, Sheri?"

A hint of true surprise showed in her eyes, but she seemed to shake it off. "Mother? How unkind of you to tease me. It's a source of great sadness for me that I've never been a mother."

She pasted a patently fabricated sadness on her face. He paused, letting her lie stand. It was cat-and-mouse getting a suspect to give up their secrets, to hang themselves, but a game he usually enjoyed. This time, though, he just wanted to grab her neck and shake until the truth fell out.

After a few moments, he pulled out the copies he had of Brandon's birth certificate, her birth certificate and various marriage licenses, his car registration, old driver's license, high school photo, and the age progression photo and lined them up next to the sketch.

Sheri's eyes went wide before she could catch herself.

"Your sweet baby boy will not be happy to hear you regret not being able to be a mother, since you've had thirty-three years to be a mother to your son. Were you *so* bad at it, Sheri?"

Jack and Chris chuckled behind him, but he maintained a straight face.

"I...I don't know why you're showing all this stuff to me." The old bat pushed the papers away. "I don't know any Brandon and don't have any children. You've gotten me mixed up with someone else."

She wasn't as good a liar as she should be, for all the years she'd been practicing. Nobody had mentioned the name Brandon, and she hadn't given the papers in front of her anything but a passing glance, looking more at the table than at the words. Apparently she had taken in the photos, though.

Just a little bit further. He could feel it and almost laughed out loud with anticipation. They had to push a little harder, but she was going to turn on sonny boy.

He stood and leaned close, his face only inches from hers. "Cut the crap. We know Brandon is your son. He is holding the two girls. Whether or not you told him to kidnap them isn't the point, at this stage."

She started to answer, "I didn't tell nobody..."

"Shut up," he yelled, as he slammed his hand on the table. He had to keep her off center; not give her time to think up more lies.

"What matters now is if anything happens to those two little girls, you are *both* going to prison for the rest of your natural lives. But if *you* help us now, tell us where he has the girls, the District Attorney will take it into consideration when it comes to your sentence."

"I've been in here for nearly two days already. I don't know what you're talking about." She folded her arms and leaned back in her chair. "I couldn't possibly have anything to do with any girls being kidnapped."

Again he slammed his hand on the table, and she

jumped in her chair. Hoping to scare her, he enjoyed the chance to hit something. He needed the outlet for the steam building inside him.

"If you keep lying to me, I'm leaving, and you have no chance at a deal. We'll lock you up and throw away the key."

He gazed deep into her eyes, seeing the hesitation mixed with the lies she was trying to get past him. She must have been able to see how serious he was, how immune he was to her story, because panic started to flood her face. A bead of sweat ran down her hairline. She'd realized the predicament she was in and might be ready to turn on her boy.

He stood up, turned to the door, and started toward it. "Come on, guys. We're out of here. The Feds are waiting for her. After all these years, and more counts of kidnapping than I could even count, they're throwing the book at her."

Jack and Chris turned to go.

"Wait!" Sheri called out in a thin, whiny voice. "What do you mean, Feds?"

He paused but did not turn around. "Kidnapping's a federal crime, Sheri." He bumped Jack's arm with his elbow. "The Feds still have the death penalty, don't they?" He forced out a laugh. "Too bad, Sheri. I guess you won't have to worry about how you get treated in prison, after all."

He walked out of the room with Jack and Chris on his heels, stopping at the two-way mirror. Sheri was the one pounding the table now. The curses coming out of her mouth would put a dockworker to shame.

He had to be patient, although it was the last thing he wanted to do. She was close to caving, he could feel it, but she needed to think she was at the end of her rope.

Within five minutes, she stopped ranting and sank into a chair. "Okay, okay, okay." She let out a breath, sounding like she carried the world on her shoulders. "Brandon's mine, the dumb shit."

Jack slapped him on the back. "Got her!"

Relief flooded through Scott, who took a deep breath and then went back into the interview room, both sheriffs right behind him.

She looked like she was eating a lemon, her haggard face awash in panic.

"Only that imbecile Jimmy was dumber than Brandon, so together they had the sense of a flea." She pushed the picture of the dead body in Marnie's driveway back toward him and picked up the age progression photo of Brandon. "I can't believe those idiots took those little girls. What the hell did they think they were doing?"

Her cavalier attitude infuriated him, but he reminded himself that everything she said was on tape. She wouldn't be able to change her story. "They didn't take the teenage girl, did they?" she asked.

"No." He saw Marnie's face in his mind, could only imagine how her panic would have intensified, Nick's too, if Carly had been home when the kidnappers got there.

Sheri shook her head, her gaze filled with resignation. "The little girls ain't got nothing to do with any of this. What a couple of dumb shits."

Holding back the laughter that threatened to spill out with shouts of triumph, he willed his mouth into a thin line.

"Where would Brandon take the girls? If he hurts them, we'll never stop looking for him. He has to know it. Where is he?"

She sat as still as a statue, her eyes not tearing but frightened. "If I tell you, you're gonna make me a deal? I give you Brandon and then I get to go home?"

What a piece of shit she was. Throwing her kid under the bus to save herself.

"Heartless, aren't you, Sheri?"

This time, she laughed, although it was almost a cackle. "Why should I care about that dumb jerk? If I don't look out for me, who else is gonna do it? Every man I've ever known thought of nothin' but himself, from my father to all those worthless husbands to this idiot Brandon."

He thought she might just spit on the floor, but instead she pounded on the table again. "It's every man and, especially, every woman for hisself, that's what I say. Nobody cares about me but me. So make me a deal."

Again, Jack and Chris barked out a laugh, but he didn't smile in the least. "You won't be going home, Sheri, not under any circumstances. But if you help us, give us Brandon's location and help us find the girls, I'll put in a good word for you with the District Attorney. That's the best I can offer, but it'll count in your favor."

Her eyes narrowed. "But if I don't help you, those girls might die, so I should get off for that, you know, saving a couple of kids."

Deliberately taking a deep breath to steady the rage building within him, he stared directly into her eyes. "You have engaged in child trafficking for the past forty years, Sheri." He held up his hand, cutting off her attempt at justification. "You can tell me how you gave babies to loving couples who couldn't adopt through traditional means, but you *sold* those babies. And you may have been selling them to child molesters, pornographers, serial murderers, or anyone else. All you cared about was making a buck."

"But…"

He slammed his hand one more time. "Stop! I don't want to hear it. You can't weasel out of what we have on you, so you might as well try and redeem yourself, both with the Feds and the god of your choice, by finally saving the lives of a couple of kids."

She opened her mouth, stared at him, and closed her mouth again, saying nothing. Her eyes were red, and there were tears in them. She must finally have grasped her situation.

"He's probably at my old house. Up on the hill above the swamp. We kept babies there over the years, you know, before placing them with a family." Her voice took on a more cultured tone on the last part of the statement, as if she had slipped into her sales pitch.

"Where's the house?" This was Jack's first question. The swamp was on the border between Schuyler and Stevens counties, so it could be in either jurisdiction.

Sheri's eyes narrowed, and her gaze darted to him. "A guy I shacked up with for a while had a house up on the east hill. He tied one on and drove hisself into a tree. When he passed, no one come to kick me out, so I stayed."

"I need an address." Scott kept his voice as hard as steel as he stood over her. "How do we get there?"

She glanced down at the table. "Okay, okay, okay. It's the first left off Rock Cabin Road." She recited the address.

"Lay it out for me. Can he see me approach, from the house? Are there any outbuildings? Where exactly will the girls be?"

Jack handed him a tablet with a map of the area pulled up on it. He shoved it in front of Sheri. "Show me."

She pointed to a small driveway. "If you pull up the drive all the way to the house, he could see you, unless he's in the basement. That's where he'll have the girls. We kept all them babies down in the basement." She glanced at him, her gaze eager for approval. He stared at her, stone-faced.

"So you gotta stop about here." She indicated on the map. "Walk the rest of the way along the trees on the side of the drive. There's a storm door into the basement on the back side of the house." She added a few more details before he had enough information and was ready to go into action.

He grabbed the tablet, slapped the cover shut, gathered up all the paperwork, rose, and turned toward the door.

"That's it, right?" she asked, her expression like a dog waiting for treat. "I done right by ya and those girls, didn't I? You're gonna tell the District Attorney, right?"

He turned back briefly. "We'll see what happens when we get to the house."

The three men filed out the door, leaving her there to stew some more, and a uniformed officer stepped up to guard the door.

"Thanks," Scott said, and walked quickly to his office. When he turned back to face Jack and Chris, he said, "Either of you want to ride with me, or are you driving yourself?"

Each man drove separately, heading out with two teams of investigators. Jack had already called to arrange for some uniformed officers to meet them there. The house rested in Stevens County rather than Schuyler, so it was his jurisdiction.

Just before he climbed into his car, Scott murmured, "Please let those girls be alive."

****

Scott drove lead up the driveway, with Jack directly behind him, followed by Chris Hoy and then cars from several different law enforcement agencies. He stopped at the bend, where Sheri Jonas had told him to stop, and waited for the others to catch up with him before going in on foot.

His heart was pounding, but in a good way. Focusing on his goal, he had a great team and was ready to go. They were going to find Brandon, and if Sheri had been telling the truth, Ashley and Deena were still alive.

The brown car sat in the driveway. He motioned to two of the uniformed officers to stand guard on the car as he led the way along the tree line to the back yard. Each hair on the back of his neck was on end. He was so close.

The house was dark from the front, but as they circled around to the back, a dim light came from what Sheri had told them would be the kitchen window. He stopped to watch for someone moving around inside.

Brandon was nowhere in sight but was likely

310

somewhere inside, armed but alone.

Scott stood next to Jack and Chris in front of the metal doors covering the steps to the basement while uniformed officers encircled the house. No sound was coming from inside. Sheri had given them the key to the doors, so once they were unlocked, he gave the signal, and the sheriffs yanked them open.

Those two officers relayed the signal around the house, and officers broke through the front and back doors and into the main floor of the house at the same time.

Once the doors were breached, he couldn't wait a moment longer. Those little girls had to be in that basement. He needed to make this case a win, for Carly, Nick, and Marnie. For Ashley and Deena. For all of them.

Scott and Jack were the first down the steps and through the interior door. He went left and Jack had agreed to go right, with Chris and the first of the uniformed officers directly behind them. The doors opened into the back of the basement, a large unfinished area. Two empty cribs were jammed against the walls to the right, with two more on the left.

An old stench of sour milk and dirty diapers made him gag, but he pushed through. The stairs leading to the main floor of the house separated this room from the rest of the basement.

The girls, curled up on a dingy mattress on the floor, started crying the minute they spied their rescuers. His breath came back in a rush, and he felt a cool trickle of sweat run down his spine.

They were alive.

The girls were both wearing their nightgowns, and no shoes. Faces streaked with tears, they had no obvious bruises or blood, but duct tape restricted their movement and kept them from talking.

His finger over his lips, he crouched down on the mattress to remove the tape over their mouths. "Are you all right?" he whispered.

They nodded, sniffling.

"Good." He smiled at them. "Are you alone or is there a man here?"

Ashley nodded toward the far side of the basement. Her eyes were solemn, encircled in red, her face pale.

"These policemen are going to take you outside, girls, and help you get the rest of the tape off. You're safe now."

Two officers came forward, picked up the barefoot girls despite the silent tears running down their faces, and carried them outside.

Then Scott signaled that Brandon was in the front of the basement. This guy had a thing for guns, from what his mother had said. Scott had to find a way to get to him without getting someone killed.

Sheri had told them there was a bathroom, a utility room, and a laundry area on the other side of the stairs. He signaled to turn on their flashlights, then turned off the overhead light at a switch by the stairs. He rounded the bottom of the staircase, taking in what must have been the bathroom door to the left, the boiler, water heater, and various pipes along the far wall, and the washer and dryer on the right.

The cool calm of training kicked in, allowing him to visualize a solution. The loser had to be in the john, which could be the best break they'd had.

He went toward the closed bathroom door, with Jack on his right. Chris came around to stand in front of the boiler, followed by several officers. After silently counting down from three on his fingers, he motioned to Jack, who kicked in the bathroom door.

Brandon Lynch sat on the toilet, pants around his ankles, a sports magazine in his hands. As the door banged off the wall behind it, he looked up startled, dropped the magazine, and fumbled with his pants.

Scott charged through the doorway into the small room, pointing his gun at the kidnapper's crotch. "Don't even think about it, Lynch."

Jack darted in, pulled the idiot's pants away from him, and fished out a gun. "We'll take this off your hands there, Brandon."

Scott leveled his gun in the surprised face. "Brandon Lynch, you are under arrest. On your feet."

"My pants!" Brandon turned from Scott to Jack. "Gimme my pants, bro."

Jack turned to Scott, who grabbed the perp's arm, pulling him to his feet. "Should I give him back his pants?"

Scott nodded. "I think you'd better. I don't want his bare bony ass sitting in one of our squad cars."

Jack chuckled. "I guess you're right."

Pulling his prisoner through the bathroom door and into the center of the room, Scott read him his rights. While all the officers watched, he motioned to his friend, who thoroughly searched the missing pants and removed a cell phone and the belt before handing them over.

"Dude, my phone?" Brandon held out his hand.

Scott snorted. This guy really was clueless. Thank God he hadn't done more damage.

"Not a chance, 'dude,'" said Jack, smirking.

Once the moron had put on and zipped up his pants, Scott yanked the kidnapper's arms behind him and slapped on the cuffs.

"You got nothin' on me," Brandon yelled. "I didn't do nothin'."

He met his gaze. "Your mother already told us everything. We know you kidnapped those two girls in the other room."

The prisoner swallowed hard, his Adam's apple bobbing up and down. Maybe he'd thought his mommy would protect him.

Giving him another yank on his arm, Scott continued. "And we know about years of trafficking in babies and children. You're going away for a long time."

"She blamed it on me?" He looked from Scott to Jack to Chris. "Seriously? She started doing it years ago, before I was even born."

Scott loved it when the criminals turned on each other. "Tell it to the judge, Lynch."

"No, no, it's true." Brandon talked fast. "Just…" He jerked his head around, trying to meet Jack's gaze. "Look upstairs. There's a laptop hidden under a loose plank in the living room. I recorded everything. You'll see it's her business, not mine."

Bingo. Scott had hoped they'd find some hard evidence to use against the pair of them, something beyond their mutual accusations.

"Okay, we'll see about that."

He yanked the scrawny arm of the criminal,

pulling the idiot through the basement and out the back steps, passing him off to one of the uniformed officers to secure in the back of a squad car. He pulled out his phone and called the forensic team, who waited back on the main road.

While he went to find the girls, the forensics van was already pulling up the driveway and into the back yard. An ambulance followed the van, stopping at the top of the drive. He was able to take another deep breath, knowing the girls were safe and the baby-trafficking ring was shut down. He closed his eyes for the briefest of moments, sending up a silent prayer of thanks.

When he got to the spot where two officers waited with Ashley and Deena, Scott knelt down, gently taking one small chilly hand of each girl.

"Are you going to lock him up?"

"Where's the skinny man?"

"When can we go home?"

"Where's Carly?"

He laughed. "Hold on there, girls. Only one question at a time."

The younger sister raised her wide and tear-filled eyes to him. "When will she be here?"

"Now, which sister are you? Carly talks about the two of you so much, I feel like I already know you."

She looked very solemn. "I'm Deena." Pointing to her sister, she continued, "She's Ashley. Where's Carly?"

He pulled the little girl closer, wrapping his left arm around her, still holding Ashley's hand with his right one. "You girls are safe now. The people behind this won't hurt you anymore. She's waiting for you at her friend Marnie's house, so once the EMTs check you over, we can go see her. She'll be so glad to see you two."

Ashley gave him a mature and worried look. "What about these guys? Brandon and Jimmy? What's going to happen to them?"

He squeezed her hand. "How did you know their names, honey?"

The girl shrugged. "They aren't very smart, are they? They argued so much, we could hear almost everything they said."

"No," he said, chuckling. "They aren't very smart. We already took care of Jimmy, and Brandon is on his way to jail. So don't you worry. He'll be behind bars for a long time."

Her big chocolate eyes filled with tears. "What about my father? Is he with Carly?"

His lips tightened, wishing again he'd been able to talk to the man. What kind of father was so out of it when his daughters were in so much trouble?

"Uh, no. He's waiting at your house. He wanted to be there in case you somehow escaped and made it home, so someone would be waiting for you."

He wasn't sure she believed him, but she let it go.

At the ambulance, he asked the EMTs to give the girls a thorough exam. While waiting for the all-clear, he jogged back to where both sheriffs were coming out the front door.

"Did you find the laptop, or anything else?"

"Yeah," Jack said. "I found the computer in the living room, hidden under a loose floorboard, right where Brandon said. It's great when the criminal morons turn on each other, huh?" His friend laughed.

Chris nodded. "I didn't find any more weapons or anything obvious, but we'll see what the crime scene techs come up with."

"Hopefully, there'll be enough on their laptop to wrap up cases against Brandon and Sheri and send them away for a long time." The EMT waved to him, so Scott headed back to the ambulance and waited for the paramedic's update.

"These girls are scared, tired, and hungry, but I don't find anything else wrong with them."

He grasped the man's hand and shook. "Thank God."

"They're good to go."

Scott couldn't wait to get these girls to Marnie's house and into their sister's arms. He was a sucker for their cute smiling faces.

Rounding the open ambulance doors, he smiled at Ashley and Deena. "Ladies, I've been told you're healthy and hungry and ready to go." Placing his fists on his hips, he let go of his built-up tension with a chuckle. "Shall we blow this popsicle stand?"

Both girls had big smiles on their faces. "Let's go," said Ashley, as she jumped down from the back of the ambulance.

Deena came to him and slid her hand into his. She tilted her head at him, her expression serious again. "I'm *really* hungry."

He smiled. "Let's get you some dinner, then."

He walked the sisters to his Jeep and opened the back door for them to climb in. "We're going to need to talk about the guys coming to your house and taking you, as well as what happened after that, but we can wait until you get something to eat. If you want, we can talk at Marnie's house, where Carly is, or we can go back to your house, where your dad is waiting for you."

"Carly. Carly. Carly," they chanted in unison.

Before he closed the door, Deena put her hand on his, and he stared into her eyes.

"But dinner first, right?"

He chuckled. She was a cutie, especially given everything these two had been through. "Yes, dinner first. Give me a minute to talk to a couple of these police officers." He closed the door and walked back to Jack and Chris.

"Thanks so much for the help and backup on this. I wouldn't want to have to go see their sister and give her any other news than that the girls are fine and home."

Jack reached out to shake Scott's hand. "Everybody loves a happy ending."

"It was good to have a coordinated effort on this, and it's good to put an end to such a long-running child-trafficking ring." Chris crossed his arms over his chest.

Scott slapped him on the back. "It'll take some more coordination through trial, but I agree. Thank you, and please pass on my thanks to your people." He glanced around the yard at the vehicles parked everywhere and the people going in and out of the house. "I'm going to take the girls to get some food and then to see their sister. I'll take their statements at the home where Carly is staying right now. If anything comes up, give me a call. Otherwise, I'll catch up with you both tomorrow."

Both sheriffs nodded and turned back to the teams

searching the house.

Scott walked back to the Jeep and climbed in. "Well, ladies, what do you want for dinner?"

He'd buy them anything they wanted tonight, just grateful all had gone well and he had two sweet girls, and good news all around, to turn over to Marnie and the kids.

Chapter Fourteen

Marnie went to the front door and opened it quickly before Matt could ring the bell. She smiled but put her finger to her lips, whispering, "Hi."

Happy to see a friendly face and have a sympathetic ear to help her clarify what to do next, she gave him a quick hug.

He walked into the entry, leaning down to speak into her ear. "Why are we whispering?"

She motioned for him to follow her into the living room, and he took a seat at the far end of the couch. Sitting in the armchair opposite him, she replied, "The kids are in the back bedroom, hopefully asleep."

"Hopefully?" He wiggled his eyebrows with a weak attempt at a leer.

She smiled, shaking her head at him. "You have a dirty mind."

"That's nothing new." He leaned back against the sofa, resting his right arm along the back of the cushions.

She waved a hand in the direction of the bedroom. "Carly is pregnant already, so it's a moot point, Matt." She just hoped both Nick and Carly, tired as they were, were sound asleep.

"True."

"More importantly, I don't want her to end up on bed rest again, or risk miscarrying. She can't stop worrying about her sisters and everything that's going on. She's been a nervous wreck. I hope she's getting some much needed sleep in there."

His expression turned serious. "So," he said, crossing him arms, resting them on his knees, leaning forward, and keeping his voice low, "what's going on with you?"

Closing her eyes, she bowed her head for a moment. How could she put the whirlwind of emotion inside her into words? "I feel guilty even talking about this right now, with everything Carly's going through, with Scott out chasing the bad guys, and those two sweet little girls missing. That's what's important right now, not my petty issues."

"Yet here I am."

Always able to see through her self-delusion and call her on it, he waited for her to continue.

"Yes, and thanks for coming. I needed to talk this out with someone. Maybe you could help me get some perspective on this. I didn't expect you to drop everything and drive down here, but I really appreciate it."

"You sounded a little frazzled on the phone, and since I had some free time, I thought we could talk in person about whatever's on your mind."

She stood, wringing her hands. "I'm going to go get my laptop. I'll be right back, but can I bring you something to drink?"

"Just water, please."

Numbness enveloped her, despite the turmoil inside. How could she go ahead with anything until the girls were home?

She came back into the living room carrying her

laptop and two water bottles. After handing one to him, she sat next to him on the couch, put her laptop on the coffee table, and opened up her email.

Detailing for Matt what she'd been through over the past couple of weeks helped clarify her options and worries. He listened carefully, without obvious judgment, when she explained that her adoption records and birth certificate were forged.

He stopped drinking his water, his eyes wide. "Forged? What?"

She explained the information she'd uncovered.

"Okay." He lifted the water bottle to his mouth again. "Wow."

"Yeah, wow." That was putting it mildly. Her whole world was upside down. "So I did some online searching about how to find birth parents and found this site for adoptees looking for birth parents, or vice versa, where you give the basic dates, location, et cetera, and see if anyone is searching for you."

"And you got a response."

"I got a response." As confusing as this all was, she couldn't help the shiver of excitement that flew through her as she pulled up her message box on the adoption search site, showing him the original message.

"Okay," he said. "Are you sure this person is talking about you? You have to be careful, Marn. There are some sick jerks out there who will say anything to get access to your personal info."

"I know." She leaned over the keyboard, but glanced at him from the corner of her eyes. "I'm not stupid, Matt, but it felt like the real thing, so I gave her my email address and phone number and asked her to contact me."

He hit his head with the palm of his right hand. "Of course you did."

She put her hand on his left arm. "I know what I'm doing." She normally might be angry at his condescending tone, but normal had gone out the window days ago. She clicked on her email. "Look at the email I got today." Her pulse raced. Could it really be her mother?

He leaned forward to read the email. "Okay. It sounds legit, but how much of it did you tell her about yourself?"

"You saw my message. I didn't tell her any of this. She knows about the VW microbus, about the cop who found me, all of it. This woman is my mother or knows her."

He read the email again and then sat back, crossing his arms. "Okay, say she is your mother, what do you see happening?"

She sighed. "I get to meet her, find out about my family history, her parents, and my birth father, whatever. I don't know." Unsure what she wanted to happen, she tried to keep herself from getting too excited.

"And what if she is not your mother but, as you said, is somebody who knew her."

She had to accept that this was possible. "Well, then, at least I learn my birth mother's name, I learn more about the day I was born and what happened after. Maybe she'll get in touch with my birth mother so we can meet."

Resting his chin on his palm, he sat silent for a moment and then touched her arm.

His dark brown eyes gazed into hers.

"If you know you have to meet this woman, one way or the other, why am I here?"

She grasped his hand, squeezing. "Because I needed a friend to talk it out with me. To hear what I'm thinking and tell me I'm not crazy. And to confirm it's not the most selfish thing in the world to think about this right now, with everything else going on."

What was going on? When would Scott call or text to tell them how the girls were? Surely, he had to have some answers soon.

"This is not the most selfish thing in the world, Marnie. You're not a selfish person." He squeezed her hand back. "You have a right to want to know who gave birth to you, and there's no reason not to think about it right now. In fact, maybe it's the perfect time, since you're waiting for news."

She wiped away a tear. "I'm scared."

Her birth mother might never want to meet her. Cold fear skittered across her skin. She might never even learn the woman's name.

Dropping her hand, he reached to rub her back. "Of course you're scared, sugar. You have such incredible parents already—there's little chance Ann, whoever she is, can compete with them. It's okay to be both excited and angry at the thought of meeting her."

She leaned toward him, placing her head on his chest. "Thanks for understanding." *He lets me ramble on and doesn't think I'm crazy. Calling him was a good idea.* "It's all too much to keep to myself. I needed to bounce it off you, to say it out loud, to be able to decide what I want to do." She smiled. "Now I know."

He wrapped his arms around her, and she pulled herself in. Overwhelmed as the tension drained, tears slid down her cheeks. He patted her back, rocking and holding her while she pulled herself together.

The front door flew open, and Scott came racing into the house. Her breath caught as she sat up straight, searching his face for an update on the girls.

"What the...?" Scott stood in the doorway, staring at Marnie as she disengaged herself from Matt's arms.

The two little girls ran past him, nearly knocking him over, yelling for their sister.

Marnie jumped off the couch and ran to him. "You found them!" She threw her arms around him, although he stood transfixed.

She closed her eyes and reveled in the relief.

"What...?"

As she stood in the entryway with her arms around Scott, Carly and Nick emerged from the back bedroom, and Carly squealed. She ran to her sisters as they launched themselves into her arms. The three sisters hugged, and rocked, and cried, and all talked at once.

Marnie kept her arm around him as she practically dragged him down the hall toward the girls. She gave him another squeeze. "Thank you so much for bringing these girls back to her." Peace filled her at the sight of total bliss on the teen's face.

Nick wrapped his arm around Carly's waist, and the four kids were talking, giggling, and happy.

Marnie sighed and leaned into him. "It's great to see them all together, isn't it?"

He didn't say anything. She grabbed his hand and pulled him back to the living room.

Matt stood at the door, pulling his coat on. "You've got a lot happening here, so I'm going to hit the road. I'll see you tomorrow."

She smiled. "Thanks for coming. Bye."

Once the door closed behind him, she pulled Scott into the living room. "What's wrong? What happened?"

His eyebrows shot up. "What was that all about?" He gestured to the couch.

She stared at him. "What? I got an email from someone who might be my birth mother. I wanted someone to discuss it with, but you were obviously busy."

"You what?"

She held up her hand. "I think the email is authentic, and she wants to meet me. So I called Kate but got no answer. I called Matt for his opinion. He stopped in and listened to me vacillate about what I'm going to do about it. Talking things out helps me even more than pro-con lists, and after you and Kate, Matt was the next best person to help me get a grip on what to do next."

He grasped her hand and pulled her to a seat on the couch next to him. "And?"

She shrugged her shoulders, opening the laptop to show him the email. "I felt guilty to even have been reading this or worrying about it, with everything else happening today."

He shook his head. "But this is incredible."

Tears coming to her eyes, she smiled. "Yeah, I think it is. I'm going to email Ann and tell her I will meet with her at Minnie's tomorrow night, as long as nothing else is going crazy around here."

He looked deep into her eyes. "Do you want me to come with you?"

She shook her head. "I don't think so, but thanks for the offer." She held his left hand with both of hers. Although grateful for his support, she also wondered if he was jealous. "I'm sorry if it made you uncomfortable to see me hugging Matt, but he's been my friend since I was young—much longer than we were married—he's my boss, and he's always going to be part of my life. I hope you can accept this."

He tilted his head down, gazing first at their joined hands and then back into her eyes. "I can't lie. I don't like to see you in the arms of another man, but I get it. I know you and Matt are close friends although you're not romantic anymore." He swallowed. "I can understand how torn you felt about the email, and I know how important it is to you to find your birth parents. I'm sorry I wasn't here for you when you needed to talk about it."

"You were doing the important stuff—bringing Ashley and Deena home." Amazed that this was just another day at the office to him, she admired him even more.

He smiled. "I wasn't alone. Jack was there, and Chris Hoy of Schuyler County, along with several other officers. We got Sheri Jonas to give up her son Brandon, the one who actually kidnapped the girls, and his location."

She shook her head. "She turned on her own son? What a cold person."

He chuckled. "No love lost between those two. Once he found out his mother told us everything, he gave us his laptop, which he says is filled with all the records we'll need to lock her away on the child-trafficking charges."

"Wow. You must be exhausted." She ran her arm over his back. Tension was clear, just under the skin.

He smiled. "There's definitely a high that comes from pulling it all together and finally bringing in the perps, but when the dust settles, I start to crash. I still need to take Ashley and Deena's statements, but I'm going to be beat by the time I take those girls home, interview them, and drive to Horseheads."

She'd lay odds they were all going to be crashing soon, now that the danger had passed.

"Why don't you set up with the girls at the dining room table, get what you need from them, and then everyone can stay here tonight? I have two more guest rooms upstairs, so there's room for everyone. We can call their father, assuming we can get hold of him, and clear it with him."

He cocked his head to the side, thinking, and then finally smiled. "Okay. Assuming I get his permission, it sounds great. I'll need to meet with Jack in the morning, to go over everything they found at the scene, before I go back to the office and talk to Sheri and Brandon again. I'll have to get moving early, but it'd be nice not to have to make the drive tonight."

She wrapped her arms around him. "I'm so relieved and happy and proud that you brought those girls home. *And* put an end to the child-trafficking ring." She sighed. "My grandmother would hate to think she played a part in the creation of such a long-lasting criminal enterprise, even if she didn't know about it."

His lips pulled into a thin line. "Her role will

probably come out in the news, if we have to go to trial, but there's nothing to imply she had any knowledge of money changing hands in exchange for babies."

While she hadn't really believed there would be, a huge weight lifted off her chest. "I'm going to take the morning off and go see my parents tomorrow. Mom needs to know what happened with all of this." She took a deep breath. "And I need to tell them both about the meeting with Ann."

"That sounds like a good idea. Maybe you can take the girls home on your way to Ithaca?"

"Sure."

He leaned in and kissed her lips, lingering a bit. "I'm glad Matt was able to help you work through all this."

She kissed him back. "I'm sorry if seeing me hugging him made you uncomfortable."

He leaned his forehead against hers. "It wouldn't bother me so much, but I do love you, Marnie."

She stilled, unprepared, unable to respond. While she had to admit their attraction was strong, they hadn't really known each other that long.

"Don't say anything right now." He sat up, pulling her hands into his again. "I fell for you right from the start. I wanted to remind you I'm not playing around here."

Still unable to speak, she simply nodded. If she was honest, it wasn't a surprise; he'd said it before. But did she feel the same?

He stood and pulled her to her feet. "Why don't I go talk to Ashley and Deena, and you and Carly can try to get in touch with her father. When I'm done taking their statements, maybe I can get a drink?" He smiled. "Something stronger than red wine?" He chuckled.

"I think it can be arranged." She smiled, the knot in her chest loosening a bit.

In the kitchen, all four kids had moved to the chairs at the table. Carly had a hand on each sister, smiling like Marnie hadn't seen her do in a long time. She appeared to have forgotten all about her cares of pregnancy, poverty, and school.

Scott made a quick call to Carly's father, who gave permission for Scott to interview the girls. Once he explained to the sisters that he needed to talk to each girl individually and Carly could be there if the girls needed her to be, Ashley volunteered to go first and said her big sister didn't need to come. They moved to the dining room, while Marnie talked to the teens about staying the night. They jumped on the idea.

"Nick." She placed her hand on his arm. "I'd feel better if you'd call home and let them know you'll be staying here."

"They won't care." The young man shook his head. "They probably won't even notice."

It was lousy to think he might be right about that. "Still, I'd feel better knowing you told them."

Still shaking his head, he stepped away to make the call.

She turned to Carly. "We need to get your father's permission for the girls to stay here tonight. Scott will have to take them home otherwise. He's responsible for them."

"Okay. Why didn't Scott ask about that when he

called my dad?"

"He was calling on official police business. I want to talk to your father about you girls sleeping here tonight."

"He has a phone, but he doesn't turn it on very often." She glanced up at Marnie from the corner of her eyes. "It's pay-as-you-go, you know, so he doesn't want to use up his minutes."

"Okay," she said. "Let's try it, and if it's turned off, you can leave a message and we can keep trying."

Carly called her father and explained they all wanted to spend the night at Marnie's house. At that point, she handed over the phone.

"Hello," Marnie said, taking the girl's phone.

"Uh, hi. This is…uh…Frank Johnson. Is this Miss Edwards?"

"Yes, but please call me Marnie."

"Okay. Thanks so much for your help in finding Ashley and Deena. I'm so grateful to everyone involved in finding them."

She smiled. "State Police Investigator Scott Randall brought them to my house a short while ago because he knew Carly was here. We were hoping to let the girls—well, really, all three of them—stay here overnight, with your permission. Everyone is thrilled to have them back, but we're all exhausted and just want to have some dinner and go to sleep."

"Uh, okay. That's fine. I 'preciate you taking care of them, the way you been taking care of my girl. She says you're a big help with her homework and all. I know the girls will be fine with you."

"Thank you, Mr. Johnson. You have wonderful daughters."

"Frank, please. You've been so good to my girls, and I know it's hard for them, without their mother, and...well, I've had some hard times. But you've been like a mother to them, especially Carly, and I know they'll always be fine with you."

She felt her eyes filling. He didn't sound like a bad man. "Thank you so much, Frank. I'm glad you think so."

"They'd probably be better off living with you. You've been so good to them."

She didn't know what to say. The poor man was overwhelmed, taking care of three girls on his own, dealing with his alcoholism, as well as everything else they'd faced. She couldn't help being moved by his honesty.

"Would it be okay if I bring Ashley and Deena home after breakfast in the morning? Is it convenient for you?"

He hesitated. "Uh, sure. But I was kind of thinking I'd like to stop down tonight, before they go to sleep, to see 'em, ya know?"

Thrilled to hear the concern in his voice, she readily agreed. "Of course. I know the girls would be happy to see you. You're welcome to stay for dinner, if you'd like. I thought maybe we'd order a pizza and some salad, so it's no trouble to have you stay."

He coughed. "I just wanna see my girls, but thank you kindly for the offer. I have another stop to make in town, so I'll be there in about forty-five minutes or so, okay?"

She smiled. "Of course. You have my address?"

"Yep, Carly gave it to me."

She nodded to Carly. "Okay, then. We'll see you

soon."

The girl's eyes were wide and her brow furrowed. "What? He won't let the girls stay?"

She brushed a hand over the girl's shoulders. "That's not it, not at all." Knowing he had disappointed these kids too many times, she had to be upbeat but honest with Carly. "He says he's happy to have you all stay here tonight, but he wants to see his girls, that's all. He's going to stop down and see you all for a quick visit. He doesn't even want to stay for dinner, although maybe we can convince him once he's here." She smiled. "He's a concerned father. There's nothing for you to worry about. Let's figure out what we want on our pizza."

The teen still seemed skeptical.

Despite the fact that Frank had barely been a father at times, maybe this was the chance for the family to start over.

****

"It's getting late." Marnie lowered her voice, leaning in close to Scott. "Ashley and Deena are so tired they're nearly asleep on their feet. I think we'll have to stop waiting for Frank to show up." So much for a new beginning.

He agreed. "I'd say Frank must have forgotten he told us he'd stop by."

She shook her head. "Maybe something came up. He sounded really worried about the girls and anxious to see them, so I'm sure something detained him or he'd be here."

He motioned behind her, and she turned around. Carly stood behind her, the girl's gaze cold and her lips in a taut straight line. "You think because your parents were reliable, responsible people, as you are, every parent is that way. You don't know what it's like to live with someone who is *never* where he says he'll be when he says he'll be there. He got a better offer, whether at a bar along the way or in the bottom of a bottle at home. He's not coming." As she turned, she twisted, looking Marnie directly in the eyes. "I'm going to tuck the girls into bed."

All she could do was nod. After Carly walked off to find her sisters, she turned back to him. "She's had to be a parent from a young age. She's mature, but it's hard on a seventeen-year-old girl to take on so much responsibility." After being let down so many times, of course the girl had stopped believing in her father.

Pulling Marnie in close, Scott rubbed her arms with his hands. "She's lucky to have you in her life, to lean on and turn to." He nuzzled her neck. "I'm impressed and proud of the way you stand up for these kids."

She smiled and leaned her head onto his. Her heart was full. "I don't do much for her but listen and ask a few questions, helping her look at things from a different angle. She's so smart and strong. She usually doesn't need much from me beyond a sounding board."

He tilted her face up so he could meet her gaze. "That sounds like a proud mom to me. Giving her wings and being there to catch her if she falls. You're not dealing with a child, and you are showing her the respect she deserves as an almost-adult. Again, she's lucky to have you."

He reached to meet her lips with his own, then wrapped both arms around her and drew her onto his lap. Before things could get out of hand, Nick cleared his throat.

She pulled away and turned to Nick.

"Carly's worried. She's trying to hide it, but I think she believed her father cared about them this time; that he'd be here. She's telling the girls a story, but I can tell she's worried."

"Have any of the girls tried calling him? Maybe he would answer a call from them. We could say the girls were asking for him."

Nick shook his head. "I'll get her phone."

Marnie led Scott to the kitchen, holding hands like teenagers, and she stopped at the refrigerator to pull out a diet cola.

"I'll never understand how you can drink that stuff this late without the caffeine keeping you awake all night." He smiled at her.

She shrugged. "It doesn't affect me that way. I don't drink any other caffeine, so maybe it's not enough to make a difference."

She pulled out a chair to sit, and he sat in the chair next to her at the table.

He shook his head. "You don't drink coffee?"

She scrunched up her nose. "Ugh, no. Can't stand it."

He chuckled. "I don't think I'm going anywhere tonight, so I'll have a beer. I was going to hold off having a drink until after Frank Johnson left, but I think that ship has sailed." He popped the top on a bottle of beer and took a swig.

Nick came out of the back bedroom with Carly's phone in his hand. "She had the ringer turned off, so she didn't realize she'd missed a call."

"Oh, good. I hope Frank called to let her know something came up."

"It's not Frank's number." Nick stared at the phone. "It says it came from the Stevens County Sheriff's Office."

A queasy sensation settled in her stomach. Why would Carly be getting a call like that at this time of night?

Scott held out his hand, and Nick gave him the phone. "Hmm. The call came in only about five minutes ago." He handed the phone back to Nick, pulled out his own phone, and dialed Jack's number, walking out onto the back porch.

Nick turned to her. "Why does he do that? I'm going to find out what the call is about eventually. He doesn't have to act like I'm a child who's too young to be part of the adult business."

She smiled. A man so much of the time these days, every now and then the boy showed through. "I think he'd have taken the call outside even if I was the only one in the kitchen right now. He probably wants privacy when dealing with police business, especially if there's a chance Ashley or Deena could come walking into the kitchen when he was on the call."

Nick shrugged. "I guess." His gaze met hers directly. "He's in love with you, you know."

Her eyes widened. "Uh, yes. He's told me." She smiled at Nick. "I didn't realize he'd told you." Somehow, that made it even more real. It wasn't just a spur-of-the-moment, caught-in-the-excitement-of-the-day kind of thing.

Again, the teen shrugged. "He didn't, but I can tell." He kicked the chair next to her and sat in the one opposite her. "He's dated some since the divorce, although not as much as he should have. But he's never been like this before. He's serious about you. I wanted you to know because he doesn't deserve to get hurt again."

"I don't want to hurt him, either." That was the last thing she wanted to do. Scott deserved to be happy.

Nick's eyes narrowed as he picked up a paper napkin and started shredding it. "If you don't feel the same way about him, if you can never fall in love with him, you need to tell him."

"I care about him, Nick. I'm not playing here." She took a deep breath before continuing. "But we have to be on the same page about more than that. And I have to get my head straight about a number of things before I can know how I feel about him. I've told him that much."

Nick wadded up the torn bits of paper and rolled them into a ball. "Bullshit." He threw the ball into the trash can and stood. "Even though Carly has been going through hell with her sisters and we've both been feeling stressed out about the baby and everything else, I know I love her. Love doesn't wait for the good times. It's either there or it isn't."

He turned and walked toward the bedroom. Just before he reached the door, he turned back to face her. "Figure out if it's there or not and tell him, either way. He's entitled to the truth."

She stared down at her hands, folded in front of her on the kitchen table. Nick didn't like the idea of Scott protecting him, but he spoke up, when he was probably nervous about doing so, to protect Scott from any more pain.

She wanted to protect Scott from more pain, too. His ex-wife had left scars, but he'd gotten past them to know what he wanted. He'd told her he loved her…and she hadn't responded. He wasn't pressuring her to say it back, but as Nick said, he deserved it.

She wanted to wait until everything calmed down with Ashley and Deena, with Carly's plans for her pregnancy, with her mother's health, and with the search for her birth mother. She wanted to be able to concentrate on him and her feelings for him, to determine how she felt, if she was in love, what she saw in their future together, and where this all was going.

She needed to think everything through, make sure she knew what she wanted, and make a plan.

They'd both been hurt; they each had scars. They'd both been divorced, and she didn't want to rush into anything. She didn't want to fail at marriage again.

But she didn't want to lose a chance at happiness with Scott because she was too busy trying to put out fires, organize her life, and put everything around her in its place. As Nick said, love didn't wait. It happened when it happened, and she'd better figure out how she felt.

The door to the back porch opened. His expression was grim when he walked into the kitchen.

"It's not good news." He crossed to sit next to her again, his voice low.

"What happened?" Her throat tightened.

He sighed. "Frank Johnson drove into Watkins Glen to meet with his lawyer at her office."

"At this time of night?"

"I know. Afterward, he took the back road around the swamp toward Harper's Glen, presumably on his way here. Somewhere on the edge of town, he swerved to avoid hitting a bicycle and ended up driving straight into the swamp. According to the witnesses Jack spoke to, Frank was unable to get the door open as the car sank into the swamp. By the time the ambulance and rescue squad got to him, he was gone."

She shook her head. "Oh, my God." Her eyes filled with tears, and she reached for his hand. "I can't believe these poor girls have to lose their only remaining parent. My heart is breaking for them." She pulled a tissue from her pocket, wiping her eyes. "What will happen to them now?" How could they tell Carly? She didn't deserve to be forced to be both parents to her young sisters when she herself was a pregnant teenager.

He pulled her close. "I asked Jack about it. Because Frank gave you permission to keep the girls tonight, there's no reason to move them right away, if it's okay with you. Jack offered to come over and give them the news, but I told him you and I could handle it."

"We can tell Carly tonight, if she doesn't end up falling asleep while tucking the girls in, but I think we should wait until morning to tell Ashley and Deena. They've already had a hell of a day."

"Agreed." He shook his head. "Jack said he'd check with Frank's lawyer, since we know who it is, and see if he made any provision for the girls. Do you know if there's any other family?"

She shook her head. "None that I've ever heard mentioned." Surely, there had to be someone out there who could help these girls.

"Well, in that case, they'll probably become wards of the state, at least until Carly turns eighteen." He turned toward the bedroom and the closed door. "When's her birthday?"

She closed her eyes briefly. "Uh, I'm pretty sure it's in about six weeks or so. That's part of what is factoring into her decision-making process about what to do with the baby. She'll be a legal adult soon and had hoped to move, with the girls, to somewhere in town, which would obviously be harder with a baby."

He shook his head. "Wow. That poor kid has way too much on her shoulders."

She leaned her head on his shoulder. Her heart was breaking for Carly and for her sisters. Nick, too. This was just too much for the kids to handle.

"Hell of a day, huh?" He sounded as tired as she suddenly felt.

"Yeah."

He pulled her in close, wrapped her in his arms, and kissed her softly. She wasn't ready to make any declarations of love, but for tonight, at least, being snug in his arms felt like home.

Chapter Fifteen

Marnie opened her eyes. Six a.m. Ugh.

She'd taken the day off work, texting Matt late last night when they found Carly had fallen asleep and they'd have to deliver the news to all the girls in the morning. While it was great to know Scott would do the official notification, and even better to have had him in her bed last night, she knew she would need to spend the day with the girls.

A headache was already building at her temples; she could hear her heart beating in her ears. Even as she lay in bed next to a warm, affectionate man, tension built in her neck and shoulders. These girls were so special, so vulnerable, and now so alone. It was enough to bring her to tears just thinking about it.

In addition to their sorrow over their father, all three would certainly be worried about what was going to happen next. So was she. She cared for the girls and didn't relish the idea of them getting tossed into the foster system, even if only for a matter of weeks.

And, of course, once Carly was an adult and able to care for her sisters, she would be in dire financial straits and any thought of college would go out the window. Maybe there was some funding available through a local organization, something to help with housing and utilities, beyond welfare and the county social services. These girls would need help, so she could start research this morning on what money was out there and available to them.

Yeah, it would be an exhausting day.

"I can hear your brain working from here." Scott's arm snaked across her stomach and scooped her in close to his chest. His stubble roughed her cheek as he burrowed his face into her neck. "It's early. Go back to sleep."

She chuckled but turned to slide her right arm around his side. "If you can really hear my brain working, you know there's no way I can go back to sleep now. Too many questions running through my mind."

He propped himself up on his elbow, looking down into her eyes. "I might have a way to distract you, at least for a little while."

He leaned in, placing his lips on hers. His kiss was the faintest of touches, a feather on her lips, but deepened slowly, waking her up in a way the worries hadn't touched. She found herself sinking into a slow warming, letting go of the knots which had been tightening her neck and shoulders.

She felt her brain let go, putting aside the sad and tough for the soft and gentle. Having someone to go through all of this with her was a luxury she could get used to.

The liquid warmth within her quickly built into a lightning heat, and she drank her fill. He met her breath for breath, touch for touch, and sigh for sigh, wanting to strengthen this intimate bond to help them weather the storm ahead. Amidst murmurs and whispered moans, they shored each other up and refilled their souls.

Once they reached the peak, she let herself float slowly back to her day, savoring her liquid bones and satiated muscles as long as she could. He didn't sleep but again pulled her into the curve of his body, nuzzling her neck and kissing her ear.

After a few moments of quiet breathing, he almost whispered, "Better?"

She smiled and nodded. "Definitely." Even the beginnings of her tension headache seemed to have eased.

He jumped out of bed. She turned, afraid he had a text of a new disaster, but he smiled. With a wink, he said, "Then my work here is done." He grabbed his clothes and raced into the bathroom, calling behind him, "Dibs on the shower."

She couldn't help but laugh. Sexy, playful, and industrious. What an incredible combination.

She pulled herself up to lean against the headboard, adjusting her pillow behind her back and taking her phone from the nightstand. Most of the email was work related, although she had one from her father. She had emailed last night, before the call from Jack, about coming over to talk to them. She had wanted to tell them about Ann, but she would need to postpone everything, at this point.

She had a text from Jack, which was unusual, so she opened it. "Need to meet with you this morning. Earliest is best."

Her pulse started racing again, but not in a good way. She responded, hoping he really meant early. "When and where?"

The answer was immediate. "How's now? I can be at your house in five minutes."

She shook her head. "Okay." *What could possibly have happened now?*

She jumped out of bed and got dressed as quickly as possible. When Scott was finished with the bathroom, she rushed in to brush her hair and teeth.

"What's the hurry?" He sat on the side of the bed to step into his shoes, watching her racing around the room.

"Jack texted he needs to talk to me. He'll be here any second."

He shook his head. "Did he say why?"

She popped her head out the bathroom door, toothbrush wedged in her mouth. "Nope."

"I'll go start the coffee." He was out of the bedroom only moments before she was.

As she descended the stairs, she caught sight of Jack coming up the front walk, so she pulled the door open before he had a chance to ring the doorbell.

"Good morning," she whispered. "Most everyone is still asleep."

He wiped his feet on the mat and stepped past her into the entryway. She led him down the hall to the kitchen. Scott poured coffee for himself and Jack but had already pulled a diet cola from the refrigerator for her.

Jack took a sip of the coffee before he motioned toward the back porch. "Can we step out there? I don't want to take the chance of the kids overhearing us."

The three stepped outside, closing the French doors behind them. They all stood around the patio table, resting their drinks on it but not sitting. She was almost bursting with questions.

Jack took another sip of his coffee and turned to

her. "So Frank Johnson's lawyer called late last night."

"You said it was somebody in Watkins Glen?"

"Yeah," said Jack. "He stopped at Jill Flack's office last night, just before the accident. He's apparently been a client since she was assigned as his court-appointed attorney for one of the DUI charges. He stopped there last night before heading over here. She said she was surprised to see him."

Scott shook his head. "He took a chance she'd be there?"

Jack shrugged. "Her office is on the side of her house. Apparently, he knocked on her house back door when she didn't answer at the office door."

Why did they need to talk about this at seven in the morning?

"And?"

Jack smiled. "Frank stopped there to drop off his will, for safekeeping."

She tilted her head to one side. "He had a will?"

"Yeah," He pulled out his phone, scrolling through. "She said he wrote it himself, which is perfectly legal, but wanted her to help him with witnesses and to keep it for him."

Frank Johnson hardly seemed the kind of man to worry about a will. Unless she was mistaken, he had no worldly possessions to worry about, either.

Scott took a sip of coffee. "I'm assuming this has something to do with the disposition of his kids, since you're over here at this hour."

Jack nodded. "Yeah. Did you tell the girls about Frank's accident last night?"

"No." Sighing, she willed her stomach to relax. "By the time we knew what had happened, the kids were all asleep, so we decided it could wait until morning."

"Okay," said Jack, looking straight into her eyes. "I hoped to catch you before you told them. You see, Frank Johnson left guardianship of his kids to you, Marnie."

Her eyes went wide, and she sank into a chair at the patio table. "Me?" Her mind went blank.

Scott pulled out the chair next to her and sat, taking her hand in his. "Did he tell you he planned to do that when you spoke last night?"

She shook her head.

Jack sat as well. "So you talked to Frank last night?"

"Yes, although it seems like a long time ago now." She shook her head. "I asked Carly to call him to get his permission for Ashley and Deena to sleep here last night. They were worn out by the time Scott brought them, and they both wanted to stay with her."

Jack waited for her to continue.

"Frank wanted to talk to me. I've never spoken with him before, which is odd, given the number of times I've stopped up at the house. But anyway, he said he knew I'd take good care of the girls and he was happy to have them stay here, but he wanted to stop down and see them before they went to bed. He told us he had a stop to make, but he would be here in about forty-five minutes. I invited him to stay for dinner."

She mumbled a bit, but was overwhelmed to think the girls had lost their father last night and didn't even know about it yet. Add on to it the fact she was now the guardian to two young girls and their teenaged sister…

Her world started to tilt, so she leaned forward, resting her head in her hands. Could she handle this? What would the girls think? How could they make it work?

Scott's arm draped across her shoulders, and he leaned in close. "Are you okay?"

She leaned into him. "I don't know." She shook her head, sitting up. "What do I know about raising these girls?" Would she be ready or able to handle two middle-schoolers and a pregnant teen?

Jack checked his phone again. "The will states that should you decline guardianship, the girls should be remanded into foster care only until Carly is eighteen, and then she would have guardianship of her younger sisters. So the choice is yours."

She squeezed her eyes tightly. "Some choice this is. Even if she ends up with guardianship, how could she possibly afford to find a place for them to live? He didn't have any money to leave them, right?"

Jack shook his head. "Jill Flack said the estate is nothing more than the few bits of furniture they have in the rented house up on the hill. Frank had trouble holding down a job, due to his drinking, so they have next to nothing, other than Frank's social security death benefit."

There was no choice here, at least not for her.

"They have to stay with me. I mean, Carly can decide for herself what she wants to do when she's eighteen, but they have to stay here. I have room. I can afford to help them. I can't turn them out."

Scott leaned in again, kissing her cheek and taking her hand in his. "Of course you can't. Frank may not have met you, but he knew you're a good person. He'd surely heard at the Youth Center or from people in town, never mind what Carly must have told him. He knew he was putting his kids in the right place."

When Carly pulled the French doors open, a sense of calm spread through Marnie's system.

"What's up?" the girl asked. "Isn't it a little cold to sit and drink your coffee out here?"

"Are the girls awake?" Marnie rose and headed back into the kitchen.

Although obviously worried, the teen nodded. "Yeah, they're using the bathroom."

"Why don't we figure out what they'd like for breakfast? I have some cereal and toast. I think there's some orange juice in the fridge, behind the milk, so why don't you pull those out?"

She busied herself looking for cereal boxes and the loaf of bread. If the girls would have her, would become her family, this would be every day. Not wanting to get her hopes up, she pushed that thought aside to deal with food and then talk.

"What's going on?" Carly stood, unmoving, in front of the table.

Marnie put the cereal on the table and went over to lay her hand on the girl's shoulder. "When the girls come out here, we need to talk, but I'd rather wait and go through everything just once."

Before Carly could object, the younger girls came out of the bedroom, followed by Nick, whose hair stood on end in several places.

"Good morning, ladies," she said to the girls, who were smiling but still mussed from sleep. She hated the fact their world was about to come crashing in.

"Good morning," said Ashley, as she slid into a

chair at the kitchen table.

Deena took a seat at the table and looked up at Marnie. "Hi."

She held up the cereal boxes. "Who wants breakfast?"

Ashley and Deena passed cereal boxes back and forth, pouring milk and juice. Someone spilled a glass of milk, but things quieted down as they began to eat.

"What's going on?" Carly repeated, sitting at the far end of the table, next to Deena, with Nick on her right.

Marnie sat down next to Ashley, folding her hands in front of her on the table. These kids were about to get terrible news and, despite her personal hope that they wanted to live with her, they'd need to adjust to one change at a time. "There's no good way to say this, girls, so I'll start at the beginning. Your father wanted to come down here last night to see you all before you fell asleep, but he never showed up, right?"

Ashley and Deena barely stopped eating to murmur agreement. Carly crossed her arms and leaned back in the chair. "What, he's got some great excuse?"

She shook her head before continuing. "He drove into Watkins for an errand, and on his way here, he swerved to avoid hitting someone on a bicycle and was in an accident." She met the girl's gaze. "I'm sorry to have to tell you...he died." Swallowing the lump in her throat, she took a deep breath and waited for the tears.

Ashley stopped eating, her spoon poised in midair. Deena turned from Marnie to her big sister, her chin quivering. Carly sat still, saying nothing.

Marnie reached out and took her hand, resting her

other hand on Ashley's shoulder.

"I'm so sorry, girls."

No one said a word. Anger and confusion flashed in Carly's gaze.

Eventually, she glanced over at Marnie, her eyes narrowed, and her lips pressed into a straight line. "What happens to us?"

Scott's gaze met Marnie's, and he smiled briefly in encouragement.

She turned back to Ashley, then Deena, then Carly. "Your father made a will and left it with his lawyer last night. He wants you girls to live with me, for me to be your guardian." She smiled at all three girls. "What do you think? Would you like to live here?"

Ashley turned to Carly. The teen picked at her cuticles, avoiding eye contact.

"You could all live here. I have plenty of space. We can work out the details later. If you don't want to live here long term, it could be just until you turn eighteen, Carly, when you could be the guardian for the girls. But I'd like for you all to stay."

The teen glanced up from her fingernails but said nothing.

Her nerves on edge, Marnie could feel tears forming in her own eyes. "There's no rush, girls. You can take some time to think it over."

Carly took a deep breath, releasing a sigh. She nodded to Nick, who held her hand. "I guess it could work." Although her eyes were red, she didn't cry.

While Marnie admired the teen's strength for her sisters' sake, Carly needed time to mourn. The younger girls got up and went to their big sister, folding themselves into her arms. She hugged them, rocked them, and let them cry on her, but her tears never came.

While the girls were huddled together, Jack smiled at Marnie, spoke softly to Scott, and then left. Scott leaned in and whispered in her ear, "He's happy to help with any legalities, so he said to give him a call." He briefly kissed her cheek before he sat up again.

Finally climbing to her feet, her tears dried and hiccups done, Deena walked over to Marnie. "Thanks for letting us live here." She tilted her head. "Where will we sleep?"

She smiled, relieved that the youngest could focus on the basics. "Well, I guess we have to talk about it and decide where everyone wants to sleep. My bedroom is the first door at the top of the stairs, but there are two more bedrooms down the hall, on either side of the bathroom."

"Plus the bedroom down here," said Ashley, sliding into the chair next to her big sister.

"Right, plus the bedroom down here. Maybe you two want to go explore the two bedrooms upstairs and you can think about which one you'd like. Once you all have ideas of who wants which one, we can sit down and talk about it. Okay?"

The girls raced up the stairs.

She turned to Carly. "Are you okay, sweetie?"

Her eyes filled with tears she refused to shed, the young mother-to-be visibly swallowed. "Yeah. I mean, there were so many nights I was sure he was dead in a ditch somewhere, but he miraculously made his way home despite being dead drunk. I've been preparing for this for a long time."

She picked up the girl's hand, cradling it in her own. "It's okay to be sad anyway. He was your father, and in his own way, he did love you girls. His last thoughts were of you."

Carly wiped away a tear that escaped her lid. "I know."

Marnie wrapped her arms around the teen, who silently cried, her shoulders shaking. She ached for the girl, but the tears were a good thing. Nick stared at her, his expression conflicted between worry at her tears and the need to hold her himself.

The girls started down the stairs, and Carly pulled herself free, wiping her face on the sleeve of her shirt. She blew her nose on a paper napkin.

Turning to face the girls, Marnie held her arms out, hoping to give their sister an extra moment to pull herself together. "Well, what do you think? Anybody have a favorite?"

"I like the one on the left of the bathroom; it looks out over the front of the house. I think we should pick that one." Ashley spoke softly, her gaze filled with excitement.

Marnie glanced at Deena. "Which one do you like best?"

The littlest sister smiled shyly. "I'd rather have the one across from yours." She gazed up into Marnie's gaze, her eyes wide. "It'd be nice to be close."

And nice to be wanted. Looking at Carly, Marnie asked, "You've already seen those rooms. Which one do you prefer?"

The girl's cheeks pinked. "Actually, I like this one best, the one down here."

Ashley and Deena shared a look. "Okay," said Ashley. "We can stay down here. That'll be okay."

"But Ashley, you each prefer a different room, so it works out perfectly." While the girls were close and didn't seem to fight much, no room negotiation was best at this point.

Deena shook her head. "What do you mean?"

Smiling, she gestured to the stairs. "You can have the bedroom opposite mine, Ashley can have the one at the front of the house, and Carly can have this one down here. Everybody's good, right?"

Deena's mouth formed a perfect O. "We *each* get a bedroom…like one of our *own*?"

Marnie chuckled. "Well, there are four bedrooms and four of us, so, yeah."

Ashley grinned, a smile that warmed her heart.

The younger girls ran back upstairs to explore and settle.

She turned to Carly. "You should put your feet up, sweetie, on the couch or on your bed, whichever. The last few days have been stressful."

"Okay. I think I'll move to the couch for a while, so the girls can come watch TV with me if they want to."

Nick stood. "I gotta make a call." He walked into the dining room, pulling his phone from his pocket.

"Oh, me, too." Marnie pulled out her own phone. "I need to let the school know you three won't be there today."

"Why don't I do it for you?" Scott picked his phone up from the table. "You can go into the school another day with a copy of the probate paperwork and establish guardianship."

"Oh, good idea. Thanks."

She poured a glass of water and handed it to Carly. "Go make yourself comfortable, and I'll bring you something to eat. How about some toast?"

"I'll try, but I'm not hungry." She wandered to the living room. Nick walked back into the kitchen.

Marnie touched his arm before he could turn around and go into the living room. "Everything okay?"

He nodded. "I asked my mom to call me off today. I told her about Mr. Johnson, and she said it was okay if I missed school today."

"Good. Carly will be happy to have you with her today." Proud at his sense of responsibility, she smiled at the boy. "You're good to her and have been mature and caring through everything that's happened." She leaned in and kissed his cheek. His face became unbearably red, and he shuffled out of the room quickly.

She found herself smiling as Scott came back into the kitchen.

"Everything's taken care of at the school. I told them the girls would be out all week. The school will arrange for someone to drop off their homework."

She walked into his embrace, wrapping her arms around his waist. "Thanks." She sighed. "It went better than I believed it would, although I know there are still storms ahead. I hope I know what to do to help all three of them with their pain, anger, and sadness over their father's death."

He rubbed her back. "If you can't handle it, get help. There are grief counselors and therapists who specialize in this type of thing."

She pulled back, looking up at him. "That's a great idea. You are so smart." He was good at this.

He smiled and kissed the tip of her nose. "Good to know you admire me for more than my rugged good looks."

She giggled and pinched his butt. "Well, those are great, too."

She laid her head against his chest, hugging tighter and relishing his strong arms around her. That's how Ashley and Deena found them when the girls came racing down the stairs.

"Oooh," Deena said.

"Shhh," said Ashley, giving her sister the evil eye.

Marnie smiled, standing next to him with one arm around his waist, his arm resting on her shoulder. She had to remember there were kids living here now. "We can go up to your house and pick up your stuff later, so you can get settled in your rooms. Sound good?"

Ashley nodded.

"Where's Carly?" Deena glanced around.

After she followed the girls to the living room, they all settled in to binge watch something she had never heard of.

Meanwhile, she stood with Scott in the hallway, peering through the doorway, watching the kids sprawled across her living room furniture, and a warmth spread through her. What a difference a day made.

He leaned down and whispered in her ear, "Nice work, honey." He kissed her neck. "I've got to get to work."

Taking his hand in hers, she led him back to the kitchen.

"I hate to leave you when so much is up in the air, but I've got to get to the office. I got a text from our IT specialists that they pulled a large number of records off the laptop, so I had Brandon and Sheri brought back in to interview this morning. I need to work on getting each of them to turn on the other."

"I'm sure it'd be best for everyone if there was no need for a trial. I'd rather Ashley and Deena don't have to testify against Brandon. Or, for that matter, Carly doesn't have to testify against either of them." She had to protect the girls.

He pulled her close for another kiss. "Already talking like a mama." He winked down at her. "I'll come back here when I'm done at the office, but call if you need me."

She smiled and agreed.

He let her go, grabbed his leather jacket, and took off.

She walked back into the living room, smiled at the pile of kids, then curled up in an armchair.

She'd never been so happy to have a roomful of people in her house, and she could definitely get used to this.

****

Marnie pulled out sliced bread and cold cuts for lunch and made a salad on the side. She stood back while the kids grabbed their food and fled to the living room, impressed with the amount of food they could consume. She'd need to do some serious grocery shopping.

She picked up her jacket, let the kids know she'd be outside, took a can of diet cola, and fled to the back porch to make a phone call in quiet.

Her father picked up the phone on the third ring. "Hello."

"Hi, Dad. How are you guys doing?"

"Marnie, sweetheart, we're good. Are you coming over after work tonight?"

She paused. How could she explain everything that had changed so quickly? "Can you put the phone on speaker, Dad? I want to talk to you and Mom, but I'm not going to be able to get away today."

"Sure." She heard him click the speaker button.

"Hi, sweetie," her mother's voice called out. "Is something wrong?"

"Huh…" She almost laughed. "Things have been wrong and not wrong and good and confusing." She took in a deep breath, letting her shoulders fall into place and releasing some residual stress.

"Tell us." The way her mother said those words opened the floodgates, and she told them the events of the past twenty-four hours.

When she was finished, there was only silence on the other end of the line.

"Mom? Dad? Are you still there?"

Her father cleared his throat. "That's a huge responsibility, sweetie. And while there's no one who handles responsibility better than you do, are you sure you want to take it on?"

"I'm sure." More sure than she'd been of nearly anything else in her life. "But there's more." She took a deep breath. "I called yesterday to say I wanted to see you because I got an email from someone named Ann, who may or may not be my birth mother." When no one gasped or cried out, she smiled and continued. "She'd like to meet me at Minnie's to talk about it.

She knows enough of the facts of the weekend that I believe she knows something. I'd planned to meet her but wanted to talk to you both first. Obviously, I had to postpone the meeting, but I want to meet with her as soon as possible."

"That's good," said her mother. "I didn't realize you'd gotten so far in your search, but I'm glad. You need to find some answers."

She had to clear her throat of the emotion welling there. More tears welled in her eyes. "You are making this easier on me, but I know it can't be easy for you." They were the best parents ever.

"Marnie…" her mother began.

The voice soothed her, but it sounded thick with tears, too.

"The hard part, at least for me, was keeping this from you all these years and the worry we'd lose you when you finally found out the truth. I'm not threatened by the idea of you finding your birth mother. I'm honored to be your mother and have this woman to thank for bringing you into this world. It changes nothing between you and me."

"Exactly," her father said. "You're expanding your family in many directions right now, but it doesn't change anything with us. It brings more blessings into our lives, too."

She couldn't speak, choked by the overwhelming love she felt for these strong, gentle, caring people. Blessed on the day her grandmother handed her over to them, she was even luckier now to still have them in her life.

She wiped her face, took a sip of her diet cola, and was finally able to speak again. "I feel exactly the same way. Thank you. I love you both so much."

Again her father cleared his throat, his usual method of dealing with an excess of emotion. "So what happens now with the girls?"

"Scott talked to Jack Finelli, who has arranged for a temporary guardianship for me, pending adjudication by Family Court. The girls have decided who is in which bedroom, and we're going up to their house to pick up all their belongings as soon as they are up to it."

"So they're already yours." Her mother sounded pleased. After a moment, however, her mother's voice changed a little, a smile obvious from the tone. "Is Scott there now?"

She never could put anything over on that woman.

"No, Mom. He's at work. He has to tie up the cases against Sheri Jonas and Brandon Lynch. He was able to track down Sheri Jonas, bring her in, get her to turn on her son, arrest him, and rescue Ashley and Deena, so he's a little busy on follow-up today. This ring has been operating for several decades, and they have a lot of work to do to uncover all the children who were involved."

"I'm sure it'll be a huge project for the police," her father agreed.

"But..." Her mother paused.

She shook her head. "Okay, so, yes, we are in a relationship. I'm not exactly sure what's going on or how I feel about it, but..."

"Marnie." Her mother's voice was firm but not stern. "You never answered my question. How do you feel about everything? How do you feel about being the guardian of the girls? Are you frightened? Happy?

Overwhelmed? Angry?"

She paused for a moment, thinking. Instantly, contentment welled within her. "Yes to all of them, except angry. I'm sad the girls had to lose their father, although life with him has not been easy for them." She sighed deeply, thinking of them all curled up in the living room. "But when I stop to think about what it will be like having them live with me, being a permanent part of my life, I'm happy. Is that weird?"

"You sound like a parent, to me." Her father chuckled.

"Exactly," her mom chimed in. "I think it's wonderful, sweetie. It will be hard, exhausting, and a lot of work, but also rewarding and filled with love. I know you'll be great at this."

Tears formed in her eyes. "Thanks, guys." Any parenting skills she possessed had come from these two wonderful people.

"But," her mother continued, "how do you feel about the meeting with Ann, the possibility of finding out more, or even meeting your birth mother? Again, are you scared, happy, angry, what?"

"Again, all of them but angry." Saying it out loud made her realize it was true. She felt bad for her birth mother, but wasn't even angry about being abandoned. The woman must have been in a terrible state for that to be the best answer she could find for her problems.

"I think everything that's happened with the girls has put it into perspective. I've had a wonderful life and the best parents possible, so everything worked out great for me. I would like to have a relationship with my birth parents, but if it doesn't happen, I'm okay with that, too."

Reassuring her parents reassured Marnie as well. Her tension over the question of her birth and identity had dissipated. If it happened, great. If not, that was okay.

"Good," her mother said. "Last question. How do you feel about Scott? I haven't heard you talk about a man this way since Matt, and you were a teenager when that started. Are you in love with him?"

"You have to squeeze every drop of emotion and energy out of me today, don't you?" She laughed, trying to stall. While he deserved an answer to his declaration of love, she'd been putting it off.

Her mother knew all her tricks, though. "Marnie…"

"Okay, okay. I like Scott, and I respect him, and he treats me well. I've seen him with the girls and with his ex-brother-in-law, who is Carly's boyfriend, Nick, and he's great with them—patient, respectful, fun. He's a good man, a hard worker, and a fierce friend. I'm attracted to him, but I'm not saying anything more about that to my parents." She chuckled, thinking of him rolling out of her bed just that morning. "He told me he's in love with me, but he didn't push me to respond. I like that he understands about all the craziness I'm going through right now and he's giving me time to figure things out."

"Answer the question, my dear."

Her mother never had patience for denial.

She closed her eyes, seeing him in her mind, joking with Nick, cradling Deena, above her in bed, holding her tight. Each image evoked emotion and excitement in her. She felt warmth and gentleness, strength and caring.

Love. It was there all the time, but she hadn't stopped spinning along in the haze of chaos long enough to notice it.

"Yes."

"Yes?" Her father asked.

"Yes, I'm in love with him."

"Well." Her mother let out a breath with a bit of a laugh. "I'm so glad to hear it. He sounds like a great guy."

"He is, Mom. I promise I'll bring him over to meet you both soon."

Her father spoke, his voice a warm sweep of softness. "And don't forget to bring over our new grandchildren, too. I can't wait to meet them all."

She smiled, a tear slipping from her right eye. "Now you're going to make me cry, Daddy."

He chuckled, although his voice was suspiciously thick as well. "We're proud of you, dear. You're going to be a great mother to those girls, and Scott is a lucky man to have you in his life. We just want you to be happy."

She smiled, unable to contain the excitement bubbling within her. "I think I am, Dad."

She thanked her parents, ostensibly for listening to her, but mostly for being there, supporting her with love, wisdom, and encouragement, for her entire life, and then she let them go so she could get back inside and check on the kids.

The teens had fallen asleep on the couch, curled together. Good. Carly had been a little pale this morning. Ashley was asleep on the floor, probably exhausted from crying. Deena was the only one still watching the show. She waved to her, one finger on her lips, hoping she didn't wake everyone else. The girl smiled, waved, and turned back to her show.

She walked back into the kitchen and opened her laptop. She dashed off an email to Ann, asking to postpone until the next night, given the sudden change in her circumstances. Before she could hit send, she got a text from Scott.

—How's it going there?—

Her heart seemed to expand. Now that she knew she was in love with him, she needed to tell him.

Not in a text, though.

—Most everyone is napping. All is good. How about you? This a good time to call?—

As soon as she pushed send, the phone rang. She answered immediately. "Hi."

"Hi. So the kids are all sleeping?"

She smiled. "Last I checked, Deena was the only one awake. She's watching TV."

"Well, the last few days have been exhausting for all of them. I expect they feel some relief, knowing they'll all have a nice place to live and whatever they need, living with you. Poverty is exhausting, even without the alcoholic parent, a stalker, and the kidnapping."

"I hadn't thought of it like that, but you're probably right." These kids were so resilient. "How are the interviews going?"

He chuckled. "Once we showed them the files we'd found on the laptops, each of them couldn't roll over fast enough on the other. It's actually pretty sad. Hell of a mother/son relationship."

"Sounds awful." She shook her head. "What a sad life."

He didn't respond for a moment.

She sent a silent wave of gratitude to the world that she couldn't imagine ever getting to the point where she and either of her parents turned on each other.

"Anyway," he continued with more energy, "I should be out of here by late afternoon. Can I pick something up for dinner?"

"That'd be great. I'll have to get some groceries tomorrow." She hesitated. "I'm sending an email to Ann rescheduling our meeting until tomorrow night."

"You don't need to," he said. "After dinner tonight, the kids and I can play some games or watch TV while you meet with Ann. I can handle it, with Nick and Carly."

"Oh. I don't know." Once she'd decided to postpone it, she'd put it out of her mind. Was she ready?

He chuckled softly. "What? You don't think I can handle two pre-teens? I have the two older kids to help. We'll be fine."

"I know..."

"Did you talk to your parents?"

She nodded. "Yes. I called them this morning."

"And?" His tone was impatient.

"They're incredible. They're excited about the girls. They can't wait to hear what Ann has to tell me. They totally support me, in everything. I'm so lucky to have them."

"They raised an incredible woman." His voice was soft and warm. "So now stop stalling. I can't wait to hear what Ann has to tell you, either."

She smiled. With backup like that, how could she

go wrong? "Okay. I'll meet her tonight, after dinner, as long as the girls are okay with me going out for a while."

"Good. I'm sure we'll be fine."

She dropped her gaze and lowered her head, before speaking. "You'll stay after, right? I mean, you'll sleep here?" She'd never been particularly shy about sex, but then, this was so much more than sex.

He chuckled. "I'll definitely stay, although sleeping is optional."

She laughed. "Okay. Good." She couldn't stop the images flooding her mind, but tried to keep it PG for her afternoon with the kids. "We'll see you when you get home, then."

Home. She liked the sound of that.

Chapter Sixteen

Minnie's was past the dinner rush, with only a few truckers at the counter and some scattered two-tops in the side room. She motioned to Ruthie, who'd been waiting tables at Minnie's almost forever, and asked if she could take a four-top in the back corner. The waitress nodded and went to deliver the order she'd been carrying.

Once Marnie had slid into the booth, Ruthie dropped off a couple of glasses of water. "Can I get you something, honey?"

She tried to stay calm as she ordered a diet cola and let the waitress know she was meeting someone. She watched the door for a woman old enough to be her mother. When a woman in her sixties came in, she figured it must be Ann. The woman walked straight to her table, leaving no room for doubt.

"Marnie?"

She stood, offering her hand. The woman who shook her hand was older, easily in her late 60s or early 70s. She was small, petite, but had a firm handshake. Her hair was wavy and mostly gray, but her eyes were the same bright blue Marnie saw in her mirror every morning.

"Please have a seat. Would you like something? Coffee? A bite to eat?"

"Just coffee."

Marnie signaled to Ruthie, who dropped off a mug and filled it from the pot in her hand and left the women to talk.

Hesitant, unsure what to say, she took a sip of her cola before volunteering, "Things were a little hectic at my house and I almost had to reschedule, but everything worked out after all."

Her companion took a sip of her coffee and smiled, staring at Marnie's face as if memorizing it.

She waited until she felt like she'd been x-rayed. "Yes?"

The older woman blushed. "You look so much like her." Tears appeared in the bright blue eyes.

Marnie felt the air escape from her lungs like a popped balloon. "Her? You mean you're not my birth mother?"

Ann's brows drew together, her mouth a worry line. "I'm so sorry. Of course, I should have worded my email more carefully." She smoothed a napkin on the table in front of her, finally looking back into her eyes. "No, I'm not your mother. I'm your aunt."

"My aunt?" She almost didn't recognize her own voice. Where was her birth mother?

"Yes, your mother was my sister Emma. She had those tight dark curls like you do, and the bright blue eyes, well, the same as you and me." Ann's eyes filled with tears. "What she wouldn't have given to be able to see you, to meet you after all this time."

She had trouble talking over the lump in her throat. "And where is Emma?"

Ann used the paper napkin to blot her tears. "We lost her about seven years ago. Breast cancer."

Marnie's stomach sank, the diet cola suddenly

acid churning in her stomach. Did this mean she was now at risk for the disease? Her hand instinctively reached across the table and joined her aunt's. "I'm so sorry for your loss."

Ann smiled sadly. "And for yours, although you didn't even know you'd lost her."

Marnie felt tears threatening to spill but took a couple of deep breaths to bring her emotions under control. "Can you tell me about her?"

Ann smiled weakly. "Absolutely." She blew her nose on the napkin and pulled another from the metal dispenser on their table. "Emma was my big sister, only two years older, and I adored her. She was kind and loving, but she had sort of a hard life." She took a sip of coffee before continuing.

While Marnie was anxious to hear the details, she almost couldn't bear to listen.

"Our mother was stern, especially with Emma. Dad was a banker over in Watkins Glen, and Mom thought it was important we, as his family, present an unblemished picture to people around town."

"Did you live in Watkins?" She tried to calm her shaking hands.

Her aunt nodded. "At first, yes. When Emma started high school, Dad lost his job. It was the early seventies, inflation was rising, energy costs were already starting to rise, Vietnam dragged on... Anyway, the bank hit on hard times, and Dad was let go. Mom was devastated and insisted we act as if nothing had changed. She hoped the bank would hire Dad back or he'd get a job at another bank in the area." She worried the second napkin, ripping it into pieces. "He didn't."

Marnie stilled, not knowing what she should say. Her own life had been idyllic compared to her mother's.

"By the time we were both in high school, money was tight. Dad finally got another job, but it didn't pay well and was only part-time. Emma was angry all the time, especially at Mom, and was sick of pretending to be something we no longer were. She got involved with a rough crowd and ended up pregnant. As you can imagine, our mother was livid."

"I'm sure. But your sister must have been so scared."

Ann smiled. "That's exactly right. She was, but our mother couldn't see it. She yelled at your mother and threatened her, but couldn't understand her. Emma didn't know what to do. I mean, you were born in 1973, just after abortion was made legal. It wasn't readily accessible, and we really didn't know anything about it. Those were the days when girls were sometimes sent away to have their babies, which Mom wanted to do, but we couldn't afford it."

"Oh, how sad." Sympathy poured through her for the frightened teenager that her mother had been.

Ann's lips thinned. "My mother was terrible to her, so Emma ended up running away when she was in her seventh month. She never told me where she went, who she met, or how she ended up going to the Summer Jam."

Marnie took a sip of her drink, but nothing could ease the dryness in her throat.

"Even though I was only fifteen, I knew about Woodstock. I had seen the way the Grand Prix races brought people and money into the area. We all thought Summer Jam would be like that. No big deal." She shook her head. "Boy, were we wrong."

"I've done some research on it. The pictures are crazy."

Her aunt laughed. "The village had no idea what it got us all into when they agreed to allow it. There were cars everywhere, parked or abandoned on the hills into town and as far away as Syracuse. There was no food to be had. The grocery store shelves were bare, and the kids who came for the concert had trouble finding anything to eat. I remember people sleeping on the parkway in front of the post office in downtown Watkins Glen. They camped everywhere and without the benefit of a tent. All those people hanging out everywhere fascinated me, but my mother was appalled, which was probably part of the reason I *was* so fascinated." She chuckled.

"And you didn't know where your sister was?"

Shaking her head, the older woman continued, "I knew she was due in late July, but we didn't know if she was even still in the area."

"She didn't tell *you* where she was at all?"

Ann crossed her arms in front of her, leaning on the table. "If we'd had cell phones, I think Emma would have texted me or called, but it wasn't like that back then. She could only call the house and never knew who'd answer, so I didn't know any more than my parents. She didn't call home until after she'd had the baby…well…you."

Marnie sat still, waiting.

Ann's gaze met hers. "She was seventeen and scared and alone. She didn't even know who the father was."

Her heart sank.

Reaching out, her aunt's hand almost touched hers, but not quite. "Looking back, I think she might have been raped, or at least she was pressured into something when she was drunk that she was too naïve to understand at the time. I don't exactly know what happened, although I tried to get her to talk about it." Her gaze filled with pain, tears threatening to spill over onto her cheeks. She cleared her throat. "Emma dragged herself to the front door that day, after making her way down the hill through all the concertgoers. She was barely able to walk and fainted into my father's arms as soon as he pulled open the door."

Tears slipped down Marnie's face as she silently absorbed the story.

"She refused to tell us what had happened to the baby. My mother railed against her, ruining any chance the two of them had to repair their relationship, but Emma refused to discuss the baby with her." Ann wiped her eyes. "Several years later, on my Christmas break from college, Emma confided in me she'd had a girl. That's all she would say, other than she hoped her daughter was warm and safe and happy."

"How did you figure out she'd given birth at Summer Jam?"

Ann sipped her coffee, probably cold by now, and folded her hands in front of her. "Our father passed away while I was still in college. After our mother died a few years later, my sister became more open about what she'd gone through. I was a teacher, Emma worked in the library, and we shared the house together. It's been a nice life, but you were always the missing part of her heart. As she got older, and especially after she got sick, she would talk about you, wonder what you were doing, or where you were. Not a day passed she didn't think of you, but we had no idea how to even try to find you."

Marnie shook her head. "But she must have done research at the library, used the internet, known about searches." Marnie knew she would move mountains to find the girls if they were missing.

"Well, now, that's the thing." Her aunt's eyes were filled with tears. "She knew nothing more than where and when you were born. She was deeply ashamed of leaving you in the minibus. The papers briefly mentioned a baby being born during the weekend, but she couldn't find any more information, nothing at all."

"My grandfather was the mayor in Harper's Glen at the time. He and my grandmother agreed to take care of the baby short term, while the police searched for the mother, but the police were swamped with control and cleanup, thanks to the concert. By the time they came back for the baby, my grandmother told them the mother had showed up and taken the baby back. They were too overwhelmed to follow up further."

"Emma didn't go back."

Marnie lowered her eyes, took a steadying breath, and then met Ann's gaze.

"No, my grandmother lied. She knew my parents were desperate to adopt and, because they were both around forty, the chances were slim. So my grandmother drove me to Tully, where my parents were living at the time, handed me to my mother, gave her forged papers, and told her to say the adoption agency had dropped me off. We lived in Tully for several years."

Her aunt leaned forward, her head in her hands. She said nothing for a few moments. When she looked up again, pain filled her gaze. "Your mother tried for years to follow the trail but couldn't find any trace of you. That's why she never knew her own daughter lived so close." She blew her nose. "She prayed every day you were safe and happy."

Unable to speak at first, over the lump in her throat, Marnie finally reached across the table, taking her aunt's hand in her own. "I was."

Ann smiled as she heard the story.

"My father never knew the circumstances of my adoption, and I didn't even know I was adopted until recently. But I had the best parents and the happiest life I could have ever asked for. Your sister gave me the gift of life, and my grandmother gave me the gift of a life with Roger and Susan Edwards. They are still the best parents and would love to meet you and to learn more about you, and Emma, and the rest of your family." If only she could have had the chance to get to know her birth mother. But how could she be angry over any of this when she ended up with so many wonderful people in her life?

"I'd like that." Ann nodded. "I don't have any family left."

Marnie smiled, shedding the panic of her search, the confusion about her identity, and any lingering anger over events she couldn't control which had shaped her life. "You do now."

Ann clutched her hand tightly, and she could feel the roots taking hold, the family bonds being formed, right there in Minnie's back booth.

****

As exhausted as she was from the day's emotional rollercoaster, contentment coursed through Marnie when she opened her front door. She had a family inside this house, waiting for her return. It was a great feeling to come home to.

Carly sat alone on the couch when she stepped in the door. "Hi."

She hung her coat on a hook, walked to the couch, and sank down next to the teen.

"How you holding up, sweetie?"

The girl's eyes filled with tears, but she held them in check. "Okay."

Marnie cocked her head and peered at her from the corner of her eye. "Okay? Really?"

Carly shook her head. "I can't believe my father is gone."

She pulled the mother-to-be into her arms and rested her head on the crown of the girl's head. "I know, sweetie. I'm so sorry."

The teen didn't say anything for a few moments but finally glanced up. "Can I ask you a question?" She spoke in a soft, younger version of her voice.

Marnie smiled. "Of course. Any time."

"Is it wrong I feel relieved, even happy, that we're going to be living with you instead of him?"

She pulled back so she could meet Carly's gaze. She could only imagine what this girl was going through, given her own conflicting emotions over Frank's death leading to her new family.

"Absolutely not. You have nothing to feel guilty about. Your father died in an accident, but his drinking took over the man you knew and loved a long time ago. He hasn't been able to really be a parent to you in years, and it's perfectly normal, smart really, to want to have food in your stomachs, a sturdy roof over your head, and someone to help you take care of the girls. You can't know what could have happened with your father, good or bad, without his accident, but having a better place for you and your sisters is not something to feel guilty about."

Carly smiled, although the smile didn't reach her eyes. Marnie pulled her back into her embrace.

"So how do you feel about suddenly having the three of us taking over your life?"

She chuckled. "Well..." How to explain the contentment that filled her?

"Wait," Carly continued. "You are a busy person, with a good job, friends, and a boyfriend. You have a lot going on in your life, and I know the girls and I are going to seriously disrupt all of that. You must be pissed."

Again she pushed the girl back to meet her gaze. "I am the furthest thing from pissed I can be."

Determined not to dissolve into tears, she took a deep breath and pulled herself together. "As I walked into the house tonight, I thought how lucky I am to have a house full of people waiting here for me. I admit it was a shock this morning to learn your father chose me to be your guardian, but I couldn't be happier. Yes, you and the girls will change my life. You know what? Life is all about change. And the most important thing in my life is the people I love, so how could I be upset to have more people to love? You and the girls will make my life full and fun and a little bit crazy, and all of it is a good thing."

Carly wrapped her arms around her neck, hugging tight. "Thank you."

She smiled into the teen's hair. "Truly my pleasure, sweetie." She closed her eyes, imprinting this joy into her memories.

After a moment, Carly sat back up, looking serious again.

"What is it?"

"I think Nick and I are going to keep the baby."

Her eyes widened, along with her smile. "Okay. When did you guys come to that decision?" And what would that mean for all of them going forward?

She lowered her eyes and her voice. "Today. And I know I shouldn't make decisions in times of stress, but we had time to talk, just the two of us, after he played Monopoly with the girls tonight. I don't know if we're going to get married or not, but I decided I want our baby to grow up in this family, surrounded by love. Is it okay with you?"

"It's your decision, yours and Nick's." She smiled at the girl. "Whatever you decide is okay with me. You two are strong and smart—you'll be great at this. And will I mind having a baby around the house? Absolutely not. One more person to love."

"Thanks. I don't know what it means for college for me, or Nick, really, but…"

She pulled the slim hand into her own. "We'll work it out. Don't worry about it now."

The girl wiped her eyes. "I love you."

She wrapped her arms around Carly again. "I love you, too, sweetie."

Carly deflated in her arms, and she realized the

girl was practically dead on her feet. She pulled back and stood up, offering her a hand. "You need to get to bed. You have got to be exhausted."

The teen yawned and then smiled sheepishly. "I am a little tired."

"Bed, then. You'll probably have some homework to catch up on tomorrow."

Her new teenaged daughter smiled. "Now I see how it's going to be, you slave driver."

She laughed, hugged the teen once more, and pushed her off in the direction of her bedroom. "You know it. Now go to bed."

Laughter followed her down the hall.

Suddenly tired beyond belief, Marnie checked the deadbolt and climbed the stairs to her own bedroom. When she pushed the door open, her heart smiled. Scott was sitting up in bed, fingers flying over the keys of his laptop, but he paused, looked up, and almost glowed when she walked into the room.

"How did it go?"

He couldn't look any sexier, sitting in her bed with his shirt off, his hair rumpled where his fingers had dragged through it, and doing his best to protect and serve.

She walked to her side of the bed, dropped her purse, kicked off her shoes, and curled up next to him. "It was good. Perfect, really. Everything is perfect."

She launched herself into his arms, dislodging the laptop and sending his notes flying.

He laughed. "Perfect is good. I can live with perfect."

She smiled up into his gaze. "That's a good thing, Investigator Randall. I think you're going to have to live with perfect." She might burst from happiness, but she'd be okay if this feeling lasted forever.

His brows drew together, his lips in a smirk. "What do you mean by that, Ms. Edwards?"

"I met you the night my world started to fall apart. My mother was diagnosed with cancer, I learned I was adopted, and that I was born and abandoned at a rock concert. You were there. I learned my grandmother forged my birth certificate and adoption papers and might have been the instigator in a decades-long child-trafficking ring. You were there. I went a little crazy, trying to figure out who I really was, all while trying to help a pregnant teenager figure out who she wants to be, and you were there. The girls were kidnapped, their father died, I inherited a teenager and two pre-teen girls, and you are still here. I literally thought my life was falling apart at the seams, and then there was you. You held on while I spun out of control, and I really hope you'll hang on for the long haul, because I'm in love with you." She placed a soft kiss on his cheek. "Want to be part of my crazy family?"

He pulled her close, his smile encompassing his entire face. "So much. I feel like I'm already home."

"Me, too," she said, as she pulled him closer to her on the bed. As he rained kisses down her neck and she dug her fingers into that rumpled hair, the idea of home became real to her in a way it'd never been before. She'd found herself, and all the love she could imagine, from the moment he'd walked into her life.

A word about the author...

Barb Warner Deane is originally from Watkins Glen in the beautiful Finger Lakes area of New York. She graduated from Cornell University, later getting her law degree from the University of Connecticut.

Barb, her husband, and three wonderful daughters have lived in the Chicago area for the past twenty-five years, other than two years in Frankfurt, Germany and two years in Shanghai, China. She draws a lot of writing inspiration from her experiences and travel as an expat.

After giving up the practice of law, Barb has worked mostly as a mom, but also as a paralegal, bookstore owner, book merchandiser, travel writer, high school media and IT specialist, and avid volunteer: for Girl Scouts, with the American Women's Club in both Frankfurt and Shanghai, as President of the Windy City Chapter of Romance Writers of America, and as high school PTA president.

In addition to writing, Barb is a genealogy and WWII buff, loves to read, of course, is a huge fan of *The Big Bang Theory* and Harry Potter, and is crazy for both U.S. and international travel. Now that she and her husband are empty-nesters, she's making plans to expand on her list of having visited 47 states and 37 countries on six continents.

http://www.barbwarnerdeane.com

Thank you for purchasing
this publication of The Wild Rose Press, Inc.

For questions or more information
contact us at
info@thewildrosepress.com.

The Wild Rose Press, Inc.
www.thewildrosepress.com

To visit with authors of
The Wild Rose Press, Inc.
join our yahoo loop at
http://groups.yahoo.com/group/thewildrosepress/

"Marnie, hi. I didn't realize you'd be here. How's your mother?"

Startled, she smiled and took a deep breath. What was he doing there? "She's holding her own, thanks."

"I'm glad." He shoved his hands into his back pockets and glanced around the suddenly quiet room.

His shoulders appeared even broader in his hunter green polo shirt than they'd been in the leather jacket. That one lock of hair slipped down over his eyes again. Realizing she was staring, and probably drooling, she quickly averted her gaze. Her tight neck muscles relaxed when Jack announced dinner was ready.

As she carried her wine glass to the table, she tried to calm her racing pulse. It had to be lack of sleep and an overabundance of stress making her picture the wild and reckless things she wanted to do whenever she got near him. She had more than enough on her mind right now without a man complicating things by starting something up between them. Even if he was a fine-looking man.

Kate took her seat and started dishing up the linguine in clam sauce. As she passed a plate to Scott, she asked, "Now, how did you two meet again?"

Praise for Barb Warner Deane...

...and the first book in the Harper's Glen series:
"*KILLING HER SOFTLY* is a fast-paced, frightening, and thoroughly enjoyable read...romantic suspense at its best."

~*Linda Castillo, NY Times Bestselling Thriller Author*
~*~

"An emotional roller-coaster ride of lost love, overcoming life-and-death challenges, and reclaiming one's self and soul..."

~*Terri Brisbin, USA Today Bestselling Author*
~*~

"5 Stars...Well-written and suspenseful. Kept me engaged to the last page."

~*Lisa Pulitzer, NY Times Bestselling Author*
~*~

"[*KILLING HER SOFTLY* is] really quite a lovely read...packs a wallop between the pages. Lots of emotion, lots of danger, lots of love."

~*Romantically Inclined Reviews*

...and for this book:
"Multi-layered wonderful story with a powerful theme-- what does make a family? Thanks for sharing this one with me. I loved it."

~*Fleeta Cunningham, Author of the Santa Rita Series and other books available from The Wild Rose Press*